Sarah Morris Remembers

D. E. STEVENSON

ISIS
LARGE PRINT
Oxford

All characters in this novel are entirely fictitious
and no reference is intended to any actual person,
whether living or dead.

First published in Great Britain 1967
by
Collins

Published in Large Print 2014 by ISIS Publishing Ltd.,
7 Centremead, Osney Mead, Oxford OX2 0ES
by arrangement with
the Author's Estate

CIP data is available for this title from the British Library

ISBN 978-0-7531-9268-9 (hb)
ISBN 978-0-7531-9269-6 (pb)

Printed and bound in Great Britain by
T. J. International Ltd., Padstow, Cornwall

Sarah Morris Remembers

For M.C. with love

Part One

CHAPTER
ONE

A small child lives in the present and takes everything for granted but to most children there comes a moment of awareness; the child wakens from its trance and becomes conscious of itself and its surroundings. This moment came to me on a Christmas morning many years ago when I discovered myself to be a little girl in a warm cashmere dress with a gold bracelet on my arm.

The dress and the bracelet were new; they were Christmas presents from father and mother. I liked the colour of the dress — a soft pinkish red — and I liked the feeling of it on my bare arms.

The boys had presents too: Lewis a big wooden sled and Willy a silver watch. We had other presents: a doll for me and books and building blocks and puzzles from the grandparents; stockings packed with sweets and crackers and fruit and queer little wooden toys from Santa Claus. The nursery floor was untidy with paper wrappings.

The boys and I were sitting on the window-seat looking out at the snow-covered garden. I didn't remember having seen snow before and I thought it was pretty. It had come in the night while we were

3

asleep, but now it had stopped snowing; the sun was shining and the long shadows of the trees fell across the glistening white lawn.

The little bracelet felt heavy on my wrist, there were charms on it which jingled when I moved my hand. I looked at my hand, opening and closing it.

"Why are you looking at your hand like that?" asked Lewis.

"I've never seen it before."

He laughed. "Silly little Sally!"

"I know what she means," said Willy. "She's beginning to find out about herself; just like I had to find out about my train — how to fit the rails together and wind up the engine."

Lewis wasn't listening; he said, "I'm glad there's snow, but it's a nuisance being Christmas Day. I won't be able to go out with my sled till after lunch."

"You wouldn't have got it if it hadn't been Christmas Day," Willy pointed out. He added, "There they are!"

There they were: Father and Mother coming back from church through the little green gate which led from the churchyard into the Vicarage garden. They had been to church early — and we would all go together at eleven — but Mother had wanted to fill up the flower-vases so she had gone over directly after breakfast and Father had gone with her to help. There they were, coming down the garden path: Mother in front, holding up the skirts of her green dress and walking carefully on the snowy path; Father shutting the gate and following her.

4

He looked up at the nursery window and waved to us. The sun shone on his thin face and smooth dark hair.

I was like Father — everyone said so. Lewis was like Mother, with fair wavy hair and cornflower-blue eyes. Willy wasn't like anyone in particular; he had brown hair (which was always untidy, no matter how often he brushed it) and thin knobbly knees. Lottie was the youngest of the family; she was very pretty with big blue eyes and flaxen curls as soft as silk. Everyone admired Lottie but at that time I wasn't interested in her, I liked being with the boys. Sometimes they were a bit rough but I didn't mind — I didn't mind what they did if I could tag along after them and share in their games.

The Fenimore Cooper period was terribly exciting and, now that I think of it, somewhat dangerous. We crept about in the woods and shot at each other with home-made bows and arrows. One day I shot Willy in the arm, it was just a graze but it bled freely. Willy didn't mind but I sat down and wept.

"You mustn't tell," said Willy, when Lewis had tied a dirty handkerchief round the wound. "If you tell we'll never be allowed to play Indians again."

"She must swear an oath," declared Lewis.

I swore a dreadful oath that I wouldn't tell — and I didn't. Of course Mother saw that I had been crying and wanted to know what was the matter but I remained dumb.

"You shouldn't play with the boys," said Mother. "They're too rough, Sarah. Why don't you play dolls with Lottie?"

"They aren't rough," I said. "It wasn't that, at all. It was something quite different."

Mother looked at me — and sighed — and said no more.

I can remember other little incidents which happened when I was a child. There was the day when Lewis was pushing me in the swing and I fell off and broke my arm. Father was in his study, writing his sermon, and came running out and carried me into the house ... and he held me tightly while Dr. Weatherstone set the bone and bound it up with splints. I remember the day when Willy's white rabbit escaped from his hutch. Mr. Blake, the sexton, was our gardener and he had told Willy that he didn't hold with rabbits except in a pie so we were terrified that he might catch Peter. We hunted madly all over the garden and at last I found Peter amongst the cabbages; I seized him by his long white ears and screamed for Willy. Peter kicked and struggled and tried to bite me but I held on like grim death until Willy came to the rescue.

St. Mary's Vicarage was a fine old house with a lovely big garden and we lived there very comfortably for in addition to his stipend Father had a small private income. The church and the Vicarage were on the side of a hill. On the top of the hill were the woods, where we played Indians, and at the bottom of the hill was the village of Fairfield. It was quite a big village with good shops so we got all our provisions there; if we wanted clothes we went to Larchester in the bus.

We knew all the people in the village and we liked them — all except the baker's boy who brought our bread. He was a sturdy individual, with a red face and ginger hair, and very cheeky. One day Lewis found him stealing eggs from a robin's nest outside the kitchen door. We knew the robins, we had watched them building their nest, and had seen the eggs in it, so when Lewis caught the baker's boy with his hand in the nest he was furious.

"Thief!" cried Lewis.

"Thief, yourself!" shouted the baker's boy. "I'm collecting birds' eggs —"

"You're not to take those —"

"Who's going to stop me?"

"I am!" cried Lewis, advancing in a threatening manner.

The baker's boy laughed. He threw the eggs on the ground and stamped on them; then he rolled up his sleeves.

"Run, Lewis!" I shouted . . . but, instead of running, Lewis went for him and hit him. The next moment they were fighting like mad dogs.

The baker's boy was much bigger than Lewis and I was so frightened that for a few moments I was too petrified to move. Then, when I saw that Lewis was getting the worst of it, I seized a stick from the herbaceous border and hit the boy on the back of his head. I was so mad with rage and fright that I hit him as hard as I could . . . he fell down on the path and lay still.

"Sarah, what have you done?" exclaimed Lewis in alarm.

"I had to," I said breathlessly.

"You've killed him, Sarah!"

"I had to," I repeated. "He was killing you — he's twice your size — it's his own fault if he's dead."

Fortunately, the baker's boy wasn't dead, he was just stunned, and after a few moments he sat up and looked about him with a surprised expression on his fat red face. Then he rose, took up his basket, and walked away.

We stood in silence and watched him go.

"You shouldn't have interfered," said Lewis at last.

"I had to — he's twice your size, Lewis!"

Lewis began to laugh. "He doesn't know what happened to him," declared Lewis. "I bet he thinks I knocked him out! Gosh, what a joke! We shan't have any more cheek from the baker's boy."

We decided not to tell anyone about the fight — not even Willy — but Minnie came into the scullery when Lewis was bathing his bruised face so we had to tell her the whole story. It didn't matter telling Minnie because she hated the baker's boy as much as we did.

Minnie Dell was our cook. She was very small but wonderfully strong for her size. She explained to us that she had had "the fever" when she was eight years old so she had never grown any bigger after that. "But three of the others died," she added cheerfully.

There had been seven little Dells. Minnie used to say the poem, "We Are Seven," and she always cried when she said it, but she wasn't really sad. She was as gay as a lark and full of fun. She came from Ryddelton, mother's old home in Scotland; sometimes she talked to us in her home tongue to make us laugh, but she could speak good English when she liked.

"You've got to mimic them, that's all," said Minnie. "You've got to listen — really listen — and watch their lips. That's how to learn a language; mind that, Sarah, when you're learning French at school."

Minnie was a wonderful needlewoman; she made her own dresses and sometimes altered things for mother. She was fond of reading and borrowed books from the library in Larchester, where she went for her afternoons off. Travel books were her favourites; she read them carefully and often came out with queer bits of information about what she had read.

"Think of this!" she would exclaim. "In Africa the blacks file their teeth into points to make themsel's look fierce!"

I can't remember a time when Minnie wasn't there, in the kitchen, cooking our meals or sitting by the fire. She was part of our lives and we loved her dearly.

Lewis, who was five years older than I was, remembered a big fat cook who had boxed his ears for taking a bun off a baking-tray which had just come out of the oven. Soon after that mother went into the kitchen and found the big fat cook lying unconscious on the floor. Mother thought she was ill and sent for the doctor . . . but Dr. Weatherstone laughed and said she was drunk and a big pile of empty bottles was discovered in the coal-cellar.

All this was a secret in the family; it was a sort of legend. Father and Mother never spoke of it so I have no idea how Lewis knew.

When the big fat cook had gone Grandmama Maitland sent Minnie Dell from Ryddelton "to be a comfort" and Minnie had been with us ever since.

When I was six years old I went to a little private school in Fairfield which was run by Mrs. Powell. She had no degrees or diplomas but she was an excellent teacher and made our lessons interesting. In addition to all the usual subjects she taught us to make little clay models and straw mats and kettle-holders in cross-stitch . . . and when we were older she gave us each a large exercise-book with hard covers and showed us how to keep diaries. We wrote about the birds and animals that we saw in the woods and about what we did in the holidays. Mrs. Powell gave us prizes for neatness and originality.

I began keeping a diary when I was ten years old and it became a habit which has remained with me all my life. The diaries are all written in big exercise-books with hard covers (like the first one, which was given to me by Mrs. Powell); some days consist of two or three closely written pages . . . and there are gaps when nothing interesting happened or when I was too busy or too unhappy to write.

When I started this story of my life I unpacked the diaries which I had kept in a large tin box and, as I turned over the pages, all sorts of things came back to me — things I had forgotten — and I realised I had plenty of material for a family chronicle. I had intended to write the story to amuse the family but I hadn't got very far before I saw that I was faced with a difficult choice: either I could write a story about the family, suitable for the family to read, or else I could write a true story about everything that had happened to us all. The choice was so difficult that I put away the pages I had written until I could make up my mind about it.

Several months passed — I had almost forgotten my "story" — then one day when I was looking for something else I came across the pages and read them and felt the urge to continue . . . and now I saw quite clearly that the story would be no good unless it was true in every detail. I would write it for myself, for my own satisfaction; no eye but mine should ever see it and perhaps when I had finished it I should be able to see some sort of pattern in my life.

As I sat down at my desk to write I realised how much I owed to Mrs. Powell. I hadn't seen her for years but I remembered her so well that when I shut my eyes I could see her round pink face and the brown fringe across her forehead and I could hear her voice saying cheerfully, "Now we'll have reading. Find your places, children."

Lewis and Willy never went to Mrs. Powell's; they went to Bells Hill, a boarding school near Larchester. On Saturdays they rode home on their bicycles and often stayed the night. When the boys were away the house was very quiet but when the boys came home the house woke up and was full of stir. Sometimes we had friends to tea and played hide-and-seek in the garden but I liked it better when we were alone and went into the drawing-room after tea for music.

On Sunday evenings we had hymns but on week-days Father sang old songs — songs which had been old when he was young — such as "A Fox Jumped up in a Hungry Plight" and "The Man that Broke the Bank at Monte Carlo," and "Ring the Bell, Watchman."

Unlike the songs of modern times they all had good rousing tunes.

I remember those evenings so well! I remember the comfortable lamp-lit room; Father at the grand piano, playing and singing in his mellow baritone; Mother sitting by the fire with her mending-basket, humming and beating time . . . and all of us standing round and joining in the choruses. Every now and then Father would put his fingers in his ears and exclaim, "Softlee, softlee, catchee monkey!"

None of us knew where the quotation came from but we all knew what father meant.

We took it in turns to choose the songs. Willy's favourite was "The Fox" and mine was an old ditty with several verses. I can't remember them now but only the chorus which came at the end of each verse:

"Dashing away with a smoothing iron,
Dashing away with a smoothing iron
She stole my heart away."

We all sang quite nicely — when we didn't shout — but Lewis's voice was beautiful; it was a boy's treble, clear as a bell. In the holidays Lewis sang in the choir. One Sunday morning he stood up and sang, "O, for the Wings of a Dove." He looked so angelic and his voice was so pure and unearthly that I was quite frightened. I was even more frightened when Mrs. Quail, who sat in the pew behind us, whispered to her sister that he was "too good for this world" ... but fortunately I remembered that only yesterday Lewis had put a small lump of mud in father's ink-pot.

Mr. Shepherd was the organist of St. Mary's so it was his duty to train the choir, but he was old and impatient and he offended people so Mother used to have the choir to practice on Tuesday evenings. She said it was better for them to be "half-cooked" before Mr. Shepherd took them.

CHAPTER
TWO

Just beyond the garden wall, on the opposite side from the the church, there was a small field. We called it "our field" but it really belonged to Farmer Rickaby; he was churchwarden and he had told father that we could play there if we were careful. We were country-bred children so we knew what that meant: not to spoil the crop by walking across it when it was growing, and never to leave the gate open. We were not likely to leave the gate open for we never opened it, but climbed over the low wall at the top of the garden. Here, there was a very old oak-tree surrounded by some enormous stones and on fine summer days we often took a picnic basket and had tea beneath its branches.

Lewis liked cricket, so quite often he didn't come home on Saturday afternoons, but Willy came home whenever he could. We used to pretend we were Dan and Una — in *Puck of Pook's Hill*. It was a good place to pretend magic for the tree was so old and gnarled and twisted that there was something very queer about it . . . and the hedge was thorn. One day we found a tiny ash-tree in the woods; it was only eight inches high, but we dug it up and planted it between two of the stones.

Our tree was magic in winter too. When the branches were bare we could see how twisted they were. Anyone might have thought the tree was dead, but every spring the buds opened and the tree was covered with fresh green leaves. It was like a miracle.

One Saturday afternoon in early June I went up to the tree by myself. There was a big cricket match at Bells Hill so Willy couldn't come home.

It was a perfect day; there wasn't a cloud in the sky; the old tree was in full leaf and the hedge was a mass of May-blossom, which smelt as sweet as honey in the warm sunshine. I could hear two cuckoos calling to each other in the woods and, far in the distance, a lamb was bleating.

I had brought *Puck of Pook's Hill* with me; it was a lovely copy with a soft red-leather cover and pictures but it had seen a lot of service since grandmama had sent it to Willy on his ninth birthday and it was almost falling to pieces. I sat down on a big stone with my back against the tree and read some of the poems aloud, trying to pretend that Willy was here, listening:

"'Sing Oak, and Ash, and Thorn, good sirs
(All of a Midsummer morn)!
England shall bide till Judgment Tide
By Oak, and Ash, and Thorn!'"

Suddenly the bushes parted and a little old man appeared. For a moment or two I stared at him in amazement; I really thought it was The Old Thing himself! Then I saw it was only Farmer Rickaby.

15

"Were you reading to yourself, Sarah?" he asked, surprised at finding me alone.

"I was pretending to read to Willy."

"You didn't know I was listening, did you? 'Oak, ash and thorn,'" he said, sitting down on one of the big stones. "There's oak and thorn but where's the ash?"

"We planted a little one; I hope you don't mind, Mr. Rickaby."

He grinned at me. He really was quite like Puck, small and thin with a brown wrinkled face and bright brown eyes. "I don't mind," he said. "I've seen you sitting here having your tea. You come here often?"

"Yes, but we're very careful; we never light a fire or leave bits of paper and we never —"

"The gate was left open on Sunday."

"Not us!" I exclaimed. "Honestly, not us! We never come in by the gate."

He nodded. "I've seen you climbing over the wall. It was one of those trippers that left the gate open — I'd trip them if I could get hold of them! If you happen to see any trippers about you might tell them to shut the gates. Ask them if they'd like Farmer Rickaby to walk into their house uninvited and leave their front door open."

"Yes," I said doubtfully. I saw what he meant, of course, but I didn't relish the idea of accosting a stranger and giving him the message.

"I like you coming here," said Farmer Rickaby. "It's a nice place to play games. Nothing grows in this corner of the field and I've been told by some that the

16

old tree should be taken down for the sake of the hay, but —"

"Oh, no!"

"No," he agreed, smiling. "In any case I can't, because a gentleman from London came to look at it and said it was ancient. He said the stones were put here by the Druids — the same people that made Stonehenge."

"Then it *is* magic!"

"I don't know about magic. It's an old place — that's what the gentleman said — hundreds of years old. He said I wasn't to cut down the tree or move the stones. Well, I never thought of it — but it's a funny thing that you can't do what you like with your own land."

"But you don't want to?"

"No, I don't want to. All the same it's a funny thing."

We were silent for a while. I tried to think of something to say because mother had told me that I was quite old enough now to talk to people and be friendly instead of sitting and looking from me as if I were dumb. (To "look from you" is a Scots expression; I can't think of anything in English which means the same thing.)

At last I said, "There's a cricket match at Bells Hill; that's why I'm here alone."

"Cricket is a grand game," said Mr. Rickaby. "I was a slogger; hit or miss was my motto. Mr. Morris used to play when he first came to Fairfield. He was a fast bowler and many's the time he sent my stumps flying . . . so maybe his sons take after him."

"Willy doesn't like cricket but Lewis is a very good bat. Lewis isn't at Bells Hill now; he's gone to Barstow."

"Barstow is a public school, isn't it?"

"Yes — and Lewis likes it. He can't come home so often because it's too far away; he only comes home for the holidays and his half-term week-end."

"That's a pity."

"Oh, Lewis doesn't mind. There's lots of cricket — he likes that better than anything — and he's hoping to get into the Colts' Eleven next summer."

"Well, well, they all grow up, and we all grow old," said Mr. Rickaby. "I'm too old for cricket now."

"Father doesn't play either."

There was another silence. This time I didn't bother to make polite conversation so we sat there for a long time without saying anything. The cuckoos were still calling to each other in the woods.

"I'll be cutting this field next week if the weather holds," said Mr. Rickaby at last.

"Oh, good!" I cried. "We'll all help! Haymaking is fun."

"But the boys are at school."

"It's Lewis's half-term holiday — and Willy always comes on Saturdays when he can — and Lottie will help too."

"Dear me, is Lottie old enough for haymaking? It seems only yesterday that she was christened. 'Charlotte Mary' — that's right, isn't it?"

I nodded. "She's got two names and the boys have got two names but I've only got one," I said sadly.

"What do you want with two names? You don't use more than one — and Sarah is a fine name," declared Mr. Rickaby. "If we'd had a girl she'd have been Sarah.

What do you want with two names?" he repeated in a grumbling voice.

"I'd have liked two names," I said. "Lewis is called 'Lewis Henry.' Lewis after mother's brother who was killed in the war, and Henry after Father. Willy is 'William Maitland' after Grandpapa. He was born at Craignethan, that's why."

"Yes, I see," said Mr. Rickaby. "I remember the day Mr. and Mrs. Morris came here with the two little boys. It was a very wet day and Mrs. Rickaby went down to the Vicarage to light the fires and air the place before they arrived. She was asked to stay to tea and came home later in very good spirits. She said Mrs. Morris was a gem. Dear me, I remember that as if it was last week."

It was so interesting to hear about things that happened before I was born that I hoped he would tell me more . . . but he didn't.

"It's time I was getting along," he said. "We've had a nice talk, Sarah. You're very like your father and you couldn't be like anyone better. He's a real gentleman, is Mr. Morris."

I smiled and said, "Yes, I like being like him."

Mr. Rickaby rose and added, "Don't forget if you see any trippers, tripping about my fields, you're to tell them what Farmer Rickaby said."

"I won't forget," I told him. It was all right to say I wouldn't forget.

Mr. Rickaby nodded and went through the gap in the hedge and I went home to tea.

CHAPTER
THREE

The weather remained fine and dry so Mr. Rickaby and his men cut the hay. It was a small field; they finished it in two days and by Saturday it was ready to turn. We had expected Lewis to come for the week-end but he had rung up to say that Tom Meldrum had asked him to spend the day at Riverside so he wouldn't be home until supper-time. The Meldrums lived about five miles from Fairfield and Lewis was great friends with Tom.

Willy came home from Bells Hill as usual, so he and I and Lottie went up to the field to help to turn the hay. It was done by hand in those days, you took a fork and turned it over to dry in the sun. The hay was light and sweet-scented and the sun was warm and golden. Lottie and I worked together; I was showing her what to do.

Presently I looked round for Willy and saw him lying under the oak-tree in the shade. I was surprised! Willy was usually a whale for work. "What's the matter?" I asked.

"It's frightfully hot and I've got a headache. Sit down and talk to me, Sarah. Did you come up here last Saturday?"

"Yes, I came by myself."

"I thought you would. I thought of you when I was watching the match and wished I was here. I hate cricket and I hate school. I hate never being alone."

"Perhaps you'll like Barstow better. Lewis likes it."

"I'm not Lewis." He sighed heavily. "Well, tell me what happened last Saturday."

"I was reading aloud, pretending you were here, when Mr. Rickaby came through the hedge. I thought for a moment it was Puck."

"Yes, he's rather like The Old Thing," agreed Willy, smiling.

We were still talking when Mr. Rickaby came by. He stopped and said, "It's warm this afternoon."

"Willy has a headache," I told him.

"A headache? That's bad, that is! You've been working too hard in the sun. Perhaps you've got a touch of sunstroke, Willy. Your face is a bit flushed. You'd better go home."

"Yes," I said. "Anyhow it's nearly tea-time." I called to Lottie and we went home.

"Don't tell mother about my head," said Willy as we went down the path.

"Sunstroke is serious, Willy."

"It isn't sunstroke. My head was bad when I woke this morning but I didn't tell Matron because I wanted to come home. I'll be all right after tea."

He seemed better after tea — more like himself — and rode back to school on his bicycle. The next day they rang up from Bells Hill to say Willy had got measles.

Nobody knew where Willy had got measles — and fortunately he didn't have it badly — but he gave it to a great many other boys at Bells Hill, and he gave it to me.

I developed a headache and a streaming cold and the following day I was covered with spots.

Mother was sure Lottie would get it — she had kissed Willy before he went away — but Lottie remained fit and well and full of the joy of life. Lottie looked fragile and fairylike, and Mother worried about her, but she was as strong as a little pony and I can't remember her ever being ill.

Measles is a horrible complaint — I felt hot and headachy and my eyes were very painful — but Mother nursed me and spent hours sitting beside my bed and reading to me, so once I began to feel a little better it was a happy time. It was a new experience to have Mother at my beck and call: Mother pulling down the blind because my eyes were painful; Mother sponging me between blankets and bringing me a drink of hot milk late at night to help me to sleep.

When I was better and able to get up and come downstairs I found I had grown thin and tall. I knew I was taller because everyone seemed smaller and because my eyes were now on a level with the chimney-piece in the drawing-room.

"She's very thin," said Father, looking at me with a worried frown.

"She's had a bad time," replied Mother. "I'd better take her with me to Craignethan this year. The change will do her good."

22

Mother's visit to her parents was an annual event and always took place in September. She went in the spring as well — after the spring-cleaning — but only for a short visit. In September she went for a whole fortnight and we had to get on without her as best we could. Father said it was good for her to get away and it was good for her parents to have her.

"It isn't good for us," grumbled Lewis.

"It's exceedingly good for us to be uncomfortable for a fortnight," said Father.

We weren't really uncomfortable — Minnie saw to that — but the comfortableness of Mother was absent.

I wasn't at all pleased when I heard I was to go to Craignethan; I hoped Father would say, "No, no, take Lottie," — but he didn't. He said, "Well, if it wouldn't be a bother to your parents, perhaps you should."

"Sarah won't be a bother," said Mother cheerfully.

Mother was always cheerful when the time came for her visit to Craignethan. She loved us all, and she loved the Vicarage, but there was a sort of gaiety about her when she set out for Scotland — a sort of suppressed excitement.

I had never been to Craignethan. One year Mother had taken Lewis, because he was the eldest, and another year she had taken Lottie, but neither of them had said much about it: Lewis because he wasn't the sort of boy who could tell you about things, or at any rate didn't bother; Lottie because she had been too young. I knew nothing about Craignethan, except that there was an old photograph of it hanging on the stairs. The house stood at the bottom of an avenue and was surrounded by trees and bushes, it looked dark and damp and rather eerie. I wanted to be at home in September (I had been given a bicycle and Willy and I had planned to go for expeditions together) but, when I was young, children were not consulted as to what they would like to do.

I had grown so tall that Mother took me to Larchester to buy some new clothes. I remember a tweed coat and skirt, chestnut-brown with little green flecks in it, and a golden-brown cashmere frock with smocking round the waist. I had set my heart on a blue frock with frills but Mother said blue was for people with blue eyes.

It was a long journey to Ryddelton, with several changes, and I was so unused to travelling that I thought we were never going to get there; my head ached and I didn't want any food. When at last we arrived at Ryddelton station I felt quite sick and dizzy; we had to bundle out of the train quickly because it didn't stop there more than a few minutes.

Grandpapa had come to meet us; he was very tall and thin with thick white hair and a small military moustache.

Mother threw her arms round his neck and hugged him.

Then he turned and said, "And here's Sarah! At least I suppose it must be Sarah."

"Of course it's Sarah!" said Mother, laughing.

"I hadn't expected Sarah to be a grown-up young lady," explained Grandpapa. "The last time I had the pleasure of meeting my grand-daughter she was very much smaller."

"Oh, Papa, don't be ridiculous!" Mother exclaimed. "You haven't seen Sarah since she was three years old; it was when you were in London for a regimental dinner and you came to Fairfield for the week-end."

"Yes, yes, so it was," agreed Grandpapa, putting his hand through my arm and leading me to the car, which was waiting in the station yard. I can remember now the feeling of that kind old hand gripping my arm firmly.

It was several miles to Craignethan House. Grandpapa drove himself, up hill and down dale. At first it was dark with the bright lights of the car lighting up the road and the hedges, but in a few minutes the moon rose from behind a ridge of hills and it was almost as bright as day. Mother chatted happily all the time but I didn't listen. I hadn't wanted to come but now I was beginning to feel excited; it was all so different from Fairfield: there were hills and rocks and a little river with the moonlight glinting on it and turning it to silver. We crossed the river by a narrow bridge, turned in at a wide entrance and jolted slowly up a steep avenue overhung by trees.

"The avenue is as bad as ever," said Mother.

"Yes, yes," agreed Grandpapa. "It's worse if anything. We got it put into decent order in the spring but no sooner was the work finished than we had a storm and the water rushed down in a torrent and washed all the metal into the road. A sheer waste of good money, that's what it was."

There were some buildings on the right, stables and barns, and then we came over the crest of the hill and saw the house below us with its windows lighted and a sweep of gravel outside the door. In the picture it had looked an eerie sort of place but the trees had been cut down and the bushes cleared away so it stood alone. At the back of the house there was a little stream amongst rocks and, beyond that, a hill with trees. The house itself was not as large as I had expected; it was a solid grey stone house with a slate roof and tall chimneys. There were no steps up to the door; the doorway was level with the ground — and the door was of heavy wood, studded with iron nails.

Of course I didn't see all that on the first night; in fact I saw very little for the door was opened by Grandmama herself. She stood, framed in the doorway, with the light shining on her silver hair . . . the next moment we were in the hall and there was a great deal of talk and laughter.

Grandmama kissed me and said, "You don't remember me, do you, Sarah?"

"But you're just like Mother!" I exclaimed. "Why didn't anyone tell me you were so pretty?"

Grandpapa laughed, "Do you hear that, Jane? You've seldom had a nicer compliment!"

"The child is tired and hungry," said Grandmama.

"Yes, she had better go to bed," agreed Mother.

"But she must have something to eat," Grandmama declared. "Can she take soup, Dorrie, or would you rather she had a bowl of bread and milk?"

Mother wasn't listening (she was looking at a picture which hung on the wall and Grandpapa had taken her by the arm and was telling her how he had bought it at a sale) so Grandmama led me into the dining-room and gave me a big cup of soup and a brown scone.

"When those two get together you can get no sense out of them," she explained confidingly. "We'll just leave them to it and have a nice little chat by ourselves. What do you like doing best, Sarah?"

"Playing with the boys," I said.

As I ate my soup, which was deliciously thick and full of barley and vegetables, I told her about the old tree and about playing with Willy and pretending we were Dan and Una. I had never told anyone before — it was a secret between Willy and me — so I was surprised to find myself telling Grandmama.

She nodded and said, "Dan and Una — that's *Puck of Pook's Hill*. Who do you have for Puck?"

"We just pretend Puck," I told her. "One day when I was there alone I thought I saw Puck, but it was only Farmer Rickaby."

"Tell me about it," said Grandmama.

I told her about it — and about the oak, and ash and thorn. We were still talking about Puck, she knew all the stories, when Mother and Grandpapa came in.

"Oh, Mama!" exclaimed Mother. "You shouldn't have given her soup so late at night."

"Well, I asked you and you didn't reply so I gave her soup. The child was hungry. I expect she could eat a wee bit of cold chicken now."

"I'll cut her a slice of the breast," said Grandpapa, taking up the carving knife and sharpening it.

There was cold chicken and salad and then there was orange sponge with cream on the top.

Mother looked at me eating and said, "Oh, well, I don't suppose it will do her any harm."

"It will do her a power of good," declared Grandpapa. "People should eat when they want and fast when they're not hungry. That's nature."

When we had finished we went into the drawing-room. Mother said I couldn't go straight to bed after an enormous meal so I sat in the corner of the big sofa. The 'grans' sat in chairs on either side of the fire with mother sitting between them on the hearthrug.

I could see now why she was always so happy to come to Craignethan: she loved them and they loved her. She wasn't like Mother, somehow; she was younger and prettier — even her voice seemed different. For a time I watched them and listened to their talk and then I couldn't keep my eyes open any longer . . .

Suddenly I was awakened by the sound of a carriage driving up to the front door. I heard the horses' hoofs on the gravel and the scrape of wheels.

"Who's that?" I cried, sitting up and pointing to the window.

"Goodness, Sarah! Why haven't you gone to bed?" exclaimed Mother.

"You didn't tell me to go to bed."

"I know — but look at the time! It's twelve o'clock."

"What about the other people?" I asked.

"What other people?"

"The people who have just arrived in the carriage."

There was a little silence. They were all looking at me.

"I heard them arrive," I explained. "I heard the carriage drive up to the door. Hadn't we better see who it is?"

"The child has been dreaming," said Grandpapa. "Dorrie had better put her to bed. We'd all be better in our beds," he added, rising and putting the guard on the fire.

"But I wasn't dreaming! I wasn't really. I heard the carriage and the horses and the wheels on the gravel."

"Come and see," said Grandpapa. He took me into the hall and opened the front door. "Look, child, there's not a creature in sight! You were dreaming."

I went out to the doorstep and looked about. The moon was bright above the sleeping hills . . . and there was no carriage, no horses, nothing.

"Are you satisfied, Sarah?" asked Grandpapa, smiling down at me very kindly.

"I suppose . . . I must have been . . . dreaming."

A big dark bird flew past on silent wings and disappeared amongst the trees.

"It's an owl," said Grandpapa. "They live in the ruins of an old tower on the other side of the hill."

"I'd like to see it."

"Yes, yes, we'll go and see it together, you and I."

"Let's go now. It's so lovely — I want to see everything!"

"Not now, Sarah. I'll take you this afternoon."

"You mean to-morrow, Grandpapa."

He smiled and replied, "It's to-morrow now."

"How can it be to-morrow now?"

"Well, it can't be, strictly speaking. To-morrow never comes."

"I don't understand."

He laughed. "We'll thrash it out when we've had a good sleep. There's your mother calling you to bed."

I watched him shut and bolt the big wooden door and then ran upstairs.

My room at Craignethan was over the front door; there was a wide view over a rolling lawn to the distant woods and hills. It was a small room but very comfortable and I loved it.

Mother was there when I went up; she was unpacking my suitcase. She said, "What were you and Grandpapa talking about?"

"He said he would take me up the hill this afternoon."

"You mean to-morrow."

"He said to-morrow never comes."

"Nonsense, you're asleep on your feet," declared Mother. "Go and wash in the bathroom next door and then get into bed. You'll see everything to-morrow."

There was a mirror over the basin in the bathroom, so when I was brushing my teeth I saw myself clearly: a thin white face, with blue marks like bruises under the eyes, framed in dark, lifeless, straggly-looking hair. Not pretty! Then suddenly I stopped with the toothbrush in my mouth . . . because I had seen it! To-morrow never comes. When you go to bed at the proper time

30

to-morrow is to-morrow, but when you wake in the morning it's to-day.

Mother was wrong! It was an amazing discovery; never before had it occurred to me that Mother could be wrong about anything.

The first few days at Craignethan were very happy; there was so much to see and I enjoyed going for walks on the hills with Mother or Grandpapa. I saw the old tower; it was a huge place with high walls, all tumbling down and covered with ivy. Grandpapa showed me the place where the owls had nested in the spring.

When Mother and Grandmama went to Ryddelton to do the shopping they took me with them and I enjoyed that too. However, after we had been there a week, I began to feel a little lonely and to wish I had someone of my own age to play with. Mother and the "grans" were happy together and talked a lot; they talked about people I didn't know which wasn't very interesting.

"How are the Loudons?" asked Mother.

"Oh, they're very well," Grandmama replied. "The boys are at school, of course. Bob is going to Sandhurst soon; he has always been keen on the Army."

"Bob is a fine lad," said Grandpapa. "He'll do well in the Service."

"I don't want our boys to go into the Army," said Mother.

"I thought Lewis was —"

"No," said Mother firmly. "That was just a childish idea. I want Lewis to go to Oxford. He's very clever."

"I don't know why people think that only morons should enter the Service," said Grandpapa sadly.

"I didn't say that!"

"No, but you meant it."

Grandpapa had been in the Army, of course. He was a colonel and "a very distinguished officer" (Grandmama had told me that) and he certainly wasn't a "moron." He loved a joke and always made his jokes with a perfectly solemn face, so it wasn't easy to know whether he meant them or not, but if you were doubtful you had only to look at Grandmama; she always smiled at his jokes.

One day at lunch Grandpapa said, "Listen, Dorrie, you must bring William Maitland next year; I want to have a look at my namesake. Bring Sarah, too, of course."

"It would be too much for you," objected Mother.

"Not a bit of it; bring them both. They'll amuse each other. By the way, what's Sarah's other name?"

"I've only got one," I said regretfully.

"You ought to be Sarah Jane."

"I don't know why we didn't call her Jane," Mother said. "It never occurred to us. Sarah was Henry's mother's name and we wanted a girl so she was Sarah before she was born."

I wondered how I could have been Sarah before I was born.

It was a fine afternoon and Grandpapa had promised to take me for a walk to the owls' tower so I went and stood on the doorstep waiting for him to get ready.

Suddenly a few drops of water pattered down on to my head. I was surprised that it was raining for there wasn't a cloud in the sky. Then, when I looked up, I saw Grandpapa leaning out of my bedroom window with my sponge in his hand.

"Sarah Jane," said Grandpapa solemnly. Then his head disappeared.

"But it isn't real, is it?" I asked, as we walked up the hill together.

"Not really real," he replied. "But pretending is fun. There's nothing wrong in pretending as long as it doesn't harm other people. Sarah Jane is a secret between you and me."

That was our last day at Craignethan; we started home early next morning and Father met us in London.

CHAPTER
FOUR

St. Elizabeth's was a big school on the way to Larchester; most of the girls were boarders but father arranged that I should go daily in the Larchester bus. At first I was frightened and unhappy — it was so different from Mrs. Powell's — but fortunately I had been well grounded so I didn't find the lessons difficult. After a bit I made friends with several of the boarders and we had them to tea on Sundays; they enjoyed going out to tea. Next year Lottie would come with me to St. Elizabeth's but meantime she stayed on at Mrs. Powell's.

It was a dull year but I was looking forward to September; Grandpapa had written to say he hoped Mother hadn't forgotten her promise to bring William Maitland and Sarah Jane when she came for her usual visit.

Father said, "It will be too much for your parents, Dorrie. They're apt to be boisterous when they get together."

"But Papa wants them," said mother doubtfully.

"It will be all right," I declared. "We won't be boisterous — honestly. Grandpapa will be very disappointed if you don't take us to Craignethan."

Fortunately Mother thought so too.

I had told Willy all about Craignethan so he was looking forward to it as much as I was; we were both wildly excited when the day arrived for us to start on our journey. Father was still a little worried in case we should be "too much for the grans": he told us that we must be good and quiet and not come into the house with muddy shoes or be late for meals . . . and of course we promised to remember.

"They'll be out most of the time," said Mother cheerfully. "They can work off their high spirits running about the hills."

This year the journey didn't seem so long because Willy had been given a travelling chess-board for his birthday and we played in the train. Willy's chess was dashing — like himself. His one idea was to take as many of his opponent's pieces as quickly as he could, so his queen came out at the very beginning and rampaged round the board, slaying her enemies indiscriminately. If you didn't know Willy's game you were apt to be taken by surprise. I knew it, of course, and had discovered that the best defence was attack — so the slaughter was frightful. Our games seldom lasted more than fifteen minutes; then we set out the pieces and started again. We must have played nearly twenty games of chess going up to Scotland in the train.

I was thirteen and Willy was two years older, so grandpapa said we were old enough to look after ourselves and we could go wherever we liked provided we stayed together. Willy wanted to catch fish so grandpapa gave him a small trout-rod and spent a whole morning teaching him how to use it. After that we went out every day and walked for miles over the rolling hills. I took a book and sat amongst the heather while Willy fished the burns. He caught a lot of small brown trout; they were delicious fried in oatmeal for breakfast.

The hills were absolutely deserted, we never saw any shooting parties, in fact we never saw anybody except the shepherd with his dog. Sometimes we lay in wait for him and, if he wasn't in a hurry, he would sit down for a "wee crack." Willy always wanted to know things and the shepherd answered his questions in a friendly way. He said it was fine to be a shepherd in the summer months but not so good in winter when the hills were covered with snow. His name was Jock Fraser and he lived in "a wee cottage amongst the hills."

"If ye follow yon burn ye'll come tae it," said Mr. Fraser, pointing. "Mebbe you'd call one afternoon; the wife would give you a cup o' tea."

"Wouldn't it be a bother for her?" I asked.

"Nae boather, she'd like it fine. The days are a bit lonesome for her," replied Mr. Fraser.

We were shy of calling on Mrs. Fraser so we put off the visit from day to day . . . but when it came to our last day we could put it off no longer.

"We must go," I said to Willy. "Mr. Fraser said it was lonesome for her — it would be unkind not to go."

Willy was very reluctant but I managed to persuade him to come with me; he took his rod and fished the burn which ran past the Frasers' cottage while I went up to the door. There was a little girl with red hair sitting on the bank so I stopped and spoke to her and admired her doll, which was made out of an old black stocking.

"Do you know the story about little black Sambo?" I asked.

She shook her head so I sat down and told her the story.

When the story was finished she came and sat in my lap and I rocked her to and fro and sang to her. I was still playing with the child when Willy came up from the burn. He was a little cross because he had had no luck.

"I don't know why you're so potty about kids," he said, standing and looking at me scornfully. Then he sat down and began to dismantle his rod.

So far there had been no sign of Mrs. Fraser. I had begun to think she must be away from home when the door opened and she came out with a dish-cloth in her hand.

"Is Mawgrit boathering you, miss?" she asked.

"Oh no!" I said. "We're having fun."

"What's the name of that hill?" asked Willy, pointing to the hill at the back of the cottage.

She looked at the hill doubtfully and then replied, "You'll need tae ask Jock."

I said politely, "You're Mrs. Fraser, aren't you? We met Mr. Fraser on the hill and he told us you lived here."

"Aye. Jock's the shepherd." She hesitated and then added, "Jock spoke about you. I'd ask you in for a cup of tea but maybe Mistress Maitland wouldna like it."

I was a little surprised but said hastily, "Oh, it doesn't matter a bit, Mrs. Fraser. We shall have to go home soon."

"Would you care for a drink o' milk?" she asked. "The cow calved three weeks syne and we've mair milk than we can use."

Willy refused the offer — he didn't like milk — but I accepted.

Mrs. Fraser fetched a cup of milk and stood and watched while I drank it.

"What lovely milk!" I said.

"Aye, she's a fine cow," said Mrs. Fraser proudly.

"Is she an Ayrshire?" asked Willy.

Mrs. Fraser hesitated.

"Perhaps she's a Hereford?" I suggested.

"You'll need tae ask Jock," said Mrs. Fraser.

By this time I had finished the milk so I rose and handed her the cup. "Thank you very much, Mrs. Fraser," I said. "I think we had better go home now. Could you tell me the time, please? We don't want to be late for supper."

"The clock's gane agley — you'll need tae ask Jock," replied Mrs. Fraser.

Willy and I managed to stifle our giggles until we were halfway down the hill; then we burst out laughing. We laughed and laughed — and all the way home we asked each other silly questions: Willy said, "How old are you, Sarah?" I paused for a few moments and then replied, "You'll need tae ask Jock." It was my turn now so I said, "Will it be a fine day to-morrow?"

We were still laughing when we went into the drawing-room and found Mother and the grans sitting there and talking.

"Hallo, you seem in good spirits!" said Grandpapa.

"Where have you been?" asked Mother.

"You'll need tae ask Jock," replied Willy, giggling.

"You've been to the Frasers'!" exclaimed Grandmama. "I hope you didn't go into the house."

"No," said Willy. "I was fishing and Sarah sat on the bank and played with the baby. I expect she's got a flea off the creature; it had flea-bites on its legs."

"Chickenpox," said Grandmama.

"Chickenpox?" exclaimed Mother in dismay.

Grandmama nodded gloomily. "There are several children and they've all got it. Janet told me yesterday."

"Goodness! Sarah will get it and give it to Lottie!" cried Mother in horrified tones.

"Calm yourself, Dorrie," said Grandpapa. "Sarah may have got chickenpox but she won't give it to Lottie."

"How do you know?"

"Because Sarah will be here and Lottie will be at Fairfield."

"Oh, Papa! I couldn't go home without Sarah!"

"Why not?" asked Grandpapa. "Do you think we couldn't look after her properly?"

"It would be a nuisance for you," said Mother, frowning.

"We should love to have Sarah," declared Grandmama.

"But she may get chickenpox!"

"That is the whole idea," Grandpapa agreed.

Mother continued to raise objections to the plan but grandpapa pointed out that if I returned to Fairfield and developed chickenpox Lewis and Willy and Lottie would all be in quarantine and therefore unable to return to school. More likely than not, said Grandpapa, they would develop the complaint one after another, in which case the whole family would be in quarantine for weeks.

This prediction scared Mother so much that she gave in and agreed to leave me behind.

"You *are* a lucky dog," said Willy as we went upstairs together. "Fancy being here, at Craignethan, instead of having to go back to school. I wish I had kissed the little brat."

"I wish you had," I told him with a sigh.

"Aren't you pleased, Sarah?"

"It won't be much fun without you."

"Better than school, anyway," declared Willy emphatically.

I said nothing. Of course it was very kind of the grans to offer to have me but I wasn't looking forward to being left behind; I thought it would be dull without Willy . . . However I needn't have worried; I was perfectly happy alone with the grans.

When Mother had been there they had talked to her all the time but now they talked to me; they discussed things with me and listened to what I said. This made me feel important. It was quite a new feeling and very pleasant.

Grandpapa and I went for walks and had jokes together and, in the evenings, he taught me to play piquet. At first he beat me every time but soon I became quite proficient and was able to give him a good game.

"It must be terribly dull for you," said Grandmama. "I wish we could ask some young people to tea. There are the Loudon boys — you'd like them, Sarah."

"We could ask them if they've had chickenpox," suggested Grandpapa.

"They haven't," replied Grandmama sadly. "The Dunnes haven't had it either. I might ask the Raeworths, but —"

"Don't worry," I said quickly. "I'm quite happy here by myself. It's so different, you see."

"Different?"

"You listen to what I say," I explained.

The grans looked at each other and smiled.

"Well, it's true," I told them. "At home nobody listens . . . everybody wants to talk. The only thing I *would* like to do is to go for a long walk over the hills. Willy and I found a lovely walk; we went up the path by the side of the burn and over Grey Ghyll and home by the old Drove Road. I could take a sandwich in my pocket and —"

"No," said Grandpapa firmly.

At first I thought it was a joke but Grandmama was shaking her head gravely so I knew he was serious.

"Why not?" I asked. "Nothing could harm me."

"You're not likely to be attacked by a wolf," agreed Grandpapa.

"Well, then," I said. "I'm quite sensible . . . you know that, don't you?"

"Oh, you're quite sensible, but even sensible people have been known to trip over a heather-root and twist an ankle — and, if they happened to be alone, they might lie out all night before anybody found them."

"I wouldn't mind," I declared. "The heather would make a lovely soft bed."

He chuckled. "That's true enough. Maybe you would sleep quite well but Grandmama and I would not."

Grandpapa never wasted words, but I knew that I must give up all idea of my expedition.

One day when we were in the garden Grandpapa said something which made such a deep impression upon me that it affected my whole life . . . and even now, many years after, I can still see him sitting on the garden seat with the September sunshine falling through the leaves of the apple-tree and making a sort of halo of his thick white hair. It was a Sunday afternoon. The grans had been to church in the morning but they had left me at home because I was still in quarantine. The sermon had been about "the lilies of the field" and Grandpapa had disapproved of it.

"Lilies don't have to toil and spin, they're just beautiful," I pointed out.

"I know," agreed Grandpapa, frowning thoughtfully. "But it isn't enough to be beautiful. I'm a soldier, not a parson, but I read my Bible carefully . . . and, to me, it's quite obvious that Jesus liked people who were enthusiastic: people who did things, looked ahead, and weren't easily turned from their purpose. Zaccheus climbed a tree because he wanted to see Jesus; some men brought their sick friend to be healed and let him

42

down through a hole in the roof; the blind man shouted at Jesus — and wouldn't stop shouting. We're told of the wise virgins who took plenty of oil for their lamps and of the woman who searched her house for the lost piece of silver . . . and of the man who wanted loaves in the middle of the night and kept on banging at the door. All these people, and many others, got what they wanted. They were rewarded for their enthusiasm, foresight, initiative and perseverance. They were go-getters, Sarah."

"Go-getters?"

"Yes," said Grandpapa, nodding. "Remember this, Sarah: you'll never get anything worth having unless you go all out to get it."

When the quarantine period was over — and I hadn't developed any spots — the grans took me to a hotel in Edinburgh for two nights; they said I deserved a little fun. We did some shopping and went to a play at the Lyceum Theatre. Then they put me into the train and I travelled to London. It was the first time I had been anywhere or done anything without Mother and it had made me feel much older, it had given me confidence in myself.

CHAPTER
FIVE

My visit to Craignethan had been delightful but I was glad to be home. They were all there when I arrived and they all welcomed me and wanted to hear what I had been doing.

"You must have eaten a lot," said Lewis. "You aren't nearly so plain and skinny."

Naturally I was charmed at this brotherly compliment.

"Yes, you're looking much better," agreed Mother.

Minnie, too, was pleased to see me and complimented me on my improved appearance. She had got a book from the library about British Columbia with pictures of gorgeous scenery and of huge wooden poles, as high as a house, carved and painted with terrifying figures.

"They're totem poles," explained Minnie. "The book says they're painted by Red Indians. I'd like fine to see them."

"So would I," agreed Willy, looking at the pictures with interest. "This one is the ugliest; I'll make a sketch of it."

Willy was clever at sketching so he made a diagram of the picture with coloured chalks before he went back to Barstow and, a fortnight later, on Minnie's birthday he sent her a little model of a totem pole about six inches high. He had carved and painted it in the school workshop.

Minnie was delighted with her present and showed it to everyone and said it was from her "jo." Willy had always been Minnie's favourite. Minnie was so grateful and wrote such a nice letter to Willy that he made her another present for Christmas: it was a little wooden stool, very strong and solid, for her to stand on when she was washing up dishes at the sink — and Minnie used it every day of her life.

While I had been away Lottie had made friends with the Meldrums. Originally they were Lewis's friends — Tom Meldrum had been at Bells Hill with him and was now at Barstow — but one day Lewis had taken Lottie over to Riverside and they had asked her to come again as often as she liked.

Lottie talked a lot about Riverside: about the green-houses and the tennis courts and the boat-house and the punts and about the large music-room which had a parquet floor and beautiful Persian rugs. Mrs. Meldrum was a widow but she liked entertaining so the house was usually full of young people, friends of Madeline and Tom and Ruth. Sometimes they rolled up the rugs in the music-room and danced. Madeline had a radiogram, Tom had a motor-bike, Ruth had a pony and they all had "marvellous clothes." I heard so much about the Meldrums that I got rather tired of them.

One Saturday when Lottie was going to lunch at Riverside Mrs. Meldrum rang up and invited me to come with her, and a big car with a chauffeur was sent to fetch us. Riverside was even more magnificent than I had expected: the carpets were thick and soft, the furniture was luxurious and there were enormous pictures on the walls. The whole effect was overpowering. Mrs. Meldrum was large and plump with pale blue eyes; she talked in a gushing sort of way: everything was "too marvellous," everyone was "absolutely wonderful" or "too sweet for words."

She fixed her eyes on me and said, "Lottie is too sweet for words . . . and of course you're frightfully clever, aren't you, Sarah?"

It made me very uncomfortable so I mumbled, "Oh, no, I'm not a bit clever, Mrs. Meldrum."

"Oh, you *are*! I know you are," she declared.

It seemed silly to argue with her so I was silent.

Then she asked me if I didn't think Madeline was "absolutely beautiful" and of course I had to agree. Madeline was the eldest of the family; she was seventeen, pretty and elegant, but certainly not "beautiful." She was spoilt by a discontented expression and an off-hand manner. If we had spoken to mother in the way that Madeline spoke to Mrs. Meldrum I don't know what would have happened.

Ruth was the same age as Lottie. She was sitting next to me at lunch so I tried to talk to her but she didn't seem to be interested in anything.

Madeline said there was a new play in London and she wanted to see it.

"Oh, what a marvellous idea!" exclaimed Mrs. Meldrum. "We'll go and stay at Claridge's and see the play and do some shopping. I haven't got anything fit to wear."

"I want a white fur coat," said Madeline.

"I want a new tennis racket," said Ruth. "I want a new frock for Daphne's birthday party and I want —"

"You had better make a list, darling," said Mrs. Meldrum.

"Oh heavens!" said Madeline wearily. "Have we got to go to London in a body? I wouldn't have suggested it if I had known —"

"Don't worry!" cried Tom. "I don't want to go to London with you. I want a canoe. Hodson has a splendid canoe, it's much better sport than a clumsy old punt."

"A canoe would be fun!" exclaimed Ruth.

"Oh, I shan't take you in my canoe," declared Tom. "You're much too silly. Canoes aren't meant for mugs. I shan't take Madeline either; she'd make a fuss if she got splashed."

"I wouldn't come in your canoe if you paid me," said Madeline loftily. "Anyhow you haven't got it yet."

"I'll ask Watkins about it," said Tom.

"Yes, ask Watkins, darling," said Mrs. Meldrum. "Watkins is absolutely marvellous; he's *sure* to know the best place to get a canoe." She rose and added, "I'll go and phone about tickets for the play. We could go next week, couldn't we?"

"Oh, you are silly!" exclaimed Madeline. "Next week is the ball in Larchester and we're having people to stay. You had better leave it to me; you'll just muddle the whole thing."

"Yes, darling," agreed Mrs. Meldrum meekly. She sat down and Madeline drifted away in her usual elegant manner.

"She'll take the stage box," said Ruth sulkily. "She'll sit in front like she always does and make eyes at the actors."

"Well, of course!" exclaimed Tom. "Madeline goes to a theatre to be looked at. Surely you know that by this time."

"She's absolutely beautiful," declared Mrs. Meldrum, smiling proudly.

The afternoon seemed very long. Mrs. Meldrum and Madeline were going to a dance so they went upstairs to rest, Lottie and Tom disappeared together and I was left with Ruth. She was still sulky and disagreeable and at last I gave up trying to talk to her; it was hopeless. We wandered about for a bit and then sat down on a seat and looked at the river.

"I hate families," said Ruth after a long silence.

I didn't know what to say so I said nothing. It was the only remark she made — except yes and no — the whole afternoon.

After tea the car was ordered to take us home. Lottie was very silent — I wondered what she was thinking — but presently she heaved a big sigh and said, "It doesn't seem fair."

"Doesn't seem fair?" I asked.

"They can have everything they want."

"Yes, but they aren't happy."

"Not happy? Whatever do you mean, Sarah?"

"They aren't nice to each other."

48

"Tom is nice," declared Lottie. "Tom is going to take me out on the river in his canoe." She sighed again and added, "Oh dear, I wish we had a lovely house like the Meldrums and lots of money! It doesn't seem fair."

The Meldrums asked me to lunch again the following Saturday but I told Mother I would rather stay at home.

"Why?" asked Mother in surprise.

"Well . . . I just don't like them very much, that's all."

"You don't like them?"

"No, not very much."

I could see that Mother was waiting for me to explain why I didn't like the Meldrums but I couldn't find a sensible reason to give her. It would be silly to say that they were too rich or that they weren't nice to each other . . .

"Lottie is very fond of them," said Mother.

"Yes, I know."

"Lottie enjoys going to Riverside."

"Yes, but I don't think it's very —"

"Perhaps you're a little bit jealous, Sarah."

"Jealous? Why should I be jealous?" I asked in surprise.

"I just thought — perhaps — you might be," said Mother vaguely.

I had been going to say that I didn't think it was very good for Lottie to go to Riverside so often, it was making her discontented with her own home, but I couldn't say it now because Mother would think I was jealous. It was silly, really: I wasn't the least bit jealous of the Meldrums in spite of all their riches — in fact I felt rather sorry for them, but I couldn't explain that either.

"I think you ought to go, Sarah," said Mother after a short silence.

"Why don't you go instead of me?" I suggested.

"Oh, I couldn't! They haven't asked me. I couldn't go without being invited."

"No, I suppose not," I said doubtfully. I wished the Meldrums would ask Mother to lunch; I felt certain that she would dislike them (and perhaps she would know the reason) but, strangely enough, they never once invited Mother to the house.

Long afterwards, when I thought of this conversation with mother, I felt rather guilty; perhaps if I had had more courage and had told her what was in my mind, she might have listened and done something about it, but I don't know . . .

Lewis had always wanted to be a soldier — it was in his blood — but Mother was so upset at the idea of his going to Sandhurst that he gave in and went to Oxford instead. He went to St. Clement's College to read Law but he spent most of his time playing cricket and he made a great many friends. Fairfield is thirty miles from Oxford and one Friday afternoon Lewis came home to see us, riding a very ancient motor-bike which he had bought for ten pounds from a man who was getting a new one.

It happened to be Willy's half-term holiday — he had come from Barstow for the week-end — and he was so interested in the bike that Lewis took him out for a run

50

to show him its paces. They went off together in tremendous spirits with Willy sitting on the pillion.

Lewis had to go back to Oxford the following morning — he was playing in a cricket match — so we all came out on to the drive to see him off.

"Do be careful, Lewis!" exclaimed Mother. "Don't go too fast, will you?"

"Oh, I'll be all right!" cried Lewis. He jumped on to the bike and tried to start the engine — but without success.

Lewis tried over and over again; he tried everything he could think of; he tinkered with the machine for nearly half an hour but nothing he could do was any use; eventually he was obliged to give up the struggle and go to Oxford in the bus.

Lewis was very hot and angry; he said he had been "sold a pup."

"Poor old pup, nobody loves you," said Willy, looking at the dirty old bike very sadly.

Willy and I had arranged to go up to the woods that afternoon; we had found a young cuckoo in a hedge-sparrow's nest and we wanted to see what was happening. I looked for Willy everywhere and at last I found him in the coach-house. He had taken "the pup" to pieces and all the bits were lying spread out on newspapers on the floor. The two wheels were propped up against one wall and the framework against the other.

"Goodness!" I exclaimed in dismay.

"She only wants cleaning, that's all," said Willy, pushing back his hair and leaving a black oily streak on his forehead. "I don't suppose anyone has taken the trouble to clean her for years. I wish you'd fetch me some old cloths, Sarah. Ask Minnie for some bits of rag."

I went and got a bundle of cloths and rags. I was terribly worried because unless Willy could put the bike together again there would be a frightful row. However, now that the bike was all in pieces, it was no good saying anything.

"You can help," said Willy. "You can wash the wheels and polish them . . . hand me that spanner, Sarah."

Willy worked all the week-end (except on Sunday morning when he had to go to church). When all the little bits had been thoroughly cleaned he began to put them together again and by Monday afternoon the job was finished.

"Now we shall see some fireworks," said Willy, standing back and looking at the machine with satisfaction. "Come on, Sarah! I'll take you for a spin."

I was rather doubtful. Certainly the pup *looked* a great deal better; it was nice and shiny . . .

"Come on," repeated Willy. He wheeled the bike out of the coach-house and after a few struggles with the pedal the engine started. I jumped on behind Willy and we roared off down the drive.

Father was standing at the church gate; he looked up in alarm as we whirled past.

It was thrilling. I clung round Willy's waist with both arms; the wind whistled in my ears.

"Are you all right, Sarah?"

"Yes," I said breathlessly.

"Not scared?"

"No, it's lovely."

"She's doing thirty-five — not bad for the old pup! I'll take you along the Larchester road where there's a downhill stretch. I want to get her up to forty."

He got her up to forty on the downhill stretch, then we went round by Brailsford and home to tea.

Father and Mother were both at the gate, waiting for us, so Willy switched off the engine and glided up to them and stopped.

"Where have you been?" asked Father sternly.

"Oh, just for a spin," replied Willy.

"You had no right to take Lewis's motor-bicycle — and less right to ask Sarah to go with you. That machine isn't safe."

"She's quite a good machine. Lewis was lucky —"

"It's a horrible contraption," interrupted Father. "The sooner Lewis gets rid of it the better. He nearly ruptured himself trying to get it to start on Saturday morning."

"If you want an engine to run sweetly you've got to look after it properly," explained Willy.

"How did you get the thing to start?"

"Cleaned it, that's all."

I said quickly, "Willy took it all to pieces and cleaned it."

"Took it to pieces?" asked Father incredulously.

"She was dirty, clogged up with oil and grit. There was nothing else wrong with her," said Willy.

"It was clever of him, wasn't it?" I said.

"Yes," admitted Father reluctantly. "Of course I know nothing at all about these machines . . ."

"It was terribly clever, Father. The engine was in little bits and pieces all over the floor, and Willy put it together again. It goes like the wind now. You saw us, didn't you?"

"Where did you learn how to do it, Willy?"

"At Barstow," replied Willy. "Oh, not in school, of course! They never teach you anything useful at school. There's a very good mechanic in the garage near the station; Romford and I go and work there in our spare time."

"You would be better employed playing cricket."

"Romford and I are keen on engines. He's going into his father's engineering works when he leaves school and Mr. Romford says he'll take me —"

"You're going to Oxford."

"No, Father," said Willy, getting very red in the face. "No, I don't want to go to Oxford. I want to go to Romford's Works and learn about engines."

"What a ridiculous idea!" exclaimed Father, turning and walking up the drive to the house.

Willy hesitated and then wheeled the pup into the coach-house.

I followed more slowly with Mother.

"You shouldn't have done it," said Mother. "I was terribly worried when Father said he'd seen you."

"I'm sorry you were worried. It was lovely — and not a bit dangerous."

"You looked dreadful! Your hair was flying and your skirt was up to your knees. You're getting too old to behave like a tomboy, Sarah."

"I'm sorry, but you see Willy has been working at it for days and I've been helping him — polishing bits and holding spanners. When he had finished and got the engine to start I was so excited that I *had* to go with him."

"You are an awful girl," said Mother, smiling. She added, "I meant to be very cross with you and give you a lecture."

I took her arm and said, "Please don't ever be very cross with me because I couldn't bear it."

"Sarah, did you know about this absurd plan of Willy's?"

"Not really. Of course I knew he was interested in mechanical things. He has always liked making things — you know that, don't you? I wish you'd seen him putting the engine together. His hands are very clever and he knew exactly how to do it. You'll let him go to Romford's Works, won't you?"

"That's for Father to say."

"But you'll help, Mother? You see, Willy isn't very good at explaining his ideas."

"Willy hasn't much tact," admitted Mother.

"But you've got masses of tact," I told her.

She laughed and said, "I need it."

This was perfectly true. Mother needed masses of tact to deal with all the troublesome people in the parish.

Nothing more was said at the time, but eventually Willy got his own way. Father wrote to Mr. Romford and it was arranged that when Willy had passed his exams he was to leave Barstow and go into Romford's Works as an apprentice.

Meanwhile Lewis was very pleased to find the pup in good condition — as well he might be! — and he wrote Willy a very nice jokey letter which began:

Dear Vet,

I enclose ten bob as a small remuneration for your valuable services. My pet is now in the best of health and spirits; his previous owner is as sick as mud at having sold him to me . . . Willy was pleased with the letter and even more pleased with the ten bob. He bought a dilapidated electric radiator which wouldn't work and put it in order and used it in his study.

CHAPTER
SIX

Now that the pup was in good condition Lewis came home quite often and sometimes brought a friend to lunch. We heard a lot about one of his friends who lived in lodgings in The High. His name was Reeder and his father had a big estate in Austria. Reeder was a good deal older than Lewis and had come to Oxford to read English literature and history.

"You must bring him home some day," said Father.

"Oh, he isn't your sort; you wouldn't like him."

"I should be sorry to think I wouldn't like a friend of yours."

"Well, he's — he's Austrian," explained Lewis. "He's a Roman Catholic so he thinks it's very queer for a priest to be married and have a family. I don't know whether he'd want to come. He might, of course, because he's a great chap for new experiences; he says they enlarge the outlook."

"Perhaps he might enlarge our outlook," said Father, somewhat dryly.

"Oh, he's a great chap," declared Lewis. "He's got a sports car and goes all over the place. Last Saturday the crazy fellow went to Limehouse 'to see what it was like' and got into a row with some dockers. He came back to college with a black eye! He got ragged about that, I can tell you!"

"He sounds very aggressive," said Mother apprehensively.

"He isn't," declared Lewis. "He's got foreign manners — very polite, you know. He's tall and broad-shouldered with blue eyes and reddish-brown hair."

"I'd like to see the young man," said Father.

"Well, I can ask him," said Lewis doubtfully.

Lewis asked him and he accepted, so the following Saturday the two came to lunch.

I was interested in Lewis's friend and had been watching from the upstairs window, so I saw them arrive in a beautifully shiny sports car. As so often happens my mental picture of "Reeder" wasn't in the least like the original. He was tall, of course, and he had dark brown hair with a reddish tinge in it . . . but still the picture didn't fit.

"Reeder" uncurled his long legs and got out of the car and stood on the gravel, stretching himself and smiling.

"Oh, lovely!" he exclaimed. "This is the real England, Morris! This is Trollope's England."

"You mean Barchester and all that," said Lewis.

"Yes, indeed! The house is old and beautiful; it has an air of its own. It has a perfume . . ."

At this moment the front door opened and Father came out; he advanced with outstretched hand. "I'm very glad to see you," he said. "It's good of you to come."

58

"It was exceedingly good of you to ask me, sir," replied the visitor.

Mother was calling to me so I ran downstairs and found her putting the finishing touches to the luncheon table, straightening the knives and forks and rearranging the bowl of roses. "Do you think it looks nice, Sarah?" she asked anxiously. "I want him to see that it's a good thing for priests to be married."

"He may think it's too nice."

"Too nice? What do you mean?"

"Roman Catholic priests live very simply."

"We live very simply," declared Mother. "And it isn't Lent. Listen, Sarah, we must have lunch punctually because we're starting with a *soufflé*. Minnie makes such delicious *soufflés*."

"They've gone into Father's study."

"I know. He's giving them sherry. I do hope he won't keep them there too long. If Father begins to talk about something that interests him he's apt to forget the time. You'll have to go and make them come, Sarah."

Mother's fears were not unjustified. They were deep in conversation when I was sent in to "make them come."

Father said, "This is my daughter, Sarah."

At once the visitor rose and bowed gravely — as if I were grown-up and important.

I bowed too; then I said, "Mother wants you to come to lunch now."

"Presently," said Father, waving his hand. "Tell Mother we'll come when we've finished our sherry."

"But it's a *soufflé*. It's a cheese *soufflé*, Father!"

Lewis's friend smiled at me. He said, "Let us go, sir! With your permission we could take our glasses with us. Time and tide and *soufflés* wait for no man."

Father laughed. "That's rather good!"

Willy was at home that Saturday but not Lottie (she was spending the day at Riverside), so there were six of us at lunch. I could see that Father liked Lewis's friend; I liked him too; he was much more interesting than Lewis's other friends, and he had much better manners. Perhaps his manners were "foreign" but they were very pleasant.

"What shall we call you?" asked Father, smiling at him.

"I have several names," he replied, "It is good to have several names because one is several different people — a different person to each of one's friends."

Father nodded. "That's true."

"I am called Ludovic Charles Edward Reeder."

"Charles Edward?"

"My mother was a MacDonald."

"An admirable reason."

"Perhaps you would care to call me Charles, sir?"

"Nobody calls you Charles!" exclaimed Lewis.

"But that is just the reason. I am a different person to-day at Fairfield."

"You speak English wonderfully well," said Mother.

"Thank you, Mrs. Morris. I spoke it with my mother, so it is not difficult to me, but I am too stiff. I wish to learn to speak like an Englishman."

"That's the reason you've come to Oxford," said Father, nodding. "How do you like it, Charles?"

"Oh, I like it very much. I find the work extremely interesting . . . and the air is free. One can say what one likes."

"I always say what I like," said Lewis.

"You would not be able to do so if you lived in my country."

"Have you made many friends here?" asked Father.

Charles hesitated and then said, "Not real friends. I find the young men . . . unripe. Is that the correct word, sir?"

"It expresses your meaning perfectly well and, after all, we speak of a 'ripe old age,' so why not an 'unripe youth'? But the word in common use is 'immature.'"

"Thank you, sir," said Charles. "Perhaps the young men are immature because England is a happy place . . ." He hesitated.

"You were going to say something more," said Father.

"Lewis has just told us he says what he likes. I find it difficult to put into words, but this is my thought: civilisation is like the crust of a pie which covers a mass of violence and barbarism. Here, in your island, the crust is so thick that you walk upon it with confidence, as if it were solid stone."

"You mean we're living in a fool's paradise?"

"Perhaps not. Perhaps the crust is so thick here, in England, that there is no need for fear."

Lewis had been left out of the conversation — and Charles was his friend. He smiled mischievously and said, "You're having a dull Saturday compared with last week."

"Dull?" asked Charles in surprise.

"You had a fight with a docker, hadn't you? He gave you a black eye. Why don't you tell us about it?"

"It was not a glorious battle," said Charles uncomfortably.

"That's nonsense!" Lewis declared. "It must have been a terrific battle. I wish I'd seen it."

"Charles doesn't want to talk about it," said Father.

"No, I would rather not talk about it," agreed Charles. "I am not fond of battles but sometimes one is obliged to fight for what is right." He sighed and added, "It is a wicked world and it is not getting any better."

"There, I must disagree with you, Charles," said Father. "I've no wish to enter into a philosophical argument — I should probably get the worst of it — but I will just ask you to study history."

"I am studying history, Mr. Morris."

"Then you must realise that the world is becoming more humane."

"More humane?" asked Charles.

"We have become kinder and more tolerant. A few hundred years ago you and I would have burnt each other at the stake; to-day you have accepted my hospitality and sit at my table, a welcome guest . . . But we needn't go back so far. Less than a hundred years ago little children were made to work in the mines and men were transported for stealing a loaf of bread to feed their starving families. Nowadays children are cared for and educated and nobody need starve. It's true that we read of dreadful things in the papers, of cruelty and violence and murders . . . but these things are NEWS. There are hundreds of thousands of people,

62

leading decent lives and trying to follow the teachings of Christ, but these people aren't NEWS so you don't hear about them."

Charles had been listening carefully. He nodded. "Yes, sir. It is true what you say. You have given me something to think about. I hope you will not misunderstand if I tell you I am surprised to find myself so happy and comfortable in your house."

"I understand your feelings perfectly, but the fact that you expected to find us less congenial saddens me. There should be more coming and going between people of different nationalities, then it would be a very much better world."

"Oh yes, how much I agree!" exclaimed Charles. "That is what I am trying to do. That is why I came to England! But perhaps it is not much use for one man to be 'coming and going'?"

"It all helps," declared Father. "You'll go back to your own country and tell your friends that you found us reasonably human."

"I shall tell them you are good and kind."

"Tell us about your home," suggested Mother; she smiled and added, "The 'coming and going' should work both ways."

"It is so different from here," said Charles slowly. "Everything is different: the people, the way of life, everything. I find it very difficult to explain."

"What does your father do?" asked Mother.

"He is a landowner. He has a castle and big estates; there are several farms and there are woods and meadows. One can ride for miles over the property. My mother died some years ago; my elder brother and my young sister live with my father. Rudolph is the heir, you understand, so there was no reason why I should not come to England; it is what my mother wished me to do."

"Have you any relations in this country?" asked Mother.

"I have a cousin in Scotland. He is a MacDonald and lives in Edinburgh. Perhaps some day I will write to him and suggest a meeting but I am a little shy. He might not like me."

"Why shouldn't he like you?" asked Father, smiling.

"There are several reasons," replied Charles seriously. "I am a 'foreigner.' I cannot speak English properly and I am of a different religion."

Mother said, "Oh, yes, you're a Roman Catholic of course."

"That seems strange to you, Mrs. Morris?"

"Well, yes . . . it does, rather," replied Mother uncomfortably. "I mean I couldn't imagine myself . . . being one."

"My dear," said Father mildly. "If you had been born of Roman Catholic parents you would most certainly have been a Roman Catholic."

"What do you mean, Henry!" exclaimed Mother. "Papa is a pillar of the Episcopal Church at Ryddelton!"

"That is exactly what I meant," said Father, nodding. He rose and added, "This has been a most interesting conversation but I'm afraid I must leave you now; I'm expecting my church-warden at two o'clock. We have one or two matters to discuss."

When Father had gone everyone began to talk at once.

Lewis exclaimed, "You see what Father meant!"

"I don't understand —" began Mother.

"It is an interesting point —" said Charles.

"You *must* see it!" cried Lewis. "If you had been born of Moslem parents you'd be a Moslem, mewed up in a harem with all father's other wives and concubines."

"Lewis, dear, I don't think —"

"But people *do* change sometimes," put in Willy. "For instance there's a chap at Barstow —"

I interrupted, "Yes, but Mother isn't the sort of person to change; that's what Father meant."

"You are right, Miss Morris," said Charles. "Your mother is a person who will always be loyal to the teaching of her childhood."

Lewis wasn't listening. He had got into his stride and was telling Mother all the different things she might have been if she hadn't been born of Episcopalian parents ... and poor Mother was trying to look amused (at what was obviously one of Lewis's clever jokes) but was really a little frightened. I used to think Mother was like a hedge-sparrow who had hatched a cuckoo amongst her brood of nestlings; she was proud of her cuckoo, because he was big and beautiful and clever, but she didn't understand him in the least.

I thought it was time to rescue Mother so I asked if I should fetch the coffee and bring it into the drawing-room.

"Yes, Sarah," said Mother with a sigh of relief. "The tray will be too heavy for Minnie."

We all rose and I ran to fetch the tray. I was surprised to find that Charles had followed me into the pantry.

"May I help you?" he inquired politely.

"It's all right, thank you. I can manage."

"But why should you carry a heavy tray when there is a strong man to help you, Miss Morris?"

"You'd better call me Sarah, hadn't you? I mean if we're going to call you Charles . . . but perhaps you just meant Father and Mother?"

He said gravely, "It will be very pleasant to call you Sarah, and I shall be honoured if you will call me Charles."

I nodded . . . I was glad I had asked him. I wanted to call him Charles. "But perhaps I shall never see you again," I said.

"Never see me again?" asked Charles in astonishment.

"I mean you've seen us now. You've seen an English priest with a family. It's been a new experience and enlarged your outlook, so —"

"Oh dear! Is that what your brother said of me?"

"Isn't it true?"

"Yes, it is true," admitted Charles, laughing. "But it is not the whole truth. My outlook has been more enlarged than I expected and enlarged in a very surprising way."

"You mean you like us?" I suggested.

"Very much," he replied seriously. "I hope we may see each other frequently."

I nodded and said, "So do I."

"Perhaps you and Mrs. Morris will come to Oxford one day and have lunch with me. There is a hotel called The Mitre —"

"It's very expensive!"

"All the same I should like it. I should like to make return for the hospitality I have received. Would Mr. Morris care to come?"

"Well, no, he wouldn't really; he doesn't like going out to lunch . . . but it would be lovely for us, of course. Do you really want us or are you just being polite? Lewis says it's a frightful bore having relations to lunch."

He laughed. "But you and Mrs. Morris are not my relations, Sarah."

"All the same, it might be a bore."

"It will not be a bore," he declared. Then he lifted the tray — it was the big silver tray and it really was very heavy — and carried it into the drawing-room.

The drawing-room was large, it was shaped like an L with a bow-window and a glass door which led into the garden. The fitted carpet, with an all-over design of roses, had faded into soft shades; the cretonne covers and pink velvet curtains had faded too. Lewis was ashamed of the drawing-room (he said it was old-fashioned) so I wondered what his friend would think of it.

"Oh, but this is perfection!" exclaimed Charles, standing in the doorway with the tray in his hands.

"You mean this room?" asked Lewis incredulously.

"Yes, indeed! But perhaps it is impolite of me to make the remark? It is just that I cannot help it."

"But, Reeder, it's terribly shabby!"

"No, no, it is right for the house — and right for Mrs. Morris. Time has been gentle here."

"What on earth do you mean?"

Father said, "Lewis, take the tray from Charles."

Lewis got up, muttering, "Well, I don't know what he means."

"Charles's meaning is perfectly clear," declared father. "Time has had a hand in the making of your mother's drawing-room; everything has been here for years and has matured gently in the sunshine. There isn't a jarring note."

"Yes, that is what I meant," said Charles. He looked round and added, "Oh, a Bechstein!"

"Are you fond of music?"

"It is what I have missed more than anything!"

"But there's plenty of music at Oxford," objected Lewis. "You go to concerts and you've got a super radiogram."

"I cannot make music," explained Charles. "At home we make music; my father plays the violin and Rudi his 'cello. Often we have friends to come in the evening and play with us. It is good to listen to music but better to make it."

"Yes, I see what you mean," admitted Lewis. "It's better to play cricket than to watch it."

Charles had crossed the room and was looking at the piano; he laid his hand caressingly on the shining wood.

"Play to us, Charles," suggested Mother.

"Not now!" exclaimed Lewis. "I'm going to take him round and show him the place. You want to see it, don't you, Reeder? You said it was like Barchester."

Charles hesitated.

"Come on," said Lewis, rising. "It's too fine an afternoon to fug indoors."

He allowed himself to be dragged away.

"Charles wanted to play the piano," I said.

"He's Lewis's friend," said Mother. "It's natural that Lewis should want Charles to himself for a nice little chat."

I had hoped that Charles would play the piano later, but I was disappointed. Lewis and Charles were late in coming back for tea and afterwards Mother showed Charles some miniatures which she kept in a glass-topped table. Most of them were old family heirlooms, and valuable, but there was one of Lottie when she was three years old. It had been painted by a good artist and was very like her.

"This is my baby," said Mother, smiling and handing it to him.

"But she is lovely!" Charles exclaimed. "I did not know you had another daughter, Mrs. Morris."

"She's my baby," repeated Mother, looking at the picture fondly. "She's much younger than the others. We're all devoted to her — and I think perhaps we spoil her a little."

"But that is natural," said Charles, smiling. "The baby is everyone's pet."

Mother always talked of Lottie like that; it used to annoy me, for Lottie was only two years younger than I was . . . and even then, at the age of twelve, she was a definite person with her own very definite ideas. She had begun to come to St. Elizabeth's with me and I had intended to look after her until she found her feet (I remembered what it was like to be "a new girl") but Lottie dropped on to her feet without any help from me; she loved school and had her own little circle of friends.

When Charles had gone I began to wonder if he had said anything to Mother about lunch at The Mitre but she didn't mention it, so I decided that he must have changed his mind.

Part Two

CHAPTER
SEVEN

When the summer holidays began Willy went to stay with the Romfords at Wimbledon; he went off very cheerfully, saying that Mr. Romford was going to show him the engineering works.

One morning I was in church with Mother, helping her to polish the brasses, when I heard the sound of music. At first I thought that Lewis had switched on the wireless . . . and then I remembered that Lewis and Lottie had gone to lunch at the Meldrums'; I opened the church door and listened. Someone was playing the piano in the Vicarage . . . and it certainly wasn't Father! I ran across the churchyard, through the little gate and down the path and peeped in at the glass door in the drawing-room. Charles was sitting at the piano and playing!

I stood on the step and listened entranced; it was tremendously exciting — I had never heard anyone play like that! The piano was sideways to the window so I could see his hands; sometimes they chased each other up and down the keys; sometimes they paused and struck a chord caressingly. He leant forward and played so softly that the piano seemed to be singing; he leant back and made the piano shout in triumph.

Presently he got up and came over to the window. "Sarah! I did not know I had an audience!" he exclaimed.

"It's only me."

"Only Sarah," he said, smiling. "Well, the audience had better come in. I was going to shut the window because it occurred to me that I was making too loud a noise. I meant to play softly . . . but then I forgot."

I went in and he shut the window.

"I hope it is all right," he said doubtfully. "Mr. Morris said I might come and play on the Bechstein when I liked; it is now the vacation so I am more free — and I came."

"Father always means what he says."

Charles nodded. "It was foolish of me to ask."

"Please go on playing, Charles."

"You like music? Perhaps you play yourself?"

"I play tinkle, tinkle, that's all. If I could play like you I'd like it."

"Oh dear!" exclaimed Charles, laughing. "You play tinkle, tinkle — and you do not like it!"

"No, it's a waste of time. I wish you would go on playing. The piano sang for you. It never does that for anyone else. It sang and shouted . . . and whispered. Why don't you go on playing?"

"Because I am having a very interesting conversation with Sarah. Let me see your hands," he added, sitting down beside me on the sofa.

I hid them and said, "No, they're dirty; I've been helping Mother to clean the brasses in church."

"Then it is good dirtiness . . . and it does not matter because I can see through the dirtiness." He took my hands and felt them carefully, stretching them out and flexing the fingers. "They are fine hands, well-shaped and strong . . . so there is no excuse for tinkle, tinkle; some day they will make the Bechstein sing."

"They won't — ever," I said hopelessly.

"What else do you do, beside tinkle, tinkle?"

"You mean lessons? We have arithmetic and grammar and history and geography and French. I like history best."

"Not French?"

"The verbs are dull, but I quite like French conversation. We have it twice a week."

Charles nodded and began to speak French . . . at least I supposed it must be French, but to me the stream of sound issuing from his lips might have been Dutch or Turkish or Chinese.

"That isn't the kind of French we have at school," I told him.

"But there is only one kind of French. The French that is spoken in France!"

He was looking at me in such bewilderment that I began to giggle feebly.

"What is this?" asked Charles. "Surely the reason for learning a language is to converse with people?"

I nodded again. "It's no good at all," I agreed. "It's worse than tinkle, tinkle. I suppose you speak German too?"

"It is my native language."

He rose and strolled over to the piano; it had a fascination for him.

"Please play," I said.

"I shall sing you a little German song about spring coming to the mountains and about a very beautiful young girl gathering wild flowers."

He was still playing and singing to me when Mother came back from church. She tried the glass door; but it was shut so I got up and let her in.

Charles stopped in the middle of a song and rose and bowed. "I hope this is not presumption, Mrs. Morris?"

"Father told him he could," I murmured.

She held out her hand and smiled. "It's delightful; please come and play whenever you feel inclined."

"That would be too frequently, Mrs. Morris, but I will come sometimes."

"You must stay to lunch," declared Mother. Then a slightly anxious look appeared on her face and she glanced at the clock. (I knew she was trying to remember what we were having for lunch.)

"How kind!" exclaimed Charles. "I should like to do so very much. Perhaps another day, when you are not otherwise engaged, you and Sarah will be my guests in a hotel at Oxford. It is called The Mitre and is a very respectable place."

"Do you really want us?" asked Mother in surprise.

"But naturally! It would be very strange to invite you if I did not want you to come. I hope you will accept my invitation?"

Mother was looking a little doubtful. She said, "It's very kind of you, Charles, but the bus takes an hour and a half —"

"I could meet you at Larchester if it would be more convenient. We could lunch at the Golden Hind."

"That would be lovely," Mother declared. "You'd enjoy it too, wouldn't you, Sarah? We could get an early bus and do some shopping."

"When will you come?" asked Charles.

It wasn't easy to arrange a day for the expedition: the Work Party met on Friday afternoons; Saturday morning was set aside for the flowers in church; on Monday the flowers had to be cleared up and the church tidied; there was a choir practice on Tuesday evening . . .

"But, Mother, we could be back in time for that!" I exclaimed.

"I like to practise the psalms before they come."

"What about Wednesday, Mrs. Morris?" suggested Charles.

"Wednesday!" cried Mother. "Oh, no, Wednesday is absolutely *hopeless*."

"Hopeless?" asked Charles, in bewilderment.

"The Bishop is coming."

"Oh, dear! Then Wednesday is indeed without hope."

"Tuesday," I said firmly. "You needn't practise the psalms, just this once."

She sighed. "Well, perhaps not . . . just this once."

"It is to be Tuesday?" asked Charles, in doubtful tones.

"Yes," I said. "We'll meet you at the Golden Hind on Tuesday at one o'clock unless something frightful happens to prevent us. That's right, isn't it, Mother?"

"Yes, dear," said Mother meekly, and she hastened away to talk to Minnie about food.

"I am learning all the time," said Charles, smiling. "I am learning that it is not an easy job to be the wife of an English priest." He chuckled and added, "I am beginning to wonder how it is possible for a parish to be properly administered without the help of a wife."

"It must be difficult," I agreed. Then I ran to see if mother wanted me to lay the table for lunch.

Father enjoyed talking to Charles. While we were having lunch they talked of life at Oxford.

"When I was there I played cricket," said Father.

"I have played cricket," said Charles. "It was only once — they did not ask me twice. It was like this, Mr. Morris: they were having a friendly game and they wanted another man. I told them I did not know how to play cricket but they said it was easy . . . and they all gave me instructions which made it more difficult. For a long time it was not my turn but I watched what they did. I saw that the batsman hit the ball and ran quickly to the other end. Then it was my turn so I hit the ball as hard as I could and ran. 'Go back!' they shouted. I saw, then, that I had hit the ball too hard, it had trickled over the edge of the field, so I went back and waited for the next ball. Alas, the next ball bounced in a very strange way so I missed it altogether — but it did not hit the stumps. I went forward to see what had made the ball bounce like that . . . it might have hit a stone. Then I looked round and saw that the man behind the stumps had picked up the ball; he knocked off the two little bits of stick and said, 'Howzzat?' — and the umpire said 'Out.' But why?" asked Charles with a bewildered air. "Why was I 'out'? The ball did not hit the stumps, I am sure of that." He sighed and added, "They were all very kind; they thumped me on the back; one man said, 'Bad luck, old chap! You'll know better next time.' Another man said, 'You've made four, that's not so dusty.'"

"Not bad for a first attempt," agreed Father, laughing.

"But, Mr. Morris, how had I made four runs when I had not run at all?"

Father tried to explain and offered to lend Charles a book about cricket.

"It is no use," said Charles sadly. "Several people have lent me books . . . but the books do not explain the essential principles. It seems that you must know all about the game before you read the books. How did you begin to learn cricket, Mr. Morris?"

"I don't know — really," replied Father thoughtfully. "I can remember playing with my father in the garden when I was about six years old."

"Then it is quite hopeless and I shall not bother about it any more," declared Charles.

After lunch, when we were having coffee in the drawing-room, the conversation took a more serious turn. Mother had gone to a Red Cross meeting and I was sitting quietly on the sofa.

"I want to ask you something," said Father. "The other day when you were here you spoke of civilisation as a crust; you likened it to the pastry crust of a pie, concealing a seething mass of violence and barbarism. The metaphor has haunted me, Charles."

"I am sorry, sir, I realised that my words had distressed you."

"Yes, I was distressed," said Father with a sigh. "But we shouldn't shut our eyes to trouble. I didn't want to pursue the subject at the time because I knew it would upset my wife. Her only brother was killed in the retreat from Mons so she dreads war and everything to do with it. If there were to be another war — which God forbid — it would be even more terrible and our sons would be in the thick of it."

Charles was silent.

"That's what you meant, wasn't it?"

"If things go on as they are doing there will be another war, but that does not mean your sons will be fighting."

"I think it does, Charles. You can't keep wars in watertight compartments nowadays. It's that man, Hitler, of course. We won the war but the peace has been mismanaged; we should have made friends with Germany."

"Perhaps even now it may be averted."

"But you think it unlikely?"

"My father knows more of these things that I; he thinks war is inevitable. He detests the man Hitler and his treatment of the Jews. My father is not careful what he says. He is a baron; he has big estates; he has enemies in high positions."

"That sounds dangerous."

"It is very dangerous," said Charles in a low voice. "My brother and I have tried to warn him but he is fearless and speaks his mind openly. Oh, well, it is useless to talk of it."

"I must go," said Father, glancing at his watch. "I have some visiting to do this afternoon, but you needn't hurry away. Perhaps you'd like to go for a walk with Sarah and come back to tea?"

"I could take you up to the woods," I suggested.

They both turned and looked at me. I think they had forgotten I was there.

Father said, "Better not mention our conversation to Mother."

"No, of course not; she would worry." Oddly enough I wasn't worried. The last war had been over before I was born so it was just a legend to me — as far off as the campaigns of Marlborough. I couldn't imagine a war with guns firing and people trying to kill each other; it was utterly incredible to a child who had led a sheltered life in the peaceful English countryside.

Charles and I set off together. We went through the garden and climbed the wall into the field. I showed Charles the oak-tree and the Druids' stones and told him what Mr. Rickaby had said about them . . . and he was very interested. Then I told him that Willy and I had found a hedge-sparrow's nest with a cuckoo in it.

"Willy knows about birds," I said. "We come up to the woods quite often and watch them."

There was no sunshine; it was a silver day. As we climbed the steep path to the woods Charles said, "There is a softness here that we do not see in my country."

"Tell me about your country."

"I wonder what you would think of it, Sarah. I told you about Schloss Roethke, did I not?"

"It's a castle?"

"Yes, a castle with towers and a path along the top of the walls. In the old days a man was always there to watch for the approach of enemies. For hundreds of years it has belonged to my family so, although it is too large to be comfortable, I am very fond of it. The Schloss stands upon a cliff at the side of a stream where the water falls over a rock into a deep pool. All round there are woods and farms which belong to my father; the people belong to us too."

"Belong to you?" I asked.

"That is one of the so different things. Your English peasants have independent natures and depend upon themselves; our people depend upon us."

"That's feudalism, isn't it? England used to be feudal."

"Oh, yes," said Charles, nodding. "You told me history was your favourite subject. It is mine also."

"I've done Queen Elizabeth's reign three times."

"Why three times?"

"Well, I never get any further." I explained. "I did it when I first went to St. Elizabeth's and then, when I moved into a higher form, they were doing it. Now I've been moved again so I'm doing it again."

82

"This seems a dreadful waste of time. Surely it would be more useful to study some other period in history."

"Yes," I said thoughtfully. "Yes, it seems silly, doesn't it?"

"It shows a lack of co-ordination and supervision," said Charles.

We walked on in silence for a few moments.

"Do you live in the castle all the time?" I asked.

"I wish we did so," he replied ruefully. "Life in the country is free — freedom to do as I like and go where I like is important to me — but my father has a house in Vienna and we live there during the season. We entertain our friends and go to parties and concerts. Oh, it is quite pleasant for a short time, but I would rather mount my horse and ride for miles over the open country. My young sister is different, of course; she enjoys the festivities; she has a gay time in Vienna."

"Is your sister older than I am?"

"Oh yes, much older. Gretchen is seventeen. Already my father is thinking of arranging her marriage."

"Arranging her marriage?" I echoed in astonishment.

"It is the custom of our country," explained Charles. "Or perhaps I should say it is the custom for people in my father's position to make a good match for their daughters." He looked at me and added, "You are very young, Sarah."

"Why do you say that? Is it because I didn't know about marriages being 'arranged' in Austria?"

"No indeed! How could I expect you to know about the customs in our country? I said it because you have the eyes of a child."

"I'm fourteen . . . but I suppose that's too young to be interesting," I said sadly.

"It is not too young to be interesting."

"Good!" I exclaimed.

"Why is it good?"

"I was afraid you might be bored . . . and I *do* want to take you up to the top of the hill. It's such a lovely view."

"I never allow myself to be bored," he declared emphatically.

"What do you mean, Charles?"

"You thought I would be bored to have you and Mrs. Morris to lunch, and you think I might be bored to walk with you in the woods, but I would not do either of these things if it bored me."

"You couldn't help it," I pointed out. "I mean you needn't have asked us to lunch, but you couldn't have got out of this afternoon's walk when Father suggested it."

"I am very clever at getting out of things that I do not like to do — very clever indeed. My sister could tell you how clever I am."

"You might have come as a sort of duty — or just to be kind."

"My sense of duty and my kindness are not so great," declared Charles, laughing. He laughed so heartily that he had to sit down on a boulder.

I was obliged to smile, though I saw nothing funny about it. Then, quite suddenly, I thought of the reason why he had come: "I'm a new experience for you!" I exclaimed.

"Quite new," he agreed, chuckling.

"You don't know any girls in Vienna."

"I know a dozen girls in Vienna."

"Then why — ?"

"My sister's friends are different," explained Charles. "It is all different. I will tell you, Sarah: *One*, no father would suggest that I should walk with his daughter in the woods; *two*, if he were to do so, I should refuse to go; *three*, if I were so foolish as to accept, we would not talk about history and Druidical stones and cuckoos."

"What would you talk about?"

"The question does not arise; I have told you that I would refuse to go."

"But if you did —" I began.

"I would not," said Charles firmly. He rose and added, "Let us climb to the top of the hill."

CHAPTER
EIGHT

When I awoke on Tuesday morning I heard the rain pattering on the sloping roof outside my window. I jumped out of bed to see whether it was just a shower or was going to be a thoroughly wet day. Alas, the sky was grey all over! Would Mother say it was too wet to go to Larchester? Oh, why did it have to be wet to-day!

Fortunately by breakfast time the skies were clearing.

"Yes, we'll go," said Mother cheerfully. "There are several things I want for the house and it will be fun to have lunch with Charles. We'll take umbrellas."

I ran upstairs to put on my tweed coat and skirt; I liked it much better than any of my other clothes because it made me look older.

"You'll be too hot in that," said Mother. "A frock and your school blazer would have been better . . . but there's no time to change now."

I had often been to Larchester before, but I thought it had never looked so pretty as it did that morning when the bus stopped for a few minutes on the ridge of hills and we saw the town below us in the hollow by the river. The rain had stopped and the sun was shining on the church spires and the fine buildings, and glittering on the windows.

Part of the town is very old and encircled by a massive stone wall, which was built when it was necessary for towns to be fortified. The wall is so broad that there is a walk along the top and, here and there, a little tower which was used as a "lookout tower" for the soldiers.

From the ridge the road winds downhill, it crosses the river by a wide bridge and enters the town through an arched gateway.

There wasn't a breath of wind this morning; the smoke from the chimneys was drifting lazily; the sky and the air and the buildings were all washed beautifully clean and fresh. In that clear atmosphere everything seemed quite near . . . the steeple of St. Margaret's looked so near that it seemed as if you could put out your hand and touch it; four fan-tail pigeons, sitting one above the other on a crow-stepped gable, looked as if they had been carved out of snow-white marble.

We had to go through the old part of the town to get to the new part where there were shops and restaurants and the Town Hall and offices. Outside the Town Hall was a park with a pond and flower-beds and trees and seats.

We had a busy morning, shopping. Then we left all our parcels at the bus office and walked down to the Golden Hind . . . and although we were a little early Charles was waiting for us in the lounge.

Charles looked different to-day; he looked older. I thought at first it was because he was wearing a brown suit, instead of grey slacks and a tweed jacket, but afterwards I decided that it was because he was entertaining us to lunch. He had engaged a round table in the big bow-window which looked out on to the garden and the river.

"I hope you are ready for lunch," he said as we sat down.

"I'm absolutely starving," I said. "I expect Mother is, too; we had breakfast early and we've been shopping all the morning."

Mother laughed and nodded. I thought she looked even prettier than usual; her cheeks were pink and her eyes were shining. One of the nice things about Mother was that she enjoyed everything so much.

"How delightful it is to feed the hungry," said Charles. "It is so sad when one asks friends to a meal and they have no appetite. Let us see what we are going to eat."

We had a gorgeous lunch. I chose veal-and-ham pie with puff pastry and Mother had sweetbreads; then we all had asparagus and strawberry mousse. The asparagus was "extra"; Charles had ordered it beforehand.

Mother and Charles talked about music.

"You must come to the Vicarage as often as you like and play the piano," Mother told him.

"You are very kind," said Charles. "But I find I must go to Austria to see my family. I hope to return to Oxford in September and resume my studies."

"Do you mean you're going soon?" I asked.

"Yes, I must go to London on Friday to see my lawyer and adjust some business matters connected with my mother's estate . . . and then I must go to Schloss Roethke. It is unfortunate; I had hoped to stay in Oxford during the vacation and improve my English but my father has written asking me to go home."

"Oh well, we shall look forward to seeing you in September," said Mother, smiling.

After lunch Charles suggested that we might like to go on the river. There were boats to be hired at a landing-stage near the hotel.

"I'm afraid we must catch the three o'clock bus," said Mother.

"But the afternoon is so fine," said Charles. "It would be delightful on the river. I could take you to Fairfield in my car."

I looked at Mother anxiously.

"Well, that's very kind of you," she said. "It would be lovely, of course — and I can see Sarah wants to go — but I must be home by five."

Charles hired a rowing-boat. He explained that he was learning to punt but was not yet proficient.

There were lots of boats on the river that afternoon, but when Charles had rowed some distance up the river it was quiet and peaceful. I had been on the river once or twice with Willy but we had always gone down-river from the landing-stage so this part was new to me.

Charles had taken off his jacket and rolled up his sleeves; he had a blue silk shirt and his arms were strong and brown. We passed meadows with cows grazing in them and there were willow-trees hanging over the water. It was so still and sunny and peaceful that we didn't talk much.

Then suddenly we heard the sound of singing and a large punt came down the river towards us. It was absolutely full of people and a tall man in grey trousers with braces over his shoulders was standing up and punting with a long pole. The river was not very wide here so Charles drew in at the side under a willow-tree to let them pass.

"He isn't very good at it," said Mother apprehensively.

She had scarcely spoken when the man looked round and waved to us, this upset his balance and he fell into the water with a terrific splash, still clinging to his pole. The punt swept on without him.

"Goodness, he's drowning!" exclaimed Mother.

"No, no," replied Charles, laughing. "The water is little more than three feet deep. I hope you do not expect me to dive in and rescue him, Mrs. Morris."

By this time the man was standing up and I saw that the water only reached his waist. He stood with the pole in his hands and shouted angrily to his friends to come back and fetch him, but as he had the punt-pole they couldn't do anything and the current was carrying them farther away every minute.

When he saw that they couldn't or wouldn't come back he began to wade towards our boat.

" 'Ere!" he shouted. "You'll 'ave ter taike me 'ome!"

"No, my friend," replied Charles. "You are too wet to be a comfortable passenger in a boat with ladies, besides it will do you good to walk." And with that

Charles pushed off from the bank and rowed on up the river very quickly.

"Oh, the poor man!" exclaimed Mother.

"Put your fingers in your ears," said Charles.

Mother did as she was told, but I only pretended . . . so I heard some of the horrible things he said.

When we had reached a safe distance we stopped and watched him climb out of the river and start walking back to Larchester, still carrying the pole.

"I am afraid you think I am very hard-hearted, Mrs. Morris," said Charles sadly. "But he would have been a very unpleasant companion for you and Sarah . . . and it is quite true that it will do him good to walk. When one is very wet it is better to walk than to sit in a boat. He is not very nice, but we do not want him to get a severe chill, do we?"

I was laughing . . . and after a moment Mother began to laugh too.

When we turned to go back Charles let me row; it was quite easy rowing down the river. We kept a good lookout for the wet man, but we didn't see him, nor did we see the other people who had been in the punt.

Then we fetched our parcels from the bus office and Charles ran us home in his car.

It had been a lovely afternoon and I had enjoyed every minute of it.

At supper Mother told Father about the man who had fallen out of the punt — she always told Father everything — and Father laughed and said Charles was right.

"He was a horrid man," I said. "He had braces over his shirt and he called us dreadful names."

"Charles told you to put your fingers in your ears," said Mother.

"Yes, but I didn't put them in tightly," I explained.

Our school reports were taken very seriously by Father. Lewis was clever so he always got good reports — without having to do much work. Willy's reports were usually "could do better" but this term they were quite good because he wanted to pass his exams as soon as possible and go to Mr. Romford's Engineering Works. Lottie didn't bother about lessons; she played games and enjoyed herself, so her school reports were poor; but Miss Bain, the headmistress, had written "*a bright, attractive girl and very popular . . . should do well when she settles down*," so father and mother were quite pleased. They still thought of Lottie as "a child."

One morning Father called me into his study and I saw my reports lying on the table.

"Your reports are good, Sarah," he said. "But I'm distressed to find you haven't started Latin. You're quite old enough to start Latin, so I've decided to take you for an hour three times a week during the holidays. I'm sure we'll both enjoy it."

Father looked so pleased with the idea that I hadn't the heart to make any objections to working in the holidays; I thanked him and said it was very kind of him.

Then he began to explain how important it was to have a thorough grounding in Latin . . . and this gave me the opportunity I had been waiting for.

I said, "Yes, I know it's important, but I want to be able to speak to people in their own languages."

"That will come later, my dear. Latin is the groundwork —"

"Yes, Father, I want to learn Latin, but I've got to live in this world with all sorts of people: French and German and Spanish and —"

"You're learning French at school."

"Not the sort of French that French people talk."

He smiled . . . but I was grimly serious. I had been thinking about it for days and days and I knew this was the only chance of getting what I wanted. "And I want to learn German too," I went on desperately. "I want to be able to talk French and German properly and understand what they say."

There was silence. Father looked at me over the tops of his spectacles. "How long have you been thinking about this?"

"Oh, quite a long time." It seemed quite a long time to me.

"Have you thought how extra tuition in languages will fit in with your work at school?"

"I shall have to leave school. You see —"

"Leave school? Really, Sarah, I never heard such nonsense! You're only thirteen —"

"No, fourteen," I said quickly. "But it isn't my age that matters. It's because I know what I want."

"What do you want?"

"I want to learn languages . . . and I know what I don't want, Father. I don't want to spend hours and hours learning things that will never be any use, like fancy dancing and embroidery and how to make lamp-shades. I don't want to spend hours learning parts in the school play; I shall never be any good at acting. I shall never be any good at drawing either, so drawing lessons are just a waste of time."

"It's all part of your education; other girls learn these things — and so must you."

"Perhaps it's all right for other girls, but not for me. I want to learn languages."

"But there are other subjects: history and —"

"I can study history at home . . . and much better."

"Better?"

"Yes, I've done Queen Elizabeth's reign three times; this is a dreadful waste of time; surely it would be more useful to study some other —"

"Sarah!" interrupted Father. "What do you mean by saying you've done Queen Elizabeth's reign three times?"

I explained what had happened and added, "It shows a lack of co-ordination and supervision, doesn't it?"

He looked at me in surprise.

"Well, doesn't it, Father?"

"Yes, it certainly does."

"I can work at home," I told him. "I can read history; I can do Latin with you; I can learn to speak French properly and Minnie can teach me to cook."

"You're learning cookery at school. We pay extra for it."

"Minnie could teach me much better; she could teach me how to make sensible things. At school we're taught to make little cakes and decorate them with icing sugar."

"Well, I must say that doesn't sound very sensible."

"It would be much more useful to learn how to make a veal-and-ham pie. You like veal-and-ham pie, don't you, Father?"

"Yes, I must admit I'm very partial to a well-made veal-and-ham pie . . . but that isn't the point, Sarah. You must continue to go to St. Elizabeth's until you've obtained your School Certificate. Later, when you're older, you might want to take some sort of post, so it's essential to have your certificate. You hadn't thought of that, had you?"

"Yes, I thought of it, but it isn't important."

"It's exceedingly important."

"No, honestly, Father! If you want a job nowadays you've got to have specialised training. Daphne Frome is learning typing and shorthand and book-keeping — she wants a job in an office. Shorthand is terribly difficult."

"So I believe."

"I help her sometimes. You see she finds it difficult to read her own shorthand notes so she reads out as much as she can and I write it down for her. Afterwards we go back and fill in the gaps."

"There are other jobs besides working in an office."

"Yes, I know. Barbara is going to be a nurse, but I wouldn't like that. I don't want to work in a shop or —"

"Of course not!" exclaimed Father in horrified tones.

"Lots of girls work in shops," I told him. "Nell is learning to arrange flowers, she wants to work in a flower shop, and Jane Riley is going to a big dressmaker's in London. Freda King wants to go on the stage; her father made a fuss about it —"

"I don't wonder!"

"But he's given in and she's going to a Dramatic Academy! You see, girls are all different and want different things. Some girls are clever at figures, others are good at drawing or music or acting . . . but I'm not. I just want to learn languages so that I can talk to people and understand what they say."

"If I were to write to Miss Bain —"

"It wouldn't be any good. The mistress who teaches us French is English, so she doesn't teach us the proper way to speak. You couldn't expect Miss Bain to change everything just for me, could you?"

"No, I suppose not," said Father doubtfully.

"And anyhow we don't have enough time to learn French. I want to leave school because they aren't teaching me the right things. The wrong things are just a waste of time."

There was quite a long silence. I didn't say any more because I had said everything that I had meant to say; I had thought it all out beforehand. This was something I wanted terribly much and Grandpapa had told me that you never get anything worth having unless you go all out to get it. I had tried to think of what Father would say and what I should reply; fortunately the conversation had gone exactly as I had expected. I had even been able to bring in the words "co-ordination" and "supervision" which Charles had used about the history muddle . . . and they had impressed father quite a lot.

"We must find a Frenchwoman," said Father at last.

"You mean I can?" I cried in delight. "Oh, Father! But will it be very expensive?"

"I shouldn't think so. Anyhow you seem to know what you want."

"Oh, I do! . . . but you aren't disappointed with me, are you?"

"It would be foolish to be disappointed. People who don't know what they want aren't much use in the world."

All the same he sounded a little disappointed so I rose and went round the table and put my cheek against his. "I'm your own Sarah," I said.

"Yes, of course you are, darling."

"It's settled, then?"

"It's settled that you're to have lessons from a Frenchwoman, but I shall have to consult Mother about your idea of leaving St. Elizabeth's. I don't know what she'll say about that."

"Yes, of course," I agreed cheerfully. I thought I knew what Mother would say. She liked having me at home and was always very sorry when the holidays were over.

CHAPTER
NINE

There was a great deal of argument in the family as to whether or not I should leave school but at last, when I had begun to feel hopeless, Father and Mother gave in quite suddenly and it was arranged as I wanted. Curiously enough it was Mother who was dead against the idea and had to be persuaded . . . and even after it was all settled she still had doubts.

"I hope we're doing the right thing," she said with a sigh.

It was a Saturday morning and we were in church together arranging the flowers.

"Of course it's the right thing," I told her. "I'm going to be able to help you in all sorts of ways. You like having me at home, don't you?"

"Yes, that's why I'm worried about it."

I was just going to ask what she meant when Mrs. Rickaby came in with a basket of roses.

"Of course you needn't use them, Mrs. Morris," said Mrs. Rickaby. "Next Saturday is my proper day for flowers, but they'll be past their best, so I thought —"

"Oh, we *must* use them!" exclaimed Mother. "They're perfectly lovely."

We had done the vases already, with flowers from the Vicarage garden, but Mother knew that Mrs. Rickaby would be disappointed if we didn't use her roses so we emptied the vases and helped Mrs. Rickaby to arrange them . . . and she went away smiling happily.

It wasn't the first time this had happened — and wouldn't be the last — for although there was a list in the porch with the names of the people who had promised to bring flowers, and the dates upon which they were to bring them, they sometimes forgot all about it or brought them too late or brought them on the wrong day — which made trouble. That was why Mother made a point of being in church every Saturday morning.

There had been trouble one Saturday morning last January when Mother was helping Minnie to make marmalade. When I went to fetch Mother she was sitting at the kitchen table cutting up the skins of the Seville oranges and the kitchen was full of the sweet tangy smell of the fruit.

"Oh, goodness! Is it ten already?" exclaimed Mother. "You had better go, Sarah. Mrs. Stanley always comes early."

"Shall I arrange the vases or wait for you?"

"Oh, just do them — unless she wants to arrange them herself — I want to finish these strips for Minnie. Don't forget the key."

I took the key of the church out of the drawer in the hall and walked up the path to church, feeling very pleased with myself (Mother had never let me arrange the altar vases before), and I found Mrs. Price waiting in the porch with a bunch of white carnations and asparagus fern.

I was deputising for Mother so I said, "Oh, Mrs. Price, what lovely carnations! Did you grow them yourself?"

"Yes, they're very fine specimens; Mr. Price grew them in his green-house," said Mrs. Price. She added, "You're late. I've been hanging about in this draughty porch for ten minutes; my feet are frozen."

It was only just after ten, but I said, "Oh, I'm sorry! You see Minnie is making marmalade this morning and Mother always cuts the strips herself; Father likes them cut very thin."

"I always put the oranges through the mincer," said Mrs. Price crossly. "I've got far too much to do without fancy touches like that. I suppose Mrs. Morris is coming later to arrange the flowers — I can't wait any longer."

"Mother said I could arrange the flowers this morning."

"Oh!" exclaimed Mrs. Price, looking at me doubtfully. "Oh well . . . but don't leave them lying about for hours."

"Of course not! I'll do them at once," I said, and I added tactfully, "I'm sure Mother will be delighted when she sees your beautiful carnations."

"They're particularly fine ones so she ought to be delighted," said Mrs. Price.

As I took the huge iron key out of my pocket and opened the church door I decided that it was a very strange thing for her to say: the flowers weren't a present for Mother; it was Mrs. Price who ought to be delighted to have her carnations put on the altar. However, you couldn't expect a stupid old thing like Mrs. Price to see that.

I put the carnations in the front pew, they would be safe there, and went through the vestry into the flower-room to get the vases ready. Four altar vases had been given to St. Mary's by Sir Clive Hudson of Brailsford in memory of his father. Sir Clive never came to church, so it was rather surprising that he had thought of giving the vases, but we were glad to have them; they were heavy brass vases and well shaped so it was easy to arrange flowers in them. We used them a lot and always kept them well polished.

I was polishing the vases when someone knocked on the outside door of the vestry. It was Mrs. Stanley with a bunch of pale pink carnations in her hand.

"Oh!" I exclaimed in dismay.

Mrs. Stanley smiled. "Did I give you a fright, Sarah?"

"Oh no, it was just —"

"I'm afraid I'm a little late."

"It doesn't matter a bit. What lovely carnations!"

"I told Mrs. Morris I'd bring pink carnations if I could get them. Is she here this morning?"

I explained about the marmalade.

"Mrs. Morris is absolutely right," declared Mrs. Stanley. "I always cut the strips myself. Is she coming later?"

"Mother said I could arrange the flowers if you hadn't time."

"Would you like to do them, Sarah?"

"Well, yes — I would. You see Mother has never let me do them before."

"I'm sure you'll arrange them beautifully," said Mrs. Stanley. She put her carnations on the draining-board near the sink and went away.

I fetched Mrs. Price's white carnations and put them beside the pink ones . . . and looked at them and wondered what on earth to do. It was all my fault, of course. I remembered now, when it was too late, that Mother had said it was Mrs. Stanley's day. I had been so pleased with myself because Mother had trusted me to do the flowers that I had forgotten . . .

Well, it was no good wasting time; I decided to see what they looked like mixed. Carnations are expensive in January, so Mrs. Stanley had only brought eight — and there were seven white ones from Mr. Price's green-house. I divided them between two vases, with the asparagus fern, and carried them into church and put them on the altar; then I stood back and looked at them.

I was still standing, looking at them, when Mother came in.

"Oh, you've done them *very* nicely!" she exclaimed.

"I hope it's all right."

"Of course it's all right; they look beautiful."

"I mean I hope it was all right to mix them. It was silly of me to get into a muddle. I didn't know what to do . . . and Mrs. Price was so cross."

"Mrs. Price?" asked Mother in alarm.

I nodded.

"Tell me all, Sarah; I can't bear the suspense."

We went into the vestry and I told her. I was afraid she would be annoyed with me but she sat down on a wooden chair and laughed and laughed.

She laughed so heartily that I had to laugh too. "But I don't know what we're laughing at!" I gasped.

"They had a frightful row at the Work Party," explained Mother. "They haven't spoken to each other for weeks." She wiped her eyes and added seriously, "I'm not laughing at *that*; it makes me feel quite sick when people are horrid to each other, but it seems funny to me that you've mixed their flowers and they go together so well and look so beautiful. I'm not clever," said mother. "Sometimes when people laugh I can't see the joke . . . but sometimes I'm obliged to laugh at a joke which doesn't seem funny to other people."

"I think this is a very funny joke," I told her.

"Do you, Sarah?"

"Yes, but I'd better change the flowers, hadn't I? They may be angry."

"No, don't touch them. They look lovely — and there's a sort of rightness about it. I don't know why, exactly."

I felt the same — so I left them. Anyhow Mrs. Price and Mrs. Stanley couldn't blame Mother because they both knew that I was going to do the flowers.

Father had promised to find "a Frenchwoman" and he set about it without delay; he put an advertisement in the *Larchester Gazette* and had several replies. Mademoiselle Bénet seemed the most suitable, she had a small flat in Larchester and took private pupils; she said she was very busy and could only take me for an hour twice a week ... but she gave me books and I worked by myself at home. Mademoiselle Bénet was used to older pupils, and at first she was impatient with me, but after a bit she realised that I was very anxious to learn and she began to take more interest in my work. She was very strict about pronunciation and made me learn poetry and say the same words over and over again until I had got them right ... then she suggested I should go to her three times a week, so I began to make better progress.

It was a busy winter for me: I worked hard at French; I read history, and Father continued to teach me Latin; I helped Minnie in the kitchen and learnt to cook quite nicely. I did the shopping for Mother, added up the accounts and paid the bills.

Lottie thought I was mad to leave school; she enjoyed dancing and games and was given quite a good part in the school play ... but I was doing what I wanted and was perfectly happy at home.

Charles came down from Oxford several times; he played the piano and we went for walks together. He told me about his work at Oxford and lent me history books. It was lovely having Charles as my friend; I missed his visits very much when the long vacation began and he went back to Austria to see his family.

CHAPTER
TEN

One day when I went to Mademoiselle Bénet for my French lesson she said, "You have been with me for nearly a year, Sarah, and you have worked well. At first I was doubtful because you were so young and your accent was deplorable. I thought it was very wrong of your parents to take you from school; I thought you would become lazy . . . but, no, you have persevered and you can speak quite nicely. You have a talent for languages, my child."

"Have I really, Mademoiselle Bénet? Could I learn to speak other languages too?"

"Why not? But I cannot teach you other languages. Listen, Sarah, we are discussing your progress in French: you have learnt quickly, it is now practice that you require. It would be a good plan for you to go to France and stay with a French family."

(We were speaking in French, of course. Mademoiselle Bénet wouldn't let me speak a word of English.)

"But that is impossible!" I exclaimed. "My father would not allow it."

"I think he would allow it if I were to explain what I have in mind," said Mademoiselle Bénet, nodding thoughtfully. "I am going to Nivennes in August to stay with my parents for a month and I would take you with me. My parents are old — theirs would not be a suitable household for you — but I have friends in Nivennes who would be willing to have you. They are very respectable people, well thought of in the district. Monsieur Delormes is a wine-grower, he has a large estate; best of all there is a daughter of your own age."

"Oh, I don't think —"

"*Ecoutez*, Sarah! You are anxious to speak fluently and well. A month with the Delormes family would be of the greatest help."

"It would be a nuisance for you to —"

"I shall be happy to take you, Sarah. It will be company for me on the long journey."

She talked to Father and Mother about her plan and they agreed to it at once. I had been quite sure they would refuse to let me go, so I was surprised . . . and a little frightened.

It was while Mother and I were buying some cotton frocks for my visit to Nivennes that I discovered why they had agreed so easily: the education of Lewis and Willy and Lottie was costing a great deal of money and my education was costing practically nothing; they felt it was unfair.

"And you've worked so hard," added Mother.

As the day of departure drew near I became more and more frightened but I was too proud to say so — and I realised that if I wanted to speak French "fluently and well" it was a wonderful opportunity — so I determined to face the alarming new experience with courage. It took every bit of courage I possessed.

It was dark when we arrived at Nivennes; we had left London yesterday morning and I felt as if we had been travelling for weeks. As usual after a train journey my head was aching so my first impression of the place was unhappy. Mademoiselle Bénet was met at the station by her parents, who fell upon her neck with cries of delight. I stood by, feeling wretchedly homesick and wishing I hadn't come.

I was almost in tears when Mademoiselle Bénet remembered me. *"Ah, la petite!"* she exclaimed, and introduced me to the two old people. Then her eye fell upon a short stout figure in a voluminous cape and a trilby hat; she pounced upon him crying, "Monsieur Delormes!" and explained that this was *"la petite Anglaise"* and she had brought me safely all the way from England and would confide me to his care.

Monsieur Delormes greeted me without enthusiasm and, taking my suitcase, led me to his car.

"She is a talker," he mumbled — in French, of course. "Her tongue never stops wagging."

"She is very kind," I said.

"Oh, you speak French? I thought you had come here to learn."

"I have come to learn to speak better. I want to speak like a French girl."

Monsieur Delormes was delighted at this news; he smiled and explained that they had been dreading the visit of a young lady who could speak not a word of their language . . . all the more so because neither he nor Madame Delormes could speak a word of English.

"This will make your visit very much more pleasant," he declared.

I wondered why they had consented to have me.

"Yvonne will be pleased too," he added.

"Yvonne is your daughter, Monsieur Delormes?"

"Yes . . . and I have a son also. He is a very fine child and extremely clever. Already he trots after me when I tend the vines. Some day the vineyard will belong to him, you understand, so it is good that he should interest himself in La Touche. Look, here is the auto, Mees Morreese! We have not far to go."

We hadn't far to go but it was uphill all the way, and "the auto" was so old and decrepit that it laboured up in low gear. Monsieur Delormes continued to talk of his son and his vineyard so by the time we arrived I was full of information. He was friendly and pleasant and I was so pleased to find that I could understand all he said that I began to feel more cheerful.

It was too dark to see the place that night but afterwards I discovered that the house stood on the side of a hill and had a wide view of the surrounding country. The vines grew in orderly rows upon broad terraces facing south and west. Monsieur Delormes explained to me that this was why the small white grapes ripenened early . . . La Touche was noted for its delicious golden wine.

Presently we passed a high bank with bushes on top of it and a large white gate; Monsieur Delormes pointed to it and told me it led to the front of the house . . . then he drove on a little farther and turned into a big yard paved with cobbles and surrounded by buildings of different sizes and shapes. The house itself was white-washed and the windows had green shutters, all tightly fastened.

Monsieur Delormes led me through a scullery into the kitchen, a large room with a red-tiled floor, an old-fashioned dresser with blue and white china upon it and a kitchen range of immense size. A small woman in a white apron was standing at the range stirring something in a pot; she gazed at me with interest . . . but Monsieur took no notice of her and walked on through another door into the front part of the house.

This seemed strange to me so I smiled and said "*Bonsoir.*"

She looked pleased. "*Bonsoir, Mam'selle; je m'appelle Suzette.*"

I nodded and said, "*Bonsoir, Suzette.*"

There was no electric light nor gas, but the house was well lighted with oil-lamps in every room. I found afterwards that one of Suzette's duties was to trim the lamps and keep them clean; what with this, by no means an easy task, and preparing vegetables and cooking, and washing the enormous piles of dishes which were used at every meal, Suzette was hard at work from early morning until late at night.

Madame Delormes and her daughter were sitting in the dining-room having supper. They rose when we went in and Monsieur introduced me and explained that I spoke French very nicely. The news was well received.

"But you are late, Jules," said Madame. "We waited for half an hour but we could wait no longer."

"Is it my fault that the train was late?" asked Monsieur. "Yvonne must take Mees Morreese to her room so that she may tidy herself after her long journey."

"Please call me Sarah," I said.

Madame nodded. "Yes, that will be better."

My room was small; it was on the top floor and had a sloping ceiling and, as the window was never opened, it was very stuffy; however it was neat and clean and the bed was comfortable. Later I managed to open my window at the bottom and prop it open with a piece of stick. This was considered very eccentric by all the female members of the household.

During the next few days Yvonne and I were together most of the time. She was a year younger than myself, short and plump with fat cheeks and smooth dark hair. Her black beady eyes gazed at me with an unwinking stare. She wanted to know all about me: why I had come to La Touche; what my home was like; how many rooms there were; whether I went to school daily; how many brothers I had; how old they were and what were their names. Then she asked if my father were very wealthy (she admired my clothes) and when I told her that he was a *curé* she was shocked and horrified. I explained that in England it was the custom for a *curé* to be married and have a family but she shook her head and replied that "*le bon Dieu*" would not like it.

Madame Delormes was tall and thin with a white face and sandy hair which was going grey. She was so colourless that she looked like a ghost; she wore felt slippers and moved swiftly and quietly so that you

110

never heard her coming. She was quite pleasant to me but sometimes I heard her raging at Suzette . . .

At home I was used to going into the kitchen and talking to Minnie and I saw no reason why I shouldn't chat to Suzette when I felt inclined — besides I wanted to find out how she cooked the vegetables — so I went in, when I could escape from Yvonne, and I got some useful tips about French cooking. Suzette was coarse and "earthy" but she was very good-natured and I liked her. I was sorry for her, too; she had a very different life from our Minnie.

CHAPTER
ELEVEN

The Delormes family seemed queer to me: at meal-times Monsieur and Madame chatted; little André was too busy eating to speak and Yvonne was practically dumb . . . but when we were alone she never ceased to ask questions. She asked the same questions over and over again in different words; at first I thought she was stupid and then I discovered that she didn't believe what I told her and was trying to trip me. I didn't like this (who would?) and I didn't like the way she treated her mother: she seemed completely under her mother's thumb and replied, "*Oui, maman*," and "*Non, maman*" — as mild as milk — but she was quite different behind her mother's back.

Yvonne had been told to take me round the farm and talk to me and show me everything. "But do not go to the village," said Madame. "I dislike that dirty little shop which sells *bon-bons*."

"*Bon-bons?*" said Monsieur, pricking up his ears. "The doctor told us Yvonne was not to eat *bon-bons*; they make her too fat."

"You hear what your father says, Yvonne?" asked Madame.

"*Oui, maman.*"

The farm was interesting. I spoke to some of the men and learned how the grapes were gathered and the various processes by which they were made into the golden wine of La Touche. I saw the cows being milked and I saw the pigs which were being fattened for bacon. The Delormes killed and cured their own bacon and the sides were hung upon the rafters in the kitchen.

I was quite happy wandering round the farm, it was all so new and strange, but Yvonne took no interest in it and one morning she suggested that I might like to walk in the olive grove.

The olive trees were beautiful, with their silvery-green foliage, and the shade was pleasant; I should have liked to linger here but Yvonne wouldn't wait. She walked on quickly and presently we emerged through a gate into a village. It was just a cluster of little cottages and a post office and a small shop which sold goods of every description: newspapers and tins of fruit and sweets and children's toys and boots and cheap jewellery and bottles of lemonade all mixed up together.

"But, Yvonne," I said, "we were told not to come to the village."

"Maman will not know. I want to send a letter to my friend . . . have you got some money, Sarah?"

I had a ten-franc note in my purse so I gave it to her and she went into the post office. Then she went into the little shop and bought a bag of sweets.

"We must hurry or we shall be late for *déjeuner*," she said. Her mouth was so full of sweets that she could scarcely speak. "You can have one if you like," she added, holding out the bag.

As she had bought the sweets with my money I took one, but it was bright pink and very sticky and tasted of cough mixture so I spat it out when she wasn't looking.

"We must hurry . . ." she repeated, glancing at her watch.

It was a very hot day and Yvonne puffed and panted as she hastened up the path.

"*Ecoutez,* Yvonne," I said to her. "If you were not so fat you could run. Why do you eat so many *bon-bons?* They are bad for you."

"They are not bad for me!"

"But, yes, they are very bad."

"I like *bon-bons,*" she gasped. "It is good to eat . . . what one likes . . ." She looked at her watch again and exclaimed, "We shall be late! Maman will be angry!"

We were very late. Monsieur and Madame and little André were half-way through their meal when we arrived.

"Oh, are we late?" asked Yvonne in a surprised voice.

"Very late; where have you been?" demanded Madame.

"It was Sarah's fault," declared Yvonne. "Sarah wanted to look at the cows. I did not know it was late; my watch is not going."

"Give me your watch," said Madame, holding out her hand.

Yvonne handed over her watch with an innocent air.

Madame looked at it and shook it and held it to her ear, then she nodded, "*Oui, c'est vrai, il ne marche* pas," she said. "It must be mended; we will take it with us when we go to Nivennes."

I was horrified. I tried to imagine the same sort of scene taking place at home . . . would Mother have asked to see my watch when I said it had stopped? Would I have expected my word to be doubted and stopped my watch so that I should have a watertight excuse for being late?

When you thought of it like that it was laughable . . . but I didn't feel like laughing.

Every now and then I was beset by a wave of homesickness, a longing not only for my home and my family but also for what I thought of as "the clean air." The clean air where you could talk comfortably and laugh and say what you thought without having to worry. All the same I was too proud to admit in my letters home that I was unhappy or that things weren't as they should be in the Delormes family. I had wanted to learn to speak French fluently . . . and I was learning fast. Another reason why I didn't complain was the discovery that Father was paying Madame Delormes a substantial weekly sum for my board and lodging . . . it was Suzette who told me this.

I wasn't unhappy all the time. Everything was new to me — and interesting. I enjoyed playing with André, who was a dear little boy and very clever for his age. I taught him to sing some English nursery rhymes and he sang them very sweetly in his shrill little treble. "Leetle Boo Peeep 'as lost 'er sheep" was his favourite.

His parents were delighted with the performance; they laughed heartily and exclaimed, *"Bravo! Encore!"*

115

. . . and André was only too pleased to sing it as often as they liked.

Monsieur Delormes was astonished to discover that I could play piquet and insisted that I should play it with him nearly every evening. I had often played with Grandpapa but Monsieur was a very much better player, shrewd and wily, so he always beat me. I thought it couldn't be much fun for him because it is much less amusing to win all the time than to lose (if you lose you have always the hope of doing better next time); but Monsieur Delormes seemed to like winning. I beat him once when the cards fell exactly right for me and he was quite annoyed.

Madame, who happened to be there at the time, said quite seriously, "No doubt Sarah was cheating, Jules."

This was so ridiculous that I wasn't even angry . . . in any case it would have taken someone a great deal more clever than I to cheat Monsieur Delormes.

Madame had promised to take us to Nivennes when she went to do her marketing so we set off in the "auto" one very warm morning. Nivennes was a delightful town; it looked very "foreign" to me with its tall houses by the side of the green, slow-moving river and its wide streets with little cafés where crowds of people sat at tables on the pavement, drinking wine or coffee. We left the auto in the car-park, Madame gave us each a basket to carry and led the way. It was terribly hot in the streets, the sun blazed down and the pavements were hot to walk on. I was wearing a thin cotton frock — and very little beneath it — but quite soon I was so hot that

116

I was sticky all over, and Yvonne's face was crimson. Madame was arrayed in a voluminous black dress with gold chains round her neck, but the heat didn't seem to worry her at all; her face was still white and she ploughed her way through the crowd like a ship in full sail.

The market was in a huge square; it was gay and noisy; there were scores of little stalls, with striped awnings, which displayed all sorts of merchandise for sale. It had been hot in the streets but here the heat was like a furnace and crowds of people were surging in all directions and talking and laughing excitedly. I was determined not to get lost so I followed Madame's tall black figure closely. She pushed her way from one stall to another, bargaining with the butcher for a joint of veal, prodding it with her fingers and decrying its quality . . . and eventually buying it for a good deal less than he had asked. At the fruit stall the same thing happened: the oranges and the grape-fruit were no good, they were wizened and light, there would be no juice in them! The stallholder became angry: the fruit was perfectly fresh — the best in the market — Madame could go elsewhere if she pleased, she would find no better! However she stuck to her point and bought what she wanted for less than had been demanded.

My basket was full by this time so Madame looked round for Yvonne. "Where is she?" exclaimed Madame. "Where has she gone? The poor child is lost. *Mon Dieu*, what shall I do?"

I said nothing. I knew quite well that she had escaped from her mother's eagle eye and had gone off to buy *bon-bons* but I had learned to hold my tongue about Yvonne's doings.

"Oh, well," said Madame with a sigh. "No doubt she will be waiting for us in the auto."

I wanted to buy some presents to take home with me, so when Madame had bought all she wanted she led the way to a stall which sold coloured head-scarves, such as the peasants wore, and little figurines and rosaries and small pictures in wooden frames. I chose scarves for Lottie and Minnie and two little ornaments for Mother; Father's present was more difficult but I found a little wooden bear which had been carved by a peasant; it was a queer little beast but I thought it would amuse Father. Madame bargained for the things and I was able to buy them for very little.

Then we made our way back to the car-park . . . and there was Yvonne, sitting in the auto and looking as innocent as a newly-born lamb.

"I got lost, maman," she bleated plaintively. "I could not find you anywhere."

"*Ah, pauvre enfant!*" said Madame in commiserating tones. "The crowds were very bad to-day."

It seemed strange that Madame's eagle eye had not observed her daughter's cheeks; they were even fatter than usual, puffed out with sticky sweets.

CHAPTER
TWELVE

One morning about ten o'clock, a car drove up to the front door. This was unusual; most of the visitors to La Touche left their cars in the yard and came in through the back premises. I was in my room at the time so I leaned out of the window to see who it was . . . and was amazed and delighted to see Charles get out of the car and stand on the gravel sweep stretching himself — as he always did when he had been driving. Then he disappeared into the house and I ran downstairs nearly crazy with excitement. Charles here! It was almost too good to be true!

I opened the door of the living-room. There was Charles, sitting at the table, talking to Monsieur and Madame, and enjoying a glass of golden wine!

When I went in he rose and bowed stiffly and said, "*Bonjour*, Miss Morris." Then he sat down and continued his conversation with Monsieur Delormes, praising the wine and asking intelligent questions about the vines.

I was so astonished at this extraordinary behaviour that I sat down on the sofa beside Yvonne without saying a word.

Charles continued to chat; he turned to Madame Delormes and complimented her upon the highly polished furniture ... it was easy to see what an excellent manager she was! She smiled and bridled; Monsieur Delormes laughed and declared that his wife kept everything up to the mark — including himself.

Charles was "foreign"; his manner was insincere. He wasn't Charles at all! He never looked at me once, nor spoke to me. I was almost in tears. It had been so wonderful to see him arrive — but it was no good; he wasn't my friend any more.

Presently he asked Monsieur for the address of a wine merchant in Paris where he would be able to buy La Touche golden wine and scribbled on a leaf of his diary. Then he rose to go. He kissed Madame's hand and Yvonne's, and turning to me said in French that he intended to write to my father, would I care to send a message?

I said in English, "Give them my love, that's all."

He kissed my hand casually and crumpled up my fingers. Then he went away.

There was something in my hand. I slipped it into the pocket of my overall and ran upstairs to my tiny room under the sloping roof. When I looked at it I found it was a little screw of paper, torn from a diary; scrawled upon it were the words, "I shall be waiting at the front gate from 1.30 to 4, but be careful."

In a moment I was transported from the depths of despair to the heights of happiness. I felt quite giddy with joy. It would be easy to escape for *déjeuner* was at midday and everyone retired to bed and rested in the afternoon.

To-day, as it happened, *déjeuner* was later than usual; Monsieur had a guest, a big coarse-looking man. They ate quantities of the good fare provided by Madame and talked about the prospects of the harvest. At any other time I would have been interested in their conversation (I could understand all they said quite easily) but to-day I was so impatient and excited that I could scarcely sit still. The hands of the big grandfather clock in the corner moved on inexorably . . . and still they continued to eat and talk.

At last the meal was over; the guest departed and Madame and Yvonne went upstairs to rest. I followed them, for although it was now half-past one I knew I must wait until they had settled down before I could escape safely.

I waited for twenty minutes; and then ran down the path to the gate and looked eagerly up and down the road. He wasn't there! He had got tired of waiting! He had come — and gone!

Then the bushes at the side of the gate parted and he jumped down on to the road.

"Charles!" I cried and flung myself into his arms.

He held me tightly for a few moments; then, taking my hand, he dragged me up the bank and through the bushes.

We sat down and he put his arm round me. "Sarah, you're trembling! I shouldn't have asked you to come."

"I'm glad you did."

"I had to, because you looked so — so lost and miserable. Your father asked me to see you and find out if you were all right; he was a little worried because your last letter sounded unhappy. I promised I would call at La Touche and find out what was the matter — and write and tell him. If you aren't happy he'll arrange for you to go home."

I wanted to go home; the unhealthy atmosphere of La Touche was beginning to get me down and the sight of Charles had raised a wave of nostalgia . . . but I hesitated.

"Well, what about it?" asked Charles.

"I'll stick it out," I said. "It's only another week. Then Mademoiselle Bénet is going home and will take me with her. That was the arrangement. Yes, I'll stick it out."

"Good girl! But why did you look so miserable?"

"You were different."

"But, Sarah, what could I do? Madame would have been horrified if I'd shown you any attention. She was suspicious, as it was. I had to be nice to the old gorgon. If I'd spoken to you or shown that we were friends she would have had a fit. Don't you understand?"

"I do, now."

"Here, in France, things are different. Girls aren't allowed to be friends with men. I don't suppose that Delormes girl has ever been allowed to speak to anything in trousers . . . and she won't be allowed until she's safely married to a man chosen by her parents."

"Yes, it's true. I was silly."

"Well, as long as you understand . . ." said Charles.

"Charles," I said. "Your English is more — more elastic."

He smiled. "That's what I want. I still find it difficult to run the words together but I'm determined to learn to speak like an Englishman."

"I'm determined to learn to speak French like a French girl."

"Yes, your mother told me that was your ambition. I think —"

"German, too," I interrupted. "I must be able to talk to you in your own language."

He looked at me strangely. "Is that the reason?"

The reason seemed obvious — it had been in my mind for months and months — so I didn't bother to reply.

"We haven't much time," I said. "Madame gets up at four . . . and I want to know such a lot of things: where have you come from, Charles? Where are you going?"

"I've been at Oxford and I'm on my way to Schloss Roethke. My father wants me to stay there for a while and help to look after the estate."

"But you'll come back to Oxford?" I asked anxiously.

"Yes, as soon as I can. Look, Sarah," he continued, taking a little box out of his pocket. "I've got a little birthday present for you. It's too late for your birthday, I'm afraid, but I wanted to give it to you myself."

It was a little gold heart, set with pearls, on a thin gold chain.

"Oh, Charles, how lovely! But you shouldn't —"

"Do you like it?"

"I love it — it's beautiful! Oh, how kind of you, Charles!"

He fastened it round my neck. "You must wear it under your frock in case Madame sees it and wants to know where you got it," said Charles, smiling.

"I shall wear it always, night and day, because I love you."

"Dear little Sarah, I wish you were older."

"I'm fifteen and a half — nearly."

"You're a child. That Delormes girl is grown-up."

"She's a year younger than I am!"

"Yes, but she's years older."

"I don't understand what you mean."

"It's because you're English," said Charles with a sigh.

"But you love me, don't you?"

"Yes, I love my child . . . and I shall love the woman she is going to be. But it isn't fair, Sarah. It isn't fair to you. One of these days you'll understand what I mean. Perhaps you'll meet someone nicer than me and —"

"There isn't anyone nicer than you in the world!"

"You've seen such a lot of the world, haven't you?"

Suddenly a thought came into my mind. "Charles, perhaps you — perhaps you'll meet someone else, someone pretty and — and charming and —" I stopped. My throat had tightened and I couldn't go on.

There was a little silence.

"You must go now," said Charles at last. "It was wrong of me to ask you to come but I had to find out what was the matter. Are they kind to you?"

124

"Yes. I don't like it much — I'm longing to go home — but I've learnt a lot, not only to speak French."

"What have you learnt?" he asked, looking at me anxiously.

It was difficult to explain and there was no time to go into details. "Oh, well, I've learnt how other people behave and — and quite a lot about vines and — and other things. I'll tell you to-morrow. You'll come to-morrow, won't you?"

"No," said Charles. "No, we mustn't do this again. It's too risky."

"Oh, please!" I cried. "I haven't said half the things I want to say. You haven't told me about Fairfield and how they all were when you saw them. I haven't thanked you properly for my dear little locket."

He smiled. "Very well, I'll be here to-morrow at the same time, but don't come unless you're sure it's perfectly safe. I shall stay in Nivennes to-night and go home to-morrow night. Now you must go, Sarah. Go quickly, it's almost four o'clock."

"Couldn't you — kiss me?"

He hesitated, but I held up my face, so he bent and kissed me very gently on my forehead. "Go quickly," he repeated.

I turned and ran up the path and round to the back door; through the kitchen and up the stairs. When I opened the door of my room Yvonne was there; sitting on the bed and waiting for me with an unpleasant smile on her round fat face.

I stood in the doorway, breathless, and gazed at her in dismay.

"Maman will be interested to hear what I have seen this afternoon," said Yvonne with a self-satisfied air.

"You followed me!"

"But yes . . . and I saw you with your lover."

"He's — he's my friend," I told her.

"*Oui, ton cher ami*," agreed Yvonne.

The word was the same; I didn't know how to explain.

She got up and came towards me. "That is a very pretty little locket. It is new, perhaps? I have not seen it before."

I put up my hand and discovered that the locket had slipped out from its hiding-place under the neck of my frock. "It is a birthday present," I told her.

"How pretty!" said Yvonne admiringly. "It is gold with real pearls. Look, Sarah, if you will give me the locket I might forget what I saw this afternoon. My memory is very convenient."

"No, no, no!"

"Such a pretty locket! Yes, I am sure it would make me forget."

"No!" I cried, slipping it under my frock.

"Well, in that case I must tell maman —"

The expression on her sly face gave me the horrors. "I shall tell Madame myself!" I cried. "Yes, I shall tell her exactly what happened. He wanted to give me a message from my father so he asked me to meet him at the gate."

"Maman will not believe that story."

"She must believe it because it's true!"

"What must I believe?" asked Madame. She had approached silently in her felt slippers and stood in the doorway, looking at us with a grim smile.

Her sudden appearance startled me and I was dumb, searching vainly for words.

Yvonne was not dumb. She burst into a torrent of explanations: she had watched Sarah at *déjeuner* and had seen Sarah's impatience — every few moments Sarah had glanced at the clock — it was obvious that Sarah had a *rendezvous*. Then from her window she had seen Sarah running down the path to the front gate — running quickly — so she had followed, but when she got to the gate there was no sign of Sarah. No sign at all; Sarah had vanished. Then she had heard voices, talking very quietly, and, looking through a gap in the hedge, she had seen Sarah and her lover sitting on the bank together. Oh, very close together, his arm was round Sarah's waist!

Yvonne had been so horrified at this dreadful sight that she had run all the way back to the house without stopping.

"*Incroyable!*" cried Madame, throwing her hands in the air. "Oh, what wickedness!"

"It isn't true!" I exclaimed.

"But I saw you!" declared Yvonne.

"I mean I met Charles because he wanted to give me a message from my father. My father asked him to see me and talk to me. He is a friend of my family. We have known him for years . . ." I went on explaining — or trying to explain — but I was so upset that most of the French I had learnt had vanished from my mind. I

127

found myself thinking in English and translating the words haltingly. Perhaps I could have explained the matter in my own language — or perhaps not. The trouble was that Madame's whole outlook was different . . . and I knew from the beginning that it was hopeless, for of course I was in the wrong. It was true that I had been deceitful; it was true that I had slipped out of the house and run to meet Charles; it was true that we had sat on the bank together and talked in low voices.

Madame scarcely bothered to listen; she didn't believe a word I said. Then, when my explanations faltered into silence, she began to rage at me, working herself up into a fury. She told me what she thought of me in plain unvarnished language; she blamed herself for taking an English girl under her roof — everyone knew that the English were immoral. They were depraved and sex-mad. It was dreadful to think that her innocent daughter had been exposed to such a wicked influence . . . but Yvonne should be exposed to it no longer. No, not a moment longer . . .

It was a terrible scene. I felt dazed and bewildered, battered by the storm of words. I had been completely ignorant of "the facts of life" but when Madame had finished with me I was no longer ignorant. The shock was frightful; I knew now what Charles had meant when he called me his "child."

"I want to go home!" I cried.

"Yes, indeed you shall go! Your father must come and fetch you instantly."

"I'll go to-morrow! If you send me to the station I can go by myself."

"*Petite imbécile!*" said Madame scornfully. "You cannot travel alone. You will remain here in your room until your father can make arrangements for you to be taken away." She signed to Yvonne and they went out together; the door was shut and the key turned in the lock.

I flung myself down on the bed and wept bitterly. I wept because I was horrified and bewildered and frightened. Yes, I was frightened; never before in all my life had I seen anyone in a furious rage. I had been sheltered and cared for; I wasn't used to roughness and violence . . . and the dreadful things she had told me had opened a pit full of horrors before my astonished eyes.

After a while my sobs grew less and I began to think of Father and Mother. What would they do when they heard I had disgraced them? What would they say? They would be angry, of course, but all the same I wanted to go home; I wanted to go now — this minute — not wait until I was fetched.

Presently there was the sound of the key being turned in the lock and Suzette came in with a tray.

"There is trouble downstairs; you are everything that is wicked," said Suzette cheerfully. "But do not distress yourself; I do not blame you! I, too, have a *cher ami* and meet him in the vineyard when the work is done. She would be angry if she knew but she does not know so she is not angry — *voilà tout!* She said you were not to have any supper but Monsieur came to the kitchen and told me to bring you food . . . so dry your eyes,

Mamselle, and sit up and eat it while it is hot. Look, it is the wing of a chicken and some salad!"

"How kind of you, Suzette!"

"You have been kind to me; you do not treat me like a machine that is good for nothing but washing dishes and cleaning lamps. I shall be sorry when you go away to-morrow."

"To-morrow? But Madame said —"

"I heard Madame arranging it with Madame Monnier. She was speaking on the telephone. Madame Monnier is going to Paris to-morrow and will take you with her in the train; after that — I do not know."

I didn't care what was to happen "after that." All I wanted was to get away from La Touche as soon as possible. I had my tickets and I could go home by myself.

Suzette put the tray across my knees. She said in a low voice, "Listen, Mamselle, I would take a message for you. He is staying at *Hôtel de la Paix* in Nivennes."

For a moment I hesitated. Then I decided that there had been too much deceit already . . . besides, Charles might do something reckless when he heard what had happened; he might come to the house and try to explain . . . and that would cause more trouble! No, it was better to leave things as they were and go home to-morrow as had been arranged.

Perhaps the chief reason why I didn't want to send Charles a message was because I had suddenly grown up and wasn't a "child" any longer. I would have to get used to my new knowledge before I could meet Charles again; perhaps I would never be able to meet him without feeling shy. I could never again throw myself into his arms and tell him I loved him.

My journey home was uneventful. Madame Monnier took me to Paris and from there I travelled to London by myself. I had my tickets, and I had travelled by myself before, so it was quite easy. Even the crossing from Calais to Dover didn't bother me for everyone was kind and helpful.

Father met me in London and we hugged each other tightly. I didn't know whether he had been told why I had been sent home . . . and he didn't mention the subject until we were sitting in the train on our way to Fairfield. The compartment was empty except for ourselves so we could talk comfortably.

"Sarah, what on earth happened?"

"Didn't Madame Delormes tell you?"

"She tried to," said Father, smiling. "She spoke to me on the phone but I couldn't understand a word. Then she got a friend to speak to me. I don't know who it was but he spoke a little English and I gathered that you had met a man at the gate and had sat on a bank with him and 'talked in low voices for a whole hour.' I didn't worry about that, of course; all I wanted to know was when and how you were coming home."

"You didn't worry?" I asked in surprise.

"I know you," he explained. "So I knew it couldn't be true."

"It was true, Father. I slipped out of the house in the afternoon while they were all resting and we sat together on the bank and had a long talk —"

"Who?" exclaimed Father in alarm.

131

"Charles, of course! I thought you knew."

"Suppose you begin at the beginning and tell me the whole story?"

I took a long breath and told him everything as clearly as I could. "That's what happened," I said. "I shouldn't have done it, of course — it was sly and deceitful — but I had to see Charles."

"It was my fault," said Father. "It was I who asked Charles to have a chat with you and make sure you were all right. When first you went to Nivennes your letters were quite cheerful but afterwards we got rather a miserable letter so we were a little worried. It seemed a good opportunity to find out through Charles if all was well. It never occurred to me that you wouldn't be allowed to speak to him. I shall write to Madame Delormes and explain."

"She doesn't understand a word of English."

"No matter," said Father cheerfully. "I shall write the letter in English and you can translate it into French. It will be good practice for you."

I began to giggle hysterically . . . and I couldn't stop.

He took my hand and held it firmly. "I believe you've been worrying, you foolish child. Did you think I would be annoyed with you?"

CHAPTER
THIRTEEN

It was lovely to be home . . . so lovely that it was almost worth while to have been miserable at Nivennes. It was September; Mother had gone to Craignethan and the two boys had taken the pup and were touring in Devonshire, so we were a small party.

Father wrote a letter to Madame Delormes; it was a good letter, polite but firm. I translated it and took it to Mademoiselle Bénet and she corrected a few small mistakes. She had heard Madame's account of the affair, so I was glad of an excuse to show her Father's version. I hadn't intended to tell her anything more about the Delormes family but she insisted, explaining that she had another pupil who wanted a month's holiday in a French household and she didn't want to recommend the Delormes unless everything was satisfactory.

When I told her about Yvonne's deceitfulness she looked at me rather strangely and said, "That accounts for your behaviour, Sarah. Deceitfulness is infectious."

I saw what she meant and I wondered if it were true. Had my own standard of behaviour been lowered by contact with Yvonne?

"Think about it seriously," said Mademoiselle Bénet. "You have seen that deceit can cause infinite trouble so be careful to avoid it in future."

I nodded thoughtfully.

"And another thing," added Mademoiselle Bénet. "You must not make the mistake of saying to yourself, 'All French people are like that.' There are bad people and good people in my country — as there are in every country under the sun."

"*Oui, c'est entendu,*" I replied. Her warning shouldn't have been necessary ... but, strangely enough, it was.

The little presents I had brought were very acceptable: Father liked his bear, and put it on the chimney-piece in his study, and Minnie was delighted with her gaily-coloured scarf.

Minnie wanted to know about my experiences and asked searching questions about the manners and the customs of the country. I told her how Madame had done her marketing, and about Suzette — and all the work she did — and I told her about Yvonne's deceitfulness and her passion for sticky sweets. If I had told Minnie that they filed their teeth into points to make themselves look fierce she would have believed it.

I had to be tactful about the French dishes which I had learned to prepare, but Minnie was eager to try them. I showed her how to cook vegetables with very little water and lots of butter, and when she saw the result she was quite pleased and consented to do them "the French way." It was a great improvement on her usual method of boiling cabbages and brussels sprouts into a green poultice.

Lottie and I had a very happy time together. She was even prettier now than when she was a small child and I found her a delightful companion. Mrs. Meldrum had given her a guitar and she was learning to play it; she practised for an hour every morning, sitting on a cushion on the floor.

I discovered that Father hadn't told Lottie why I had come home from Nivennes, but had just said I was unhappy there . . . which was perfectly true as far as it went. It was kind of Father but I decided that I should like her to know so I told her the whole story myself.

We had taken a picnic tea up to the field and were sitting on the stones under the oak-tree.

Lottie listened to my tale in silence and then exclaimed, "The old woman must have been crazy! Why shouldn't you talk to Charles?"

"Things are different in France; girls aren't allowed —"

"What is he like?" she interrupted.

"You mean Charles?"

"Yes, I've never seen him. I've heard a lot about him, of course, but that doesn't give you any clear idea of a person."

I was surprised to hear that she had never seen Charles. I knew that while I was away he had come to the Vicarage quite often to talk to mother and play the piano.

"Oh, well, I'm at school all day," explained Lottie. "And I often go and spend the week-end with the Meldrums. We have fun," she added with a little smile.

"You haven't been to Riverside since I came home."

"They've all gone for a cruise to the Mediterranean, that's why. Mrs. Meldrum wanted to take me but she couldn't get a cabin. She said she would take me next time . . . or perhaps to Switzerland at Christmas for winter sports. Mrs. Meldrum thinks it's very wrong for you to have left school, Sarah."

"Mrs. Meldrum doesn't understand," I said quickly. "It was the right thing for me to leave school because I want to study languages."

"It must be so dull!"

"It isn't dull at all."

"I should hate it."

We were silent for a little, drinking tea and eating scones and honey.

"You haven't told me about Charles," said Lottie at last. "What is he really like?"

I tried to describe him to her.

"Sarah — I believe — you're in love with him!" she exclaimed, gazing at me with wide blue eyes.

"There's nobody like him in the world."

"Oh, Sarah! And does Charles . . ."

"He said I was a child."

"So you are," declared Lottie, nodding seriously. "You're younger than I am in lots of ways. I've got several admirers."

She said it with such a self-satisfied air that I had to laugh.

136

"You needn't laugh, Sarah. I meet lots of boys at Riverside, and it's better to have several admirers because it keeps them up to the mark. I've learnt a lot from Madeline; she's grown-up now, and very pretty and attractive, so she has a string of young men . . . and she keeps them guessing."

"Keeps them guessing?"

"Madeline says a man gets tired of a girl if she makes herself too cheap . . . so she keeps them guessing. That's what I'll do when I'm older — and that's what you ought to do. Charles will get tired of you if you let him see that you think there's nobody like him in the world."

I was silent. I thought of the way I had thrown myself into his arms and hugged him — I had been so pleased to see him that it seemed the natural thing to do — I had told him that I loved him and asked him to kiss me! Perhaps Lottie was right; perhaps he would get tired of me; perhaps already he had become tired of the affection of a "child" and had found someone else; someone pretty and attractive, like Madeline, who would keep him guessing.

"What's the matter, Sarah?" asked Lottie.

"Nothing. I was just thinking."

"Does Charles write to you?"

"No, he's very busy. He's in Austria with his father, helping to manage the estate."

"Is it a big estate?"

"Yes, it stretches for miles and miles; there are farms and woods and fields and a huge castle which stands on the edge of a cliff; it has belonged to his family for generations."

"What fun. Perhaps you'll go there some day." She sighed and added, "I'd like to see Charles."

I had told Lottie that Charles didn't write to me but a few days later I received a long letter from him; it was a warm friendly letter.

Charles began by explaining that he had found his father's property sadly neglected and he was trying to put things right. He was in the saddle all day, riding to outlying farms and arranging for the repair of roofs and barns and a proper supply of water to the peasants' houses.

"All this should have been done long ago but my father cannot be bothered with these things and Rudi, who ought to be looking after his inheritance, has no *drive*. He is vacillating so people do not attend to what he says. The people here are pleasant and kindly but they need an iron hand in a velvet glove. Alas, Rudi has neither so he does not get on with them well; I hope he will gain confidence in himself when he is married. He is now engaged to be married to a young girl whose parents have been friends of our family for many years, so the match is suitable and our father is pleased. Anya would not suit me; she cannot talk of Druids' stones and cuckoos and the reign of Queen Elizabeth of England. However Rudi is devoted to her and they are to be married in

November. The wedding is to be a very grand affair, both families have large connections in Vienna, so I must be here to help Rudi through the ordeal and I must stay with my father and Gretchen while Rudi and Anya are away for their honeymoon (which is to consist of a cruise round the world). This means that I shall not be able to return to Oxford for some time.

"It is sad that I shall not have the joy of seeing all my good friends at Fairfield but it is important that I should be here. We are living in my father's house in Vienna — as you will see from the address — but things are so unsettled that I am anxious for my father's safety. I want my family to return to Schloss Roethke as soon as possible and live there quietly and try to keep clear of political affairs. I think I told you that my father speaks his mind too freely? That is dangerous here where the pie-crust is thin . . . but at Schloss Roethke he will be amongst our own people who are faithful to the family.

"Unfortunately Anya finds the Schloss cold and damp so it has been agreed to instal central heating and to make several alterations in the west wing, including a self-contained flat for the newly married couple; all this must be done while they are away and I must be here to keep an eye on the work. Once this has been done, and my family is comfortably settled, I shall be able to leave them with an easy mind.

"I have explained these matters fully so that you will understand why I cannot return to England as soon as I had hoped . . . and now I must explain what happened at Nivennes. When you did not appear at our *rendezvous* I went up to the house and had an interview with Madame Delormes — it was an unpleasant interview! Alas, I made trouble for you! It was foolish and impulsive of me to ask you to meet me; my only excuse is that you looked unhappy and this made me lose my wits. I hope you will be kind and forgive me.

"Please allow your parents to read this letter; I ought to write to them and thank them for all their kindness to me but I am very busy.

"Take care of yourself, little Sarah. I am glad you are not here, but safe in England where the crust is thick.

"Yours ever,

"Charles."

When I had read the letter and digested it I handed it to Father and he read it carefully.

"It's a very good letter," said Father. "Charles is a good son. It's a pity he isn't his father's heir; the brother doesn't sound much use."

I didn't reply. It was true that Rudi didn't sound much use, but I was glad Charles wasn't his father's heir.

"We'll show the letter to Mother when she comes home from Craignethan. Meanwhile keep it safely," added Father.

140

I answered Charles's letter, of course, and after that we wrote to each other fairly regularly. He told me about his brother's marriage, which was a gorgeous affair, and he told me about the troubles he was having with the builders. The walls of the old castle were so thick and strong that the instalment of the central heating was much more difficult than anyone had expected and the other alterations which Anya wanted were even more troublesome. In one of his letters Charles wrote, "I have a feeling that Anya does not want to leave Vienna." This simple little sentence told me a good deal.

It was not until Christmas 1937 that I had a short letter from Charles to tell me that the Schloss was ready and they were on the point of moving. Once he had seen his family comfortably settled he would be free to do as he wanted.

All this time I had been going to Mademoiselle Bénet twice a week for French conversation and had been having German lessons from the organist of St. Margaret's in Larchester. He was a German — Herr Müller — but he had become a naturalised British subject and had changed his name to Mr. Miller. He was thorough and conscientious so I enjoyed my lessons with him.

CHAPTER
FOURTEEN

The Anschluss took place at the beginning of March 1938; Hitler marched his troops into Austria and took over the country. I was dismayed when I heard the news: where was Charles and what was happening to him?

Strangely enough there seemed to be little trouble in Austria — some people said it was better for Austria to be amalgamated with Germany and now Hitler would be satisfied. Was this true or was it wishful thinking? I talked to Mr. Miller about it but found him very reticent; however, when I pressed him he said, "There is great power for evil in the man."

By this time Father had read *Mein Kampf*, which had been translated into English, and he was of the opinion that sooner or later there would be war. The queer thing was that a great many other people had read the book but very few of them seemed to believe that Hitler meant what he said.

Life at home went on as usual: Lewis was still at St. Clement's College and came to see us now and then; Lottie was still at St. Elizabeth's and Willy had left Barstow and was in Mr. Romford's engineering works. He was very happy there and Mr. Romford was pleased with him but his hours were long and he didn't get home very often.

We had a reunion for my eighteenth birthday. All the family came. We hadn't been all together for a long time so it was lovely. Lewis and Willy were very friendly to each other, much more so than when they were younger.

It was a fine March day so we all went for a walk together in the woods and then sat down to a splendid tea; mother and Minnie had made a cake and decorated it and put eighteen candles on it. They all chaffed me and we had jokes and were very happy. Afterwards, when I looked back and remembered my birthday, I wished I could have it all over again.

I received some delightful presents, including a new bicycle from Father, a gold wrist-watch from Mother and fifty pounds from the grans. Grandmama wrote and said they were sending me money as I might like to buy "some pretty frocks." I had hoped for a letter from Charles but was disappointed.

A few days later Mother suggested we should go to Larchester to spend some of my "birthday money" and I agreed. It was always fun going for an expedition with Mother and I wanted some new clothes.

We had an early lunch and caught the one o'clock bus. It was a dull misty day, not very pleasant, but we did our shopping satisfactorily. I bought a very pretty rose-red frock with some of the grans' money; it was a colour that suited me and Mother said it was very becoming, then we had tea together at a small tea-shop before coming home.

The tea-shop was run by two Scottish ladies who made the scones and cakes themselves. We had been there before several times and they had discovered that mother was a fellow-countrywoman. To-day we were rather late so the tea-shop was empty and Miss Ferguson came and sat at our table.

At first she and Mother talked about Ryddelton; Miss Ferguson said she knew it well, she used to stay there sometimes with an old aunt.

"It's still the same as ever, very quiet and peaceful," said mother.

"Peaceful?" said Miss Ferguson with a sigh. "It's nice to think of somewhere peaceful in these troublous times. That Hitler is a dangerous man; you never know what he'll do next. He has swallowed Austria but that won't satisfy him."

"What do you mean?" asked Mother in surprise.

"My sister says if he attacks Poland there's sure to be another war."

"Another war! Oh, there could never be another war — that would be dreadful!"

"Haven't you read his book, Mrs. Morris? My sister and I got it the other day; it's quite terrifying. He says Germany is encircled by enemies and he wants 'lebensraum.' He means to take it by force if he can't get it any other way."

"There couldn't be another war," repeated Mother in a breathless voice. "You must be wrong, Miss Ferguson! War is terribly wicked and . . . and dreadful. It couldn't happen again! I must ask Henry . . . yes, I must ask Henry."

144

Miss Ferguson looked at me and I shook my head so she began to talk of something else but Mother didn't listen. She sat there for a few minutes as if she were turned to stone and then rose and said we must go.

We had never spoken about the possibility of another war in Mother's hearing — Father had warned us not to mention the subject — but she saw the papers every day so it seemed strange that she hadn't realised the danger. I have wondered about it since, and have come to the conclusion that to Mother the last war was "the last war" and the idea that there could be another had never entered her head.

Coming home in the bus I tried to talk to Mother about our afternoon's shopping expedition but she didn't answer . . . and when we arrived in Fairfield she got out and walked very quickly up the hill to the Vicarage. I collected the parcels and followed. It was unlike Mother to leave me to carry all the parcels, but she wasn't thinking of parcels; she was thinking only of getting home to Father as quickly as she could.

When she got to the Vicarage gate she staggered . . . and would have fallen if I hadn't dropped all the parcels in the road and seized her in my arms.

"I feel . . . so . . . queer," she said vaguely.

"You're tired," I said. "You've been hurrying up the hill."

I managed to get the gate open and made her sit down on the bank at the side of the path. I was frightened; I didn't know what to do — whether to stay with her or go for help — her face was quite grey and she was breathing heavily.

"You'll be all right in a minute," I told her. "You were racing up the hill — that's what's the matter."

I waited, holding her hand, but she seemed to be getting worse. "Just sit there quietly while I run and get Father," I said.

Fortunately Father was in his study and between us we managed to carry her into the drawing-room. We laid her on the sofa; her eyes were open but she seemed only half-conscious. She was clinging to Father's hand as if she were drowning.

"Ring up Dr. Weatherstone — quickly," said Father.

Mother was terribly ill; her left leg and arm were paralysed and most of the time she was unconscious, but occasionally she emerged from the mists and recognised us and spoke to us. Dr. Weatherstone sent for a nurse; Father and Minnie and I took turns in sitting by her bedside and helping to lift her.

I told Father and the doctor exactly what had happened; the doctor said it was not the mental shock which had caused the seizure, it was hurrying up the hill when she was tired. I thought he was wrong but it was not for me to argue with a doctor . . . and in any case it didn't matter. The only thing that mattered was for Mother to get well.

Nurse Ede was kind and capable; she was very attentive to mother and gave little trouble in the house but she talked too much and too cheerfully. At meals nurse chatted happily about her other patients and told us how she had "pulled them through" when the doctor had given up hope. Of course Mother was just another case to her — so it is unfair to blame her — but father and I were in agonies of anxiety and apprehension so we found it almost intolerable.

We had asked Dr. Weatherstone whether we ought to send for Lewis and Willy and he had replied that we could do as we liked, but it was better for Mother to be kept very quiet; excitement would be the worst thing possible . . . so Father decided not to send for anyone. I felt worried about it (if I had heard that Mother was desperately ill I should have wanted to go to her), so I sat down and wrote to the boys and told them all about it; I wrote to the grans and to Lottie.

There was no question of Lottie coming; she had gone to Monte Carlo with the Meldrums for the Easter holidays, but I thought she ought to be told.

For five days Mother's condition was unchanged; she lay in a coma, her arm and leg were limp and useless, but on the morning of the sixth day I thought she seemed better; her face was less grey and drawn and her eyes brighter. When I was giving her a drink of warm milk she looked up at me and smiled.

"You're feeling better, aren't you?" I said.

"Sarah, I can't . . . remember what happened. Did I fall down and . . . and break my arm?"

"No, darling. Your arm isn't broken, it's just rather stiff."

"It's heavy and limp . . . but I can move my fingers."

I looked at her poor hand and saw that it was true; she was moving her fingers. She was getting better!

147

"I was hurrying," said Mother. "I wanted to talk to Henry . . . about something . . . but I can't remember what it was. What was it, Sarah?"

"You didn't tell me."

"It was something important," said Mother, frowning.

"Don't worry about it. Just drink your milk."

"What a nuisance I am! Sarah, I must be better before the Sale of Work."

"Yes, of course, darling."

At that moment Nurse Ede came in with a rustle of her starched apron. She said, "Oh, you're a lot better this morning, Mrs. Morris . . . and I see you've been a good girl and finished all your milk! We'll soon have you running about like a two-year-old."

Nurse Ede and I had established a routine. She preferred to be on duty for the first part of the night and wakened me at four. I sat with Mother until eight, then had breakfast with Father and did anything that had to be done in the house and the parish. In the afternoon Minnie took over while nurse went out for a walk and I rested. Father always sat with Mother in the evenings. In addition to this arrangement of duties one of us was available to help nurse if we were wanted.

Now that Mother had begun to get better she was improving every day; even Dr. Weatherstone, who had been very gloomy, was pleased with her progress . . . but Father still went about looking dazed and miserable. The only time he was cheerful was when he was sitting with Mother; when he was with her he showed her a smiling face.

One morning at breakfast I said to him, "She's better, you know."

"What did you say, Sarah?" he asked, waking from his unhappy dream.

"She's better. She slept quite well and nurse is giving her a lightly boiled egg this morning."

"That's good," said Father miserably.

"Dr. Weatherstone is pleased."

"Yes, he's pleased . . . but there's no chance of her making a complete recovery. I asked him. She'll always be a helpless invalid, Sarah." He rose, leaving his breakfast half finished, and added, "I'll go up and sit with her for a little before I go out."

I thought about what he had said. It was terribly sad that she wouldn't be able to go about in her usual energetic way, but to me the most important thing was that Mother should be here. I would look after her; I would sit and read to her and bring her flowers; I would do all I could to make her happy.

Mother had now been ill for nearly a fortnight and she was so much better that Dr. Weathersone was talking of getting her up for a little to sit in a chair. She said she would like to see Lewis so I rang him up and arranged for him to come to lunch the following day. I felt so happy when I went to bed that instead of lying and worrying I went straight off to sleep.

Nurse Ede woke me at four as usual; it is a ghastly time to be wakened but I was getting used to it now.

"She's been a little restless," said nurse. "It's nothing to worry about — everyone has their ups and downs — but you can call me if you want me."

Mother was asleep when I went in, so I sat down at the table near the shaded light and took up the book I was reading. It was very quiet; the fire, which was kept burning night and day, was flickering cheerfully.

Suddenly I heard a little gasping sound and turned to see mother staring at me with frightened eyes. Her lips moved as if she were trying to speak. She was trying to tell me something! My heart was hammering with fright. I bent forward and took her hand.

"What do you want, darling?"

She looked at me . . . and suddenly I knew. "You want Father, don't you? I'll run and get him."

I ran to his room; he was awake in a moment. There was no need to tell him what was the matter. He put on his slippers, seized his dressing-gown and struggled into it as he followed me along the passage.

He knelt down and took her hand. "Dorrie," he said. "Darling Dorrie."

"Hen — ry," she said in a slurred voice.

"Yes, dearest, I'm here. Don't try to speak."

"The Lord — is —" she began.

He knew what she meant; he always knew what she wanted. He began to say it slowly and clearly:

"'The Lord is my Shepherd, therefore can I lack nothing. He shall feed me in a green pasture and lead me forth beside the waters of comfort . . .'"

His beautiful clear voice never faltered.

150

"'Yea, though I walk through the valley of the shadow of death, I will fear no evil: for Thou art with me . . .'"

When he got to the end he kissed her very gently on the forehead and closed her eyes.

CHAPTER
FIFTEEN

We had all known that Mother was popular in Fairfield, but we hadn't realised how much everyone loved her. All sorts of people came to the Vicarage with flowers: old people and young children, people we knew and people we had never seen before. Some of them brought wreaths but most of them brought flowers from their gardens. We were nearly smothered in flowers. We put them on dust-sheets spread all over the drawing-room floor . . . masses of spring flowers!

Lewis and Willy came. We were glad to have them for they were kind and comforting and steady.

When Lewis saw the heaps of flowers — and more arriving every few minutes — he said, "She wouldn't like to see them like that, you know. They'll wither without any water."

"But what can we do?" I exclaimed.

"We can't do anything," said Willy. "And I think she would like to see the flowers. Not because of the flowers but because of all the people who knew she was fond of flowers and wanted to bring them to her. Three little children came half an hour ago with bunches of cowslips . . . Mother would like that."

"Yes, she would like that," I agreed.

"There's the bell again!" said Willy. "I told Minnie I'd answer the door — she has enough to do."

"Can I do anything to help?" asked Lewis.

"Just being here is a help," I told him.

Father had telegraphed to Mrs. Meldrum and had received a reply saying that they had broken the news to Lottie and she was so dreadfully upset that they thought it unwise for her to attempt the long journey home; they would do their best to take care of her and keep her from moping and they sent their love and heartfelt sympathy to us all. It was more like a letter than a telegram.

The next day two enormous wreaths arrived from a florist in London: one from the Meldrum family and the other from Lottie. The Meldrums' wreath was in the form of a harp; it was made of orchids and arum lilies and was twice the size of any other.

Willy unpacked it and stood it against the drawing-room wall. He said, "I didn't know Mother was very friendly with the Meldrums."

"She wasn't," I replied. "I don't think she ever saw them. She would have liked to go to Riverside but they never invited her."

"Queer people," said Willy. He looked at the harp and added, "How Mother would have disliked that thing!"

"I wonder what it cost," said Lewis.

Father sighed and said, "It's kindly meant."

The day of the funeral was fine and sunny — which seemed all wrong. (I felt it should have been a miserable, wet day for mother's funeral.) Mr. and Mrs.

Heath came over from Limbourne and Mr. Heath helped Father to take the service. The church was quite full; Mr. Rickaby had to bring some wooden chairs from the vestry for people who couldn't find an empty seat. There were people in church that morning who had never been to church as long as I could remember, people like Mr. and Mrs. Wilbraham, who were supposed to be atheists.

I sat with Lewis and Willy and Minnie and Mrs. Heath in the Vicarage pew. I can't describe the service; I was in a sort of trance, I didn't even want to cry.

Afterwards when it was all over and people were going away I noticed a group of women standing beside the grave. They were members of mother's Work Party: Mrs. Rickaby and Mrs. Price and Mrs. Stanley and half a dozen others. I knew them all, of course. I was looking at them and wondering what they were going to do when they began to sing:

"Abide with me; fast falls the eventide;
The darkness deepens; Lord, with me abide."

They sang it all through very softly and sadly.

Lewis and Willy and I stood and waited until they had finished; then I began to cry . . . and I couldn't stop.

Lewis and Willy took me home and Minnie helped me to go to bed; I lay there and cried until there were no more tears left in me.

154

* ★ *

Lewis and Willy stayed at the Vicarage for the week-end, but they were obliged to leave on Monday, so I pulled myself together and went with them in the taxi to see them off at the station.

When I got home there was a car standing on the sweep of gravel outside the door. I wasn't surprised; people often came to see Father. I went round to the back and found Minnie in the kitchen, beating up eggs.

"There's a visitor," she said. "Mr. Morris told me to make cheese straws for supper."

"Who is it, Minnie?"

"A gentleman. I didn't see him properly — just the back of him going into the study. He's been here nearly an hour."

"Oh, goodness, what a bother!" I took off my hat and coat and flung them down on a chair. I was tired and miserable; in no mood to talk to "a visitor." If the man intended to stay I should have to change for supper.

"It's no good standing there," said Minnie. "If he's staying you'll have to light the drawing-room fire. I'm too busy."

I tapped gently on the door of the study and went in; Father and his visitor were sitting in the two old-fashioned high-backed chairs which stood at either side of the fire.

Father looked up and said, "Here's a friend to see us, Sarah."

It was Charles! He got up and took my hand. "Sarah, I hope you're pleased to see me."

"Yes! Oh, yes! I haven't seen you for such a long time!"

"Not since we met at Nivennes. I hope you've really forgiven me for all the trouble I caused you? It was very bad of me."

"It was unwise," said Father mildly. "However, there was no harm done; I wrote to Madame Delormes and explained that I was to blame."

"You, sir?" asked Charles in surprise.

"It was I who asked you to see Sarah and make sure she wasn't unhappy; it didn't occur to me that you wouldn't be allowed to speak to her."

"Where have you come from?" I asked.

"From Austria. My family is comfortably settled in the Schloss, so I'm at liberty to attend to my own affairs."

"You've given them a great deal of your time," said Father, nodding. "What are your plans, Charles? Are you going back to Oxford?"

"Yes, but not to resume my studies; there has been too long a break. I intend to write a book about Oxford."

"A book . . . about Oxford?" asked Father incredulously.

"No wonder you're surprised, sir," said Charles, smiling. "Scores of books have been written about Oxford by scholars and historians — but, as far as I know, there hasn't been a book about Oxford written by a man like me: a man half Austrian and half Scottish, who came to Oxford on a voyage of discovery."

"Go on," said Father encouragingly.

"Yes, I want to tell you about it because it was you who gave me the idea. You said to me that I should go home and tell my friends that you were 'reasonably human'; you said the more 'coming and going' there was between people of different nationalities the better."

"I remember saying something like that . . . so the book is destined to tell your friends in Austria about your adventures in England?"

"Yes, and especially about Oxford: about its beautiful buildings and its history and about the impression it made upon the heart and mind of a stranger. I shall tell of the kindness and hospitality I received; I shall tell of rowing on the river and drinking ale in the pubs and the walks and talks and the lighthearted 'rags.' My book will be a hotchpotch, a strange mixture of old and new. Probably it will be no good at all, but I want to try."

"It sounds as if it might be very interesting," said Father. "You'll have to do a good deal of research, won't you?"

"Yes, I must get permission to visit the Bodleian Library — but the Master of St. Clement's College will arrange it; he's a good friend."

"I must go now," said Father. "I should like to hear more about it later; you'll stay and have supper with us, I hope."

"Thank you, sir, but I won't stay," replied Charles. "I just looked in on my way to Oxford. I should like to come some other time, if I may."

"Any time," said Father, nodding. "It's always a pleasure to see you." Then he went out and shut the door.

I felt a little shy of Charles; so much had happened since I had seen him. I said, "It was kind of you to come, Charles."

"Not kind! I wanted to see you."

"We're very — very sad — just now."

"Yes, Mr. Morris has just told me — I didn't know before. Oh, Sarah, what can I say to you except that I'm sorry? And it isn't enough! Your mother was a wonderful person. I was very fond of her — and I know you were devoted to her. I can see you're very unhappy."

"Yes, very unhappy," I murmured. "I loved her dearly but — but I could have been nicer to her. That's what's — making me — so miserable."

"We all think we 'could have been nicer' when we lose a dear friend."

"You didn't feel like that, Charles! You told me that you and your mother were 'very close together'."

"Yes, and it was true, but I remembered times when I was impatient inside."

I was silent. That was exactly what was troubling me: I remembered times when I had been "impatient inside"; times when I had thought Mother was "a little bit silly."

"We're all human, Sarah," said Charles at last.

"Oh, Charles! If only I could see her, just for a few minutes, to tell her how much I loved her!"

158

"I know your feeling . . . but she knew you loved her, and she loved you dearly. Listen, I want to tell you something: while you were at Nivennes I came here several times and played on the Bechstein. One afternoon Mrs. Morris happened to be free from all her duties and she sat on the sofa and listened. She was so quiet that I forgot she was there and went on playing for a long time. Then, at last, I remembered my hostess and sat down beside her. She talked about you. She asked me if I thought it had been right for you to leave school when you were still so young; I said I thought you were old enough — and sensible enough — to know your own mind. 'I thought that, too,' she said. 'But, you see, I *wanted* Sarah at home; she's such a comfort to me. I wanted her so much that I couldn't look at it from the outside. I felt sure I was being selfish.' I told her she was one of the most unselfish people in the world."

"She was."

"Yes, she spent her life doing things for other people. Don't cry, Sarah! I've upset you, talking like this, but perhaps it will comfort you to know that she wanted you so much."

"Oh, yes, it does! But I wish I hadn't left her and gone to Nivennes."

"Mrs. Morris spoke of that, too. She said, 'I miss her dreadfully, of course, but it shows she has a talent for languages . . . and it shows she has courage, doesn't it?' I agreed.

"'Yes, it was brave,' said Mrs. Morris with a sigh. 'It was a big adventure and she was frightened, but she made up her mind to go. Sarah is like her father — not like me. Henry is full of courage.' "

After that we were silent for a little while. There were all sorts of things that I wanted to ask Charles, but I was dreadfully tired and it was comforting to sit beside him in silence.

Presently he said, "Sarah, this isn't the right time to speak of my own affairs . . . so I must go away quickly." He took my hand and kissed it and went to the door.

There was a lump in my throat but I managed to say, "Come back soon."

CHAPTER
SIXTEEN

Several days passed; Father and I were alone, except for Minnie, and the house felt very empty. I had expected father would be utterly miserable — I had feared a complete breakdown — but he was wonderfully good and brave; going about as usual, talking to people and taking all the services in church. In the evenings when I sat with him in his study he spoke of Mother quite cheerfully.

"I'm glad she has gone first," he said. "My dear Dorrie would have been lost without me . . . and she has been spared a great deal of suffering, not only physical pain but mental agony. She was a gentle creature; she hated violence and cruelty so she was very miserable during the last war. This coming war, which I fear is inevitable, will be ten times worse: Britain will be devastated by bombs and all the young men will be conscripted. Our boys will be in the thick of the fighting." He sighed and added, "Yes, God has been merciful to Dorrie."

Suddenly I realised that my prayers for Mother's recovery and my plans for taking care of her had been completely selfish. I had been thinking of myself, not of her. I murmured, "Yes, but I was afraid you would be terribly unhappy."

"I was terribly unhappy when she was ill; the future seemed wretched. I imagined her a complete invalid, not able to go about and do all the things she enjoyed doing; I imagined her confined to her room, anxious and miserable . . . but now she's at peace. She's safe and happy and some day we shall be together again. I know that, Sarah."

I, too, believed it, but not with such confidence — such wonderfully happy confidence.

I was trying to do some of Mother's work in the parish. The Work Party and the choir were beyond me, but I could do the flowers and clean the brasses. On Saturday morning I took the big key and went up the path to church. I felt anxious because it was Mrs. Price's day for flowers and, since the episode of the carnations, she hadn't spoken to me. One day when I had met her face to face coming out of the butcher's and had said, "Good morning, Mrs. Price," she had turned her head in the opposite direction.

When I got to the church door Mrs. Price was waiting for me with a huge bouquet of sweet peas. I said, "What lovely sweet peas, Mrs. Price! They're very early, aren't they? Ours are only in bud."

"Yes, they're early," she agreed. "Mr. Price grows them in his green-house. Would you like me to arrange them, Miss Morris?"

I hesitated.

"I just thought you might be busy," she explained. "I could arrange them if you show me what to do."

162

"That would be very kind of you, Mrs. Price."

I opened the door and we went in together; I showed her the flower-room and the sink and took the vases out of the cupboard.

"There isn't anything to say at times like this," said Mrs. Price. "I mean nothing that's any good. She was so gay and pretty that it seems very sad. She was a saint if ever there was one. She was too good for this world so I expect God wanted her in heaven. I mean, heaven would be dull if only old, ugly people were there. You needn't say anything, Miss Morris. I just wanted to tell you what I thought when I heard she had gone. You needn't say anything," she repeated.

I couldn't have said anything if my life had depended on it.

I gave her the vases and took out the cleaning materials.

"I could clean the brasses," suggested Mrs. Price. "I could do it when I've finished the flowers — if it would be a help."

I managed to say it would be a help.

"That's right, dear," said Mrs. Price. "Just put the cleaning things on the table and go home. It will take me some time but if you give me the big key I'll lock the door and leave the key at the Vicarage."

As a matter of fact I would rather have locked up the church myself, but she was being kind so I couldn't refuse her offer. "Thank you very much," I said. "Perhaps you think it's a pity to keep the church locked; we used to leave the door open all day but

163

someone came and stole the money out of the alms box."

"How dreadful!" exclaimed Mrs. Price. "That's worse than Ananias and Sapphira." She had taken off her coat and was putting on an overall which she had brought with her in her bag . . . and she looked so capable and sensible that I felt I could leave her quite safely.

I paused at the door and said, "I'll tell Father what you said about Mother; I think he would like it."

"Oh, I don't know," she said doubtfully. "Mr. Morris would think it very childish."

It was childish, of course, but all the same it was comforting. "I think he would like it," I repeated.

"Well, you know best," said Mrs. Price.

My eyes were full of tears when I came out of the church into the bright sunshine. There was a man standing on the path, but everything was blurred and I didn't recognise him . . . then my heart gave a bound and I saw it was Charles.

He came forward and took my hand.

"Have you been waiting long?" I asked.

"I've been waiting for nearly three years. I've been waiting for you to grow up, Sarah. You're grown-up now, aren't you? Are you old enough to know whether you love me enough to marry me?"

My heart was racing so madly that I was breathless.

He took my arm and we walked up the path to a wooden seat beneath an apple-tree and sat down.

"Sarah, why don't you speak to me, darling? Have you met someone else — someone nicer than me?"

I took a deep breath and said, "How could I? There isn't anyone — nicer than you — in the world."

"That's what you said before."

"Yes."

"Are you sure, Sarah?"

"Certain sure."

He put his arm round me. "I loved you the very first moment I saw you, when you came into your father's study and said, 'But it's a soufflé! Father, it's a cheese soufflé.' You looked so sweet and innocent; your lovely hazel eyes were big with anxiety."

"You stood up and bowed as if I were someone important . . ."

"You'll always be the most important person in the world to me."

"I've always belonged to you, Charles."

"I know, darling."

We were silent for a few minutes. There was a soft breeze and the apple-blossom was falling, one of the pink petals fell into my lap, and the scent of the honeysuckle which grew in the hedge was warm and sweet in the sunshine.

At last I said, "You've always known I loved you. I told you that day at Nivennes and you said I was a child. You must have thought me very foolish."

"Foolish? What do you mean?"

"Listen, Charles: a girl I know says that if you love a man you should 'keep him guessing.' You should have fun with other men and not make yourself cheap. She

165

says a man gets tired of you if you allow him to know that he's the only man in the world."

Charles laughed.

"I mean it," I told him seriously. "You've known for years that for me you're the only man in the world."

"But I haven't become tired of you, Sarah. I must be different from your friend's admirers for that sort of treatment wouldn't suit me at all. I should be too proud to compete with other men for favours. In fact if the girl I loved began to 'have fun with other men' I should retire from the contest and give them a clear field. I want all — or nothing." He was smiling at me as he spoke but I could see he really meant it.

"I think I should feel the same," I said thoughtfully.

"Of course you would! But we needn't worry; you and I belong to each other. When will you marry me, darling?"

"We aren't properly engaged yet."

He drew me into his arms and kissed me. It was a different kiss from the gentle brotherly kiss he had given me at Nivennes; there was something fierce about it . . . and a little frightening.

"We're properly engaged now," he said, smiling. "I shall buy a ring on Monday. I've got to go to London on Monday. You'd like diamonds, wouldn't you? I think a solitaire diamond —"

"I want your signet ring."

"But it's a man's ring! You must have diamonds."

"I want this," I said, trying to pull it off his little finger.

"But, Sarah, I've worn it for years!"

166

"That's why I want it: because you've worn it for years."

"But, Sarah —"

"You shall have it back," I promised. "You shall have it back when you put a plain gold band in its place."

He laughed. "What a determined person you are!"

It was a struggle for him to get the ring off his little finger but it slipped on to the third finger of my left hand very comfortably.

"Does that satisfy you?" he asked teasingly.

"It will do very nicely in the meantime."

"Sarah, I love you!"

"Are you sure, Charles?"

"I'll kiss you again, just to show you —"

"No, not now," I said hastily. "I want to talk to you sensibly. What are your plans?"

"I've been thinking a lot about plans," replied Charles thoughtfully. "When I was here before, at Oxford, I became very fond of England. I enjoyed the feeling of freedom; I liked the natural friendly manners and the lack of convention. You know that, don't you?"

I nodded. "You said it was a happy place."

"Yes, that's what I felt. When I went back to Austria, I felt frustrated. I felt like a fish out of water, I couldn't breathe freely. Then came the Anschluss when Austria was betrayed by her government and surrendered without a blow! That decided the matter: I couldn't live in a country dominated by a man like Hitler."

"What do you mean, Charles?" I asked in surprise.

"My mother was a MacDonald, as you know, so already I am half British by birth. I want to become a

British subject. I have been in touch with the authorities and have applied to be naturalised. I had hoped to be able to tell you that it was fixed but there are various 'snags' — as Lewis would say. However I've got several good friends who are willing to vouch for me and on Monday I'm going to London for an interview, so I'm hoping the matter will be settled before long."

I was so astonished that I was speechless.

"Aren't you pleased, Sarah?"

"Oh, yes! Yes, of course I'm pleased! Terribly pleased! But, Charles, are you sure you want to become a British subject?"

"Quite sure. I've told you the principal reason; there are other, personal, reasons why I shall never go back to Austria."

"Never go back?"

"Perhaps that sounds rather strange to you."

It sounded very strange. I knew he loved his home. He had told me so much about Schloss Roethke, the fine old castle standing on the rocks above the stream; he had told me about his horses and how he loved cantering for miles over the fields and meadows of his father's estate and he had told me about the kind friendly peasants and the little children who ran to greet him when they saw him coming.

Charles sighed. He said, "I spent two years riding about my father's estate and putting things in order. My father asked me to do it — and it had to be done because it had been neglected. I talked to the people

168

because I liked them — and understood them — and I always took a few sweets in my pocket for the children."

"You made friends with them, Charles."

"Yes, but afterwards I discovered that my popularity with my father's tenants was a cause of offence to Rudi. I found he was jealous. He's the heir, so he — and not I — should be popular."

"Oh, but how childish! If he wanted to be popular he should have gone about the place himself — not left it to go to rack and ruin."

"Yes, of course," agreed Charles. "I explained that, and he accepted my explanation. Rudi couldn't quarrel with me for I had only done what my father asked me to do (and I must admit he was very grateful to me for my work in getting the Schloss put in order), but I saw quite clearly that it would be better for everyone if I came away and never went back."

"Oh, Charles, how sad!"

"Yes, it's a little sad but it can't be helped." He hesitated and then added, "There's another, personal, reason why I can never go home: it's because of Anya."

"Your brother's wife! Isn't she nice to you?"

"At first she was a little too nice to me; then, when she found I wasn't interested, she was . . . not very nice. Oh, it wasn't serious," declared Charles. "Anya is just a silly girl who likes a lot of attention but Rudi is devoted to her and I was afraid he might see what was happening."

"How awful for you!"

"Yes, it was very difficult; I was walking on eggs. Sarah, I've told you of these unhappy affairs because

169

we're going to be married and I don't want to have any secrets from you. When we're married it would be the natural thing for me to take you to my home and introduce you to my people . . . but, alas, I shall never be able to take you to Schloss Roethke!"

"No, I can see that."

"I can never go home," repeated Charles. "So the best thing to do is to accept the fact like a sensible man and make a new life for myself."

"With me," I said.

"Yes, with you, darling. It will be a good life, we shall be happy together, I shall have no regrets. It is easier for me to do this because my mother left me all her money and it is here, in this country, invested in good securities. We shan't be wealthy, but we shall be able to live comfortably on the income."

"She left all her money to you?"

"There was no reason why she shouldn't: Rudi will have more than enough. My mother was wise," said Charles thoughtfully. "Now that I look back and consider the matter I believe she realised that some day there might be trouble between Rudi and me. My father is not wise. Sometimes, when he was angry with Rudi, he would say foolish things."

"You were his favourite," I suggested.

"Yes," said Charles with a sigh. "Yes, but he shouldn't have shown favouritism. Rudi can't help it that his nature is soft and pliable. We can't help our natures, Sarah."

"No, I suppose not," I said doubtfully.

170

"Well, that's enough about my family troubles," said Charles in a different tone of voice. "You and I must look to the future. As I told you I've applied to become a British subject . . . and the moment I hear that my application has been granted I shall enlist as a private soldier in the British Army."

"Enlist!" I exclaimed in alarm. "But, Charles, you might have to fight against your own country — your own people!"

"I shall be fighting against Hitler and all his works," said Charles grimly.

Somehow this seemed to bring the war very near. I had thought of it and talked of it but now the awful horror invaded my mind; for a moment or two I was afraid I was going to faint. I leaned forward and rested my head on my hands.

Charles's voice seemed to come from a long way off. "Sarah, what's the matter? Are you feeling ill?"

"Yes . . . no, I'll be all right in a minute."

He put his arms round me and held me tightly. "My poor darling, you've been having a bad time! Perhaps something I've said has upset you?"

"About — enlisting and — and fighting. It seemed to bring the war — so horribly near."

"I don't think it's very near," said Charles thoughtfully. "It's coming, but it may be months — or even years — before Hitler takes a step which will precipitate a crisis. That's one of the reasons why I want to marry you as soon as possible, so that we can have a little time together."

"Yes," I said, sliding my hand into his.

He held it firmly. "Will your father agree?"

"I'll ask him to-night."

"Shall I ask him?"

"No, I'd rather do it, Charles."

"Just as you like," said Charles doubtfully. "There's the difference of religion; that will be a sorrow to him, I'm afraid."

"What will your father say?"

"He'll be furious with me," said Charles frankly. "However, I'm not his heir . . . and, as I told you, I'm never going home."

"We shall have to be married in your church," I said. Strangely enough this thought had only just occurred to me: we couldn't be married by Father in St. Mary's.

"Does it matter very much, Sarah?"

"Not . . . very much."

"We shall be happy," said Charles earnestly. "We shan't interfere with each other's religious beliefs. That's understood, isn't it?"

"Yes, that's understood," I agreed, smiling at him.

CHAPTER
SEVENTEEN

Father was fond of Charles. I knew that, so I didn't expect any trouble, but I waited until we were having tea together in his study.

"Charles was here this morning and he asked me to marry him," I said.

"I was afraid of that," said Father.

"Afraid? I thought you'd be pleased; I thought you liked him!"

"I'm very fond of Charles — he's a fine man — but the world is going mad and you'd be safer with an Englishman."

"Charles is the only man for me," I said earnestly. "I loved him when I was a child — in a childish way — but now I love him differently, as a woman. You won't make any objection, will you?"

"It wouldn't be much good, would it?"

"Yes, it would; I'm under twenty-one."

"I shan't make any objection to your engagement."

"But I want more than that, Father. I want you to be happy about it; I want your blessing."

"Dear child, you always have my blessing, but I can't feel happy about it; Charles's future is so uncertain. However if you're quite sure it's the right thing I'll give my consent to your engagement . . . but you'll have to wait until the war is over before you marry him."

"What!" I exclaimed in dismay. "Oh, we can't wait! We want to be married at once — as soon as possible!"

"That's out of the question."

"But, Father —"

"Listen, Sarah: if war breaks out between England and Germany Charles will be interned as an enemy alien."

I saw then that I had gone about it in the wrong way. I should have begun by explaining that Charles had registered an application to become a naturalised British subject . . . however it was not too late. I explained it now.

Father's reaction to the news was much the same as mine had been. "I can't understand it," he declared, with a worried frown. "Charles has often spoken to me of the old castle and the estates which have belonged to his family for hundreds of years; I was under the impression that he loved his home and was proud of it."

"His brother is the heir," I pointed out.

"I know, but all the same I can't understand it . . . and what will his family say? They'll be very angry with him, won't they?"

"Yes, but he says he will never go back to Austria."

"Never go back?" asked father incredulously.

"He detests Hitler."

"Yes, I know, but —"

"Charles intends to make a new life for himself here, in Britain, so there's nothing to prevent us from being married, is there?"

174

"You must wait," said Father firmly. "You really must wait until Charles hears that his application has been granted."

"He expects to hear quite soon."

"All the more reason why you should wait." Father took up the newspaper which he had been reading and I saw it was useless to say any more.

Charles came to see me on Tuesday morning; he had been to London the day before and had had his interview. I wanted to hear all about it so we went out together and sat on the seat in the garden.

"Tell me your news first," said Charles. "Did you speak to your father about our marriage?"

"Yes, but he was rather — rather difficult about it. He's very fond of you but he said your future is uncertain."

"Everyone's future is uncertain!"

"He wants us to wait until you hear about your naturalisation."

"But that may take weeks!" exclaimed Charles in dismay. "Oh, Sarah, what are we to do?"

"Perhaps you should speak to him."

"Yes, I will," agreed Charles.

"What happened yesterday at your interview? Was it all right?"

"I don't know," he replied doubtfully. "In some ways it was better than I expected — they took a lot of trouble and went into my case very thoroughly — but in other ways it was not so good."

175

Charles had been interviewed by a Board consisting of five members. This was unusual. There was a 'spy-scare,' so applicants for naturalisation were being very carefully screened. He was told that if his application hadn't been very strongly backed by influential people it wouldn't have been considered at all.

When he was shown into the room Charles saw the file of papers, relating to his case, lying on the table. Some of the papers were given to him to read and he was questioned about them. The file included a letter from the Master of St. Clement's College and several other letters, all of which bore witness to his good character and sound opinions.

Two members of the Board seemed particularly interested in Charles's home in Austria and asked why he had spent such a long time there with his family and had now decided to give up all connection with them. Charles replied that he felt he owed a duty to his family — especially to his father — and had wanted to do all he could for them. He now felt that he had repaid his obligations to his family and was free to live his own life.

They asked a great many questions, some of which seemed irrelevant, but Charles answered them all. He told them that his idea of becoming a British subject had been conceived while he was at St. Clement's College, reading history and English literature; it had been in his mind for years. He repeated that his mother was British and that he found Britain very congenial; everyone was kind and friendly.

"But that was several years ago," said an elderly member of the Board. "After that you went home to Austria. Why have you suddenly made up your mind that you want to become a British subject?"

"I couldn't bear to live in a country dominated by Hitler, sir," replied Charles. "If my application is granted I intend to enlist in the British Army."

"It does you credit, Mr. Reeder, but you would be more useful as an interpreter."

"I'm sure that was the key to the puzzle, Sarah," said Charles. "I saw them looking at each other and nodding. They wouldn't have taken all that trouble over my case if I hadn't been fluent in French and German."

"Did they seem friendly?"

"At first they were very stiff and starchy, but towards the end of the interview they thawed out and became more friendly . . . all except one man who said little but looked disagreeable. Eventually I was dismissed and told that my case would be carefully considered and I would hear the result in due course. As I was coming away I said I would be very grateful if I could be informed of the result as soon as possible as I was engaged to be married to an English girl. They were interested to hear that and asked several questions about you."

Charles sighed and added, "I'm sure it would be all right if it were not for that one man. He didn't like me."

Charles had just finished telling me about his interview when Father came through the little green gate which led to the churchyard.

"I'll speak to him," said Charles, rising and walking towards him across the lawn.

I got up and followed.

"Mr. Morris," said Charles. "May I have your permission to marry Sarah? Perhaps this is not the correct way to ask (we do things differently in my country) but please forgive me and give your consent."

"I've told Sarah I'm willing to give my consent to an engagement."

"Thank you, sir. We want to be married as soon as possible."

"Sarah is only eighteen. I should like you to wait —"

"I've loved Sarah for years," said Charles earnestly. "I shall do my best to make her happy. I'm not a wealthy man but my mother left me sufficient capital to ensure a reasonably comfortable income. I can give you details —"

"It isn't your financial position," interrupted Father. "It's the uncertainty of your future. You're hoping to become a naturalised British subject, aren't you? Well, you must wait until it's settled."

"But we don't want to wait!" exclaimed Charles, in desperation. "I had my interview yesterday and they promised to let me know the result 'in due course.' It might be to-morrow or it might take weeks; you know what these Government departments are! Sarah and I want a little time to be happy together before — before anything happens."

"You mean before there is war."

"Yes, sir."

Father hesitated and then said, "No, Charles. I'm sorry but I can't give my consent. You must wait until the matter is settled."

I signed to Charles to say no more; I knew it was hopeless.

"I'm sorry," repeated Father, then he turned and walked away and disappeared into the house.

CHAPTER
EIGHTEEN

There was a wooden seat in the churchyard, quite near Mother's grave; I had gone there several times and had sat there doing the mending. I wasn't good at mending — Mother had always done it — but it had to be done. The seat was at the edge of the churchyard and had a pleasant view over a low hedge to the fields and the village of Fairfield.

One fine Saturday afternoon when I was sitting there I heard the roar of a motor-bike coming up the hill, and a few minutes later Lewis came striding up the path towards me; he was in khaki uniform.

"Hallo," he said. "I suppose you're surprised to see me dressed up as a soldier-boy?"

I was too surprised to answer.

"Well, there's nothing very startling about it. I've always wanted to make the Army my profession, but there was such a hullabaloo when I wanted to go to Sandhurst that I gave in and went to St. Clement's College instead. The first thing I did when I got there was to join the Officers' Training Corps. So now you know," added Lewis, sitting down beside me and taking off his cap.

"You never told us!"

180

"I didn't want another hullabaloo."

"But, Lewis —" I began.

Lewis didn't listen. He continued earnestly, "It was the wisest thing I ever did in my life. There will be conscription, of course, so it's better to be a trained officer — better for me and better for my country. Besides it's what I've always wanted. Willy is good at machinery so he'll be roped in to make munitions. You ought to join the Wrens."

"Leave Father all alone!"

"Minnie would look after him."

"I couldn't possibly! He depends on me — he would be miserable alone with Minnie. You must be mad, Lewis!"

Lewis looked surprised, but he just said, "Don't lose your wool; I was trying to help you, that's all. What will you do if women are conscripted?"

"I don't know," I said. "I only know that my duty is to look after Father."

"There's going to be war, sooner or later," said Lewis . . . and went on to talk about it. He was excited at the prospect; he didn't remember the last war so he wasn't dreading its horrors.

"Don't talk about it," I said at last. "I can't bear to think of it. Thousands of people will be killed! We've had one war casualty in the family already."

"You mean Mother?"

"Yes."

"Do you often come here?" asked Lewis after a short silence.

"Yes, quite often. I suppose it's silly but I have a feeling she likes me to come. I feel peaceful and — and comforted."

He nodded understandingly. "I miss her dreadfully, Sarah. I liked to feel she was here, at the Vicarage. It was a sort of anchor. We've been out on an exercise to-day — that's why I'm in uniform — and I thought I'd come and sit here for a little before going back to Oxford. I brought some flowers; they're just wild flowers that I picked in the hedges, but she liked wild flowers, didn't she?"

He showed me what he had picked: dog-roses and honey-suckle. Then he got up and put them on her grave.

As I watched him standing there, bare-headed, I thought how pleased she would be if she knew . . . perhaps she did know.

When he came back we were silent for a while and I went on with the mending.

"Charles seems under the weather," said Lewis at last. "I met him the other day coming out of the Bodleian; he told me you and he were engaged and wanted to be married but Father was being obstructive. I don't wonder, really. Charles is an Austrian, which means he's an enemy alien."

"Charles has applied to become naturalised."

"Oh, that's the idea!"

"Yes."

"Well, I'm not really surprised," said Lewis thoughtfully. "We've had talks about political matters . . . and he likes this country. I remember him saying 'the air is free.' It would be ghastly to live in a country where the air wasn't free and you couldn't say what you liked."

Lewis was looking at the matter from a slightly different angle; but it was Lewis's nature to think of his own personal comfort . . . and it was quite an interesting angle.

"In that case," said Lewis. "I mean if Charles becomes naturalised there's no reason why you shouldn't marry him."

"Will you talk to Father about it?"

"Talk to him?"

"Yes. I want to marry Charles now, as soon as possible, so that we can have a little time together before war comes. Could you stay here to-night and try to persuade him? Please Lewis! He might listen to you."

"All right. I don't suppose he'll listen to me but I can have a try."

Father was very pleased to see Lewis, as I knew he would be. At supper he talked about his plans for the future.

"I can't stay here if war breaks out," said Father.

"You can't stay here?" I asked in astonishment.

"They don't really need me here; Fairfield is a backwater. I shall be more useful in London."

"London may be bombed," said Lewis.

"It will be bombed. It will be Target Number One; that's why I want to be there, to help people in distress. Sarah and Lottie can go to Craignethan; they'll be safe there. I shall take lodgings in London and help Mr.

Hetherington in St. Rule's parish. He'll be glad of my help."

"But, Father —" began Lewis.

"Oh, I dare say you're surprised," interrupted Father. "You look upon me as an old man, but I'm only fifty-eight — and perfectly strong and healthy. I can't sit here doing nothing if the country is at war; I want to be in the thick of it. Of course if your mother were here it would be different; she would be my first consideration."

"Have you told the vestry about your plans?" I asked.

"I told them I was thinking of it; they said I was mad."

To me it seemed quite mad: Father, who had lived in a quiet country parish for twenty years, to be thinking of giving up his home and taking lodgings in London! However my own plans were so uncertain that it was no good saying anything.

After supper I said I was tired (it was perfectly true; I was tired all the time. I was tired of waiting and wondering when Charles would hear about his future; tired of thinking about it). I went upstairs, leaving father and Lewis to have a talk.

For some time I lay in bed reading *Greenmantle*. I found I could read Buchan's adventure stories; my mind was so full of worries that I couldn't read any other kind of book. It was nearly midnight and I was just going to turn out the light when there was a gentle tap on my door and Lewis came in.

He sat down on the end of my bed. "Well, I've done it, Sarah," he announced. "Don't ask me how I did it because I don't know. At first he was adamant. He said you must wait until Charles heard definitely whether his application for naturalisation would be granted; he said that if you were to marry Charles you would take his nationality. You see the point, don't you?"

"Yes, but it's only a question of time. I mean, he's sure to get it sooner or later."

"Father thinks it's doubtful. He said he was responsible for you and it would be wrong for him to give his consent. It seemed hopeless to pursue the matter further so I began to talk about his crazy plan of leaving Fairfield and going to London."

"It is crazy," I agreed.

"Absolutely crazy — at his age. I tried to tell him so, as tactfully as possible, when suddenly he interrupted me and said, 'You think I'm mad, Lewis. Everyone thinks I'm mad to give up a good living and a comfortable house and go to London, but I'm determined to do it . . . and, if I'm going to do what I want, I've got no right to prevent Charles and Sarah from doing what they want. Both plans are mad — the world is upside down — so you can tell Sarah in the morning that they can go ahead with their arrangements and we'll all be mad together.' That's what he said. I didn't wait till the morning because I thought you might be wondering . . . and there was a streak of light under your door. Why on earth are you crying, Sarah? I thought you'd be pleased."

"I always cry when I'm pleased," I declared hysterically, and I put my arms round him and hugged him.

"Silly old Sally!" said Lewis, giving me a brotherly hug.

We decided to be married in a Roman Catholic church in Oxford. It was a "mixed marriage" so it must be quiet and simple, with only the family present and Minnie Dell and a few of Charles's Oxford friends. I wrote to the grans and told them all about it and asked if they would come but they said they were too old. They both wrote very kind letters and sent me a hundred pounds, and said they would like to see Charles. Would it be possible for us to come to Craignethan for a few days?

I showed their letters to Charles and he agreed that we ought to visit them. We had arranged to go to Skye for our honeymoon so we could easily spend a couple of nights at Craignethan on our way home.

Charles was busy making arrangements for the wedding and working at his book. He wanted to get all his notes for the book completed before we were married. We had made up our minds to "forget" about the naturalisation (we were tired of thinking about it). If the application was granted before we were married so much the better, if not it couldn't be helped.

In spite of all his work, Charles came to Fairfield nearly every day; he took me for spins in his car and we went for walks together. It was a very happy time.

One morning, when I had been doing the shopping in the village, I returned to find Charles in the garden.

We sat down and talked for a few minutes and he told me about his book. He had finished the historical

186

part, which was the most troublesome; the rest of it, which was to consist of his own experiences, could be done later.

"You've been talking to Minnie," I said.

"Witch!" exclaimed Charles. "How did you know?"

I knew because he had caught Minnie's intonation. Her voice had a Scottish lilt. Charles, with his "musician's ear," was very susceptible to accents and intonations. Sometimes he spoke — almost — like an Englishman, but when he had been in Austria for a time his foreign accent was quite noticeable and if he were upset or excited his English became less "elastic."

"Well, that's all very interesting," said Charles, smiling. "But it's a lovely day and I was going to suggest we should have a walk in the woods."

We climbed over the wall at the top of the garden and went up past the old oak-tree and the Druids' stones.

"Do you remember the first time we came this way?" asked Charles.

"What a donkey I was!"

"You were a very sweet little girl."

"I was 'a new experience' for you."

"You were, indeed," said Charles. "You were friendly and natural; there was no silly nonsense about you. I knew then, quite definitely, that you would grow up into a wonderful woman and I made up my mind to marry you. I've had to wait a long time but it has been worth while."

I took his arm. "I've always known that you were the nicest person in the world."

187

Our plans were settled now: the wedding was arranged for next week and after that we were going north in Charles's car. I showed Charles the letter from the hotel in Skye saying they would reserve a room for us.

"It's wonderful," said Charles, with a little sigh. "My mother talked to me about Skye when I was a child; she used to come and sit on my bed and tell me about the jagged Cuillins and the white sands and the soft mists and the smell of the sea-wrack — I think she was homesick for her island — and to me it has always been a place in a dream. Now it has become real."

"This letter has made it real."

"You always understand, Sarah! Yes, that letter saying that there's a room reserved for us — a room in Skye! I'm going there at last and I'm going with you."

As he was going away I asked if he were coming to-morrow.

He nodded. "I'll come at tea-time if I can manage it. If not I'll come on Saturday. Will that be all right?"

"Yes, of course," I said. "Just come when you can."

CHAPTER
NINETEEN

Charles didn't come to tea on Friday but I knew he was busy so I wasn't surprised. I, too, was busy; there were many things to arrange before the wedding; Mrs. Price had offered to come to church every Saturday morning while I was away to arrange the flowers and clean the brasses and I had accepted her offer gratefully . . . but with a hidden smile (a little saying of Grandpapa's had come to my mind: "a poacher makes the best keeper"). I had settled with Minnie about meals for Father; I had bought some new clothes and two suitcases and I was making some nightgowns.

Father had a vestry meeting on Friday evening. It was the beginning of July and, as it was still quite light, I sat by the drawing-room window, sewing. Gradually the light faded and the garden grew dim except for a bed of tea-roses. They were Mother's roses — Father had given them to her some years ago for her birthday, twelve beautiful little bushes of tea-roses! I thought of Mother as I looked at them and remembered how much pleasure they had given her. In the dusk of the evening each little bloom seemed to glow with a light of its own.

Presently Father came home from his meeting and went up to bed. It was now quite dark so I switched on the standard lamp above my head but I was too lazy to go on with my sewing. I sat there with the half finished nightgown in my lap, thinking of Charles and feeling happy. In six days we would be married . . . it was almost too wonderful to be true. I thought of our honeymoon in Skye and I thought of taking him to Craignethan to see the grans; I was longing to show them my Charles, I knew they would love him.

It was quiet and peaceful. My heart was quiet and peaceful too. Then, in the distance, I heard the sound of footsteps approaching and for some reason I was suddenly frightened . . .

A moment later the tall figure of Charles emerged from the gloom; he came in at the glass door, sank on to his knees beside me and exclaimed, "Oh God, what am I to do!"

"Darling! What's the matter?"

"My father has been arrested!"

"Your father —"

"Rudi has written to tell me and begs me to come at once. The letter was written a week ago but he was afraid to post it. He sent it to Switzerland with a friend. It's a desperate letter, badly written, badly expressed. He begs me to come. He's frantic! What am I to do?"

"Charles! Tell me properly, darling."

"Yes, I must," he said, taking a deep breath. "I must try to be calm. I was calm before — I had made up my mind that we must put off our marriage — but seeing you like this has — has upset me. I was out in the dark and I saw you sitting here with the light shining on your dear head. It was like — like being a wanderer and seeing a vision of love and home and happiness. Oh, Sarah, I don't want to leave you! I've waited so long for you, and now — now when I thought the waiting was over — and our troubles were over —"

I took his hand and held it firmly. "Tell me what has happened."

"Here's Rudi's letter," he said, taking the envelope with the thin crumpled sheets of paper out of his pocket and giving it to me.

I took it and looked at it. I could read German now — but not Rudi's frantic scrawl!

"You'll have to tell me," I said.

"They left the Schloss and went to Vienna for the marriage of Anya's brother. Naturally Anya wanted to be there, but it would have been wiser if she and Rudi had gone by themselves — instead of opening the town house and going en famille — but what's the good of talking about it! They all went to the marriage and in the evening they went to the opera with a party. When they got home the Secret Police were waiting for them; my father was arrested and taken away. The house had been searched, the servants had fled in terror — all but old Hans and his wife."

"Why was he arrested?"

"It's what I've been afraid of for years! I've told you about my father — about the way he spoke of Hitler. He's fearless and impatient; he comes of a proud Austrian family; he despises Hitler, calls him an upstart, a low-born guttersnipe — and other worse things. It's a wonder this hasn't happened before!"

"Charles, listen! Why must you go?"

191

"Rudi says I could influence my father and persuade him to behave reasonably."

"But he's in prison, isn't he? You couldn't —"

"Oh, it isn't a dungeon. He's a political prisoner in the State Prison in Vienna. Rudi is arranging for him to be properly looked after, and can visit him at certain times. His friends are making every effort to get him released. If he would be patient and reasonable, they might succeed . . . but he isn't reasonable. He's as angry as a caged lion. It's dangerous, that!"

"Dangerous?"

"At any moment they may lose patience with him and decide to — to end his life."

"Oh, Charles! But what could you do?"

"He would listen to me."

"Why? Why would he listen to you if he won't listen to Rudi?"

"He would listen to me," repeated Charles.

I knew the reason. He would listen to Charles because Charles was vigorous and determined . . . and because Charles was his favourite son. I said, "Isn't there any other way? You said you would never go back."

"I didn't mean to go back."

"If you go they'll keep you there! They can't get on without you!" I exclaimed.

"No, no! I shall only go for a few days."

"How long?"

"I'll come back to you as soon as I can," he said desperately. "As soon as I can, Sarah. I shall find out how things are and have a talk with my father, and I shall see a friend who has a good position in the new *régime*. He might be able to help us. Oh, darling, you understand, don't you? He's my father . . . and his life is in danger."

At first I had been angry, perhaps a little jealous. Why should Charles always have to go to the rescue when his family was in trouble? But now I realised what I should feel if my father were in danger of his life.

"Yes," I said sadly. "Yes, I understand."

He sat down beside me on the sofa and put his arm round me and I rested my head against his shoulder.

For a little while there was silence.

"I wonder," said Charles doubtfully.

"What do you wonder?"

"I wonder if I could wait and go to Vienna next week . . . after we're married. It would just mean putting off my visit for a very short time. If I could wait and go after our marriage you would belong to me, Sarah. That's what I want."

It was what I wanted more than anything in the world, and for a few moments the burden on my heart lifted. Then I realised the danger. I could keep him — yes — but if he waited and something dreadful happened he would never forgive himself.

"That's what I want," he repeated. "I'd feel safer if we belonged to each other. I could wait and go to Vienna after we were married, couldn't I?"

Somehow the knowledge that I could keep him made it easier for me to let him go. "I think perhaps you'd better go," I told him.

"Yes, perhaps —"

"It just means putting off our marriage until you can arrange things satisfactorily. There isn't any danger, is there? Danger for you, I mean."

"Oh no, I don't envisage danger to myself. I've always been careful not to offend people; I'm well known in Vienna as a man more interested in the improvement of his father's property than in political matters."

"You aren't just saying that to comfort me?"

"I wouldn't lie to you, Sarah — not even for your own good — there must always be truth between you and me. If I thought there was danger I wouldn't go; I promise you that. No, the only reason I'm so upset is because I hate leaving you."

"When must you go?"

He sighed. "My plan is to catch the boat at Dover to-morrow morning. I left my car at Fairfield to have a tyre changed; the man said he would do it to-night."

"I wondered why you didn't come in your car. Charles, will you be able to write to me?"

"Yes, I'll write, but I shan't be able to tell you much. My country is now a Police State and letters may be opened."

"Just a few lines will do."

We went on talking quietly. Sometimes not talking, but just being together in silence.

"Charles."

"Yes, darling?"

"If we had been married to-day instead of next Wednesday . . ."

"I couldn't arrange it any sooner."

194

"I know, but — but we could pretend. We could pretend we were married this afternoon."

"Sarah! Do you know what you're saying?"

"I just thought . . . if you wanted to pretend."

"Oh, darling! Are you sure?"

"We've belonged to each other for years."

"We've always belonged to each other," said Charles softly.

We came downstairs together in the early dawn; the cold grey light was creeping in through the drawing-room windows. Charles unfastened the glass door and we went down the path to the gate. There was a damp mist rising from the ground and the trees were dripping.

When we got to the gate he stopped. "Say good-bye here, darling. I haven't left myself much time; I shall have to run."

"Charles! Oh, Charles, come back to me soon!"

He took me in his arms and kissed me. He held me so tightly that it hurt. "I'll come back as soon as I can," he said desperately. "As soon as I can, Sarah. You know that, don't you?"

"Yes, I know."

"*Auf wiedersehn*, my own darling girl."

"*Auf wiedersehn*, Charles."

He turned and ran.

The mist was thick under the trees and in a moment he had disappeared but I could hear his footsteps running quickly down the road. The sound grew fainter and fainter in the distance until at last I could hear it no more.

Part Three

CHAPTER
TWENTY

Here there is a blank in my diary . . . and a blank in my mind. I suppose I must have gone about as usual: eaten and slept and talked to people, but I can't remember anything about that time. There was no letter from Charles and no news of him; it was as if he had gone away in the grey mist of dawn and vanished from the earth.

When war was declared I began to come to my senses. I had to make the effort for there was so much to do. Father was determined to leave Fairfield and go to London; he repeated all he had said to Lewis and added that Lottie was to remain at St. Elizabeth's for another year and I was to go to Craignethan.

"I shall come with you," I told him.

"It won't be safe, Sarah. I don't want you in London; you would be an anxiety to me."

"I'm sorry, but you'll have to bear the anxiety as best you can."

He looked at me and sighed but said no more. Perhaps he realised that in my present queer state of mind it would be better for me to be in London.

"We'll find a flat and live there together," I said. "It will be more comfortable for you than lodgings."

"I'm not going to London for comfort," said Father, but he said it meekly and I took no notice.

After some difficulty I found a furnished flat; it was very small and rather dark but it was conveniently near St. Rule's. There was no question of taking Minnie with us — I could run the flat myself — so Minnie decided to go home to Ryddelton and live with her youngest sister. Father gave her a small annuity which would make her independent.

I couldn't leave Fairfield without saying good-bye to some of the people who had been kind to us, so I went to call on Mrs. Powell and had a chat with her.

When I was a child I had thought Mrs. Powell "quite old" but now she seemed younger . . . which was strange. Another strange thing was that, although I knew her so well, I knew nothing whatever about her. I looked at her sitting there, plump and cheerful, with the brown fringe and the lively brown eyes, and wondered what had happened to her husband and whether she had ever had a child and why she had settled down in Fairfield to teach other people's children. When I was a child I had accepted Mrs. Powell at her "face value" — as children do — but now I felt that there was something mysterious about her and I should have liked to know her history.

"Do the children still write their diaries?" I asked.

"Yes, of course," replied Mrs. Powell. "It's a good habit to keep a diary and once you get into the way of it you can't stop. I've kept a diary all my life; it's very interesting to look back and remember what has happened."

200

"I suppose it is," I said with a sigh.

"You've had a bad time lately," said Mrs. Powell. "There are bad times in our lives — and good times as well — and it all makes a pattern. The pattern is very important, Sarah. Remember that."

"I can't see any pattern, Mrs. Powell."

"You will, some day," said Mrs. Powell, nodding. "Meanwhile it would be good for you to get a job in London. When you're anxious and unhappy it's better to keep busy; I know that from experience."

When I was coming away I kissed her and thanked her for all she had done.

"But I haven't done anything!" she exclaimed in surprise.

"You taught me that lessons are interesting."

"Did I, Sarah? Well, you couldn't have said anything that would have pleased me better," declared Mrs. Powell, smiling.

I called on Mrs. Stanley and Mrs. Price and Mrs. Rickaby and several other people who had been friends of Mother's; it was a struggle to make myself do it but they were all so pleased to see me that it was well worth while.

There were various other matters to be settled before we left Fairfield. Father was giving up the living and was going to St. Rule's in a voluntary capacity; everyone thought it very unwise but he was determined to do it and he said we would have enough to live on if we were careful. All this took time but at last the arrangements were completed; we put all the furniture

201

in store in Larchester and left St. Mary's Vicarage for ever.

We were saying good-bye not only to the dear old house and garden but also to memories — happy memories and sad ones. I was saying good-bye to the whole of my life. It was almost incredible that St. Mary's Vicarage was no longer my home: strangers would be living here; sitting in the drawing-room, walking about the garden and picking mother's roses!

It was surprising that I didn't feel more unhappy but already I was so miserable that my feelings were numbed, nothing seemed to matter any more.

I had been against the move, like everyone else, but soon I realised that it was good for Father to make a clean break with the past and begin a completely new life. He was welcomed cordially by Mr. Hetherington, the vicar of St. Rule's; he took many of the services, visited people in the parish and made new friends.

Mr. Hetherington was tall and thin with grey hair and dark eyes. He was spiritual and other-worldly and the services in St. Rule's were beautiful, but people didn't come to him for help and comfort — as the Fairfield people had come to Father. To me there was something inhuman about Paul Hetherington but Father had a great admiration for him.

Mrs. Hetherington was kind but she was so much older than I was that we seemed to have little in common. I thought her plain and uninteresting. Her complexion was very pale; she had large brown eyes and smooth dark hair which she wore parted in the middle and pinned into a "bun" at the back of her

202

neck. We knew nothing about the Hetheringtons when we went to London but we had not been there long before someone told Father that their only child, Gilbert, had been in the Navy and had been drowned at sea in an accident. Nobody seemed to know any details about the accident and the Hetheringtons never mentioned him.

My first few months in London were unhappy ones. The flat was so small and easily run that I hadn't enough to keep me busy. I couldn't have left Father alone but I could have managed a part-time job — and this was what I wanted — but Father was anxious about me and wouldn't hear of it. I had been losing weight and Father had consulted old Dr. Weatherstone before we left Fairfield. Dr. Weatherstone had come to see me and had poked me and prodded me and given me a tonic and had said I must rest as much as possible . . . which was quite the wrong advice. I had too much time to sit and think and worry about Charles; I missed all the coming and going at St. Mary's Vicarage and I was lonely.

There had been bombing raids in the north but so far none in London, and apart from the black-out and the rationing and the uniforms in the streets there was little to show that we were at war. Some people were of the opinion that the Luftwaffe would never bomb London, but Father thought otherwise and persuaded Mr. Hetherington to allow him to make the huge crypt beneath the church into an air-raid shelter. The walls were strengthened and several large stoves were put in.

When it was ready Father took me to see the place. He had paid for everything himself and had made it wonderfully comfortable; there were cupboards full of cups and saucers and plates, cupboards full of tinned food and biscuits and tea and sugar, and there were wooden bunks with mattresses and blankets. He had provided books and packs of cards and games for children. It was all very clean and neat . . . and empty. I wondered if it would ever be used.

No sooner were we settled in London than Father received a short note from Lottie to say she had left school and was living with the Meldrums. Father rang up and spoke to her and told her she had no right to leave school without his permission . . . but Lottie said she was sick of school and "there was a war on"; (this was an excuse for anything and everything!) She said Mrs. Meldrum needed her because there was a battalion of the Downshire Regiment in the old barracks at Larchester and the Meldrums were "holding open house" for the officers.

I thought this sounded unsuitable for Lottie, who was only seventeen, and I told Father that he should go to Fairfield and see her and send her back to school. But he sighed and said, "The child seems happy with the Meldrums; they've always been very kind to her, you know."

"It would be better for her to go to Craignethan."

"Yes, I told her that, but she said it would be dull; there are no young people at Craignethan. At any rate she's quite safe at Riverside."

204

Lewis had been drafted into an infantry regiment and was in training on Salisbury Plain; he came to see us now and then, and he looked so smart and soldierly and was so cheerful that it was a pleasure to see him. As usual he was full of his own affairs and not particularly interested in other people's.

"The war won't last long," said Lewis. "I only wish I could get to France and see some active service before it's over. It's sickening to be kept kicking my heels on Salisbury Plain. However once the battalion is up to strength we'll probably be on the move." He smiled and added, "Have you seen Father's air-raid shelter? It's pathetic, isn't it? The Germans don't intend to bomb London."

He was so full of confidence that, while he was there I believed him.

Willy had completed his years of apprenticeship in Romford's Engineering Works, but Romford's Works were not making munitions, so when war broke out he was transferred to a new factory which was making tanks. I never really understood the ins and outs of the matter (Willy was very reticent about his affairs and disliked interference), but one day he said somewhat bitterly, "I'm doing unskilled work; I'd have been more use to my country with a gun in my hand."

"Did you try to enlist?" I asked.

"Of course!"

"Why wouldn't they take you, Willy?"

"You'll need tae ask Jock," he replied with a grim smile.

It was useless to say any more but I realised that there had been a muddle. Willy was a skilled mechanic so they had refused to take him for the Army . . . but he was doing unskilled work and eating his heart out over it.

I was very unhappy about Willy: the factory was completely blacked-out, so he seldom saw the light of day, and his hours of work were long and arduous; he was pale and haggard and depressed; his clothes were shabby and dirty. Sometimes he turned up at the flat, looking like a tramp, and I made him have a bath and gave him a good meal. I washed his clothes and mended them and tried to cheer him up.

"Lewis says the war will be over soon," I told him.

"Lewis is wrong," said Willy. "This phoney war will turn into a real war and London will be bombed. Hitler is just biding his time. He can break through the Maginot Line whenever he likes. The French have 'no stomach to this fight'; they'll crumple up and leave us in the soup. Before we know where we are the German Army will be at Calais."

"My dear boy!" exclaimed Father in alarm.

"Well, you'll see," said Willy.

We did "see." Not many months passed before Willy's prophecies all came true

CHAPTER
TWENTY-ONE

One morning when I was in St. Rule's air-raid shelter, putting things in order after a bombing raid, Mrs. Hetherington came in to help me. She asked how I liked living in London. Usually I replied cheerfully, and not very truthfully, to this question (because people didn't really want to know), but to-day I was feeling so depressed that I told her I was lonely and hadn't enough to do.

"How would you like to help me with an Augean labour?" asked Mrs. Hetherington, smiling.

"You mean . . . cleaning stables?"

"Worse," she replied. "Dirty people are worse than dirty animals. Don't bother about it, Miss Morris. It was silly of me to mention it."

"But I'd like to help you!"

Mrs. Hetherington looked at me doubtfully.

"Please tell me about it," I said.

"Oh well . . . it's a girl called Susie Dowles. I've known her for years — she was in my Sunday School class when she was little — so I've always been interested in her. Her parents are both dead but they left Susie their basement flat so she took her grandmother to live with her. It was very good of Susie — at least I think so."

"Is the old woman bed-ridden?"

"Oh, dear me, no! She's very spry." Mrs. Hetherington sighed and continued. "Susie works in a munitions factory and gets good pay. She keeps the flat beautifully clean — she's proud of it, you see."

I nodded.

"Well, about three weeks ago Susie was knocked down in the street and was taken to hospital. I've been to see her several times and I'm glad to say she's better and she's going home to-morrow . . . but unfortunately Mrs. Dowles is a dirty old woman, so Susie's nice little flat is sure to be in a mess."

"You're going to clean it up for her?" I suggested.

"Yes. I just thought Susie won't be feeling very grand and it would be horrid for her to come home and —"

"Of course it would!" I exclaimed. "I'd like to help you, Mrs. Hetherington."

"It won't be a very nice job," said Mrs. Hetherington in warning tones.

Mrs. Hetherington drove me to the scene of our Augean labour in Mr. Hetherington's little car; she had brought pails and scrubbing brushes and other cleaning materials and a box of groceries. Old Mrs. Dowles was out when we arrived but a neighbour had the key of the little flat and let us in.

"I've cleaned up Susie's bedroom," said the woman. "It wasn't too bad, reely, but I just couldn't stomach the kitching. That old woman is a reg'lar slattern — an'

208

I don't care who 'ears me say it! You ain't goin' ter do the kitching with your own 'ands, Missis 'Etherington?"

"Yes," replied Mrs. Hetherington.

"Well, rather you than me!" said the woman.

It was a small basement flat and quite nicely furnished . . . but when we opened the door of the kitchen the smell of dirt and decaying vegetable matter came out to meet us in a wave.

Mrs. Hetherington threw open the window and said, "Go home, Miss Morris."

"Did you say 'go home'?" I asked in astonishment.

"Yes, it's even worse than I expected. The floor is filthy; the sink is full of dirty pots and pans and dishes; the smell is intolerable."

"I know, but —"

"It isn't a stable, it's a pigsty — no, it's worse! Please go home."

"I'm going to help you."

"No. It isn't fair."

"Isn't fair?" I asked. "What do you mean?"

"I mean Susie is a friend of mine but she isn't a friend of yours, so it isn't fair. I shouldn't have asked you to —"

I laughed and took off my coat.

"I'd rather you went home," said Mrs. Hetherington earnestly.

I put on my overall and tied up my hair in a clean duster.

"Oh well," said Mrs. Hetherington with a sigh. "If you really feel you can bear it . . . but if we're going to scrub the floor together you must call me Pam."

Half an hour ago I couldn't possibly have called her "Pam" but now I felt differently. "That will be lovely," I said. Then, when I saw her looking at the mess in despair, I added briskly, "Come on, Pam! We must do the cupboards first, then clean the dishes and put them away. After that we'll scrub the floor."

"I would have started with the floor — but of course you're right, Sarah," replied Pam, smiling.

Fortunately there was a gas-geyser which produced plenty of good hot water so we got on none too badly. We scrubbed out the cupboards, washed the dishes and put them away, and sat down to have a cup of coffee before tackling the floor. There is no better way of making friends than working together, so by this time we were very comfortable.

"I never thought you were like this," said Pam, as she helped herself to sugar from a packet.

"Neither did I."

"You mean you didn't think I was like me?"

"No. I mean, yes, that's what I mean."

"I'm shy," she explained. "It's wrong and silly but I can't help it. Sometimes I feel as if I were tied up with cords."

"Surely you weren't shy of me?"

"I'm always shy until I get to know people and you looked as if you were miles away — as if you were lost! Don't tell me why, unless you want to."

I wanted to . . . so I told her about Charles.

"Oh dear, how dreadful!" said Pam, looking at me with soft, velvety-brown eyes. "No wonder you have that tragic look! It's so awful not to *know*, isn't it? I can sympathise because of Gilbert. If I knew exactly what had happened to Gil it would be so much easier to bear."

"I thought you knew what had happened."

"Everyone else thinks he's dead."

I understood what she meant. Other people thought Charles was dead but I was sure he was still here in this world — somewhere — and that some day he would come back to me. I was sure . . . otherwise I couldn't have borne to go on, day after day, month after month . . . but just sometimes, in the middle of the night, I wasn't quite sure and I was swamped in a wave of misery and despair.

"Gil was 'lost at sea,'" said Pam. "It sounds so — so forlorn, doesn't it? 'Lost at sea.'"

"Yes," I said sadly.

"Gil and I have always been close together. Even when he was a tiny baby we understood each other perfectly . . . and we went on understanding each other; we didn't need words. Gil is part of me — just like my hand." She looked at her hand and added, "I would know if my hand were dead, wouldn't I?"

"Do you think that kind of feeling can be trusted?"

"Yes, I do," she declared. "I think that kind of feeling is absolutely real . . . so if you feel in your bones that Charles is alive *I'm sure he's alive.*"

For a few moments I couldn't speak.

"Gil was in the Navy," continued Pam. "He always wanted to be a sailor. He had just got his commission as sub-lieutenant — he was so pleased and proud! His first voyage was in a destroyer bound for Malta. One night in the Mediterranean he disappeared. Nobody saw him fall overboard. He just . . . wasn't there . . . in the morning. 'Lost at sea.'"

"Oh, Pam! Was it a storm?"

"No, it was dark and misty." She hesitated and then continued, "There were two of them. Gil's great friend, Sam Liston, was in the same ship and disappeared at the same time. I mean they were both . . . gone. The Listons have no hope. They accepted the official statement that the boys fell overboard and were drowned."

"Perhaps they were picked up by a fishing-boat."

She sighed and said, "Perhaps. At any rate Gil wasn't drowned. When he's in the water he's in his element — like a seal. Besides, I'm sure he's alive."

"Pam, are you sure all the time? Even in the middle of the night?"

"Yes, all the time." She hesitated and then added, "Thoughts that come in the middle of the night aren't your own real thoughts."

"What are they?"

"Whispers from the devil."

"I'll remember that."

"Remember it in the middle of the night," said Pam, nodding.

We were silent for a few moments.

"Come on!" cried Pam, jumping up. "We'll divide the floor in half and have a race."

"But we must be thorough," I reminded her.

Minnie would have cleaned that floor in half the time but she couldn't have done it more thoroughly. We

212

discovered that beneath the dirt there was good sound linoleum so it was worth doing well. The race was a dead-heat and we were just about finished when the door opened and a young woman walked in. She stood and looked at us — and looked round the kitchen — then she sat down on a chair and burst into floods of tears.

"Susie!" cried Pam, throwing down the scrubbing brush and rising from her knees. "Susie — dear — what's the matter?"

"Angels," sobbed the girl. "Angels in my kitching — that's wot's the matter! Angels straight from 'eaven!"

"It wasn't much," declared Pam earnestly. "We were just — just tidying up a bit, that's all. Susie, don't cry like that; it wasn't anything — really."

"Wasn't it!" cried Susie. "Wasn't it nothin'? Don't I know wot this plaice looks like when Granma's bin 'ere alone for a week — never mind three! All the w'y 'ome in the bus I wos thinkin' wot it would look like, with the floor grimed an' the sink full of stinkin' dishes! All the w'y 'ome in the bus I wos thinkin' wot a pity there wasn't no miracles nowerd'ys . . ."

"Don't cry, Susie!" said Pam, patting her back gently. "Please don't cry. Look, this is Miss Morris —"

"It ain't!" exclaimed Susie hysterically. "It ain't Miss Morris an' it ain't Missis 'Etherington. It's two angels stright from 'eaven that's bin doin' a miracle in my kitching, that's wot it is! If I lives to be a 'undred I won't never forget this day. It's the wonderfullest thing that ever 'appened to me . . ."

Pam and I were very silent going home in the little car but presently she said, "It has made me feel very humble, Sarah. I wonder why."

"It's always humbling to get more than you deserve."

"Yes, you're right. We were overpaid."

I certainly was overpaid a hundred-fold for my part in the cleansing of Susie Dowles's kitchen; I had made a friend. Never before had I had a friend like Pam Hetherington, a friend much older than myself, intelligent and well read, a friend to whom I could say anything I liked and be sure of finding sympathy and understanding. Why had I thought her plain and uninteresting? I realised now that, in her own unusual way, Pam was beautiful.

I wasn't lonely now and when I woke up in the middle of the night I remembered what Pam had told me and said a prayer to exorcise the devil and all his works.

Our friendship wasn't one-sided; I was able to help Pam quite a lot in the parish of St. Rule's. Sometimes in the evening, when Father was at the air-raid shelter, Pam came and brought her mending-basket and we sat by the fire and talked. She knew I was "safe" so she could tell me things she wouldn't have mentioned to anyone else.

One evening, when we had been sitting together for some time in companionable silence, she said, "You're lucky, Sarah. I mean lucky to have your father. He's a good kind human man; it isn't easy to live with a saint."

"Father admires him tremendously."

"Oh, so do I!" declared Pam. "And I love him tremendously, too . . . but his standard is too high for an ordinary, worldly mortal like me. That's the trouble."

CHAPTER
TWENTY-TWO

It was September and the Battle of Britain was at its height when Lottie rang up and said she would come to lunch.

"I suppose you can give me lunch?" she said doubtfully.

"Yes, of course, Lottie! It will be lovely to have you."

"I want to see you, Sarah."

"Yes, do come, Lottie."

I felt quite excited at the prospect of seeing Lottie. I hadn't seen her since we left Fairfield. I had asked her to come several times but she had said she was much too busy.

Lottie arrived in a taxi at one o'clock. She was beautifully dressed and her manners were sophisticated.

"What a ghastly little den!" she exclaimed when she saw the flat. "I don't know how you can *bear* to live in such cramped quarters."

"I've got used to it," I replied. Compared with Riverside it was a "ghastly little den."

Fortunately she enjoyed her lunch (I had provided her favourite food) and afterwards when we were having coffee together she became more like herself and chattered happily about all she was doing . . . but she had said she wanted to see me, and I had received the impression that it was not just sisterly affection, so I asked if she were still quite happy with the Meldrums or would she rather go to Craignethan.

"It would drive me raving mad to go to Craignethan," she replied. "Besides, I'm busy with war work."

This was the first I had heard of Lottie's war work.

"I thought Father would have told you," said Lottie. "The Fourth Downshires are in Larchester and the Meldrums are keeping 'open house' for the officers; I'm helping to entertain them. It's war work to entertain the boys."

She went on talking about her war work and presently said in an off-hand manner, "You needn't be surprised if you hear I'm engaged."

"Engaged to be married!" I exclaimed.

"Yes, of course."

"But, Lottie, you're only seventeen!"

"I'm nearly eighteen — and there's a war on. Don't be stuffy about it, Sarah. I came to-day because I want you to help me; I want you to prepare Father for the news . . . not say I'm engaged, of course, because I'm not, but just tell him I have a great friend. You could —"

"I suppose it's Tom Meldrum."

"Goodness no! Tom is all right to have fun with, and he dances divinely, but there's nothing glamorous about funny old Tom."

"Who is it, then?"

"Ian Macnab," said Lottie. "He's marvellous, Sarah — absolutely marvellous. He's Scottish, of course, everyone calls him Mac. He's very tall and good-looking with dark hair and beautiful hazel eyes and he's got a slight Scottish accent — most awfully attractive. He's madly in love with me and very earnest. It's terribly thrilling."

"Lottie, you shouldn't —"

"We had a concert the other night, just an impromptu concert in the music-room; Mac sang Scottish songs and I accompanied him on my guitar. He has a deep bass voice, it sounded marvellous; we had to give three encores."

"You'll have to speak to Father and see —"

"We have fun together. Mac takes me on his motor-bike and we buzz about all over the country. We went to Brighton and had dinner at a marvellous hotel."

"But, Lottie, you're too young — *really*. Who is he? Where is his home? You aren't serious about it, are you?"

"Oh, I don't want to be engaged just yet. Madeline says I ought to have some fun before I settle down with a 'steady' . . . but all the same he's terribly sweet," added Lottie, smiling in a faraway manner.

"Where is his home?"

"At a place called Elgin; it's hundreds of miles away in Scotland. He's getting leave soon, and he wants me to go with him and meet his people. I can't make up my mind whether to go or not."

"You can't go without telling Father and asking his permission."

"I've told you I haven't decided. Mac is sweet, of course, and he wants me to go with him terribly much, but . . . Oh, I don't know!"

"You will have to ask Father."

"Oh, Sarah, you *are* stuffy!" she exclaimed. "Things are different now."

"What do you mean?"

"Girls can do as they like. They can go about and have lots of fun and nobody minds."

Lottie seemed so irresponsible that I felt quite desperate. "What does Mrs. Meldrum say?" I asked.

"Mrs. Meldrum thinks he's sweet."

"Does she know anything about him?"

"I don't think so. You see there are so many of them — I mean so many officers — but she thinks he's terribly sweet."

I tried to find out more about "Mac" but it was hopeless. She was like water slipping through my fingers; she just repeated what she had said before: Mac was sweet and thrilling and his home was in Elgin. At last she became annoyed with me and rose to go.

"I wish I hadn't told you!" she declared. "You're so stuffy, Sarah. You don't realise there's a war on."

I didn't realise there was a war on! It was so funny that I had to laugh.

"What are you laughing at?" she asked.

I didn't answer; if I had begun to tell her what it was like to live in London with sirens wailing and bombs falling I wouldn't have been able to stop — and I didn't want to quarrel with Lottie — so I just kissed her good-bye and told her to be sensible.

"Oh, sensible!" said Lottie scornfully. "Who wants to be sensible? Madeline says you're only young once."

Lottie had said I was to "prepare Father" (and of course it was only right that he should be told of her affairs) so at supper that night I informed him that Lottie had come to lunch.

"What is the child doing? I wish I had seen her," he said.

"She's having fun."

"Having fun?" echoed Father.

No wonder he was surprised. His war work wasn't fun; he was out and about all day long, visiting people who were in distress or had been injured and taken to hospital. St. Rule's shelter was full nearly every night and Father was there himself, two nights out of three, welcoming people and trying to comfort those who had seen their homes fall in ruins and had lost their dear ones and all their possessions. The Hetheringtons helped in this work and a small band of "helpers" had been organised to come and cut sandwiches and make tea and coffee. I had volunteered as a "helper" and went to the shelter twice a week and at other times when extra hands were needed. My chief job was to look after the small children; I played with them and told them stories and tucked them up in the bunks.

The nights in the shelter were exhausting — and terribly distressing. All night long people kept on coming in, half dazed with the frightful things that had happened to them, or searching frantically for a lost friend. All night long we could hear the crash of bombs — dropping on someone's home, smashing someone's life! The explosions sounded like dull thumps in the underground crypt.

At first I had been very anxious about Father; he did so much, he was on his feet for hours at a stretch and never spared himself, but curiously enough he seemed to thrive on the work. Usually he slept for a few hours in the afternoon and awakened rested and refreshed.

"Did you say Lottie was having fun?" asked Father incredulously.

"Yes, that's what she told me. I'm worried about her, Father. I've never thought the Meldrums were the right kind of friends for Lottie."

"You've never thought . . . but they've been so kind to her!"

"I know they're kind, but they're too rich and — and pleasure-loving. It isn't good for Lottie."

"Sarah, you're trying to tell me something."

"She seems to be allowed complete freedom and goes buzzing about all over the country with young men on motor-bikes."

"Young men — or one young man?"

"A young Scotsman called Ian Macnab."

"But she's just a child!" exclaimed Father in dismay. "Who is he? Where does he come from?"

"His people live at Elgin. That's all I know. I tried to find out more about him from Lottie but she wouldn't tell me — or couldn't."

"Do you think I should ring up Mrs. Meldrum?"

I considered the question before answering. Then I said, "I don't think it would be much good. Mrs. Meldrum keeps open house for the officers; they have dances and concert parties nearly every night. Lottie says it's war work to entertain the boys."

"I don't like it, Sarah! I had better arrange for her to go to Craignethan."

"It's too late."

"Too late? What do you mean?"

"She wouldn't go," I said.

We discussed the matter further; I tried to convince Father that he had lost control over the movements of his younger daughter but he didn't believe me and at last he decided to go to Fairfield the following day and see Mrs. Meldrum.

"It's my fault," said Father miserably. "I should have taken better care of the child."

Father was always ready to think that any untoward happening was his fault. In this case the trouble had begun when Lottie was a child and had been allowed to make Riverside her "second home." However it was useless to say that now, so I said in soothing tones, "She left school without your permission and went to stay with the Meldrums, so why is it your fault?"

"I should have taken better care of her," he repeated. "If Dorrie had been here this would never have happened."

Father went to Fairfield early in the morning and returned in time for supper.

"How did you get on?" I asked anxiously.

222

"Lottie was out so I didn't see her but I had a talk with Mrs. Meldrum. My dear, you're right; she's a foolish woman and utterly irresponsible. I asked her about the young man but she seemed quite vague."

"Vague?"

"Yes, I can't describe her attitude in any other way. She said, 'Oh, yes, he's a dear boy. He sings charmingly.' When I asked if she knew anything about his people she said, 'Oh, he's Scottish, you know, so I expect they live somewhere in Scotland.' I said I thought she ought to know something about the young men who came to her house and she was quite surprised. She said, 'But there are so many of them and they know they can come to Riverside whenever they like! We want to give them a good time before they go abroad . . . and it's fun for the girls too.'"

I couldn't help smiling at Father's account of the conversation. I hadn't seen Mrs. Meldrum for years but obviously she was exactly the same as ever.

Father sighed, and added, "It was hopeless to get any sense out of the woman so I came away."

"Did you have lunch?"

"No, I didn't bother. I went to the barracks in Larchester and I was fortunate enough to find young Macnab. I liked him, Sarah. I liked him very much indeed . . . but he's a boy, not yet twenty, far too young to think of marriage."

"Is he thinking of marriage?"

"Yes, he seems devoted to Lottie. He wants to take her with him when he goes on leave and introduce her to his parents. I said Lottie was just a child but he didn't agree. He said, 'Lottie isn't a child in the way you mean, sir. She's grown up and she loves me — I know she loves me — but she's having a good time, that's the trouble.' We talked some more and he said, 'Lottie is the most wonderful girl in the world, but it isn't doing her any good being here with the Meldrums.'

"Well, I had just seen Mrs. Meldrum so I was in agreement with him about that. I asked him how I was to get her to come away and he said, 'You can't, because she's enjoying herself.'"

"He sounds sensible," I said.

"Yes, he's serious-minded; not the sort of young man to do anything foolish. I told him he had better consult his parents. He said he would. Then he asked my permission to take Lottie with him to Elgin when he goes on leave. He said that if his parents could see Lottie he was sure they would love her and agree to an engagement. 'Just an engagement,' he said earnestly. 'I'm willing to wait as long as you like before getting married. I just want to feel safe.' He seemed serious and sensible so I told him that if his parents gave their consent I wouldn't withhold mine. Perhaps I was wrong," said Father doubtfully. "Perhaps I allowed myself to be persuaded too easily, but I liked the boy immensely. It's war-time and young people feel unsettled; they don't know what's going to happen to them and they want a sort of anchor."

"I think he sounds very good value."

"Yes, he's made of the right stuff. If only Lottie were older I'd be quite happy about it."

I was glad that Father had seen "Mac" and had liked him so much. Nothing was settled of course; nothing could be settled until Mac had been home and consulted his parents.

Several days passed. Then one night, when Father had gone to the shelter and I was alone in the flat, Mac rang up.

"Oh, is that Sarah?" he said. "I hope it's all right for me to call you Sarah. I've heard such a lot about you from Lottie that I feel as if I know you quite well."

"Of course you must call me Sarah."

"That's fine," he declared. He had a deep voice and a slight Scots accent, just as Lottie had said.

"Look here," said Mac. "I rang up to talk to Mr. Morris, but perhaps you could tell him. I'm terribly happy, Sarah, I'm feeling on top of the world. I'm away home to-morrow *and Lottie is coming.* Isn't it grand? I wrote to Mother, and Mother rang up Lottie and persuaded her to come. I meant to go north on the bike but Mother says I must bring Lottie by train and they'll meet us at Inverness. Mr. Morris gave his permission for Lottie to come so it will be all right, won't it?"

"Yes, I'm sure it will be all right. It's a good plan for your parents to see Lottie."

"That's what I thought. The parents won't be able to help falling in love with Lottie; she's so beautiful and sweet. Tell Mr. Morris I'll take the greatest care of her."

"I'm sure you will."

"And, Sarah . . . if the parents say we can be engaged, Mr. Morris won't mind, will he? I mean he said he would agree if they agreed, but I just wanted to make sure."

The voice sounded anxious so I replied reassuringly.

"It's almost too good to be true!" exclaimed Mac. "I'm sure it's going to be all right. The moment the parents see Lottie they'll realise how lucky I am. Lottie is so wonderful; I don't know what she can see in an ordinary sort of bloke like me."

"I think you sound nice, Mac."

"You sound very nice," he declared. "It will be fun having a sister — I'm an 'only,' worse luck! Mother wanted a daughter but she didn't arrive. Well, Mother is getting a daughter now: the most wonderful daughter in the world."

CHAPTER
TWENTY-THREE

We heard no more from Mac and Lottie for a fortnight. This didn't surprise me; they were probably much too happy to think of anyone but themselves.

Then one morning, when I was out shopping, Lottie rang up and spoke to Father. He told me about it at lunch.

"They're engaged," he said. "Apparently the Macnabs were delighted with Lottie. She said they were sweet."

"That's what we expected, isn't it?"

"Yes, but it was Mac's embarkation leave and the battalion is moving to-morrow. Lottie is quite frantic; I couldn't get any sense out of the poor child. Apparently Mac didn't tell her it was embarkation leave — he wanted her to enjoy herself at Elgin — but I think it was a mistake."

"Where are they going?" I asked.

"Lottie doesn't know. The movement of troops is 'top secret,' but my guess would be the Middle East." He sighed and added, "My poor little Lottie! This is a dreadful time for the young."

I rang up Riverside that evening. Mrs. Meldrum answered the phone and said that Mac had been there to say good-bye; Lottie was so upset that she had gone to bed.

"You must come to-morrow, Sarah," said Mrs. Meldrum. "You had better stay for the week-end."

"I'll come to-morrow, but only for the day."

"Lottie wants you to stay. The poor girl is quite shattered."

"I can't," I said. "There would be nobody here to look after Father."

"Couldn't the servants look after him?"

"I haven't any servants."

"None at all?" asked Mrs. Meldrum in surprise. "Really, I don't know how you manage! Oh, well, you must come to-morrow by the early train. I'll send Watkins to meet you at Larchester, that will save you taking the bus to Fairfield."

Lottie was in bed when I arrived; she hugged me desperately.

"Oh, Sarah, it *is* good of you to come! I wish you could stay. I'm so miserable."

I held her in my arms. Her airs and graces had vanished and she was the little sister of long ago.

"How shall I bear it?" she whispered. "I love him frightfully. We had a wonderful time together at Elgin. They've got a lovely house and his mother is a darling. She's terribly good-looking — just like Mac — and she was sweet to me. She said she had always wanted a daughter. Mac's father is nice too; they both agreed that we could be engaged." She sighed and added, "Darling Mac! We were so happy together — and now he has gone."

228

"He'll write to you, Lottie."

"Oh, yes, of course! It will be lovely getting his letters and I shall write long letters to him and tell him everything. I wish I weren't so silly."

"Silly?"

"Yes, I'm rather a silly girl — not nearly good enough for Mac — but I'm going to turn over a new leaf. I'm going to read sensible books and improve my mind so that when we're married I shall be a companion for Mac — he's very clever, you know. I wish you could have seen Mac before he went away, but there wasn't time."

"I'll see him when he comes home."

"Yes, when he comes home," agreed Lottie. She added, "Oh, dear, I'm so miserable! I wish I could go to sleep — and stay asleep until Mac comes home."

I nodded sadly. I knew, only too well, what she was feeling.

"Yes, you know what it feels like," declared Lottie. "That's why I wanted to see you. I never realised before how frightful it must have been for you when Charles went away . . . but I do now. We can sympathise with each other; we're in the same boat, aren't we?"

I was silent.

"Do you still love Charles?" she asked.

"Yes, and I always shall."

"How do you manage to bear it? I want to know because it might help me."

I sat on her bed and told her how I managed to bear it. I had found it was useful to try not to think about Charles; it was better to think of other people. It was bad to be sorry for yourself; it was better to be up and doing and keep busy. The best thing of all was to have a definite aim in your life.

"What do you mean by a definite aim, Sarah?"

"My aim is to learn to speak German really well so that when he comes back — as I'm sure he will some day — I shall be able to talk to him in his own language; the language he spoke as a child. You've told me your aim, haven't you, Lottie? You're going to read history and travel books and —"

"Yes, I shall start straight away," she declared. "I shall go to the library to-morrow and ask the man what to read."

I knew she would start straight away but I wondered if she would continue; it takes a good deal of perseverance to keep on reading by oneself . . . however my advice had comforted her; she had stopped crying and was talking quite sensibly.

Father had told me to suggest she should go to Craignethan, so I mentioned it.

"Oh, no!" she exclaimed. "I couldn't possibly! You said it was important to keep busy and help people, didn't you? Well, I shall be busy here. Mrs. Meldrum really needs me because Madeline has joined the Wrens and Ruth is half engaged to Eric Corder and is being silly about it. There won't be much entertaining, now that the battalion has gone, but the under chauffeur has been called up and Watkins is old and not very strong so I can drive Mrs. Meldrum to Larchester when she wants to do some shopping; I can arrange the flowers for her and chat to her and keep her happy; she isn't the sort of person who can be happy by herself."

"Yes, I see," I said doubtfully. It wasn't the sort of job I should have liked.

"I know you think Mrs. Meldrum is silly," continued Lottie. "But she's been very kind to me — and she likes me — so I couldn't leave her in the lurch. I don't know how I could have managed if Mrs. Meldrum hadn't given me presents: frocks and stockings and things."

"I thought you got an allowance from Father."

"Yes, but it isn't very much. I mean, not when you go to a lot of parties and want to look nice. Does Father give you an allowance, Sarah?"

I hesitated and then said, "Not a dress allowance, just housekeeping money."

"He ought to," declared Lottie. "That coat is terribly shabby. Why don't you ask him for money and buy some decent clothes?"

The sisterly candour didn't upset me; I knew my coat was shabby — I had worn it for years.

"You don't care what you look like," said Lottie, nodding wisely. "It's because of Charles, of course . . . but you ought to care. I don't intend to go about looking like a drab because I'm miserable about Mac."

I couldn't imagine Lottie going about "looking like a drab." "All right," I said. "You take my advice and I'll take yours. I shall ask Father for money to buy some decent clothes. It's a bargain."

She smiled. It was rather a wan little smile but it was better than nothing.

I spent the day at Riverside. Lottie and I went for a walk together in the afternoon. Then I was sent to Larchester in the car and caught the train back to London.

The dim blue light in the compartment was hopeless for reading, and all the villages and towns were completely blacked out for fear of air-raids, so the train seemed to be hurtling along through Stygian darkness and there was nothing to do except think. I thought of Lottie and all we had said; I was glad I had seen her for I knew I had helped her. She had been wonderfully good and sensible. Her engagement seemed to have steadied her.

Lottie had said we were "in the same boat" (and I hadn't contradicted her) but it wasn't true for she and Mac could write to each other; she would know where he was and what he was doing. Mac would have friends round him to keep him cheerful and share any dangers that might befall . . .

"Oh, Charles, where are you? What has happened to you? Oh, my love, my dearest love, you'll come back to me some day when the war is over! You'll come back to me, won't you? I must go on believing that, I must go on hoping, because it's the only way I can bear it."

CHAPTER
TWENTY-FOUR

I was tired when I got home from Larchester and was delighted to find the table laid for supper.

"Have the brownies been here?" I asked.

"It's just tinned tongue and salad," said Father, smiling proudly. "A box of eggs has come from Craignethan but I didn't know how long to boil them. I made coffee — I've watched you making it, Sarah."

The coffee was very good; I complimented the cook and we sat down together. When I had told Father my news about Lottie he produced a letter which he had received from Colonel and Mrs. Macnab.

It was a warm friendly letter, saying how much they had enjoyed Lottie's visit and what a dear girl she was . . . so natural and unaffected and so delightfully pretty. The letter continued:

"At first we thought they were much too young to be engaged, but when we saw how devoted they were to each other we could not withhold our consent. Mac told us that you would give your consent to an engagement, if we would give ours, and when he explained that this was his embarkation leave and the battalion was being

233

sent abroad we felt we could deny him nothing. We are afraid you must be feeling anxious about the engagement; your little daughter is so young and you do not know much about Mac, but we would like to assure you that our dear boy is wonderfully sensible and responsible. He has always been a good son, thoughtful and considerate, so we are sure he will be a good husband. Mac asked us not to tell Lottie that the battalion was under orders — he wanted her to have a happy time while she was here. Our hearts were heavy at the prospect of parting with Mac, and at the thought of the dangers lying ahead, but we were glad that he should have this brief period of happiness before he went away. It is sad that the two dear children are to be parted, but we must hope and pray that all will go well and they will be spared to enjoy a long and happy useful life together."

When I had read the letter I handed it back to Father. "They must be very nice people," I said.

"Yes, it's a kind, sensible letter," he agreed.

There was no time that night for me to mention clothes to Father, but the next morning at breakfast I asked him if he could give me some money to buy a coat and a few other things that I wanted.

"My dear, do you need new clothes? You always look very nice," said Father in surprise.

"I want a warm coat for the winter."

"Of course you must have a coat!" He frowned thoughtfully and added, "But you're getting a dress allowance, aren't you?"

"No, you just give me money for housekeeping expenses. I really need some new clothes, Father, so if you could —"

"I thought I had arranged it with the bank . . . but that was for Lottie, of course! Oh, dear, I'm afraid I've been very inconsiderate, Sarah!"

"It doesn't matter," I told him.

"It does matter! I must go to the bank this morning and find out how much there is in my account. Dorrie always managed our financial affairs. I'm not very practical about money."

This wasn't news to me. I had no idea what Father's income was (it was doubtful if he knew it himself), but he had a small private income which should have been enough for us to live on in moderate comfort, but he could never refuse a request for money; sometimes he ran himself so short that he hadn't enough at the end of the week to give me to pay the rent and the very small bills for our living expenses. Lately this had happened more often for it had got about amongst the less desirable elements, who came nightly to the shelter, that Mr. Morris was always ready to listen to a hard luck story, and was "good for a fiver" if the hard luck story were sufficiently heart-rending.

When I hinted gently to Father that we ought to try to save a little he had reminded me that we should "take no thought for the morrow" . . . which had silenced me completely. Now, however, Lottie's advice had made me think again and I had come to the conclusion that if Father was "a lily of the field" I had better become a "wise virgin" or we should soon be left without any oil for our lamp.

At supper that night Father told me he had been to the bank and had discovered to his surprise that there was a nest-egg on deposit receipt; so he wrote a cheque for fifty pounds and gave it to me. "I've been selfish and thoughtless," he said remorsefully. "You do all the work in the flat and make me very comfortable so it's only right that you should have money to spend. I shall open an account for you and tell the bank to pay in fifty pounds every quarter."

"It's too much."

"No, no! It's what I give Lottie."

I thanked him suitably and made no more objections. It was more than I needed but I could keep it safely and have something to fall back on if necessary.

We were both unusually cheerful that evening; Father because he loved giving and I because I was looking forward to my shopping expedition.

"Where will you go for your coat?" asked Father.

"Barrington's," I said. I had often dawdled past the huge block of buildings, looking in at the plate-glass windows. Several times I had gone in and wandered round. It was a "luxury store," warm and comfortable; even in war-time Barrington's had a wonderful display of goods. On the ground floor there were wide, carpeted corridors with stalls on each side upon which were displayed gloves and stockings, perfumery and soap, ribbons and laces. There were large halls with

236

tiled floors where one could buy meat and fish, fruit and flowers and groceries. Upstairs there were departments for coats and hats and suits, children's garments, shoes and underwear. There were furniture departments with whole rooms furnished in different styles; there were departments for books and toys and pets. There was a Gentleman's Department, a Wine and Tobacco Department and several large restaurants. It was Barrington's boast that they had "Everything You Want."

"Oh, Barrington's," said Father, nodding. "It's a big place, isn't it? I'm afraid it wouldn't be much use for me to come with you; I know very little about ladies' clothes, but I shall be interested to see your coat. Be sure to choose a nice warm one, Sarah."

It was not until I was going into the store that I began to wonder what I should do about the cheque. How could it be turned into money? Then my eye fell upon a notice which was written in several different languages, "Bring Your Problems To Us," so I took a lift and went up to the office. Here I found a broad shiny counter divided into sections for "Inquiries," "Accounts," "Complaints," "Foreign Exchange," etc., etc.

The young man in the "Inquiries" section was very attentive.

"It's about a cheque," I told him. "My father gave it to me to buy some things I want, but I haven't got a bank account so I've brought my problem to you."

He smiled and said, "Quite right! If you don't mind waiting for a few minutes I'll send for Mr. Duncan."

237

I sat down on a comfortable sofa and waited. It was amusing to watch people coming in and looking round and making for the different sections of the counter; most of them were women, but not all. A fat man with a very disagreeable expression made a bee-line for "Complaints." "It's disgraceful!" he announced loudly.

Unfortunately I never learned what was disgraceful, for at that moment Mr. Duncan appeared and invited me to come into his private room. Mr. Duncan was of medium height and strongly built; he had smooth brown hair, brown eyes and very white teeth. His voice was clear and incisive. He was well dressed in a brown worsted suit . . . altogether he looked a very pleasant capable man. His private room was an exceedingly comfortable apartment with a sofa and two easy-chairs; in the middle of it stood a very large table with an enormous blotter, a case of stationery, two baskets full of neatly clipped papers, and three telephones.

Mr. Duncan placed a chair for me on one side of the table and sat down opposite me.

My problem was no problem to Mr. Duncan. "Yes, I see," he said. "We can deal with this in several ways, Miss Morris. First I'll ring up your father's bank and have a word with the manager — it won't take five minutes — and then we can either cash the cheque for you or else you can leave the money with us and buy what you need in the store."

I said I would leave the money; I didn't want to walk about with fifty pounds in my handbag.

Mr. Duncan nodded. He picked up a telephone receiver and in less than five minutes he had arranged

238

matters with the bank manager. He took the cheque, made out the receipt and handed it to me.

"Now that you have opened an account at Barrington's, Miss Morris, I should like to explain the advantages," said Mr. Duncan. "For one thing —"

There was a tap on the door and the young man from "Inquiries" looked in.

"Not now!" exclaimed Mr. Duncan, waving him away.

"It's important, sir. I wouldn't have interrupted you if —"

"This lady's business is important."

The young man looked at me imploringly.

"I can easily wait a few minutes," I said.

"That's very kind, Miss Morris. Well, Marriott, what's the trouble?"

"It's a foreign lady, Mr. Duncan. She speaks a few words of English but we can't understand what —"

"Get Mademoiselle Claire."

"She said she wasn't feeling well and went home."

"She's never here when she's wanted!"

"The lady is very excited, Mr. Duncan. She asked for someone who could speak German —"

I said, without thinking, "Perhaps I could help."

They both looked at me.

"I can speak German," I explained. "Not as well as French, of course, but I might be able to —"

"Why should you be bothered?" said Mr. Duncan. "Listen, Marriott, you'll just have to tell the lady —"

"Let her try, sir!" exclaimed Mr. Marriott. "The lady is very excited. I'll bring her here."

"No, please!" I cried in alarm . . . but Mr. Marriott had vanished.

Mr. Duncan smiled at me. He said, "It will be very kind of you, Miss Morris. Don't look so frightened. If you can't make anything of her it won't be the end of the world."

There was no time to say any more before Mr. Marriott returned with a very large lady in a very expensive mink coat. I saw at once that Mr. Marriott had understated her condition; she was furiously angry. She stood in the doorway and glared round the room. "I am a Dutchwoman," she announced in German. "If anyone here could speak my language there would be no need for me to soil my lips with the language of my country's enemies. I ask for someone who can speak German because it is written over the doorway that German is spoken here. Does that mean I am German?"

I shook my head and said, "*Nein.*"

"Oh, you understand, do you?" she asked, frowning at me.

I nodded and said, "*Ja.*"

With that she burst into a torrent of abuse. She was so angry and so voluble that I couldn't understand all she said, but I gathered that she was furious because she had seen the notice over the doorway, written in large letters, "Bring Your Problems To Us." It was written in English, French and German . . . but there was nobody who could speak German in the place. No, nor French either!

When at last she paused, breathless, I spoke to her in German and explained that the interpreter had been taken ill and gone home.

She glared at me.

"I regret that I cannot speak German well," I said.

"You speak quite well."

I smiled at her and thanked her and asked her to sit down. "I should like to help you," I told her.

It was gratifying to find that I was able to understand the lady, for my German lessons with Mr. Miller had ended abruptly when we left Fairfield. I began to wonder whether it would be possible to make friends with this lady and arrange to have conversation with her. However it was useless to think of that at the moment; it took me all my time to cope with the situation.

She sat down on the sofa and I went and sat beside her. "I should like to help you," I repeated.

"Who are you? Do you belong to this god-forsaken place?"

"No, I came to speak to Mr. Duncan on a private matter, my name is Sarah Morris."

"Mees Mawriss?"

"Yes."

"My name is Mevrouw Zumbach. Can you deal with my problem?"

"I hope so; I shall do my best."

She had calmed down now, and began to explain what she wanted. Her son had a post in the Netherlands Chamber of Commerce and she and her daughter had escaped from the Netherlands before the

German troops overran the country. Her son had many friends in London and she wanted to give a luncheon party to make some return for the hospitality he had received. She had been told that Barrington's had a private room which could be hired for parties.

I looked at Mr. Duncan. "Is that right?" I asked.

He was sitting there, smiling at me. "Is what right, Miss Morris?"

"Oh, I'm sorry! I forgot you couldn't understand. She wants to hire a room and give a luncheon party. If you give me a jotting pad I'll make notes about it."

"But, Miss Morris, why should you bother? Just tell her that we'll be delighted to do it for her; the details can be settled —"

"Give me a pad and a pencil!" I interrupted impatiently. "If I don't do it now she'll probably get into another rage and go somewhere else."

He took a pad and a pencil out of his drawer and brought them to me. "It's very good of you," he said.

I made notes of what she wanted: the date, the hour, the number of guests, the food and the wine and various other details. It took quite a long time, she was very unbusinesslike, but at last it was all settled.

"I hope it will be a very successful party," I told her.

"Would you like to come, Mees Mawriss?"

"Would I like to come?"

She nodded. She was smiling now and her face looked quite different, round and fat and kindly. "Please come," she said. 'It would be a pleasure . . . and my other guests would like to talk to an English lady."

242

I laughed and thanked her and accepted the invitation; it would be a good opportunity to practise my German.

When she had gone Mr. Duncan said, "I've been sitting here watching you tame a tiger."

"She was more like a bear."

"She was a wild animal of some sort," he agreed, laughing. "I couldn't understand a word but I gathered she was extremely rude."

"I didn't understand all the rude things she said."

"Perhaps that was just as well."

We looked at each other and smiled. Then I drew a chair up to the table and made a fair copy of my notes for him.

"This is excellent," he declared. "I'm extremely grateful. You see we've just made some rooms on the top floor into a suite for parties. There's a very large room for dances and wedding receptions and a smaller one for luncheons and dinners. The English Rose Suite is a new idea of mine; I'm tremendously keen on new ideas. It isn't only that the Zumbach party will be a paying proposition, it will also be an advertisement. We'll do it well, of course, and the guests will tell their friends — that's how things get known."

I nodded and rose. "I expect you're busy, Mr. Duncan, so —"

"Just a minute," he said quickly. "The fact is I've been wondering . . ." he paused.

"Wondering?"

"I suppose you're a business woman, Miss Morris?"

"A business woman? What do you mean?"

"You're a secretary, I expect. You've got a post in some firm? I mean . . ." he paused again.

"What do you mean?" I repeated in bewilderment.

"I'm trying to offer you a job," said Mr. Duncan.

CHAPTER
TWENTY-FIVE

I waited until after supper before breaking the news to Father. I waited until I had washed up the dishes and we were comfortably settled by the fire. I was just going to begin . . .

"By the way," said Father, "you haven't shown me your coat; I hope you got a nice one."

"Goodness! I forgot all about it."

"But I thought you were going to Barrington's?"

"Yes, I did, but something happened which —"

"Something happened?" interrupted Father in alarm. "Not anything unpleasant, I hope?"

"No, it was rather amusing. I was just waiting until we were comfortably settled to tell you about it."

"Go ahead," he said, taking his pipe and filling it carefully. "Go ahead, Sarah. I'm all ears."

I told him the whole story from beginning to end and added, "I want that job, Father; I want to start to-morrow."

"But, my dear girl, there's no necessity for you to take a job. You've got plenty to do at home — and at the shelter. To-day's experience was amusing, but other experiences might not be so pleasant. Anyhow I don't like the idea of your working in a shop; it would be too exhausting for you."

"It wouldn't be exhausting; Mr. Duncan said I'd be in the office most of the time, translating letters. Then, if a customer comes to one of the departments — someone who can't speak English — they'll send for me."

"I don't like it at all."

"It won't affect you, Father. Mr. Duncan knows I can't be there until eleven o'clock so I can do all the housework and the shopping before I go."

"I wasn't thinking of my own comfort, my dear. Sometimes I feel you make me too comfortable. I'm thinking of what's the best thing for you. No, no, Sarah, it won't do. You must ring up that man and tell him —"

"This is the best thing for me," I said earnestly. "I want something to do that will use my brain and prevent me from thinking. Cleaning and cooking aren't any use."

He looked at me sadly. "I was hoping you were beginning to get over it."

I shook my head.

"But you're happy with the children. Why not come to the shelter more often? You're so good at amusing them and keeping them quiet."

It occurred to me, quite suddenly, that Lottie never argued with Father; she just went ahead and got her own way without any trouble at all. Why should I have to fight like a tiger for anything I wanted?

"And another thing," said Father. "You don't *need* a paid job; I've given you an allowance for your clothes."

"Yes — and it's very kind of you — but it isn't really the money. I'm keen on languages, as you know, and if I take this job I shall be able to make use of my one small talent and be helpful to people who are strangers in a strange land."

He looked at me in astonishment.

"I've been thinking about it," I explained. "I tried to think why it was that I wanted this job so much. That's the reason."

"If you put it like that I can't say anything more. You must do as you want, Sarah. If you find the work too arduous we can —"

"It won't be. It will be quite easy, and I know I can do it satisfactorily. That's half the battle, isn't it?"

He smiled and replied, "It's nine-tenths of the battle. Well, if you're going to Barrington's to-morrow don't forget your coat."

Mr. Duncan was in the office when I arrived. He welcomed me warmly and explained that he had been wondering if I would come; it had seemed too good to be true. He asked, somewhat diffidently, if I would mind wearing a uniform.

I suppose I looked a little startled.

"Of course if you have any objection you can wear what you like," said Mr. Duncan hastily. "I just thought it would give you a sort of status. A plain black charmeuse dress would suit you, Miss Morris."

I replied that I had no objection to wearing a plain black charmeuse dress; I had imagined that he meant me to be attired in a page-boy uniform.

He laughed and said, "Let's go and choose it now. Then you can start work to-morrow."

"Wait a moment!" I exclaimed. "What about Mademoiselle Claire. I don't want to take her job."

"Oh, she just comes 'to oblige.' She'll be quite pleased to hear we've found someone. Anyhow she isn't satisfactory, is she, Marriott?"

"Never here when she's wanted," agreed Mr. Marriott. "And what's more everyone hates her like poison."

"Why do they hate her?" I asked apprehensively.

"She puts people's backs up."

"We were in a jam," explained Mr. Duncan. "We had an excellent man, Herr Straker. He can speak half a dozen languages, but he's been interned as an enemy alien. Come along, Miss Morris. We mustn't waste time."

I soon discovered that Mr. Duncan never wasted time.

We went up in the lift to the dress department and Mr. Duncan explained to the manageress — a very grand lady — exactly what he had in mind:

"Miss Morris has a beautiful figure so the dress must fit her perfectly, Miss Fitzroy."

"Yes, of course, Mr. Duncan."

Various dresses were produced for his approval but he approved of none of them. "I don't like all those bits and pieces — buttons and frills and bows. I know exactly what I want for Miss Morris; you'll have to make it for her, that's all. I want a perfectly plain black

248

charmeuse dress with a round, closely-fitting neck and long sleeves."

"Yes, of course, Mr. Duncan."

"We'll choose the material and you can take her measurements."

"Yes, certainly. We're very busy in the work-room but I think I can promise it for next week."

"It must be ready at eleven o'clock to-morrow morning."

"To-morrow morning!" echoed Miss Fitzroy in dismay.

"Yes," said Mr. Duncan. "And put your best dressmakers on to the job. The dress must fit Miss Morris like a black skin."

The grand lady looked so astonished that I was obliged to hide a smile . . . and smiles did not come easily to me at the time.

When my measurements had been carefully taken and the material chosen I told Mr. Duncan that I wanted to buy a coat.

"Your coat!" he exclaimed. "That's what you came for, of course! I forgot all about it. Shall I come and help you to choose it? They pay attention to what I say."

I said I had noticed this.

Mr. Duncan chuckled. "Miss Fitzroy is very high and mighty, isn't she? But she's good at her job. I like people who are good at their jobs."

I wasn't very anxious to have Mr. Duncan with me when I was choosing my coat for I was sure he would insist on my having the best and most expensive in the department. Mr. Duncan was paying for my dress — or

249

at least Barrington's was paying for it — but I would have to pay for the coat. However a very smart little page pursued us into the lift and informed Mr. Duncan that he was wanted urgently in the "Ladies Underwear."

"It's the buyer, I suppose," said Mr. Duncan with a sigh. "He's a fat man with pudgy hands, quite unsuitable for frillies, but he's good at his job."

The manageress of the Coat Department had heard all about me and was helpful and kind. Her name was Maud Renfrew — later I got to know her well. She chatted to me as she brought out the various coats to show me:

"You'll be very useful, Miss Morris. We often have trouble with foreigners, especially since the war started; there are hundreds of people of different nationalities in London now. I'm so sorry for them when they come in here to buy something and we can't understand what they want. It makes me feel such an idiot. I learnt French at school, like everyone else, but it hasn't helped me to understand French people talking."

"It doesn't," I agreed.

"Mr. Marriott says you're *very* clever. You can speak French and German like a native."

I wondered how Mr. Marriott knew, since he was unable to speak a word of either language.

"Mr. Barrington told me we were to ring up the office if we needed you," said Miss Renfrew.

"Mr. Barrington?" I asked.

"Mr. Duncan Barrington," she explained. "He's the grandson of old Mr. Barrington, of course. Old Mr.

Thomas Barrington started the business and is still on the Board of Directors. He's too old to take an active interest — over ninety I believe! — but he comes in now and then and has a look round. Mr. Duncan is the manager; he's very capable and go-ahead. Some people call him 'the Dictator' but I don't blame him for liking his own way; a big place like this needs someone with a firm hand to run it properly. If you do your best he'll always back you up."

"The customer isn't always right?" I suggested.

"Oh, she is — while she's there," replied Miss Renfrew. "When she has gone he'll tell you it's all right and you aren't to worry."

This concerned me because I was going to work here and the sooner I got to know the ins and outs of the business the better.

I chose my coat, a very nice dark-brown tweed with a fur collar, and discovered to my surprise that I was to get ten per cent off the marked price.

"We all do," explained Miss Renfrew. "It's one of Mr. Duncan's bright ideas. He says if you treat your employees well they work all the better. You should get a hat while you're about it, Miss Morris. A little fur cap to match the collar would be nice . . . and if you want a perm you can get ten per cent off that," she added with a glance at my hair.

She was quite right; my hair was a mess; I hadn't bothered about it for months.

The hair-dressing department was on the top floor. Here, too, I was kindly received and told that I would be very useful . . . and I was given an invitation to "drop in" any afternoon at four-thirty for a cup of tea.

"We don't go down to the restaurant for tea," explained Miss Balcombe. "It takes too long. We just make tea ourselves in the wash-room and have a cup and a slice of cake between shampoos and perms. Several of my best girls have enlisted in one or other of the women's services, so we're frightfully under-staffed, but if you come this afternoon I'll fit you in somehow."

My duties at Barrington's were erratic. At first I was sent for two or three times a day and spent the rest of the time in the office, translating business letters, but soon my work became much more active. I was in constant demand as an interpreter; sometimes I was sent for by several departments at once and was obliged to hurry from one end of the building to the other.

Mr. Marriott explained this by saying, "They didn't like Claire so they managed without her whenever they could."

Neither he nor Mr. Duncan was in the habit of wasting words.

I remember my first customer particularly well. It was my first day on duty; I had arrived in the office at eleven o'clock, my hair had been cut and permed and I was wearing my new dress.

Mr. Duncan examined me carefully. "It's exactly right," he said. "It's elegant and it's businesslike . . . but just to finish it off you must have a long gold chain with a medallion on the end of it. They've got some in the Jewellery Department."

"They want Miss Morris in 'Footwear,' " said Mr. Marriott, emerging from his post in the telephone-room. "It's urgent. Shall I take her, Mr. Duncan?"

"I'll take her," replied Mr. Duncan. "We can stop in 'Jewellery' on the way." He set off at a brisk pace; I followed, half walking, half running. We stopped in the Jewellery Department for my chain and then rushed on to "Footwear." By this time I was quite breathless and had begun to wonder whether I should be able to stand the pace of my new job . . . and whether I should ever be able to find my way about the enormous building.

"Here you are!" said Mr. Duncan. "You can manage by yourself, can't you? Come back to the office when you've finished . . . I'm wanted in 'Millinery.' " He was gone before I could reply.

A well-dressed lady in a blue hat was sitting on a chair with one shoe on; the assistant was standing with the other shoe in her hand. Both were flushed and heated.

"She doesn't understand," said the assistant, turning to me in desperation. "I've told her we don't stock threes in that make of shoe. We could get her a pair of threes, of course; it wouldn't take more than a few days. That's a four she's got on and it's much too large — she could never wear it with any comfort — but she won't take it off. She really is awfully silly."

I looked at the lady in the blue hat — her eyes were blue, too — she was petite and elegant and, in spite of her mulish expression, she was very attractive.

She said, *"Elle est imbécile, cette jeune fille."*

I smiled at her and replied in French, asking her why she wanted to buy shoes which were too large for her "so elegant little feet."

She threw back her head and laughed merrily and burst into a torrent of explanations: the shoes were not for herself — no, indeed, they were much too large! — she intended to give them to her sister. It was to be a surprise for her sister so she had come by herself to buy them and would hide them away until her sister's *anniversaire*. She knew nothing about "trees an' fours" — that girl was an imbecile — but she had tried on a pair of her sister's shoes this morning before she came out, so she was aware that if a shoe were a little too large for herself it would fit Cécile very nicely. That imbecile girl had tried to prevent her from trying on the shoe but it was essential for her to try it on; how otherwise was she to know if it would be the correct size? Surely I would understand that it would be a thousand pities if, when she gave the shoes to Cécile, they did not fit her perfectly?

I assured her that I understood and explained the matter to the assistant.

"Well, what d'you know!" exclaimed the girl. "I never heard of such a crazy idea in all my life! I'd like to see my sister's face if I went and bought her a pair of shoes!"

I admitted that it was a strange idea and that my sister would certainly not appreciate such a gift.

"Supposing the lady's sister doesn't like the shoes?" asked the girl doubtfully.

254

"They can be changed, can't they? I'll explain that to her; meanwhile you can do up the parcel and make out the bill."

While we were waiting I chatted to the lady; it was pleasant to air my French, which had been in cold storage for so long. She told me that her name was Madame Breuchaud and her husband was in the Free French Forces. Her sister had come to England and was living with them in lodgings. "Cécile can speak English, not too badly, so it is good to have her with us. She can speak Dutch, too; our mother was *Hollandaise*."

"Do you like being here?" I asked.

"It is a little strange. We do not know many people here in London."

It was not always so easy to sort out the muddles — and on several occasions it was impossible to smooth things over and make everyone happy.

For instance, I was summoned urgently by the glove department, where I found a very irate lady displaying a glove which had split between the fingers. There was a very young gentleman with a very red face behind the counter.

"Thank goodness you've come, Miss Morris!" he exclaimed in relief.

The lady turned to me and explained volubly in French that she had bought the gloves only last week — and look what had happened when she had put them on for the first time! Just look! Was it not disgraceful? She had been told that this was a good store but I could see for myself that it sold rubbish. Could I not see that

255

the glove was badly fashioned, badly finished? The gloves must be replaced instantly by a new pair.

I turned to the young man behind the counter. "It seems rather an inferior make of glove," I said.

"It is," he agreed. "It's a very cheap make of glove . . . but it wasn't sold here. Barrington's has never sold this make; we only stock the best. Can you explain to the lady that she must have bought the gloves somewhere else?"

This was neither easy nor pleasant; the irate lady knew she had bought the gloves here — yes, here at this very counter! She remembered the occasion distinctly; she remembered that stupid boy with the red face. Could I, or could I not, replace this rubbish with a new pair of gloves?

I could not.

In that case the manager must be summoned.

Mr. Duncan was sent for and the matter explained, but even he could not accomplish the impossible and after a lengthy argument — translated by me — the lady went off in a rage, saying she would never again cross the threshold of this third-rate establishment.

"We had better put up the shutters right away," said Mr. Duncan. He winked at the assistant, grinned at me . . . and strode off at his usual pace.

CHAPTER
TWENTY-SIX

It was the day of the Zumbach luncheon party. Mr. Duncan sent for me to come to the English Rose Room and showed me all the arrangements: the long table looked very festive, with cut glass and silver and flat bowls of flowers and fruit down the centre.

"Oh, how lovely!" I exclaimed. "I'm so glad you haven't put large arrangements of flowers in the middle; it's nice to be able to see people on the other side of the table."

"Can you suggest anything else?" he asked anxiously.

I looked round the room. "What about a big jar of chrysanthemums over there in the corner?"

"You're right! That corner looks bare. Go down to 'Flowers' and get as many as you want. Tell them I said so."

I glanced at my watch and saw that I had less than half an hour to accomplish my assignment . . . and wished I had held my tongue!

Fortunately the manager of the flower department was very friendly and entered into the spirit of the affair; he allowed me to choose a great armful of bronze and gold chrysanthemums and several large sprays of beech leaves; he gave me an enormous chinese jar with dragons on it and detailed his best assistant to help me.

"Kitty will carry up the jar for you," he said. "And I'll lend you a sheet to spread on the floor. You won't be popular if you make a mess of the place."

"I hope that jar isn't terribly heavy," I said, as Kitty and I went up in the lift.

"Oh, no, it's a little bulky, that's all," she replied, smiling cheerfully. "This is fun, Miss Morris; the other girls will be awfully jealous when they hear I've been helping you."

Kitty's words gave me a fleeting glimpse of the monotony of her daily life; anything that was different from usual was a treat to be welcomed with delight! These glimpses into the lives of other people were interesting. I should have liked to hear more about Kitty's life, but there was no time to think of that now.

We spread the sheet and arranged the flowers in the jar and we were just gathering up the debris when the Zumbachs arrived. I had intended to change for the party and had brought my rose-red frock with me but there was no chance of escape. Mevrouw Zumbach greeted me warmly and introduced me to her son and daughter — both of whom could speak English.

"Oh, what a pretty room!" exclaimed the girl. "The table looks lovely, doesn't it?" She turned to her mother and repeated her remarks in Dutch.

Then the guests began to appear in twos and threes and were regaled with cocktails.

"Do you like schnapps, Miss Morris?" asked young Mijnheer Zumbach.

"I've never tasted it," I replied.

"It is *nice*," he declared, smiling at me and handing me a glass.

It wasn't nice — or at least I didn't like it — however, I had to pretend I was enjoying his national drink.

Many of the guests were Dutch but most of them could speak English, after a fashion, and insisted on speaking English to me. I had hoped that some of them would speak German, but I was disappointed; there was so much rage in these people at the way their country was being treated that they preferred to remain silent rather than to speak the hated language of their enemies. There were some Belgians who spoke French, several Polish officers who spoke their own language to each other and French to me ... and a dark-skinned Spaniard (who looked like my idea of a hidalgo) was conversing gravely in Spanish with an elderly Frenchwoman.

It crossed my mind that the Tower of Babel must have been something like this.

At luncheon I found myself sitting next to a young Dutchman with very fair hair and light blue eyes.

"Food goot," he said, tucking into his hors d'œuvres with obvious enjoyment.

"Yes," I agreed.

"Blooms pretty," he suggested, pointing to the flowers.

"Yes, very pretty."

"I luff goot food and pretty womans," he declared with zest.

259

I couldn't help laughing.

"What this name?" he asked, holding up his spoon.

"Spoon."

"Schpoon," he said, nodding.

"Fork," I told him, pointing to it.

"Fawk?"

"Yes."

Seeing that a lesson in English was taking place the hidalgo and two of the Polish officers joined in and, pointing to their noses and their arms and various other parts of their anatomy, wished to know the English names ... and roared with laughter at each other's efforts to pronounce the words.

The talk and the laughter became louder and louder. There was no doubt about it: the Zumbach party was exactly like the Tower of Babel.

Mr. Duncan had given me the afternoon off but by three o'clock I was so exhausted that I came away. It was a splendid party and was still going strong ... it looked as if it might go on for hours.

Father was interested in my doings and encouraged me to tell him about my work. I think he realised that it was good for me to spend my time sorting out the muddles.

"You're the girl with the smoothing iron," he said.

I remembered the old song. "Yes, that's rather a good description of me and my job."

"Have you stolen anyone's heart away?" he asked teasingly.

"No. At least ..."

260

Father was serious in a moment. "Whose heart, Sarah?"

"Well, I don't know — really. I have a horrid sort of feeling that Mr. Duncan is — is getting interested in me."

"Why horrid?"

"Because it would spoil everything; I should have to give up my job."

"It would be interesting to see the young man."

"He wants to meet you," I admitted with reluctance.

"But you don't want us to meet?"

"I want to keep things on a business footing."

"Yes, I see. Well, if you change your mind about it . . ."

We left it like that. In any case there was no time to say more for the sirens had begun to wail hideously and it was my night on duty at the shelter. I ran to put on my warmest and oldest clothes.

Father was waiting for me in the little hall; he was dressed in his "siren suit."

"It's your night off duty," I said.

"Yes, but I'm coming with you."

"You needn't," I told him. "You're tired. Why not go to bed?"

"I don't like your going out alone."

"I've often done it! I really think you should go to bed and have a good night's sleep."

"I'm not happy about it. I'll come to the shelter with you and if there's nothing much doing I'll come home and go to bed."

I said no more. I wasn't sorry to have him with me for there were prowlers in the darkened streets and I had been accosted several times in a very unpleasant fashion. I hadn't mentioned my experiences to anyone but perhaps Father had guessed.

He took his torch with the shaded light and we set off together.

By this time the guns had begun to fire and away to the east we could see bombs exploding. When we got to the shelter we saw people hurrying in the same direction as ourselves.

"It will be full to-night; I'd better stay and help," said Father.

It was useless to protest so I followed him down the flight of stone steps to the crypt.

How difficult it is to describe London during that time of war! It is even more difficult to describe our feelings. If I were to say we weren't frightened I don't suppose anyone would believe me, but all the same it was true. We had become used to the raids and took them calmly. It was exhausting to be kept awake night after night by the noise; it was heart-rending to see women and little children, whose homes had been destroyed, crowding into the shelter; but we were so busy trying to comfort them and giving them food and putting them to bed in the wooden bunks that we had no time to think of our personal safety . . . and on our nights off duty we were so tired that we went to bed in our own homes and plugged our ears and slept. I spoke to scores of people who helped in our shelter — and in other shelters — and they all agreed that after the first few raids they had ceased to be frightened.

That night was one of the busiest we had had: people kept coming in all the time; we spread rugs on the floor for them to sit on; we listened to their tales of horror; we gave them tea and sandwiches. Some of them stayed and tried to sleep, others snatched a hasty meal and went out again to look for a lost husband — or wife — or to see whether there was anything to be salvaged from their ruined homes. Two children were brought in by a fireman who had rescued them from a burning house. "Can you cope with them?" he asked. "Their parents have disappeared. The kids were alone in the house, screaming their heads off."

"Do you know who they are?" I asked. This was the most important thing to know about stray children; hundreds became lost in the confusion.

"I haven't the foggiest idea," said the fireman and went away.

The children were toddlers; they stood looking round the shelter and blinking in the light. I took them to a corner which had been set apart for small children and gave them milk and biscuits. Then I sat down and put my arms round them and tried to find out their names. Sometimes children had names sewn on their clothes, but these children had not.

"What's your name?" I asked the little boy.

"Teddy."

"Teddy . . . what?"

"Jus' Teddy."

"What's daddy's name?"

It was useless, of course. I talked to them for a little while and then tucked them up in a small bunk and told them a story until they went to sleep.

Pam Hetherington came and looked at them. "They're awfully sweet, aren't they?" she said. "Their wretched parents will be frantic . . . however, we can't do anything about it to-night."

Sometimes the police were able to restore lost children to their frantic parents but there had been several occasions when the parents had disappeared completely, and were never found.

It was five o'clock in the morning before the "All Clear" signal was given and people began to drift away. Soon only the sleeping children were left — and the "helpers."

As usual we made coffee for ourselves and sat down and finished the remains of the food.

"It's been bad to-night," said Mr. Hetherington wearily. "A man told me the docks got the worst of it."

"There's a good deal of damage in the city," said someone else.

"I'm off home," said Mr. Martin. "I want a few hours' sleep before I have to be in the office." Mr. Martin was an elderly man who had lost a foot in the First War but, in spite of his disability, he was one of our most valuable helpers and not only came when there was a raid but also in the early evening to prepare the food.

"We had better be off, too," said Father. "Come on, Sarah, you look tired."

I was exhausted — but so was everyone else.

When we came out of the crypt dawn was breaking in the east with a sad grey light. We saw flames shooting up in various directions; a chill wind blew scraps of charred paper along the street and there was a smell of burning in the air. Two fire engines dashed past at top speed.

As we turned the corner of Picton Street I stopped and clutched Father's arm.

"It's gone!" I cried.

It had gone completely; the whole big block of Picton Mansions was a heap of ruins.

For a few moments we stood in silence, looking at it.

"I told you to go to bed," I said at last.

"It isn't on fire," said Father calmly. "We had better see if there's anything left."

"I told you to go to bed, Father." That was all I could think of: I had told Father to go to bed.

A policeman came up and said, "It's a mess, isn't it? A direct hit — that's what it was."

"Our flat was there," said Father.

"Nobody in it, I hope?"

"No, it was empty but I had some valuables. I'd like to have a look —"

"I'm sorry, but my orders are to keep people away. It isn't safe . . . and you can see for yourself there's nothing left. If you take my advice you'll get rooms at a hotel; there's a small place in the next street. The young lady looks all in."

We took the policeman's advice and were fortunate enough to get two rooms and they gave us a reasonably good breakfast. By this time it was nine o'clock so I rang up Barrington's and told Mr. Marriott what had happened. He was very sympathetic and took down the address of the hotel and promised to explain to Mr. Duncan why I couldn't come.

Then I went to bed and slept like a log.

It was seven o'clock in the evening when I awoke to find Father standing beside my bed.

"Oh, you're awake!" he said cheerfully. "I've been in to look at you several times. You had better get up and have some food. This isn't a bad little place; they gave me quite a good lunch. We were extremely lucky to get these rooms ... and the proprietor says we can stay until we find another flat. That's splendid, isn't it?"

I looked at him standing there, so good and kind and cheerful ... and I remembered that I had told him to go to bed. I put my arms round him and hugged him.

"You're all right, aren't you, Sarah?" he asked anxiously.

"Yes, but what about you? Have you slept?"

"Yes, I had a good sleep and then I went along to the shelter and helped the Hetheringtons to clear up the place. They very kindly offered to have us to stay but it would be a nuisance for them; we're better where we are in the meantime. Mrs. Hetherington said I was to tell you that Teddy's mother has been found, alive and well, and they're being evacuated to Wales. She said you would know who Teddy was."

"Yes," I said. "But what about Teddy's daddy?"

"Mrs. Hetherington didn't mention him. You had better get up," repeated Father. "Willy is coming to

266

supper with us. I thought I'd better ring him up and tell him what had happened; he seemed a little worried about us."

"How strange!" I said, giggling feebly.

"It isn't any good worrying," Father pointed out. "It's over and we're both alive. We aren't the only people whose homes have been destroyed. I said that to Willy but he still seemed rather upset. That's why he's coming to supper."

I got up and washed and put on the clothes I had taken off; it was an odd sort of feeling to have nothing belonging to me except the clothes I was wearing. I combed my hair with the little comb I had in my handbag.

When I went downstairs Willy had arrived and was talking to Father in the lounge; he got up and greeted me with unusual fervour.

"Well, we had better have our meal," said Father, and led the way to the dining-room.

Willy was still holding my arm. He said in a whisper, "I believe he's quite pleased about it."

"Pleased?"

"Yes, I think he felt a bit guilty because other people were getting it in the neck and he was safe and comfortable. Now that he's got it in the neck and lost his possessions he feels happier. It sounds mad, of course, but you know what Father is."

It sounded quite mad but probably Willy was right.

The supper was plain but adequate and I began to feel much better. Father had ordered a bottle of claret which helped to liven up the occasion. Soon we were all talking quite cheerfully and discussing plans.

"Why not have a holiday?" asked Willy. "You could both go to Craignethan, couldn't you?"

"I can't," said Father. "There's a great deal to do at the shelter."

"I can't either; I've got a job," I said.

"Oh, of course!" agreed Willy. "I'd forgotten for the moment that you were one of the world's workers. How are you getting on?"

"It's very interesting."

"She's the girl with the smoothing iron," said Father, chuckling.

"You mean that song we used to sing?"

"Yes, she irons out all the muddles. Go on, Sarah, tell Willy about the lady who bought the shoes for her sister."

I smiled and said, "You've spoilt that one, Father. I'll tell you about the Polish lady."

"But you can't speak Polish!"

"No, and I could never learn; it's terribly difficult."

The Polish lady wasn't really my business but the managers of the various departments at Barringtons had acquired the habit of sending for me in almost any emergency; they would have sent for me if a Chinese gentleman had arrived on the scene and would have expected me to find out what he wanted. This was gratifying, of course, but it made a great deal of extra work. The Polish lady could speak a little English and had asked for a sleeping-suit for her boy but shook her head violently when she was shown children's pyjamas.

"No, no! Sleeping suit for my boy — six years big," she exclaimed in accents of desperation.

"She keeps on saying that," declared the assistant, turning to me helplessly. "She says her boy is six years — and big. These pyjamas are suitable for a boy of eight; he can't be bigger than that."

"Six years big," repeated the Polish lady.

"Very big?" I asked.

She nodded violently.

"How big?"

She stood on tiptoe and held her hand above her head.

Light dawned upon me. "He's a man?" I suggested.

"Yes, my boy is man. Six years . . . no, six yards big," said the Polish lady triumphantly.

I took her by the arm and led her to the department for gentlemen's underwear.

Willy was chuckling. He said, "Do they sell slumber suits for giants at Barrington's?"

"He was six feet tall," I explained. "That was easy! I have much more difficult problems to solve every day of my life."

Father and Willy were both laughing when the dining-room door opened and Duncan Barrington walked in.

It was kind of him to come but I wasn't particularly pleased to see him. However, I shook hands with him and made the introductions.

"Well, well," he said. "I just dropped in for a few minutes to see how you were — but you all seem very cheerful."

Willy smiled. "It takes a bigger man than Hitler to get my family down."

"Will you have something to eat?" asked Father.

Mr. Duncan replied that he had had his meal but would like some coffee. He sat down and began to talk to Willy.

As a rule Willy was difficult to draw so I was surprised to see him emerge from his shell and answer Mr. Duncan's inquiries.

"I'm in a tank factory," explained Willy. "I wanted to enlist, of course, but it's supposed to be a 'reserved occupation.'"

"Is it an interesting job?"

"My work isn't interesting; it's dirty and monotonous. However someone has got to do it so I mustn't complain."

They talked for a few minutes and then Mr. Duncan turned to Father. "Marriott said you had lost everything, sir. I wondered if we could help. We can let you have clothes coupons, for instance."

"That would be marvellous!" I exclaimed.

"It's good of you," said Father. But we don't want anything 'under the counter.'"

"Oh, it's fair and square," Mr. Duncan replied. "We have a special arrangement with the rationing office for people who have lost their belongings . . . and we might be able to find you another flat."

Father wasn't interested in clothes coupons (though how he thought he was going to exist, when he had nothing but the clothes he stood up in, was more than

I could see) but the offer to find us a flat was a different matter. He accepted it with alacrity.

"How about getting a bigger flat?" suggested Willy. "I could come and share it."

Father and I were both delighted at this idea.

"Just tell me what you want and we'll see what we can do," said Mr. Duncan, taking out his note-book.

After Mr. Duncan had gone we went on chatting.

"That fellow is a live wire," said Willy.

"It's his job," I explained. "He wants people to bring their problems to Barrington's."

"I like the man," declared Father.

CHAPTER
TWENTY-SEVEN

Barrington's solved all our problems satisfactorily. They found us a partially furnished flat in Bolingbroke Square; it was much larger than the other flat but as Willy was coming to live with us, and was able to share the expense, the rent was well within our means. We got some of our furniture out of store and moved in without delay. I was much happier in the new flat; there was more room to move about and it was delightful to have some of our own nice furniture around us; best of all we had Willy. It was good for us and it was good for him. He was better fed and housed so he put on a little weight and became more like his old self.

Soon after Willy came to live with us he bought an enormous wooden table and put it in one of the empty rooms; he also bought sheets of drawing-paper and tracing-paper and coloured inks. One evening when I went to tell him supper was ready I found him hard at work.

"What are you doing?" I asked.

"Oh, it's just an idea of mine — a sort of gadget."

"What sort of gadget?"

"Listen, Sarah! Nobody is to come into this room."

"But I've got to clean it."

"Oh, I don't mind you or Father; neither of you knows a hawk from a handsaw," said Willy, smiling. "But nobody else is to come in here . . . and when I say nobody I mean nobody."

"If it's as secret as that you'd better lock the door and keep the key in your pocket," I said sarcastically.

"Yes, that's what I'll do."

"It'll get awfully dirty if I don't —"

"It won't, because I shall clean it myself."

After that Willy worked at his gadget nearly every evening.

If I were writing a history of the war I should have plenty to say about the next eighteen months but this has been done by a great many other people and I have no intention of attempting the task. I am merely trying to put together an account of what happened to the various members of the Morris family . . . but the war was with us all the time and it wasn't in the background. As everyone knows, the first three years of the war were a gruelling time for the British, we lost ground in every theatre, and it wasn't until the Battle of Alamein that the tide began to turn.

Meanwhile Father and Willy and I each had our own work to do — usually at different hours. We came and went; it was not often that we were all at home together. Occasionally, when Willy had a free Saturday, he and I went for an expedition to Kew or Hampton Court or, if it were wet, to a picture house. There was a strange sort of monotony in our lives. The raids continued and the shelter was full nearly every night but the bombs didn't fall on us.

Lewis was still in England. Much to his disgust he had been seconded from his battalion and was in a hutted camp helping to train crews for armoured cars. We saw him now and then when he happened to be in London and had a few hours to spare. Lottie was still at Riverside with the Meldrums; she never wrote but I rang her up occasionally and had a chat with her.

I had told Father that Mr. Duncan was "interested" in me. We both spent our days running about the huge store and interviewing people in different departments so we didn't meet very often, but when we did happen to meet he always stopped and spoke to me. One day when I was having lunch by myself in the downstairs restaurant, which was the cheapest place for meals, he came and asked if he might sit at my table. It was impossible to refuse so I accepted the inevitable with a good grace.

I knew he never lunched in the downstairs restaurant; the head-waiter knew it too. He arrived breathless with haste and excitement and suggested that Mr. Duncan might prefer to move to a more secluded table.

"All right, Benson," said Mr. Duncan. "Miss Morris is lunching with me to-day so we'll both move." He added, "I just wanted to see what sort of a meal you're serving in this place."

Several waiters were summoned and we were moved to the "secluded table."

274

"This is delightful," said Mr. Duncan. "We shall have time for a chat. I never see you except when we're both running to someone's rescue but I hear about you, of course. You seem to be popular with everyone."

"Nearly everyone is very nice to me."

"Nearly everyone?"

"Yes, one or two people aren't so pleasant. They think I have an easy time."

"Jealous?"

"Yes, perhaps."

"Who are the idiots?"

I smiled and replied, "That would be telling."

We talked "shop" for a little. It was interesting to hear about some of his plans — he was always thinking of plans for making Barrington's bigger and better. I never knew anyone so full of enthusiasm for his work as Duncan Barrington, and he had the power of kindling a flame of enthusiasm in the bosoms of his employees.

We had an excellent lunch. It was a good deal better than the usual meal which was served in the downstairs restaurant; I wondered how this had been achieved but I made no comment.

When we had finished and were having coffee (which also was a good deal better than usual), Mr. Duncan changed the subject.

"I see you're wearing a ring," he said.

"Yes, I'm engaged to be married."

"It's a signet ring."

"Yes. He wanted to give me a diamond engagement ring but I said I'd rather have this."

"I suppose when you're married you'll desert us?"

I hesitated and then replied, "I don't see much chance of our being married until after the war."

"He's in the Forces, I suppose? Is he in this country?"

"No, he's abroad at present."

Mr. Duncan waited for a few moments; I knew he was hoping for more information but I was silent.

At last he said, "Are you quite comfortable in your new quarters, Miss Morris?"

"Very comfortable . . . and it's lovely having my brother to live with us."

"I liked your brother," declared Mr. Duncan. "I'm sure he's good at his job, but I had a feeling that he wasn't very satisfied with the work he was doing. Am I right?"

This was a safe subject, and I enjoyed talking about Willy, so I told Mr. Duncan all about him: how he had been in Romford's Engineering Works but had been moved to his present uncongenial employment when the new factory was opened. "He's wasted there," I said. "He's doing work that could be done by an unskilled man."

"That's bad. Why doesn't he write to Sir Edgar Romford? They might take him back. Romford's are making precision instruments for aeroplanes, so they could get him back quite easily."

"Did you say Sir Edgar Romford?"

"Mr. Romford has been given a K.B.E. I saw it in the Honours List."

It was amazing how much Mr. Duncan knew. He was terribly busy but he found time to keep himself informed about everything that was going on.

276

"Tell your brother to write to Sir Edgar," said Mr. Duncan, nodding. "That's the best way. Well, I suppose I'd better get a move on. We're making alterations in the furniture department and I promised to be there about two o'clock. This has been a delightful little break, Miss Morris. We must do this again. Do you lunch here every day?"

"No, very seldom," I replied. This wasn't strictly true (it suited me to lunch there) but I didn't want to lunch with Mr. Duncan again. For one thing I was determined to keep our relationship on a business footing, and for another I had discovered that Barrington's enjoyed gossip ... the news that Miss Morris had been entertained to lunch by the boss would be a juicy subject of conversation for days.

All the way home I was thinking of the best way to put the matter to Willy, so that he would write at once to Sir Edgar Romford. However when I arrived at the flat Willy was busy with his gadget and after supper Father wanted a game of piquet ... so I could do nothing about it that night.

The following morning we had breakfast earlier than usual, and Father went along to the shelter to see about putting up some extra bunks, so Willy and I were left to finish our breakfast alone.

"I saw Lewis yesterday," said Willy. "He said he would come and see you as soon as he had a moment. He's at a camp somewhere in Essex."

"Yes, I know."

"Oh, he writes to you, does he?"

"Yes, now and then. Where did you meet him?"

"I met him face to face in Regent Street. He was glowing with health and vigour. Lewis has always had the best of everything; he's one of Fortune's Darlings."

I didn't reply. It was sad that Willy should feel like that.

"You needn't look so disapproving," said Willy. "You know it's true. Father and Mother gave Lewis everything he wanted because he was 'so handsome and clever,' and Lottie could do as she liked because she had blue eyes and yellow curls. You and I were the ugly ducklings."

It wasn't fair of Willy . . . but I knew he was overworked and miserable. "I didn't know you felt bitter about it," I said.

"I can see you don't believe me, Sarah, but if you look back you'll realise that it's true. I felt bitter about it at the time but I'm glad now; spoiling doesn't prepare you for present-day life. If I'd been spoilt when young I couldn't have survived the last two years: the long hours in the workshop, the grinding monotony of the work, the foul language and the friendlessness . . . and Mrs. Black's cooking. Sometimes when I felt at the end of my tether I came to you for a little spoiling, didn't I?" He grinned at me and helped himself to another cup of coffee.

"Oh, Willy! But things are better now?"

"Quite a lot better in the domestic line," nodded Willy. "For one thing you haven't got a drunken husband coming home in the early hours of the

278

morning and raising hell. I'm glad you haven't got a drunken husband, Sarah."

"So am I," I said with an involuntary chuckle.

"You see," said Willy, rising and taking his pipe off the chimney-piece and filling it with his long clever fingers — which, alas, were so engrained with oil that no amount of scrubbing would clean them. "You see, Sarah, one of the hardest things I have to bear is the enmity of the other chaps in the workshop. They've had a down on me from the very beginning."

"Why?"

"Because I'm different from themselves. For one thing I don't like foul language and for another the foreman holds me up as a shining example of punctuality — and all the other virtues. It's rather sickening for them, so they take it out on me when they can. That's all; I didn't mean to whimper about it."

"You never whimper!"

"I seem to be whimpering a bit now, for some reason or other. All the same I'm glad I've had the misery and grind."

"You're glad?"

"I've stuck it out," he explained. "Sticking it out has been good for me; it has stiffened my backbone. I shall go on sticking it out (they've got me by the short hairs so there's nothing else for it) but it won't be so bad, because —"

"Willy, listen: you could go back to Romford's."

"My dear girl, there's not a hope! I've told you —"

"Listen!" I said loudly. "Romford's Works have gone over to munitions; they're making precision instruments for aeroplanes and Mr. Romford has got a K.B.E."

"What!"

"It's true."

"Precision instruments?"

"Yes."

"And may I ask how Miss Morris happens to know all that?"

"Miss Morris heard 'all that' from Mr. Duncan Barrington."

"That man again?"

"Yes."

"What else did Mr. Duncan Barrington say to Miss Morris?"

"He said Mr. William Morris should write to Sir Edgar Romford."

"Did he, now? He seems to take a lot of interest in the Morris family."

"His interests are very wide."

Willy stood and looked at me for a moment or two but I didn't say another word. I knew Willy too well: he hated to be ordered about and told what he ought to do.

"Lordy, look at the clock!" exclaimed Willy. "I'd better be off!"

He went off like a rocket; I heard the front door bang and his feet clattering down the stone stairs.

Part Four

CHAPTER
TWENTY-EIGHT

My work at Barrington's had become more arduous but my domestic arrangements were easier for I was able to enlist the services of a woman who lived in the flat below us. She helped me in the mornings and she was willing to come for an hour in the evenings if I wanted her. It was a comfort to come home and find supper prepared instead of having to set to and prepare it myself after a strenuous day's work. Mrs. Raggett was a quiet mouse-like little woman — I never got to know her well — but she was very useful to me.

All this was good. The only disadvantage in our new flat was its distance from St. Rule's: instead of five minutes' walk it took twenty minutes in the bus to get from door to door, which was less convenient for Father. For me it meant that I didn't see Pam Hetherington so often. However we met when we could in the evenings and I still went to the shelter two nights a week. Even when there wasn't an air-raid the shelter was used by people who liked company for themselves and safety for their children. We were obliged to make a small charge for refreshments, otherwise we couldn't have carried on, but they didn't seem to mind. Sometimes I dropped in on my way home from

Barrington's and helped Pam to make sandwiches; she was usually there at half-past six and we sat at a table together and chatted as we worked.

One Thursday I was earlier than usual.

"Mrs. Hetherington isn't coming," said Mr. Martin. "I've got two other ladies on the job . . . by the way you can talk French, can't you, Miss Morris? There's a man here — rather a queer sort of customer. He was hanging about outside the church so I brought him in out of the rain. I don't know what he wants."

The man was dressed in rough clothes with a muffler round his neck; he looked sullen but his face brightened at the sound of his own language and he asked if I were "Madame Heddington."

"No, but I am her friend. Do you want to see her?"

"The letter is for the wife of the curé of St. Rule's. I was told to give it into her hand but already I am late." He was searching in his pocket as he spoke and after producing a rolled-up coil of twine, several nuts and screws and a pocket-knife, he found a very dirty crumpled envelope and showed it to me. It was addressed: *Mrs. Hetherington, Wife of the Rev. Paul Hetherington, Vicar of St. Rule's Parish Church, London, S.E.*

"I have come to the right place?" he asked, looking at me warily.

"Yes, but Mrs. Hetherington is not coming to-night."

"Then I must return another day," said the man crossly. "It is a nuisance but he said I must give it into her hand."

"Who gave you the letter?"

"They call him Gene."

"Can you take an answer to Gene?"

"No, I am not going back."

"Where is Gene?"

He answered rudely, "How do I know? I agreed to bring the letter — not to answer questions. I am in a hurry." Then he crammed the envelope into his pocket and turned away.

He was so careless that I was afraid he would lose the letter — or perhaps not bother to come back — and I was beginning to think that it might be important. "Wait!" I exclaimed, seizing his arm. "Mrs. Hetherington is my friend, why not give the letter to me?"

He shook his head. "No, that is no good."

"I can give it to her."

"Gene said she would reward me with English money if I gave it to her safely."

I opened my bag and took out a pound note. He eyed it greedily.

"Look," I said. "This will save you the trouble of returning another day."

The transaction was completed in the twinkling of an eye; he ran up the steps and disappeared.

"You got rid of him pretty quickly," said Mr. Martin.

"He was in a hurry," I explained. "He brought a letter for Mrs. Hetherington. I had better take it across to the Vicarage in case it's important."

"Not likely," he replied. "It's probably a begging letter; she gets dozens of them."

I ran across the road and rang the bell at the Vicarage. As I waited on the doorstep I began to

285

wonder if I had been foolish and had wasted twenty good shillings, but when Pam opened the door and I gave her the letter I saw that the money had been well spent.

"Gil . . ." she said in a hushed voice. "Gil's writing! Sarah, where did you get it?"

"From a Frenchman who came to the shelter. Oh, Pam, I'm terribly glad! I'll go away and leave you to read it."

"No, stay! I'm frightened . . ."

She was trembling and her eyes were full of tears, so I took her firmly by the arm and we went into the study together. "It's all right," I said. "There's nothing to be afraid of."

"A letter . . . from Gil!"

"Yes, it's lovely. Shall I open it for you?"

She handed me the dirty crumpled envelope and I opened it with a paper-knife which was lying on the table. When I unfolded the thin sheet of paper I saw that the letter was written in shorthand.

Pam looked at it in dismay. "Goodness!" she exclaimed. "I can't read this."

"But I don't understand! Why did he write it in shorthand unless he thought you could read it?"

"I used to be able to read it," she explained. "Years ago, when Gil was fifteen, he broke his leg so badly that he was laid up for several months. It was boring for him so I got a girl to come in every morning and teach him shorthand. We learnt it together — it was more fun for Gil — and we wrote each other silly letters, like a game, you know."

286

"You'll remember," I told her. "I'm sure you'll remember. Just make a start and read out what you can; I'll write it down as you go along. If you don't know a word we'll leave a space and fill it in afterwards — that's the way."

"Well . . . perhaps," she agreed, looking at the letter doubtfully. "Gil and I could always read each other's squiggles. It begins 'Dearest Mam' — that's what he calls me. He called me 'Pam' when he was little but Paul didn't like it so we compromised."

"'Mam' is nice," I said, seizing a block of scribbling paper. "Go on, Pam. What next?"

The first part of the letter seemed to be an account of the accident but Pam was so worried and upset that all she could do was to make out a few words here and there.

"Oh, dear, I can't read this!" she exclaimed. "He says, 'Sam was backing about' . . . no, that can't be right!"

"Leave it," I said. "Go on to the next bit."

It was very difficult but we persevered and when we were half-way through Pam began to remember and to read it more easily. I found a magnifying glass in the drawer of the desk which was a help.

When at last we came to the end she looked up and said, "It's a hopeless muddle, isn't it? But he's alive and well — nothing else matters."

"The beginning is a muddle," I agreed. "We can go back to that later. The last part is fairly clear. Wait a moment and I'll sort out my scribble so that you can read it for yourself."

When I had written it out the last part of the letter read as follows:

"... so that you will ... why I could not ... before. I am afraid you must have been ... I am O.K. now so you need not worry ... I cannot come home ... got a job ... with our old friend Percy Blakeney ... we export merchandise over the mountains ... Spain ... this letter ... by that route ... has promised to ... and give it into your hand ... I hope he will ... safely ... I am useful here ... speak the lingo ... get on well with ... chaps ... better not tell ... I am alive. Safer for me ... you must tell father ... make him understand ... top secret ... very important ... write again if possible ... no time ... Pierre and ... just starting ... lots of love from Gil."

When Pam had read it she held out her hand to me and said in a shaky voice, "I thought it was a hopeless muddle — but it makes sense. How did you know the way to do it?"

"There was a girl at school who was learning secretarial work; she had difficulty in reading her own shorthand notes and I found I could help her by writing it down like this. It's easy to fill in the spaces afterwards. Who is Percy Blakeney? I seem to know the name?"

"Of course you do! He was the Scarlet Pimpernel."

"The Scarlet Pimpernel!" I echoed in surprise. "Then that means —"

"It means that Gil is helping people to escape from France . . . over the mountains into Spain."

"Merchandise?"

"Human beings were the merchandise exported by the Scarlet Pimpernel."

"Yes, of course," I murmured. It was years since I had read the books.

"It's the sort of thing Gil would enjoy," said Pam in thoughtful tones. "He's very . . . adventurous. Percy Blakeney was his hero; he adored *all* the Scarlet Pimpernel books. We used to read them together, so he knew I would understand. Oh, Sarah, isn't it wonderful! My own darling Gil! I wonder why he couldn't write to me before. Perhaps he was ill."

"Perhaps," I agreed. "But he's all right now. He says you needn't worry . . . and he couldn't do a job like that unless he was perfectly fit."

"It must be dangerous," said Pam apprehensively.

I couldn't deny this. "But he's happy," I said. "You can tell from the way he writes that he's in good spirits. He's useful because he can speak the lingo and he gets on well with the chaps."

"*That* must have been Pierre! I mean the man who gave you the letter. Do you think he could take an answer?"

"I asked him but he said he wasn't going back. I couldn't get much out of him; he was a surly individual."

"Oh well, perhaps it's safer," said Pam with a little sigh.

We talked some more about it and presently Pam exclaimed, "Oh, it's wonderful! I've just begun to realise it properly. It's as if a dark cloud had rolled away and the whole world was full of sunshine. Everything looks different!"

"But you were sure he was alive, weren't you?"

"Yes, I knew he was alive . . . but now Paul will know it, too. Paul won't keep on wanting to give away Gil's clothes."

"Give away Gil's clothes!" I echoed in dismay.

"It has been . . . difficult," she explained. "You see the Listons have given away all Sam's belongings — and Paul thinks it's the right thing to do. It distresses me when Paul thinks I'm being silly and sentimental and selfish."

I managed to remain silent but it wasn't easy.

"Oh, he doesn't say it, of course! He just thinks it," said Pam hastily. She added, "And you can see his point of view, can't you?"

I looked at her and wondered . . . I wondered whether Paul Hetherington had been jealous of the love between his wife and his only son.

"Let's try again," I suggested. "Now that you've got into the way of it you might be able to decipher the first part of the letter. It's an account of the accident."

Pam nodded. "Yes, we must find out what happened. I want to make a fair copy of the whole letter for Paul."

We went over it again and this time we made better progress, but even with the help of the magnifying glass there were a good many gaps in the narrative. We filled them in as best we could by guessing. It took a long time but when we had finished the fair copy read as follows:

"This letter is very secret. Nobody must know about it. That is why I have written it like this. We could always read each other's squiggles so I hope you have not forgotten. First I must tell you about the accident. It happened on a dark misty night. Sam was larking about and fell overboard. I shouted for help but nobody came and I was scared stiff because I knew he was a poor swimmer so I kicked off my shoes and dived in after him. I hunted about but he had disappeared. I could not find him in the mist. At last I realised that it was hopeless — you can imagine my feelings! The ship was miles away by this time so the only thing to do was to look out for myself. I struggled out of my clothes and swam ashore in my underpants. It was a long exhausting swim but I made it and crawled out of the water on to a sandy beach. I knew I was somewhere on the south coast of France. After resting for a bit I started to climb a cliff but I was tired and dizzy so I fell and injured my head. When I regained consciousness I was lying in bed in a fisherman's cottage. They had found me on the beach. I was ill for a long time and the injury to my head made me lose my memory. I did not know who I was nor where I had come from. The fisherman and his wife were very kind to me. Their son had been killed at the beginning of the war and they felt I had been sent to them to take his place. It was rather pathetic. His name was Eugene so they called me Gene. I did not know my name. When I recovered I was able to help them with the fishing. As you know I am pretty useful with a boat. Gradually my memory began to return. It came back in flashes like switching on and off an electric light. It has come back completely now and I am perfectly fit. I have explained all this so that you will realise why I could not write to you before. I am afraid you must have been dreadfully worried . . ."

When we had got thus far Pam said, "Don't bother any more, Sarah. I can do the rest of it myself. Oh dear, it's dreadful about Sam, isn't it? He was such a fine boy, so full of life and fun!"

"It was dreadful for Gil," I said sadly.

"Yes, dreadful. Sam was his best friend, they had known each other for years —"

"But you don't know what happened to Sam!"

"He was . . . drowned," said Pam with a little sob. "Gil would never have given up hope and swum ashore until he was quite quite sure."

"You don't know for certain."

"No," she admitted doubtfully. "But you see he wasn't a good swimmer — not like Gil. Gil has always been keen on swimming; he has won dozens of cups and prizes for swimming and diving."

"You told me he was like a seal."

"Yes, just like a seal. That's one of the reasons why I knew he was alive."

We were silent for a few moments.

"What about Pierre?" said Pam at last. "I ought to give him something for his trouble."

I told her what I could — there wasn't much to tell — and added that I had rewarded him. She wanted to repay me but I refused to take the money . . . and she didn't press the matter. Instead she said softly, "'Cast thy bread upon the waters: for thou shalt find it after many days.'"

"Yes," I said. "Yes, that's what I feel! You always understand!"

Pam smiled rather sadly. "I understand because I've been casting my bread upon the waters for months and months; giving away money I could ill afford, pinching and scraping so that I need never refuse a begging letter. Oh, I don't take any credit for it! I mean it isn't a Christian idea — to give, in the hope of being repaid. Paul would say it was a pagan superstition."

"But it's in the Bible," I pointed out.

"There are lots of things in the Bible which aren't Christian," replied Pam. "'Bread upon the waters' is one of them. I knew that all the time, but the idea had taken root in my mind and I just — just couldn't get rid of it."

I nodded. I knew from experience how difficult it was to get rid of an idea which had taken root in one's mind.

"I haven't thanked you," said Pam. "It isn't because I'm not grateful, it's because I haven't words. Oh, Sarah, if you hadn't been there and made that man give you the letter he would have gone away and lost it! I

293

know he would! How can I ever thank you enough? It's silly to say, 'thank you.' I wish I knew —"

"Don't over-pay me, Pam."

"I couldn't! . . . but I won't say any more." She sighed and added, "You must go now, darling. I've made you terribly late for supper but Mr. Morris won't mind if you tell him why."

"'Safer not to tell anyone,'" I reminded her. "I shall just say I've been helping you, that's all."

Pam followed me into the hall and kissed me. She said, "Don't worry too much, Sarah. Perhaps Charles has lost his memory — it's possible, isn't it?"

I shook my head.

"Well then, it's some other reason," said Pam earnestly. "It's something we haven't thought of. You'll find your bread, my dear."

Then she opened the front door and I went home.

CHAPTER
TWENTY-NINE

One morning at breakfast Father received a letter from Lottie; he read it carefully and exclaimed, "I can't believe it! Lottie must have gone mad!"

"What has she done now?" asked Willy.

"She's going to be married."

"But, Father, that's good news!" I said. "It means that Mac is coming home. Has he got leave? I suppose his parents have —"

"It isn't young Macnab."

"What do you mean? She's engaged to Mac!"

"Apparently she has changed her mind. She intends to marry Sir Clive Hudson."

"Sir Clive Hudson!" I echoed incredulously. "You mean the man who owns Brailsford Manor? I thought he was quite old!"

Father didn't reply; he was re-reading the letter. Then he handed it to me and got up and left the room.

"The old boy seems upset," said Willy. "Funny, isn't it?"

"Funny!" I cried.

"Well, he wasn't upset when a bomb fell on his flat."

"Of course he's upset — frightfully upset! So am I! She's engaged to Ian Macnab — you know that as well as I do! He's in the desert — fighting! What does it mean? What on earth can have happened?"

"It's no good getting upset about Lottie's vagaries. Read the letter," suggested Willy. "Read it aloud. I haven't much time and Lottie's fist is difficult with all those whirls and twirls. I can't bear affected handwriting. Go on, Sarah, we may as well know the worst."

I took up the letter and read it aloud:

Riverside,
Fairfield

"Dear Father,

This letter is to tell you I am going to be married to Sir Clive Hudson. He has been taking me about a lot since Mac went away and yesterday he asked me to marry him and I said I would. I expect you will be surprised, but Mrs. Meldrum says you will be very pleased about it. He has a lovely place called Brailsford Manor. It is only about five miles from Fairfield so you probably know about it. His mother lives with him, but she will go and live somewhere else when we are married. I have been to Brailsford Manor several times and it really is a lovely place. There are stables for hunters and green-houses and lovely gardens and a lake with swans. Clive is a good deal older than me of course and he is a widower but he says I need not be jealous of his first wife because they were not happy together. He has given me a lovely sapphire ring — and he said what did I want for a wedding present. I can have anything I like. I think I shall have a little car. It would be nice to have a car of my very own. We are going to be married in London — and of course I want you all to come. You will be getting a proper invitation soon. I have not told Mac yet, but I thought you could write and tell him. It would be easier for you to write. I am afraid he will be rather surprised, but I have waited a long time and it is no good waiting any longer. It will be nice to live near Fairfield where I know such a lot of people — and Brailsford is a lovely house for parties. I have written to Lewis to see if he can get leave and come to the wedding. It would be nice if Lewis could come.

  With much love from your loving
Lottie

"P.S. I am enclosing Mac's address. You can tell him I still want to be friends with him."

"Good lord, what a letter!" exclaimed Willy. "It's practically illiterate. Didn't she learn anything at that posh school? She always was a spoilt brat — but that's the limit. She's going to marry a lovely house and a lovely garden and a lovely lake with swans and a lovely sapphire ring. I hope they'll make her happy."

I was so shattered that I couldn't speak.

"Don't worry, Sarah," said Willy, helping himself to marmalade. "You worry far too much about the family."

"It's Mac I'm worrying about."

"You needn't. He's had a lucky escape."

"She was such a dear little girl."

"She was always utterly and absolutely selfish. Mother and Father spoilt her — I've told you that before — and the Meldrums seem to have finished the job." He got up and added, "That letter ought to be put in a gold frame studded with diamonds ... no, sapphires. Well, I'm off, Sarah. I may be late for supper; I've been summoned to an interview with Sir Edgar Romford."

"Oh, Willy, did you write to —"

But Willy had gone.

I cleared the table and was washing up the dishes when Father came in.

"Have you read the letter?" he asked. "It's a dreadful letter, Sarah. It's a selfish, heartless letter. I can scarcely believe our own little Lottie can have written it."

"Yes, I feel the same."

"I should have taken her away from those people," said Father wretchedly. "I knew that woman was foolish, but I left my child in her care."

"You couldn't help it," I pointed out. "Anyhow it's too late to think of that now. Do you know anything about the man?"

"Only by hearsay. He must be forty-five or more; he was married before, but his wife left him. She's dead now." Father sighed heavily and added, "I wouldn't mind so much if Lottie had fallen in love with the man."

"She has fallen in love with his possessions."

298

"What am I to do? Would it be any good for me to go to Fairfield and see her?"

"Well, would it?" I asked.

He took up the letter which was lying on the kitchen table and read it again. Then he put it down.

It was time to take a strong line, so I turned from the sink and faced him. "Listen, Father, you can't do anything. You can see from the letter that Lottie is quite determined to marry the man, can't you? If we don't want to lose Lottie altogether you'll have to accept it and put a good face on it —"

"She won't be happy!"

"Perhaps not . . . but that's all the more reason why we should stand by. She may be glad of our help some day."

He looked at me in astonishment. "You're wise," he said.

"It isn't wisdom, it's experience," I told him. "If you're in trouble — lonely and miserable and anxious — it's a good thing to be able to fall back on your family. I'm sorry for people who haven't got families to fall back on."

He took up the cloth and began to dry the dishes. As a rule I didn't allow Father to do any household chores, but to-day I made no objection. He did it very carefully and took a long time over the job. However I hid my impatience.

When the dishes were all dried and put away he said, "I shall have to write to that boy. It will break his heart, Sarah! What am I to say?"

299

"Do it now," I suggested. "I expect they'll put the engagement in the papers and he might see the announcement. It will be less frightful for poor Mac to hear about it from you."

"Yes, I had better write to his parents too," said Father miserably. He added, "I never thought I should have cause to be ashamed of Lottie."

A few days after we had received her letter Lottie rang up and spoke to me; she asked with some anxiety what Father had said.

I was glad she had the grace to be anxious and, as I had made up my mind to be agreeable to her, I answered amicably, "Father was surprised and upset, but if you're quite certain you want to marry Sir Clive Hudson he won't make any objection. You'll want Father to marry you, of course."

"Well . . . no," said Lottie. "You see we're going to be married in a big fashionable church . . . and Clive's uncle is a canon . . . so we thought . . ."

"You don't want Father to take any part in the ceremony?" I asked incredulously.

"He won't mind, will he? You see, Clive's uncle —"

"Is a canon," I said. "You told me that before."

"You can explain to Father, can't you, Sarah?"

I felt inclined to tell her to do her own explaining. Then I realised that it would be easier for Father if I were to tell him. Lottie had said he wouldn't mind but I thought he would "mind" a good deal.

"Sarah, you'll explain, won't you?"

"Very well," I said.

"He won't mind," repeated Lottie. (It was always easy for Lottie to deceive herself when she wanted to get her own way.) She added, "Oh, Sarah, I nearly forgot! Has Father written to Mac?"

"Yes, and also to his parents."

"Good," said Lottie with a sigh of relief. "You see, Clive wants us to be married quite soon and it's sure to be in all the papers because of his being a baronet."

"Yes," I said. "Well, good-bye, Lottie."

"Wait, Sarah! There's another thing: you'll be getting your invitation, of course, but I wondered . . . I mean would you mind if I didn't have you as one of my bridesmaids? You see, I'm going to have Madeline and Ruth and Betty and Daphne. All of them are tall and fair and Mrs. Meldrum thinks —"

"Mrs. Meldrum thinks it would make a better show if you didn't have someone small and dark."

"How did you know?"

"A little bird told me."

"You don't mind, do you, Sarah?"

"Not in the least," I replied cheerfully. The idea of being one of Lottie's bridesmaids had never occurred to me and I could think of nothing I should dislike more.

There was another sigh of relief. "That's all right, then. Clive says we must have the reception at Barrington's; they've got a lovely big room for receptions, haven't they?"

"Yes."

"You'll all come, won't you?"

"Probably; unless we happen to have a previous engagement."

"Sarah, you aren't being stuffy, are you?"

Perhaps I had been a little stuffy . . . but what was the use? I decided that I must make an effort to be friendly so I asked Lottie to come and have lunch. I couldn't give her lunch at the flat but I could meet her at Barrington's in the Dutch Room.

"Yes," said Lottie. "Yes, that would be lovely. I'm coming up to town to-morrow, and I've got a lot to do, but I could easily meet you for lunch."

We arranged to meet at one o'clock.

The Dutch Room was more expensive than the big restaurant and therefore much less crowded. I was there at one o'clock, as arranged; Lottie was late so I sat down and began my meal.

Then I saw her come in and stand in the doorway, looking round the room. She really was a beautiful creature, tall and slender and elegant, with a blue cap perched jauntily on her flaxen curls.

I waved my hand — and she saw me and came towards me, smiling. "Oh, you've begun!" she said.

"I get an hour for lunch," I explained. "That means I'm on duty at two o'clock."

"Oh, what a bore! Couldn't you have got the afternoon off?"

(I could have done so, of course. Mr. Duncan wouldn't have minded but I was unwilling to ask for favours.)

"What a bore!" she repeated. "It doesn't give us much time, does it? I couldn't get here before; I was trying on my wedding dress. Mrs. Meldrum is giving it to me — it's perfectly lovely."

She sat down and put some parcels on an empty chair.

"You're having lunch with me," I said, handing her the menu.

"Oh, thank you, Sarah!" She ordered her lunch and then looked at me critically.

"This is my uniform," I explained.

"Oh, I wondered. It's very unusual and becoming — and it fits you beautifully. I suppose you got it here?"

"Yes."

"I wouldn't mind a frock like that."

"I expect they would make one for you."

"Sarah, listen, it's a bit difficult," said Lottie confidentially. "Mrs. Meldrum is giving me my wedding dress, as I told you, but Clive and I are going to a big hotel at Bournemouth for our honeymoon and I must have some nice clothes."

"You want me to give you some money?"

"Just lend it," she said hastily. "Once we're married I can pay you back. I don't want to ask Clive for money before we're married."

It was not unreasonable, so I offered to lend her a hundred pounds.

She opened her eyes wide. They were very blue and innocent. "Can you really?" she asked in surprise. "That would be marvellous."

"It's all I've got," I told her. "I've been saving up for a rainy day — but you'll pay it back, won't you?"

"Of course I will," she replied. "Clive is very generous so there won't be any trouble about it. Oh, Sarah, you're a friend in need!"

"I'm your sister."

She nodded, "Yes, of course."

Having made my point I said very earnestly, "Lottie, I've been worrying about you. Are you sure you're doing the right thing? You were fond of Mac, weren't you? What has happened to change —"

"I don't want to think about Mac!"

"But, Lottie —"

"I don't want to think about him . . . or talk about him. I'm going to marry Clive."

"Have you considered seriously what it will mean?"

"Of course! I'm not a child. Mrs. Meldrum says I'm a lucky girl and I know I'm lucky! Clive loves me and he's very kind and sweet — so it's quite all right. Please don't keep on at me about it, Sarah."

"Well, I can't," I told her. "I've got to go now; it's nearly two."

"It doesn't matter if you're late, does it?"

"Yes, it does . . . and anyhow you've got what you wanted, haven't you? I'll send you a cheque to-morrow."

"Now you're being stuffy," said Lottie, smiling at me. "You aren't a bit nice when you're stuffy."

I got up and she kissed me affectionately. "You're all coming to the wedding, aren't you?" she said.

"Father and I are coming. I don't know about Willy."

"Oh, well, it doesn't matter! Lewis is coming; that's the main thing. Lewis is going to give me away."

"Not Father!"

"I'd rather have Lewis. He looks so marvellous in his uniform. Let's hope it's a nice fine day," added Lottie cheerfully.

CHAPTER
THIRTY

It was September now and the weather had been dull and cold for nearly a week, but Lottie's wedding day was as mild and sunny as any bride could wish.

I had taken a good deal of trouble over my wedding garments. Maud Renfrew had helped me to choose them: a soft rose-pink silk frock and hat to match and a long blue silk coat. It sounds garish but the colours were so soft that they looked well together, and Maud had insisted that I should have a little cluster of soft blue feathers sewn under the brim of the hat. Perhaps it was foolish of me but I was determined to make a good appearance amongst Lottie's grand friends.

It was difficult to know whether or not Father was disappointed at not having been asked to play his proper part in the wedding ceremony — he said nothing about it and neither did I. We had lunch early and were ready and waiting long before it was time to go.

Willy was there to see us off. He had a free afternoon, so he might have come with us, but he had refused the invitation, explaining to me that he had nothing to wear. This was perfectly true; Willy's clothes were in a deplorable condition, but I knew he didn't want to go to Lottie's wedding so I hadn't bothered.

Willy was in very good spirits; he was full of jokes. When he saw me, dressed for the occasion, he pretended to be dazzled by my "beauty" and declared that Sir Clive would change his mind at the last minute and insist upon being married to the elder Miss Morris.

"Go and change, Willy," said Father. "The taxi won't be here for another ten minutes; you can manage it if you hurry."

"I refused the invitation," Willy pointed out.

"That doesn't matter. I should like you to come, and there will be plenty of room in the front pew."

"What am I to wear?"

"Clothes!" exclaimed Father scornfully. "It doesn't matter about *clothes*! Lottie is your sister so you ought to be at her wedding."

"I'll come if you like, Father. I can wear my boiler-suit; I've had it washed so it's nice and clean. I shan't be wearing it again."

"Oh, Willy!" I cried. "Are you going back to Romford's?"

"That's the idea. I don't quite know how it was managed; you'll need tae ask Jock."

"For Jock read Edgar!" I said, laughing.

"I don't know what you're talking about," declared Father irritably. "We've no time for your silly jokes . . . and there's no time now for you to change. The taxi is at the door so we'll have to go without you —"

"What a pity!" said Willy, heaving a deep sigh. "I'm sure Lottie would have liked to see me sitting in the front pew wearing my boiler-suit."

"Come on, Sarah!" exclaimed Father. "Come on, we mustn't be late!"

I stayed for a moment to congratulate Willy and then ran after Father down the steps.

The church was large and fashionable. Elegantly clad guests were flocking into the building in a constant stream. Father and I were met at the door by Tom Meldrum. I hadn't seen Tom for years, and scarcely recognised the one-time bouncy schoolboy in the tall Guards officer, but he recognised Father and, greeting us cordially, escorted us to the front pew.

The church was warm, scented with masses of flowers, the organ was playing softly and people were chatting to each other more as if they were in a theatre than in church.

None of us had seen Sir Clive. A meeting had been arranged but had been cancelled at the last moment because Sir Clive had "important business in the north." ("He's gone to see an Eskimo about an igloo," said Willy irreverently.)

Now that I saw him, standing at the chancel steps, I could scarcely believe that this was the man Lottie was going to marry: he was small and thin and pale, and his smooth dark hair had receded from his forehead. Willy had discovered in *Who's Who* that our prospective brother-in-law was forty-nine but he looked more . . .

308

and it seemed a mistake to have chosen a tall good-looking nephew to act as his best man.

These reflections were cut short when the choir began to sing "All Things Bright and Beautiful." It is a children's hymn, not really suitable for a wedding, but it had always been Lottie's favourite. The choir sang it well, with various charming descants, and certainly all things were bright and beautiful at Lottie's wedding . . . except the bridegroom.

Lottie, walking up the aisle leaning on Lewis's arm, was a dream of loveliness in white satin, embroidered all over with crystal beads, and a flashing diamond tiara on her flaxen hair. Lewis, too, was beautiful. They were alike and both were aglow with youth. The four bridesmaids were dressed in filmy green and carried bouquets of roses.

All went well: Charlotte Mary and Clive Warren were joined together in holy matrimony for better, for worse.

As a spectacle Lottie's wedding was a tremendous success . . . but I couldn't help thinking of Mac.

There was a great crush coming out of church and it was some time before Father and I could find a taxi, so we were a little late in getting to the reception. It was taking place in Barrington's English Rose Room, and when we arrived the large beautiful room was full of guests. The bridal party was grouped near the door beside the towering wedding cake; we were announced inaudibly, greeted them and wished them happiness . . . and passed on in the queue.

This was another slight to Father! The bridegroom's mother was standing there, greeting the guests — so why not Father? However I don't suppose Lottie had thought of it and Father was completely oblivious of any slight. He was wearing a dazed expression as if he had suddenly awakened to find himself in China or Peru.

I kept hold of his arm and tried to steer him through the ever-increasing crowd of well-fed, beautifully dressed people, all of whom seemed to know each other intimately and were talking at the tops of their voices. We knew nobody, and soon I began to have a queer feeling that we must be invisible, for people kept pushing us aside, without noticing we were there and greeting each other over our shoulders.

I released my hold on Father's arm to loosen my collar, and a waiter pushed between us with a tray of glasses, so we were separated — and I lost him. I tried to find him again, but it was hopeless. By this time I was so hot and bothered that I made my way to a corner of the room where there was a palm tree. No sooner had I reached this comparatively quiet spot than I was hemmed in by a group of half a dozen ladies and gentlemen who had been making for the same haven. They all had champagne glasses in their hands and, as I was still invisible, their conversation was cheerful and uninhibited.

"Well, here's to them!"

"Lottie has done pretty well for herself, hasn't she?"

"She's been endowed with plenty of worldly goods — if that's what you mean."

"Poor old Clive looks a bit yellow."

310

"I don't know how she *could!*"

"Oh, Clivey isn't too bad."

"He isn't my idea of a 'handsome husband.'"

"You can't have everything. Lottie prefers 'ten thousand a year.'"

"More like twenty."

"Not really?"

"Well, say fifteen, and plenty more rolling in."

"I thought it was his father that made the pile."

"How long will it last?"

"Which? The marriage or the pile?"

"Oh, both, of course! The marriage is balanced on the pile."

Shrieks of laughter interspersed this curious conversation. I had tried several times to escape, but I was still invisible so they didn't move to let me by.

At last I said loudly, "May I pass, please?"

Evidently I wasn't inaudible for one of them moved about six inches and I pushed through the gap . . . to find myself face to face with my brother-in-law.

He didn't know who I was, but replied politely to my greeting.

"I hope you're enjoying yourself," he said. "I see you haven't got anything to drink."

"It doesn't matter," I told him.

"If I could see a waiter . . ."

"Please don't bother. I'm Sarah, Lottie's sister."

"I'm afraid I didn't hear what you said."

The noise of chatter was so overwhelming that I wasn't surprised. I shouted, "I'm Lottie's sister."

"Oh yes, how foolish of me! You were sitting in the front pew. I remember thinking your hat was very pretty . . . but you aren't like Lottie."

"I know."

"I ought to speak to your father. I suppose he's here — somewhere?"

I supposed he was, unless he had been trampled underfoot, or had been deafened by the noise and gone home without me.

"We ought to have met," said Sir Clive, with a worried frown. "I'm very sorry I couldn't manage it but I had business in the north."

I nodded and said, "I know." It would have been fun to ask about the igloo — and probably quite safe because he wouldn't have heard what I said — but I didn't risk it.

"You must come and visit us at Brailsford when we get back from our honeymoon."

"Yes, I should like to come."

"We'll have a party for you."

"It would be nicer to come when you're alone."

"Don't you like parties, Miss — er — Sarah, I mean?"

"Not awfully."

"Neither do I, but I expect I'll get used to them. Lottie says Brailsford will be a good place for parties. Do you think this is a good party?"

"Splendid."

"I suppose it is. I'd enjoy it more if I hadn't a headache."

"It's the noise."

"Yes . . . but Lottie says 'the more noise the better the party.' I wonder when we'll be able to get away. We're going to Bournemouth, you know. It's a big hotel and they have dances every night so Lottie is sure to enjoy it, isn't she?"

"Yes, she's sure to enjoy it."

"What did you say, Miss — er — Sarah, I mean?"

"She's sure to enjoy it," I shouted.

This seemed a very odd conversation — a sort of Alice-in-Wonderland conversation — and, now that he had mentioned his headache, I discovered that I had a headache too. I had already congratulated him and wished him happiness and I couldn't think of anything to say. I kept on looking at him and trying to make myself believe that this careworn little man was Lottie's husband. Lottie's husband! He looked as old as Father and not nearly so full of life . . . but all the same I liked him and, strangely enough, I felt very sorry for him.

We stood for a few moments without speaking; it is difficult to find something worth saying when you have to shout loudly and clearly to make yourself heard.

Suddenly he said, "If you wait here I'll go and find a waiter. You must have something to drink." Then he turned and pushed his way through the crowd. They were his guests — one imagined they must be his friends — but nobody noticed him or spoke to him; it seemed as if he, too, must be invisible. I waited for a few minutes, but he didn't come back, so I made my way to the door . . . and discovered Father in the vestibule talking to Mr. Duncan.

"Are you ready to go home, Sarah?" asked Father. "I should have liked to have a word with Lewis but I couldn't stand the noise a moment longer — I've got an appalling headache — but I don't mind waiting for you if you're enjoying yourself."

"Is everything all right?" asked Mr. Duncan anxiously. "Is the party going well, Miss Morris? Is there enough champagne — or had I better send up another dozen?"

They were both looking at me so I said wearily, "Judging by the noise the party is going like a rocket — but I've had enough. Let's go home, Father."

"Would it be rude? I mean, shouldn't we say good-bye?" asked Father, hesitating.

"We shall never be missed," I replied.

CHAPTER
THIRTY-ONE

Now that Willy was a white-collar worker we got his hands cleaned and I made him buy some new clothes; he looked quite different, and was very cheerful. He told me little about his work but he had taken away all the papers connected with his "gadget"; he said Sir Edgar was interested in it.

Soon after Lottie's wedding I was sent for by the China Department and on arriving there found a little lady with very blue eyes awaiting me eagerly.

"Oh, Mees Morreese," she said, in careful English. "I do not want you for translation. I have learned, as you see! I hope you have not forgotten me?"

"Madame Breuchaud!"

She nodded happily. "Yes, yes! I asked for you to come and speak to me because you were kind. It would be so nice if you will come and have lunch with us one day. Is this possible?" Then, before I could reply, she made a gesture of impatience. "*Oh, c'est trop difficile!*" she exclaimed. "*Parlons français, Mees Morreese!* Can you have *déjeuner* with us to-morrow here at Barrington's? I know you are busy but no doubt you are allowed time for *déjeuner*. My sister will come and my husband also. I have spoken of you so much that

315

they want to meet you. I have told them of your kindness to me when I could speak no English and the girl was stupid about the shoes."

I told her that I should be delighted to have *déjeuner* with her, and to meet her husband and her sister, and added that I hoped the shoes had been a success.

"Oh, Cécile was so pleased," said Madame Breuchaud, nodding. "Cécile laughed, she thought it a good joke, and the shoes fitted her perfectly. Shall we say twelve-thirty in the so charming restaurant on the top floor? You will like Cécile — and Jules also, of course. How glad I am that you will come!"

My official lunch hour was from one to two, but there was no reason why I shouldn't have lunch a little earlier, so the matter was settled and I met them as arranged. Cécile was a delightful girl; she resembled Madame Breuchaud but was younger . . . and a size larger, as was to be expected. Jules was not so pleasant; he was a natty little Frenchman with a dark moustache and a roving eye. His eye roved in my direction rather too often and his foot touched mine once or twice under the table . . . but I took no notice of his advances.

He admired my black charmeuse dress and declared that only a woman with a perfect figure could wear it. (We were speaking French, of course, so the flattery didn't sound so blatant.)

"It is my uniform," I said coldly.

"But it is extremely becoming," said Cécile, nodding. "And how interesting it must be to have such a wonderful post!"

"It is because she is clever and can speak half a dozen different languages," declared Madame Breuchaud admiringly.

I laughed and said, "Not half a dozen — just French and German."

"Is it permitted for one to inquire why you are not in one of the women's services?" asked Jules Breuchaud, twirling his moustaches.

I had been asked this question before, several times. The answer was that I was keeping house for my father and working in the air-raid shelter. Mr. Duncan had managed to get me exempted. I was glad of this because I didn't see how Father and Willy could have got on without me.

"Ah!" exclaimed Jules. "It is one of your famous English 'wangles'!"

I didn't reply. As a matter of fact I had never felt guilty for having avoided conscription; I was doing three jobs and working to the limit of my capacity.

Perhaps it was unfair to dislike Jules Breuchaud so heartily, for at that time officers in the Free French Forces were finding life somewhat difficult. (France had let us down, so many of them assumed an aggressive manner to hide an inferiority complex.) Anyhow, I didn't bother about Jules, I was much more interested in Cécile, who continued to question me about my work and repeated that it must be interesting and amusing. She was an attractive creature, intelligent and full of vim, and it occurred to me that she would make a valuable assistant. I could say nothing until I had spoken to Mr. Duncan, but I had become so busy that I really needed someone to help me.

For some time I had been trying to avoid Mr. Duncan — and had met him frequently — but now, when I wanted to speak to him, he was extremely elusive. I was nearly run off my feet that afternoon, but near closing time I had a respite so I asked Mr. Marriott where Mr. Duncan could be found.

"Furniture," said Mr. Marriott. "If he isn't there he may have looked in at 'Groceries' about the latest consignment of tea; failing that you might try 'Bed Linen.'"

To cut a long story short I pursued Mr. Duncan from one end of Barrington's to the other and eventually discovered him in the Pets Department talking to the vet, who had been summoned to have a look at a sick monkey.

"Hallo, Miss Morris!" he exclaimed in surprise. "Haven't you gone home?"

"I wanted to speak to you for a minute," I told him.

"Yes, of course! This is Mr. Player . . . Miss Morris. Mr. Player has come to see poor Jacko. I'm afraid poor Jacko's days are numbered. I'm not going to have any more monkeys. Children love them, of course, but this climate doesn't suit the poor little beasts."

"They're delicate," put in Mr. Player. "I'll take Jacko home with me and see what I can do . . . but I can't hold out much hope, Mr. Duncan."

He wrapped up the monkey very carefully, put it in a covered basket, and went away.

318

"Poor Jacko," said Mr. Duncan with a sigh. "He might have lived to be a great grandfather if he'd been left peacefully in his native jungle."

"Or he might have been eaten by a tiger," I suggested.

"That's true," agreed Mr. Duncan, more cheerfully. "Well, what's the trouble, Sarah?"

It was the first time he had called me Sarah — and it gave me a slight shock of surprise — but we were alone in the Pets Department and it was "after hours", so no doubt he felt that our strictly businesslike relationship could be relaxed.

"It isn't trouble," I replied. "It's just that I think it would be a good plan for me to have an assistant; there are more and more strangers in London and I feel I can't cope with the work satisfactorily. I simply haven't time."

"I was wondering about that," admitted Mr. Duncan. "I've watched you trying your best to be in three places at once. I'd have suggested before that you should have help, but you've *made* this job — it's a very personal job — and it would be difficult to find you an understudy. However, now that you've raised the subject, I'll tell Marriott to advertise for —"

"Mr. Duncan, I know someone who might agree to come."

"In that case you had better fix it up."

"You mean I'm to fix it up?"

"Yes, of course."

"But I haven't told you anything about her!"

He smiled. "You've told me all I need to know. You're anxious to have her, therefore she's the right person for the job. See what I mean?"

I saw what he meant. Obviously I wouldn't be anxious to have an "understudy" unless I was sure she would do.

"Well, that's settled," he said. "I'll speak to Marriott about it. You can get her dress from Miss Fitzroy and she can have a silver chain — not a gold one. She can start with two-thirds of your salary and we'll raise it if she makes out. Is that all right?"

I laughed and said, "It's all right except that you're going too fast. I haven't asked her yet."

"I'm always being told I go too fast," declared Mr. Duncan ruefully. "But it's my considered opinion that other people go too slow. They make such a song and dance about things instead of going ahead and getting on with the job." He added, "Ask her, Sarah. Persuade her to come. She can have a bigger pay-packet if there's any trouble about that. Now tell me about your brother: did he write to Sir Edgar Romford?"

"Yes, and Sir Edgar asked him to come for an interview. Willy went to see Sir Edgar and took some blueprints of a gadget which he has been working at for several months —"

"What sort of a gadget?"

"I don't know."

"Really, 'don't know' or 'top secret'?"

"Both," I said, smiling. "Anyhow, Sir Edgar was interested and in some way managed to get Willy out of that horrible tank factory and has put him into the

320

drawing office in Romford's. Willy is ever so much happier — it's splendid! I can't thank you enough for your help."

"I did nothing except hand on a few scraps of information."

"You may think it was nothing, but it has meant a great deal to me, Mr. Duncan."

"Need it be 'Mister Duncan'?"

"Yes, you're the boss and I'm an employee."

"Here in Barrington's I'm the boss; but supposing we had a little jaunt together? We could go to the Savoy and have dinner and dance . . . if that would appeal to you?"

I wondered how to get out of it without being unkind.

"It doesn't appeal to you," said Mr. Duncan sadly.

"Not really," I told him. "I have a lot to do and I get very tired. I help to run a shelter, which means being there two nights a week. It's very kind of you, but I really need a good deal of sleep or I couldn't carry on; besides, as you know, I'm engaged to be married."

He sighed and said, "Does that prevent us from being friends?"

"No, it needn't prevent us from being friends."

"And you can call me Duncan, can't you?"

"Well, perhaps . . . after office hours, Duncan," I replied, smiling at him.

"Good," said Duncan. "We'll shake hands on that."

We shook hands solemnly.

I was glad we had had this talk for now I knew exactly where I was. He, also, knew where he was and would keep his side of the bargain: Duncan was the last man on earth to go back on his given word. We were friends, no more and no less, so I needn't avoid him in future; it had been difficult to avoid him and I liked him so much that I wanted to be friendly.

"You look happy," said Duncan.

"It's good to have a friend."

"I shall always be your friend, Sarah. If ever there happens to be anything that a friend can do . . . well, you know what I mean, don't you? That's part of the bargain."

He was gazing at me anxiously so I nodded and said, "Yes."

"Good," said Duncan.

We came down the stairs together — six flights of stairs; the lifts were not working as the lift-men had gone home. Everyone had gone home: the huge building was empty of life; everything had been tidied up for the night and most of the stalls were covered with white dust sheets. As we walked through the Grocery Department our voices echoed eerily from the tiled walls.

"How queer it is to see the place like this!" I exclaimed.

"I like it," replied Duncan. "It sort of belongs to me — if you know what I mean."

"You're king of all you survey," I suggested.

"Are you laughing at me, Sarah?"

"No, indeed! Why should I? You *are* a king and you take good care of your kingdom. I've always thought so."

322

He was silent for a few moments. Then he said, "I've come here to live. I've got a little flat on the top floor. Had you heard about that?"

Of course I had heard about it! The news had gone round Barrington's in a few hours: Mr. Duncan had taken over a suite of rooms on the top floor; he was having them done up; he was making a bathroom and a kitchenette — all by Barrington's, of course. At first it was rumoured that the bijou flat was for display, it was going to be furnished by Barrington's and shown to customers. Then, one night after everyone had gone home, Mr. Duncan moved in (with his own furniture) and in the morning he was actually in residence. Mr. Duncan was here, in residence! The news was so exciting that the war news paled in comparison.

I told Duncan all about it and he laughed delightedly. "It's fun to get inside knowledge of Barrington's Babblings. I had no idea my movements were so important . . . but it's not a bad idea, you know," he added thoughtfully. "We might have a small flat done up to show people."

"But don't you think people would prefer to choose their own decorations?"

"No, I don't," he declared. "People have no imagination. You must help me, Sarah."

"Miss Cole, in the Furniture Department, is surely the right person —"

"No," said Duncan. "The flat must be a comfortable home, not a showroom furnished with a suite. It must be the sort of place that people will want to live in. See?"

I saw — but I wasn't very keen to help him. Miss Cole would be annoyed and Barrington's was a hot-bed of gossip. However I didn't take the matter seriously for Duncan was a person who liked choosing things himself.

"Why did you come to live here?" I asked, changing the subject.

"It worried me when I heard the bombs exploding in all directions — I kept wondering if THAT ONE had got Barrington's — I sleep a lot better, now that I'm on the spot. Sometimes at night I wander round to see if everything is all right and have a word with the night-watchmen. It keeps them up to the mark."

Duncan walked with me to the main exit and opened the door to let me out. He reminded me to "fix it up with the understudy" and we said good night.

"Oh, Mees Morreese, but this is too good to be true! To work with you at your so interesting job and to receive such good remuneration! No, no, I cannot believe it!" Cécile's voice had risen to an excited squeak at the end of the telephone.

"The job is yours if you want it," I told her. "I've spoken to Mr. Duncan Barrington and he said I was to persuade you to come."

"Persuade me!" cried Cécile. "No persuasion is necessary . . . but will I be able to do it nicely? That is the trouble. I have had no secretarial training — no training at all — and my English is not good."

"Your English is adequate and it will improve."

"Yes, yes, I shall work very hard to improve!"

324

"Listen, Cécile. It's only fair to warn you that you will be rushing about from one end of the building to the other, sorting out muddles. You may find it tiring."

"No matter! I am strong and active . . . but how shall I learn, Mees Morreese? I have never done anything like this before."

"Neither had I, but I soon discovered that tact and common sense was all that was needed. We'll work together for the first few days until you get into the way of it and learn to find your way about."

"Mees Morreese, shall I have a black gown — like you?"

"Yes, and a silver chain."

"Oh, this is wonderful! I have been wanting a job so much. You see, I have not any money. My sister and my brother-in-law are very kind but I do not like to be dependent. I have taken some pupils but they pay very little."

"Will you be able to get rid of the pupils?"

"I shall not get rid of them," declared Cécile, laughing. "My sister will be glad to take them and she will teach them better, so everyone will be pleased. When shall I come, Mees Morreese?"

"Come to-morrow at a quarter to eleven. I'll wait for you in the office . . . and you had better call me Sarah."

"But you are to be my boss!"

It was true that I would be her boss but I couldn't bear to be called "Mees Morreese."

I had told Mr. Marriott that Miss Dubonnet was coming and he must have passed on the news for when I arrived at twenty minutes to eleven, Mr. Duncan was

325

in the office. Cécile came in punctually at a quarter to eleven, so I introduced them and Mr. Duncan shook hands with her.

"All serene?" he asked cheerfully.

"All serene?" echoed poor Cécile in bewilderment.

I said quickly, "Mr. Duncan means, 'is everything all right?'"

"Oh yes," said Cécile happily. "Everything is very serene; I am so pleased to work here in this beautiful place with Sarah and I hope I shall be able to do it very nicely."

"Good," said Mr. Duncan, nodding. "Very good indeed." He turned to me and added, "You'll see Miss Fitzroy and fix up about Miss Dubonnet's uniform, won't you, Miss Morris?" Then he sped off before I could reply.

"He is very fast!" exclaimed Cécile in astonishment.

I laughed and replied, "He says everyone else is very slow."

"One sees that he might think so," she admitted.

"It's this new Display Flat," explained Mr. Marriott. "The boss wants it to look like a home . . . with a pipe on the mantelpiece and a pair of slippers warming at the fire."

"Oh!" I said, somewhat apprehensively.

"It's not a bad idea," declared Mr. Marriott . . . and disappeared quickly into the telephone room.

I soon discovered that Cécile was all I had hoped. She was full of enthusiasm; she was intelligent and had a keen sense of humour. It was all to the good that she was untrained, for she had no stereotyped ideas; she watched how I dealt with the various situations and copied my methods. In a few days she was able to work by herself . . . and she was so charming and unassuming that everyone liked her.

It was just as well that I had "an understudy" for Duncan was quite determined that I was to help him make his Display Flat into a home. In a way I enjoyed this new commitment (what woman wouldn't have enjoyed choosing papers and cretonnes and carpets and pieces of furniture — not to speak of bathroom equipment and all sorts of pots and pans and dishes for a small kitchen?) but it brought me into too close contact with Duncan and it made Miss Cole my enemy . . . last but not least I was well aware that Barrington's was babbling about me.

However I had no choice but to live it down and once the flat was finished, and I returned to my old ways, Barrington's found something else to babble about — all but Miss Cole, who would never forgive me as long as she lived!

Now that I had Cécile life wasn't such a rush: there was more time to give to individual customers, and we arranged the work so that now and then we could take it in turns to have a whole day off.

CHAPTER
THIRTY-TWO

"Sarah, I must see you! Something ghastly has happened!" It was Lottie's voice on the telephone, a fluttering, frightened voice.

"My dear! What is it?"

"I can't tell you — like this. I must see you! Will you be there if I come now?"

"Now?"

"Yes, I'm in town. I'll get a taxi and come — now."

"But, Lottie, what's the matter? Why do you . . ."

The line was cleared; she had rung off.

It was March, and I had arranged with Cécile to have a day off to do some spring cleaning, otherwise I wouldn't have been at home at half past eleven in the morning. I was in my oldest clothes and an overall, with my hair tied up in a duster, but fortunately I had finished turning out the sitting-room.

I lighted the fire, made some coffee and rushed to my room to change. I was worried about Lottie but all the same I didn't want to receive her "looking like a drab."

When the bell rang I was ready; the fire was burning brightly and the tray with the coffee cups was on the little table.

For once in her life Lottie was pale and dishevelled, she collapsed into a chair and burst into tears.

"Lottie, darling! What on earth has happened?"

"I'm caught!" she sobbed. "It's all his fault — he promised faithfully that it would be all right. He said I needn't worry — I hate him!"

"Who?" I asked in alarm.

"Clive, of course! He promised me . . . and now *this* has happened."

"What has happened?"

"I'm going to have a child."

"Oh, Lottie! That's lovely!"

"It isn't!" she cried. "It isn't 'lovely,' it's horrible. I'm frightened and miserable, it's making me ill and — and ugly. I'm ugly now — and it's getting worse! I won't go through with it — I won't have a child, it's revolting!"

"Lottie, be quiet! You mustn't talk like that."

"I hate Clive," she repeated frantically. "I told him I didn't want children and he said it would be all right. It's his mother's fault! He goes to lunch with her in town and they talk about me — I know they do! She hates me because she's had to leave Brailsford. She's told him he ought to have a son and heir."

"Well, of course! It's quite natural that he should want —"

"At first I couldn't believe it!" she interrupted in a hurrying, breathless voice. "It was too bad to be true — it couldn't be happening to *me*! But I've just been to see Sir Wilmot Slayne — that's why I came up to town — and he — he said it was true. He was horrid to me, Sarah!"

"Horrid?"

"Yes, dreadfully unkind. I told him I was frightfully delicate. I told him it would kill me to have a child; I told him he must do something about it."

"Do something?" I exclaimed. "Lottie, you're crazy! No doctor would dream of such a thing; it's against the law!"

"I don't care! He *must* do something! It would kill me! I'm terribly delicate; I've always been delicate, haven't I?"

I was speechless.

"Sarah, why don't you answer?"

I moistened my lips and said, "It isn't true."

"It *is* true! I've always been frightfully delicate ever since I was a child. You know that, Sarah. I want you to help me. You're my sister — you *must* help me!"

"Help you? I don't know what you mean."

"Listen, Sarah," she said urgently. "I want you to ring up that horrid man. You must tell him that you're my sister and I've always been very delicate. He'd have to do something if you told him. He'd *have* to listen to you!"

"No." I said it very softly.

"But I've always been terribly delicate!"

"No."

"Yes, I have!"

"No, Lottie."

She flung herself about in the chair and sobbed hysterically. "Why are you so beastly to me? I thought you'd be kind! You want me to die! That's what it is! I wish Mother was here! Mother understood me! Mother knew I was delicate — she used to call me her little fairy — and Mrs. Meldrum says I'm terribly highly strung! I told him all that but he wouldn't — wouldn't believe me."

"You'd like some coffee," I said. "I'll go and fetch it. A cup of coffee will do you good."

"No, wait!" cried Lottie, seizing my hand. "You must ring up that man. You *must*, Sarah! He wouldn't believe me; he laughed — yes, laughed — and said I was a strong healthy young woman and it would do me good to have a child! When I told him I'd go to someone else he said, 'Yes, go to someone else, Lady Hudson' and opened the door . . . but he'd have to listen to you, Sarah. You must ring him up and tell him —"

"No, Lottie."

"All right, I'll go to someone else!" she cried wildly. "There are people you can go to — I know there are! If you won't help me I'll ask Madeline. There was a girl in the Wrens — Madeline told me about her. She knows a woman who . . ."

I couldn't bear it a moment longer. I left her talking and went to get the coffee and the milk; the coffee had got cold and it took me a minute or two to heat it up. When I went back to the sitting-room, with the two jugs in my hands, she was gone.

When Father came home that evening I told him that Lottie was going to have a child.

"Ha, ha!" he exclaimed. "So the little monkey is going to make me a grandfather; that's good news, isn't it? How do you like the idea of being 'Aunt Sally'?"

331

"I thought you'd be pleased," I said . . . and added, "You're awfully wet, Father. You had better give me your coat and I'll hang it up on the pulley in the kitchen. Why didn't you take your umbrella?"

"It was perfectly dry when I left home," said Father, taking off his coat and handing it to me."

"You'll find a pair of socks and your slippers beside the sitting-room fire."

"Oh, thank you, Sarah! Grandfathers have got to be cosseted, haven't they? What's for supper?"

"I'm afraid it's just cauliflower au gratin."

"Well, what's wrong with cauliflower au gratin?" said Father cheerfully.

There was nothing wrong with it, of course, except that we had it too often. Food was difficult and becoming more so every week. Sometimes it was impossible to get even the scanty rations to which we were entitled without standing in a queue for hours. Fortunately my two men were easy to feed: Father had never bothered about food and Willy had been fed so badly when he was boarding with Mrs. Black that he enjoyed every dish I put before him. All the same, I don't know how I could have managed without an occasional parcel from Craignethan.

There was more chaff when Willy came in:

"Hallo, Uncle William!" said Father.

"Oh, I'm to be Uncle William, am I? I've been wondering when that world-shaking event was going to take place. When are we to expect the heir of Brailsford Manor to make his appearance on the scene?"

They were both looking at me and waiting for an answer. "You'll need tae ask Jock," I said lightly . . . and went to fetch the supper tray.

I could hear Willy explaining the joke to Father; they were both laughing when I returned.

The war news was good that evening and Willy had brought a paper so the topic of Lottie's baby was shelved while they discussed the advances made by the Russians.

"The German troops in South Russia are being hard pressed," declared Willy. "If Hitler wants to save them from annihilation he'll have to transfer some fresh divisions from another front."

"We'll get out the map after supper," suggested Father.

When we had finished our meal I cleared the table and went to wash up the dishes. Usually Willy came and helped me, but to-night I didn't expect him; the two were so intent upon the strategies of war that they had scarcely noticed what I was doing.

I was wrong, however, for after a few minutes Willy followed me and taking a cloth off the pulley began his usual task.

"What's up, Sarah?" he asked in a low voice. "I thought you'd have been as pleased as Punch about Lottie's infant . . . and here you are, dripping tears into the sink."

"I'm not dripping tears into the sink!"

"Well, you don't seem wild with joy. How did you hear about it? Did her ladyship ring up and prattle about layettes?"

"She was here this morning. She doesn't want the child."

"Whew! So that's the trouble? I might have guessed! Bad for the figure, of course."

"She says it will kill her."

"Not a bit of it! Our dear little fragile Lottie has always been as strong as a horse. You aren't worrying about that, are you?"

"No."

"Well, what the hell are you worrying about?"

"I don't know what she's going to do."

"You don't mean she's thinking of . . ."

"I don't know," I said desperately. "She talked so wildly — and I wasn't any good to her. I was terribly upset — horrified at the things she said — and instead of — of trying to make her see sense I was beastly to her. It seemed so dreadful that she didn't want a child — so unnatural and — and horrible. I was so — so disgusted that I couldn't be kind. I've been thinking about it all day, worrying about it. If I'd been kind and gentle I might have got her to — to listen. She *does* listen to me sometimes. If she goes and does something — frightful — it will be my fault — because I failed her."

Willy was standing with a plate in one hand and the cloth in the other. He said thoughtfully, "She won't do anything frightful."

"She talked so wildly!"

"I dare say she did — I can imagine the scene! — but it's all talk with Lottie. She won't 'do anything frightful'

334

because it's dangerous and she's too jolly careful of herself."

"What am I to do?"

"Do? You can't do anything except stop worrying about the silly little fool. Lottie will produce the infant on the correct date without the slightest trouble — if I know anything about her."

"If you'd seen her, Willy!"

"If I'd seen her I'd have given her a bit of my mind," said Willy cheerfully. "I don't know why you're so upset. I don't mind betting you tuppence that the infant will arrive safely. It will be isolated on the top floor of Brailsford Manor so that its screams won't be heard. The nursery will be thoroughly hygienic, with bars in the windows, and a thoroughly competent nurse will be engaged to look after it and see that it causes no trouble to its parents."

"An unwanted child!"

"Oh," said Willy, looking at me. "Oh, I see! You've always been potty about children; you'd like one of your own."

"You see a lot, don't you?"

"That's why you're so upset — that's why you were horrified — that's why you couldn't be kind."

"Yes, that's why."

"I wish you wouldn't cry," said Willy crossly. "It's upsetting me."

"I'm sorry. It's just — just because it makes me want Charles rather badly."

"He'll come back, Sarah. He tried to get his father out of prison and got caught in the act."

"What! How do you know?"

"Well, it's obvious. I don't pretend to be a seer or anything; I just look at the facts and draw the logical conclusion. He went to Vienna to try to get his father out of prison and when he found he couldn't manage it legally he arranged an escape. It's the sort of thing Charles would do. I can imagine him letting his father down out of the window at the end of a rope . . . or perhaps he gave a feast for the warders and doped their wine. Then all he had to do was to get the keys out of their pockets and open all the doors and lead his father out of the prison disguised as an old crone."

"You ought to write thrillers," I told him.

"But something went wrong," said Willy thoughtfully. "I don't know what went wrong . . . perhaps the warders weren't sufficiently doped and recovered too soon and Charles was caught red-handed and clapped into prison with gyves on his wrists like Eugene Aram."

"You're talking nonsense!"

"I know, I wanted to cheer you up."

Oddly enough Willy's nonsense had cheered me up. "What do you really think?" I asked.

"I really think Charles may have fallen foul of the authorities and been imprisoned. Once we've settled Hitler's hash Charles will come back."

"Honestly?"

"Yes, honestly. Charles has always seemed to me . . . indestructible," said Willy thoughtfully.

CHAPTER
THIRTY-THREE

Mr. Hetherington and Father took it in turn to celebrate Holy Communion at St. Rule's. On the first Sunday in June it was Mr. Hetherington's turn for the early services; I got up at six and went at seven o'clock. For the last few days there had been a queer sort of tension in the air; everyone knew that huge concentrations of troops and materials were being assembled all around the south coast; everyone knew that this could only mean one thing: we were preparing for the invasion of France. Last but not least, everyone knew that the less said about it the better.

I had gone at seven o'clock because I had thought the church would be quiet at that hour . . . but it was full of people; there was scarcely a vacant seat, and the service was wonderfully sincere and moving; many of the women were in tears.

When I got back to Bolingbroke Square and climbed the stairs to the flat I found Lewis sitting on his suitcase on the landing.

"Hallo, Sarah!" he said. "I wondered what had happened to everyone. I've been ringing the bell for ten minutes."

"Oh, Lewis, I'm sorry! Father and Willy don't hear the bell and I've been to church. Have you come to stay?"

"I can't stay long."

Now that I had time to look at him I was alarmed. He was pale and haggard, he looked years older. "Is something the matter?" I asked.

"The weather, that's all."

"The weather?"

"Well, I suppose you know there's something up . . . a very big something. Everyone knows, even Hitler, but he doesn't know when or where. I just thought I'd like to see you, and I brought some of my clothes that I shan't be wanting. You can keep them, can't you?"

"Are you going, Lewis?"

He nodded.

"You look awfully tired."

"I haven't been in bed for three nights."

"You had better come in and have some breakfast; then you can go to bed and sleep."

"That sounds good . . . but you'll have to waken me at three."

"At three this afternoon?"

"Yes, but don't tell anyone."

I opened the door and we went into the kitchen together. Lewis sat down on a wooden chair and leant his elbows on the table and watched me getting things ready. "Where are Father and Willy?" he asked.

"In bed and asleep. They won't want their breakfast until later, so you and I can have ours together. I suppose I mustn't ask questions?"

338

"Better not." He sighed and added, "Oh, I know you're all right; you aren't a gas-bag."

"Will you be able to let me know . . . how you get on?"

"I'll let you know when I can, but don't worry; no news is good news, see?"

"Yes."

"It'll be all right. Everything has been planned to the last trouser button. It's bound to be all right — if only we get the right weather. If we don't get the right weather it'll be all wrong. Gosh, I'm glad I haven't got the responsibility of deciding!"

"Can't you wait for the right weather?"

"No, at least . . . that's one of the things you mustn't ask."

"Am I allowed to ask what you've been doing?"

"Acting chauffeur and dogsbody to a bloke in the commissariat department. I've been attached to him for temporary duties, that's why I've had such a lot to do. The bloke finds me useful and wants to keep me — but he can't do that. I *must* be with my own chaps when . . . well, when the whistle blows."

"The armoured cars?"

"Yes. I've trained them and they're a splendid lot of chaps. It would be frightful if I couldn't go into action with them."

While I flew round, making coffee and toast and boiling eggs, Lewis went on talking. Perhaps he told me things he shouldn't have mentioned but he knew I was safe and he had got to the stage of tiredness and tension when he had to unwind. He talked about "logistics," which was a word I hadn't heard before, and explained that it was the provisioning and maintenance of an expedition. In the old days armies were able to live off the country in which they were operating, but to-day every fighting man had to be fed and clothed and taken care of; every gun had to be provided with ammunition, every machine with petrol and spare parts — and mechanics to service those that were damaged — and everything had to be ferried across the Channel under the protection of air-cover and be available in the right place at the right moment.

"It sounds impossible!" I exclaimed.

"It's going to be done. It's the biggest thing that has ever been tackled in the history of the world. Some people call it the modern Armada; they're talking through their hats! The Armada was child's play compared with this show. All the same if that man — what's his name? — had paid proper attention to logistics he'd have conquered England."

"Medina Sidonia," I said. There wasn't much I didn't know about the period. I added, "But it was the gales that destroyed the Armada."

"The weather finished it off," admitted Lewis. "But if the fleet had been properly equipped before he left Spain Medina Sidonia could have landed his troops and made a bridge-head before the weather broke. Goodness, Sarah! Where did you get such enormous brown eggs?"

"Craignethan eggs; Grandmama sends them to me."

"Why do Craignethan hens lay huge eggs?"

"Peaceful surroundings and lots of good food."

340

"I wouldn't mind being a Craignethan hen."

"Wouldn't you, Lewis?"

"Yes, I would," he declared, sitting up and pulling himself together. "I'm glad I'm me. I'm glad I've been chosen to play a part in the greatest adventure in history. Remember that, Sarah, whatever happens . . . *and I mean whatever happens.*"

I sat down and began to eat my egg — but I hadn't much appetite. "Lewis, do you remember when you were Henry V in the school play?"

"I've been remembering it for the last three weeks, saying Harry's speeches to myself whenever I had a moment to think:

" 'On, on, you noblest English!
Whose blood is fet from fathers of war-proof! —
Fathers that, like so many Alexanders,
Have in these parts from morn till even
    fought . . .
I see you stand like greyhounds in the slips,
Straining upon the start. The game's afoot:
Follow your spirit; and upon this charge
Cry — God for Harry! England! and Saint
    George!' "

We were silent for a few moments.

"It's great stuff, isn't it?" said Lewis. "It's a pity Shakespeare isn't alive to-day . . . but his inspired words are alive. I wonder if Churchill will quote some of Harry's speeches. He's expected to-day at Portsmouth. Can I have some more butter, Sarah?"

"Yes, of course," I said, passing him the dish.

"Have you got a proper shelter in this building?" asked Lewis.

"I believe there's a cellar but we don't bother about air-raids; we go to bed except when we're on duty at St. Rule's. Anyhow there haven't been many lately. I expect the Germans are too busy —"

"You'll have to go down to the cellar every night. These new secret weapons are going to be nasty . . . flying bombs, you know. It will be all right once we get to the rocket-sites but, until we can get there and destroy them, London is going to have a bad time."

I passed him a jar of marmalade which I had made with some sugar saved from our rations. "Is that a secret too?" I asked.

"Everything is secret," he replied thoughtfully. "I mean it all hangs together. Better not say anything about anything for a few days. Of course once we get going you can say what you like. This marmalade is jolly good."

"Have some more," I suggested.

He finished the jar, piling it on to his toast in large spoonfuls. He had another cup of coffee and I emptied the sugar bowl into his cup; I knew he had a sweet tooth. Then he sat back and smiled at me.

"You look better," I said.

"I feel a whole lot better," he replied. "It isn't only the good meal and the Craignethan eggs; it's talking to you, Sarah. I'll have a bath and go to bed but you must waken me at three."

"Yes, I will, but what am I to say to Father and Willy?"

"Tell them nothing. You see, sometimes people give away bits of information without meaning to. For instance, Father might mention to someone that I'd been here but I'd had to dash back to Portsmouth in the afternoon. At the moment everything is terribly secret," said Lewis earnestly. "Hitler has spies everywhere and he'd give his ears to know just when and where we intend to make our landings. You realise that, don't you?"

I nodded. "Yes, of course. Do you want to see Father? Because, if so, you had better see him now. He has to go to St. Rule's this afternoon."

Lewis hesitated . . . and then said, "Better not; it would be difficult to say good-bye to him without letting the cat out of the bag."

I thought Lewis was wrong — and said so — but Lewis thought he knew best. "I'll write to him as soon as I can," he promised.

I turned on the bath and put two hot-water bottles in the bed. Then I waited until he was in bed and drew the curtains.

"Three o'clock, Sarah," he said with a huge yawn. "Not a moment later . . . promise faithfully?"

"Yes, three o'clock," I replied.

He was asleep in a moment.

When I went back to the kitchen Father and Willy were there in their dressing-gowns, looking at the remains of the feast.

"Have you been entertaining the King or only Mr. Churchill?" asked Willy, pointing to the pile of egg-shells, the empty marmalade jar and butter dish and sugar basin.

"Lewis is here."

"Lewis? He seems to have scoffed all our rations."

"Yes, he was hungry."

"Well, I'm blowed; don't they give him anything to eat in the Army?"

"He was hungry," I repeated.

"It doesn't matter," said Father. "If Lewis was hungry —"

"There's plenty to eat," I told them. "You can have boiled eggs and bread and coffee and milk."

"Where is Lewis?" asked Willy, sitting down and helping himself to a slice of bread.

"In bed in the spare room. He was tired."

"Yes, I gathered that much. I mean where has he come from?"

"I don't know."

"Is Lewis going to France?"

"I don't know."

"I believe he is . . . and you *do* know. That's why you fed him like a fighting cock."

"I fed him because he was hungry and tired." That was true, anyhow.

"What has he been doing to get so hungry and tired?"

"Sarah has told you that she doesn't know," said Father. "It was quite right to give Lewis a good meal and it will do us no harm to eat our bread without butter for once in a way."

"And there isn't any sugar," Willy pointed out.

"No, it's finished," I said.

"Is Lewis going to stay here long?" asked Willy. "Because, if so —"

"I don't know," I said. Then I gave them their eggs and went away and left them to finish their breakfast.

Willy went to lunch with the Romfords, as he often did on a Sunday so Father and I had lunch by ourselves, then he got ready to go to St. Rule's shelter.

As he was going out of the door he said, "I'm not going to ask how long Lewis is going to stay with us, Sarah."

I knew then that he had guessed. I said, "No, Father, please don't ask me."

He hesitated for a few moments and then sighed. "Give him my love, Sarah — my dear love." Then he went away.

At three, when I went to waken Lewis, he was sleeping soundly. I hated wakening him, but I had to do it.

He got up at once and dressed and had a cup of tea and a slice of plum cake — which Grandmama had sent in the last parcel of food from Craignethan — and I told him what Father had said.

"Give him my love, Sarah, and ask him to pray for us."

"Yes, I will — but he prays all the time."

"Take care of yourselves."

"I suppose it would be silly for me to say that to you?"

"It would be, rather," he replied, smiling. "But all the same it's nice to know that people are a little bit silly."

"I'll be — thinking about you, Lewis."

"Don't worry too much . . . and don't forget that no news is good news."

"Yes, I know."

"And don't ever forget that whatever happens I'm glad and proud to be in it. Cry 'God for Harry! England! and Saint George!' "

"I won't forget — ever."

"That's right," said Lewis. Then he gave me a big hug and went away.

When he had gone I dried my tears and went along to the church at the corner of the street and stayed there for a long time, praying that all would go well for England and Saint George . . . and for Lewis.

CHAPTER
THIRTY-FOUR

The next few days were anxious ones for everyone in Britain. Nobody knew what was happening. It was only afterwards that we heard the invasion had been delayed owing to weather conditions. Then at last we heard that the huge fleet had crossed safely; the troops had landed and made their bridge-heads and had fought their way to their objectives. We listened to the news on the radio with breathless excitement.

The Americans had encountered more opposition but their troops fought splendidly.

On the following Monday Mr. Churchill and some of his staff and a party of American Generals crossed over to France and met General Montgomery and made a lightning tour of inspection. This news gave a tremendous boost to the morale of the whole country for, rightly or wrongly, we took it to mean that all was going well. It was amazing to see how the tension relaxed; people smiled as they went about their work and chatted cheerfully to perfect strangers in the streets and in the buses.

A few days later father received a field postcard from Lewis to say he was well and "going strong."

I see in my diary that it was on the night of the 12th June that the "flying bombs" began to arrive in London. Lewis had warned me that they would be "nasty" but at first they did little damage. Afterwards when they began to come at all hours of the day and night they were noisy and destructive, but Londoners with their usual courage found a denigrating name for Hitler's Secret Weapons.

"We've got to bear them," people said. "It won't be long now. Once Monty gets to the launching sites there will be no more doodlebugs, meanwhile we've just got to bear them . . . and the news is good, isn't it? Our boys are wonderful."

The news from Lewis was good too. He wrote quite often; sometimes his letters were very short, at other times they were longer, but they were invariably cheerful:

> Somewhere in France,
> Sometime

"Dear Sarah,

Thank you a million for the socks; they're just the thing for this sort of job. I'm delighted with them. I didn't know you were a knitter! Do you think you could manage a pair of mittens? They would be awfully useful. The chocolate was very welcome too, but don't send food because you need it for yourselves and the logistics of this affair are better managed than Medina Sidonia's. We are issued with cartons which contain tip-top food which only has to be heated up to provide good solid nourishing meals . . . and whenever we stop, at any hour of the day or night, our chaps brew up char (which is another name for TEA, in case you don't know!). Do you remember that song about 'Tea in the morning, tea in the evening, tea in the afternoon'? We used to shout it at the tops of our voices — and Father put his fingers in his ears! What fun we had — and what a long time ago it seems! One evening when we had stopped and were having our usual brew-up I started singing the song to my chaps and I soon had them joining in the chorus. I couldn't remember all the words so you might ask Father to write them out — he's sure to remember. My chaps love singing; you would laugh if you could hear us. I bet Father would put his fingers in his ears! We were stuck for a bit after the landings but we're going strong now and we aren't going to get stuck again. My chaps are grand. We're the modern cavalry, you know, which makes life very interesting — a bit too interesting at times. The French farmers and peasants aren't awfully keen on being 'liberated'; they don't fall on our necks with cries of joy. You see, they had settled down during the occupation and our arrival means more fighting and more destruction of barns and crops. You can't blame the poor wretches when you see the mess that war makes of their land. Talking of 'mess' I see in the papers (which roll up with astonishing regularity) that the buzz bombs are making a mess of London — and I just hope you and Father are taking proper care of yourselves. I can't tell you anything interesting but I'm keeping a skeleton diary and I'll show it to you one of these days.

Lots of love and again 'thank you' for the socks.

Yours ever,

Lewis

"P.S. Don't forget the mittens, will you?"

CHAPTER
THIRTY-FIVE

One evening towards the end of August I returned home to find Willy waiting for me.

"Great news!" he said.

"I know! I heard it on Duncan's wireless at one o'clock. Paris is liberated, Marseilles isolated; Montgomery says it's a decisive victory!"

"It's the beginning of the end," agreed Willy. "There's still a long way to go but we've got them on the run all right. As a matter of fact there's another piece of news for you."

"What's that?"

"It's in *The Times*. Listen, Sarah: 'The wife of Sir Clive Hudson, Baronet, of a daughter, Frederica Doris, both well.' What do you think of that? I told you her ladyship would produce the infant without any bother," added Willy, chuckling.

"You're always right, aren't you?"

"You owe me tuppence."

I took two pennies out of my purse and handed them over.

"Frederica Doris," said Willy thoughtfully. "Doris after mother of course, but why Frederica? Silly name!"

"Wasn't Sir Clive's father called Frederick?"

"I believe he was! He was the bloke who made the Hudson millions in the last war. He dealt in hides or something. Yes, you've got it! I bet they're as sick as mud that the wretched infant isn't a boy."

Father was late for supper that night; he had managed to get an evening paper and was so excited over the marvellous news about Paris and the thousands of German prisoners and the "complete enemy collapse in Northern France" that Willy forbore to mention his "family news."

"Listen to this!" exclaimed Father as we sat down to supper. "Lewis Hastings says, 'Victory is not a strong enough word.' Pétain has left Vichy — nobody knows where he has gone — the Falaise pocket has been cleared of Germans. American troop movements are secret. Where are they, I wonder? What are they doing? I expect they've got an unpleasant surprise for Hitler up their sleeves! Get out the map, Willy, and let's have a look!"

I said firmly, "*Do* eat your fish before it gets cold."

It was not until supper was over and the map had been spread on the table and the war news had been thoroughly discussed that Willy produced *The Times* and pointed to the announcement in the births column.

"Dear me!" exclaimed Father. "That's good, isn't it? 'Both well.' I must write and congratulate Lottie. I'm glad she has called the child Doris."

We asked Father about "Frederica" and he confirmed our guesses; it was Sir Frederick Hudson in whose memory the four big brass altar vases had been donated to St. Mary's. How well I remembered those vases! I

352

could see myself polishing them until they shone like new-minted gold! I could see myself arranging flowers in them! It was astonishing to think that Lottie's child was to be called after the legendary Sir Frederick.

Lottie's child! I hadn't heard from Lottie since that day in March when she had called to see me. Perhaps I should have done something about her but the fact was I had been so absorbed in the war news, and in the letters I had been getting from Lewis, that Lottie's troubles had seemed unimportant. I had thought of her now and then and had hesitated beside the telephone, wondering if I should ring her up and find out what was happening . . . but what should I say? I didn't know what to say to Lottie — and I was afraid of what she would say to me — so I had let the matter drift. But now all was well and there was no reason why I shouldn't get in touch with her. The best way would be to buy something nice for Frederica Doris and write a congratulatory letter. Knowing Lottie I felt pretty certain that she had forgotten all about her unwillingness to have the baby and was basking happily in her husband's smiles and the satisfaction of a difficult job successfully accomplished.

"Sarah, wake up!" exclaimed Willy. "I've asked you three times when you're getting your holiday. I'm getting ten days at Christmas and I thought it would be fun if we could go to Craignethan together. What about it?"

"I'm afraid not," I replied regretfully. "Christmas time is always terribly busy at Barrington's. I hope to get ten days or a fortnight in January . . . but you can go to Craignethan, of course."

"Not much fun without you," grumbled Willy.

I sent Lottie some little things for the baby, and wrote a friendly letter but I had no reply. At first I didn't bother — Lottie was never a good correspondent — but after a while I began to feel anxious. Obviously Lottie was still angry with me. What could I do to heal the breach?

Then, one evening, Lottie's nurse rang up and spoke to me: Lady Hudson was very pleased with the little garments; she sent her love and would like to see me. Could I come to Brailsford Manor on Wednesday and spend the day? A car would be available to meet me at Larchester.

I accepted the invitation. I wanted to see Lottie . . . and I knew Cécile wouldn't mind if I took a day off.

Brailsford Manor was a beautiful old house, beautifully furnished, but unlike Riverside the richness was restrained. The deep pile carpets, the curtains and the comfortable chairs and sofas did not leap at you and shout 'Look at me! I'm expensive.' Everything had been carefully chosen and was in good taste.

I was conducted upstairs by a very old butler and found her ladyship lying in bed in a large and very beautiful room.

"Oh, Sarah! How nice of you to come!" she exclaimed. "It was sweet of you to send the little frocks and things for Frederica. I ought to have written — but you understand, don't you? I've been so dreadfully ill that I haven't been able to write to anyone."

354

I kissed her and said, "It's lovely to see you, Lottie."
I was delighted to find that bygones were bygones.

"You understand, don't you?" repeated Lottie.

"Yes, of course! Letters are a bother when you're ill."

She didn't look as if she had been "dreadfully ill."
She looked as charming as ever in a pink silk bedjacket,
trimmed with swansdown, and a little pink cap on her
shining flaxen curls. The eiderdown was pale pink and
there was a large bowl of roses on a gate-legged table
which stood in the middle of the room.

"I had a dreadful time," continued Lottie plaintively.
"It was too frightful for words; I thought I was going to
die. Clive was terribly anxious about me."

"I'm sorry," I said. "But you must forget about it
now. It's all over and you've got a darling little
daughter. I'd like to see her, Lottie."

"You'll see her later. As a matter of fact nurse is
going out this afternoon so I thought you wouldn't
mind coping with her. You like babies, don't you?"

"Yes."

"Nurse isn't going until after lunch and she'll be
back about six. You can stay till then, can't you?"

"Yes."

I thought she was going to tell me not to be stuffy,
but she didn't. She was too anxious for me to stay and
look after her baby.

"It *is* kind of you, Sarah," she said with a sigh. "You
see I'm still so weak. It gets on my nerves when she
cries. She seems to cry a lot but nurse says there's
nothing the matter with her so I suppose it's all right."

"Haven't you asked the doctor?"

"Oh, nurse is very experienced! She knows all about babies."

"Is the baby like you, Lottie?"

"No, she's an ugly little thing."

"She's only two months old, so perhaps —"

"I was pretty from the very first; Mother used to tell me that I was 'just like a little doll'; I can remember her saying it."

"Lottie," I said, "do you think you could let me have the money I lent you?" It was uncomfortable to have to ask, but I had made up my mind that I must.

"Oh yes!" she exclaimed. "I've thought of it several times . . . and then I forgot. I'll give you a cheque to-day. By the way, Sarah, do you ever hear from Lewis? He never writes to me; he didn't even write when Frederica was born, which was rather beastly of him."

"Perhaps you don't write to him," I suggested.

"I've been so ill that I couldn't write to anyone."

"I can give you his address if you like."

"Where is he?"

"Somewhere in France."

"Perhaps he's in Paris," said Lottie with a sigh. "I've always wanted to go to Paris. It's lovely to think that we'll be able to go to Paris after the war."

I had lunch by myself in the enormous dining-room, waited on attentively by the old butler. It was a very good lunch: soup and casserole of chicken and mushrooms, followed by chocolate mousse. I was enjoying a cup of coffee when my brother-in-law came in, full of apologies for being late.

"I'll just have coffee," he told the butler.

"Have you had lunch?" I asked.

"No, I don't want anything to eat; it has been a very troublesome morning. I hope they've given you a good meal, Sarah."

"Yes, the chicken is particularly good. Why don't you have some, Clive?"

He looked surprised. "Oh, it's good, is it? Well, perhaps I'll change my mind."

The butler, who had been hovering in the background, hastened away to get it . . . and I was glad to see that when the casserole was handed to him Clive helped himself to the wing of the chicken and proceeded to eat it.

"You're right, Sarah," he said, smiling at me. "It's delicious. The fact is I don't feel hungry when I've had a lot to worry me. This morning has been exceedingly upsetting."

It was common knowledge that Sir Clive Hudson was a very wealthy man but it seemed to me that his riches were a burden to him; he would have been happier with less money and a wife of his own age who would look after him properly.

"I suppose your business is very complicated," I suggested.

"Some of it is," he admitted. "But there was nothing 'complicated' about my business this morning; it was just . . . infuriating."

"Tell me about it, Clive."

"I don't want to bore you."

"It wouldn't bore me. I'm always interested when people talk about their work."

"One of my factories makes boots for the Army, but we get the laces from a factory in the Midlands. The boots and the laces have to be packed up together and sent off at exactly the right time to be shipped to France. This morning, quite by chance, I happened to be there when they were being packed and I had a look at them. Would you believe it, Sarah, the laces were too short? The laces were too short and the man who was responsible for the consignment hadn't noticed! What do you think of that?"

"If you hadn't happened to be there . . ."

"If I hadn't happened to be on the spot they would have been sent off!" declared Clive. "I don't often lose my temper, so they were considerably startled when I let fly. I asked the manager how he would like to be issued with boots and laces that didn't fit; I told him his 'blue-pencil' carelessness might have resulted in the loss of a battle . . . rather fanciful, perhaps, but I was angry. To tell you the truth I quite enjoyed letting myself go and laying into the the man . . . but it has upset me."

"What happened?" I asked.

"Oh, the laces had to be sent back and, after a good deal of telephoning up and down the country, I managed to collect suitable laces and the consignment was dispatched . . . but it just shows you can't trust anyone. I'm afraid this must be boring you, Sarah."

"Oh no, logistics interest me!"

"What do you know about logistics?"

I smiled and replied, "Not very much, really. Napoleon said his army marched on its stomach but you've got to have boots and laces too. Lewis told me that everything from a tank to a trouser button has to be in the right place at the right moment. That's logistics, isn't it?"

He laughed. "You've got hold of the essential principle! I forget who it was made the statement that to keep a fighting man supplied with all he needs you must have sixty men behind him."

"Sixty!"

"Personally I think that's an underestimate," said Clive thoughtfully. "Consider the manufacture of all the requisites 'from tanks to trouser buttons,' not forgetting food and newspapers and postal services . . . and the packing of all the goods . . . and the complicated organisation . . . and the transport . . ."

We were still talking about logistics, and Clive was enjoying a second helping of chicken, when the butler interrupted us.

"Excuse me, miss," he said in confidential tones. "Nurse has asked me to inform you that she will be glad if you will go upstairs to the nursery as soon as convenient; she is anxious to catch the bus to Larchester."

"What's that?" asked Clive in annoyance.

I rose and said, "Nurse is going out this afternoon and Lottie wants me to look after the baby."

The nursery was exactly as Willy had foretold: it was a large bright room on the top floor with bars in the windows, a frieze of Noah's Ark animals round the walls and white-painted furniture. Nurse was middle-aged and chatty.

"I'm so glad you've come, Miss Morris," she said. "I want to show you everything before I have to run for my bus. This is the day-nursery, of course; baby is asleep in the night-nursery. I have a room of my own and a nice bathroom and a kitchenette."

In the kitchenette there was a row of sterilised milk bottles on the shelf and a row of nappies hanging on the pulley. Nurse's room was adorned with photographs of babies in various stages of development. "They're all my babies," she said proudly. "I'll tell you about them some day. There isn't time now. Perhaps you could come earlier next Wednesday."

"Next Wednesday?"

"Lady Hudson said you would come every Wednesday so that I can have my afternoon off duty."

"I'm afraid that's impossible; I've got a job in London."

Her face fell. "Oh, what a pity! Lady Hudson said you were very fond of babies and would come whenever we wanted you. I can't get out much because there's nobody here to look after baby except the under-housemaid — and she's only fifteen so I don't feel very happy about it. Most mummies like looking after their babies themselves, but Lady Hudson wanted a boy so she isn't interested," added nurse confidentially.

This seemed dangerous ground. I said, "Lady Hudson is still very weak, so perhaps she finds it too tiring —"

"Weak?" exclaimed nurse. "Whatever makes you think that? She's simply splendid."

"She's still in bed."

"Oh, she felt a little tired after last night so she thought she would have a day in bed. The party was a great success; Lady Hudson looked lovely."

"Oh, I see."

"Baby has her bottle at four," said nurse. "Usually I take her out in her pram in the afternoon, but it's too wet to-day, so just let her sleep. She's in here," added nurse, opening the door of the night-nursery.

My niece was asleep in her cot; she was a dear little creature. Her round head was covered with silky down; her cheeks were pink and her nose was squashy. One tiny hand was grasping the blue cellular blanket.

"Oh, what a darling!" I whispered.

"Yes, she's a nice little baby," said nurse. "She cries a good deal but that's good for her lungs. It's better not to lift them when they cry. If you once begin that sort of thing you're done for."

"You don't think babies need love?"

Nurse laughed. "What a funny idea!"

"Rather an old-fashioned idea, perhaps?"

"Very old-fashioned. We were taught in hospital that the less a baby is handled the better."

"Oh, I see."

"It's a great mistake to spoil babies. I hope you aren't a spoiler, Auntie Sarah," said nurse archly.

Fortunately there was no need to answer. Nurse glanced at her watch, gave an exclamation of dismay and ran to catch her bus.

I had been slightly annoyed to discover that the reason I had been invited to spend the day at Brailsford Manor was to deputise for nurse but my annoyance didn't last long; I was very happy with Freddie . . . I couldn't call her Frederica.

After nurse had gone she slept for about half an hour; then, when she wakened and cried, I lifted her and changed her and sat down in the big nursery chair and cuddled her. I was aware that nurse would disapprove but I didn't care a rap: Freddie was warm and soft and cuddly and obviously she enjoyed being cuddled. I thought we were entitled to our fun.

She gazed at me with an unwinking stare — her eyes were hazel, like Clive's. I sang to her and I walked about the room with her and talked a lot of silly nonsense. I told her that her name was Freddie and I loved her dearly and I would come and see her whenever I could.

"You won't forget me, will you, Freddie?" I said.

Freddie blinked at me solemnly so I kissed the back of her neck which is the most delightful place to kiss a baby — and the most hygienic.

We spent a very old-fashioned afternoon.

At four o'clock precisely I warmed Freddie's bottle and gave it to her; at five my tea was brought to me on a very large tray by a very young footman; at six, when nurse returned, Freddie was back in her cot and sleeping peacefully.

"I hope she's been good?" asked nurse anxiously.

"Good as gold."

"She cries a lot when I leave her with Maureen."

"She didn't cry at all with me."

Nurse looked somewhat taken aback. She was not altogether pleased to hear that all had gone well during her absence . . . but, on the other hand, she realised that as all had gone well there was more chance of my coming again soon to relieve her. These two incompatible emotions, struggling in nurse's bosom, produced a very curious effect.

"Good-bye, nurse," I said, smiling blandly. "I wish I could stay and see her in her bath but I've got to catch my train."

We shook hands cordially.

Lottie was still in bed when I went to say good-bye to her.

"Good-bye," I said. "I've enjoyed my afternoon with Freddie. She's a darling."

"Frederica," said Lottie, frowning.

"No, Freddie."

"I don't like it."

"Well, I do," I said cheerfully. "Freddie likes it too."

"What nonsense! She doesn't know anything."

"She knows a lot more than you think. She's a dear little baby and very clever for her age. Lottie, why don't you look after her and have fun with her when nurse goes out? You used to like playing with dolls. Freddie is a real live doll."

Lottie was silent for a few moments. I knew why, for I had just seen the same thing happen to nurse: two incompatible emotions were struggling in Lottie's bosom; she was annoyed with me . . . but she wanted me to come back.

"Oh well," she said at last. "It doesn't matter. It was very kind of you to come. You'll come again, won't you? Perhaps you could come for a week-end? Nurse wants to go to Devonshire to see her mother. You're so clever with babies, aren't you?"

"The best butter."

"No, really and truly," declared Lottie, opening her blue eyes very wide. "It's a wonderful gift to be clever with babies. Do come for a week-end, Sarah."

"I'll see if I can arrange it, but I've got a job, you know."

"Oh, are you still doing that Barrington job? I thought you'd given it up ages ago." She added, "Look, here's the cheque and thank you very much for lending me the money."

I was surprised that she had remembered.

"You *will* come, won't you, Sarah?" said Lottie, as she kissed me good-bye.

As I went home to London in the train I thought it over seriously and decided that if father were willing — and if Mrs. Raggett could come to the flat on Sunday — I had better go to Brailsford. It would have to be soon, of course, for once the Christmas rush began I should be too busy to get away for a week-end. Barrington's was always terribly busy at Christmas time. Yes, I had better go. Nurse wanted to see her mother and wouldn't be happy until she had accomplished her object . . . and although nurse was too stiff and starchy for my liking, she was fond of Freddie in her own way and obviously efficient. It would be unfortunate, to say the least of it, if nurse decided to look for another post where she would have more freedom.

When I explained the matter to Father he agreed at once; Willy was not so amenable.

"Why should you?" he said crossly. "Oh, of course we can manage all right — but Lottie ought to look after her baby herself. Why should you have to bother? You're working all week; you need a quiet Sunday to rest . . ."

He went on like that but I took no notice. It was for Freddie's sake that I was going to Brailsford.

I went on the following Friday night and stayed until Monday and I had a very happy time with Freddie; she was no trouble at all.

On Monday morning nurse walked in while I was giving Freddie her orange juice.

"Oh, Freddie, look who's here!" I exclaimed rapturously.

Fortunately Freddie played up, she smiled and held out her arms in a most endearing manner.

Nurse picked her up and kissed her. "That's the worst of babies," said nurse apologetically. "You can't help getting fond of them however hard you try."

"Boo!" exclaimed Freddie, blowing an orange juice bubble.

It seemed to me an apt comment.

Part Five

CHAPTER
THIRTY-SIX

In November large notices were put up in Barrington's advising people to SHOP EARLY FOR CHRISTMAS but it wasn't until the beginning of December that the Christmas rush started in earnest.

One afternoon when I was in the office Duncan came in and spoke to me and said he was raising my pay. When I told him I was getting enough already he replied rather crossly that none of his employees got more — or less — than they were worth. So I smiled and thanked him.

"That girl you've got is good value. I've raised hers too," said Duncan.

I was glad of this; Cécile would be pleased.

"Would you like another understudy?" asked Duncan. "It seems to me that things are getting a bit beyond you . . . and you're looking tired, Sarah."

I was very tired but I didn't say so. "There's a lot to do," I admitted. "Cécile and I are on the go all the time."

"Shall I tell Marriott to advertise?"

"No, don't do that. Cécile has a great many friends in London; she might know of someone suitable."

"That's an idea. I'll ask her," said Duncan, nodding.

We were still discussing the matter when Mr. Marriott came out of the telephone room and interrupted our conversation.

"Miss Morris is wanted in 'Photography,'" he said in his usual brisk way. "It's a Danish gentleman. His English is poor but he speaks German."

The Danes were the only people I had met who were willing to speak German; their country had offered little resistance to the German invaders and, for that reason, it was well treated by the occupying forces. Denmark, a land of bacon and butter, was used by the conquerors as a holiday resort.

These were my thoughts as I went down in the lift to the second floor where the Photography Department was situated. Afterwards it seemed strange that I had no premonition of what was in store for me . . . it was just an ordinary afternoon at Barrington's and I was on my way to cope with one of my usual jobs.

When I arrived at the Photography Department I was pleased to find that there hadn't been any unpleasantness; there was no "muddle" to be smoothed out; they were awaiting me in amicable silence. The assistant was elderly and competent; the Dane was tall and fair and handsome, though slightly over-weight, and only wanted a golden hat with horns to transform him into a Viking.

"The gentleman wants a film projector," explained the assistant. "We've got two different makes of projector and I thought it would be a good plan for you to tell him about them."

"I'm afraid I don't know anything about film projectors."

"No, but I do," replied the assistant, smiling. "And here's the book of instructions, Miss Morris."

The task was not as difficult as I had feared; the assistant demonstrated the working of the projectors; we examined the diagrams in the book and I translated the instructions.

One of the projectors was "a better job" than the other; it was also more expensive but after some consideration the Viking decided to buy it and produced a large wad of pound notes. When the transaction had been completed he thanked me very politely for all the trouble I had taken.

"It has been a pleasure," I told him.

Then I turned to come away and found my way was blocked by a very tall man, in a grey overcoat, who obviously had been listening to the conversation. I looked up at his face . . . and my heart gave a wild leap!

It couldn't be Charles! It couldn't possibly . . . but it was . . . or was it? This man looked older than Charles and less full of vitality. Could I be mistaken? No, I couldn't be mistaken, for it was not only my eyes that recognised him, it was the feeling in my heart. It was . . . *it was Charles*!

All this happened in a moment — it happened in a split second — my lips were forming his name when he swung round and walked away.

I was so astounded by conflicting emotions, that I was stricken dumb; my heart was hammering madly, my feet seemed rooted to the ground.

Then, as I saw the tall figure disappearing, I suddenly came to my senses and dropped the book I was holding and ran after him. I pushed through the crowd at the Christmas card counter like a mad-woman and ran down the wide space between the displays of Fancy Goods. Ahead of me was the tall figure in the grey overcoat. I saw him turn to the right, where there was a tiled vestibule with lifts on each side. When I arrived, breathless, in the vestibule I caught sight of him entering one of the lifts and rushed forward. I was too late; the lift was full; the sliding gates were slammed in my face, the lift moved downwards and vanished . . . but again I had seen him, head and shoulders above the packed crowd of women and children, and for a moment he had looked straight at me! I was certain now, certain beyond any possibility of doubt, that it really was Charles for I saw that he had recognised me.

The next lift was filling up so I walked into it, confident that I should find Charles waiting for me on the ground floor. The lift went down and stopped; I was the first to get out, I stood looking this way — and that.

"Can I help you, miss?" asked a lift-man.

"I'm looking for a tall gentleman in a grey overcoat."

"That way," said the lift-man, pointing. "He asked me the way to the nearest exit; I said through the 'Wine and Cigars.'"

I turned and ran. I wasn't thinking of anything; I wasn't even wondering why he was here in London; there was only one idea in my head: *I must catch Charles*.

372

When I got to the Wine Department I paused for a few moments and gazed round . . . he wasn't here! I hurried to the exit, pushed my way through the revolving door and looked up and down the street. It was a side street and empty except for a lady and gentleman standing on the pavement and a taxi disappearing round the corner.

I said breathlessly, "Oh, please tell me! Did you see a tall man in a grey overcoat?"

"He took our taxi," replied the gentleman. "I mean the taxi that brought us here. He said he was in a hurry, so —"

"I've lost him!" I cried.

The lady and gentleman were gazing at me in astonishment but I was so frantic that I didn't care. "I've lost him!" I repeated. "Oh, what shall I do? He's a friend. I haven't seen him for years — he disappeared before the war. I saw him — so I ran after him — and now I've lost him! What am I to do?"

The Commissionaire had come out on to the pavement by this time. He said, "Oh well, you can't help it, miss. You did your best to catch him — it wasn't your fault that he got away — the right thing for you to do is to go straight up to the office and report it. I suppose you know what he took?"

"Know what he took?" I echoed stupidly.

"You've got it wrong," explained the gentleman. "It isn't a case of shop-lifting. This young lady recognised a friend whom she hadn't seen for years . . ."

"Never mind," said the lady, taking me by the arm. "It's too cold to stand here — and you're dreadfully upset — you must come and sit down quietly until you feel better."

We went back into the Wine Department and they brought me a chair. They stood and looked at me and talked. I was so stunned at having seen Charles — and lost him — that I had no idea what they were saying. I sat there like a stone image. Charles had been within my grasp — I could have touched him — but I had let him go! Charles was here, here in London! Why hadn't he got my address from Fairfield and come to see me?

I was roused from my bewilderment by the gentleman, who put a small glass into my hand. "Drink it," he said.

I drank it. The liquid was as hot as fire and almost choked me but it helped me to pull myself together.

"Thank you," I murmured. "It's very kind. I don't know why you should bother. It was just — just that I hadn't seen him for years — or heard of him. I didn't know what had — had happened to him. We're friends — that's why I tried to — to catch him."

"Well, you know he's all right anyhow," said the lady comfortingly.

It was true: I knew now that Charles was alive and well but I found little comfort in the knowledge. Charles had seen me — he had recognised me — but he had fled from me. What did it mean?

"Listen, Ben," said the lady, turning to her husband. "We must get a taxi and take her home. That's the best thing to do."

I told them that I was not free to go home until six o'clock.

"That will be all right," said the Commissionaire. "You're Miss Morris, aren't you? This is Mr. and Mrs. Ainger. I know them well. They often come to Barrington's. If they're willing to take you home —"

"Of course we shall take you home!" exclaimed Mrs. Ainger.

I objected, somewhat feebly, but Mrs. Ainger was one of those small but determined women who sweep all obstacles aside and insist upon getting their own way. Mr. Ainger was aware of this, of course; he pressed something into the Commissionaire's hand and told him to get Miss Morris's coat and to report at the office that Miss Morris was unwell and had been taken home by friends.

"It's very kind of you," I said. "If I got a taxi I could go by myself. Why should you bother?"

"You're dreadfully upset," replied Mrs. Ainger. "You aren't fit to go by yourself. If I let you go by yourself I shouldn't sleep a wink all night."

"Don't let's risk it," said Mr. Ainger, smiling. "We can easily see Miss Morris safely home."

"It's very kind of you," I repeated.

Presently the Commissionaire returned with my coat, a taxi was ordered and my new friends took me home.

CHAPTER
THIRTY-SEVEN

"But, my dear, it can't have been Charles," said Father.

He had said the same words over and over again, sitting beside me on the sofa and holding my hand.

"I've told you, Father. I've told you all that happened."

"I know, but you must have made a mistake."

"It was Charles. It was, really!"

"People sometimes resemble each other — not often, I admit, but there are such things as 'doubles' — and you saw him only for a moment in a crowd."

"I saw him twice!"

"But only for a moment."

"It wasn't only seeing — it was the feeling I had."

"You were upset," said Father. "It was natural that you should feel upset at the resemblance."

"It wasn't a 'resemblance'; it was Charles himself."

"You said he looked older, so perhaps —"

"It's natural that he should look older!"

"Listen, Sarah! You had been thinking about Charles. Then you looked up and thought you recognised him."

"I wasn't thinking about him; I was telling the Dane about the film projector."

"You often think about Charles, don't you?"

"Yes, but not when I'm busy. That's why it's so good for me to have the job at Barrington's."

"It was someone like Charles and you thought —"

"There's nobody like Charles in the world!" Suddenly I was shaken by sobs, horrible sobs that seemed to come from deep down in my body.

"There, there, darling," said Father, patting my back. "It's been a shock to you. Better soon!"

"You said that when I fell off the swing and broke my arm!" I cried hysterically.

"Did I? Well, perhaps I did. Your arm was very painful and I wanted to comfort you. It's a pity we have so few words in which to express our sympathy." He sighed and added, "If there were anything I could say or do that would be any comfort —"

"You are!" I exclaimed. "You're the greatest comfort! Oh, how lucky I am to have you! Go on talking to me."

"Sarah, if I'm to go on talking to you I must tell you what's in my mind. It's this, my dear; if Charles were alive he would have come back to you."

I said desperately, "Father, he isn't dead. I saw him!"

"You thought you saw him because he was in your mind. Couldn't you put him out of your mind? Couldn't you leave the past behind you and make a new life for yourself?"

"I know what you mean."

"Yes, you know what I mean. I've been hoping for it so much, my dear. Duncan is such a good fellow; he's kind-hearted and dependable and he loves you dearly."

"I know, but —"

"Sarah, you're wasting your life. You're fond of Duncan, aren't you? Why can't you leave the past behind and think of the future? I'm sure you and Duncan would be happy together."

"It wouldn't be right to marry Duncan."

"What do you mean?"

"I mean if Charles wanted me I would go to him . . . even if I were married to someone else."

"Sarah, what are you saying?"

"Don't you understand! *I belong to Charles.*"

"Charles won't come back."

"He *has* come back — I saw him to-day!"

"If it was Charles — which I very much doubt — why didn't he speak to you?"

"I don't know!" I cried. "I don't know! That's what's so frightful — *I don't know!*"

"I shall make some fresh tea," said Father, rising. "A cup of tea will do us good. Go and wash your face and brush your hair while I boil the kettle."

I did as I was told, and we had tea together, but my trouble was too deep, my anguish too real to be alleviated. I went to bed and lay there, tossing and turning restlessly, trying to find some reasonable explanation for what had happened that afternoon . . .

Charles had seen me; he had recognised me but instead of speaking to me he had turned away . . . and, now that I had time to think, I realised that his extraordinary behaviour was not just a sudden impulse. Charles was here in London but he had made no attempt to get in touch with me. He had only to go to

Fairfield — everyone there knew our address! He had only to write me a letter — our letters were still being forwarded.

When I thought of all this I realised that it was absolutely hopeless and my bewilderment gave way to despair. I must face the fact that it was all over between Charles and me.

I looked at the signet ring on my finger . . . I should have to take it off! But it had been there so long that I couldn't bear to part with it. Later, perhaps, when I got used to the feeling that we didn't belong to each other any more, I would take it off and put it away . . . but not yet. Charles had loved me dearly — I knew that — so the past still belonged to me and was full of happy memories. Perhaps some day I would be able to stop loving Charles but he was so much a part of my being that it didn't seem possible . . .

There was no sleep for me that night; the hours passed slowly and miserably. When at last the morning came, and I tried to get up, I felt so ill, so sick and giddy, that I could scarcely stand on my feet — and I couldn't stop shaking — so I was obliged to crawl back to bed.

Father rang up Barrington's and explained that I was ill. Duncan was very sympathetic, he said he wasn't surprised, I had been doing far too much and had been looking very tired; I must take my holiday now, instead of later, and there was no need for me to come back until I was perfectly fit. Cécile knew a girl who could come and help her.

"So that's all right, isn't it?" said Father, looking at me anxiously. "You can go to Craignethan. It always does you good to go to Craignethan, doesn't it?"

I was too tired to argue with him — and it didn't seem to matter what happened to me — so it was settled that I was to go to Craignethan when I was well enough to travel.

Pam came to see me. She sat down beside my bed and took my hand. "Do you want to talk or shall we just sit here quietly?" she asked.

"I saw him, Pam! Father says it couldn't have been Charles but it was — really — and he saw me — so it's all over. I've thought — and thought — but there's only one possible explanation."

She looked at me doubtfully.

"He has met someone else," I said in a low voice. "He has met someone — he likes — better. Perhaps he's married."

"Yes," said Pam sadly. "That's what I thought when your father told me."

"There's no other explanation, is there?"

"I can't think of any."

"It's all over, Pam. I've got to face it."

She squeezed my hand. "Yes, darling, I'm afraid so. It will be terribly hard to bear, but gradually it will become easier, gradually you will be able to think of him —"

"I shall always love Charles!" I burst out defiantly. My other comforters had both tried to persuade me that I must stop loving Charles. (Father had said, "Forget him, Sarah. Put him out of your mind." Willy had raved against him furiously . . . which was even harder to bear.)

Pam's reaction was different. "Yes, that's the best way," said Pam, nodding. "Go on loving Charles and feeling sorry for him."

"Feeling sorry for him?" I echoed in surprise.

"He has lost his way," she explained. "Poor Charles has taken the wrong turning and missed the road to happiness. I'm terribly sorry for Charles."

Her fear was that I might feel resentful. She didn't say it in so many words but I knew Pam so well that words were unnecessary. It was one of Pam's tenets that resentment and jealousy are venomous snakes, poisonous to the heart and mind and spirit.

"It's all right," I said, trying to smile. "There are no snakes in my heart. I love Charles too much to be angry with him."

We talked some more — and I felt comforted.

Presently I said, "Now tell me about Gil: have you any news?"

"I'll tell you about Gil another day."

"No, now!" I exclaimed. "Please tell me! I can see you've had good news."

She was reluctant to speak of Gil but when I pressed her she told me that she had just received a short letter from him saying that, as there was no more need for the mountain road to freedom, he and "Percy" had shut up shop and were coming home together. Gil would have to report to the Admiralty and explain what he had been doing but he didn't anticipate serious trouble.

"Serious trouble?"

"Technically Gil is a deserter."

"But, Pam —"

"It will be all right," said Pam. "I'm not worrying." Then she kissed me and added, "We've talked enough. Go to Craignethan soon, darling. That's the best thing for you."

I realised that Pam was right: it would be better to get up and pack my suitcase and go to Craignethan, rather than lie in bed feeling miserable, so I made the effort. Father took me to the station and put me into the train.

CHAPTER
THIRTY-EIGHT

No sooner had the train begun to move than I regretted my decision to leave home. There was Father, standing on the platform waving to me — his figure receding farther into the distance every moment! Pam was in London, too — and Pam was the only person who understood! I felt quite frantic. Why, oh why had I consented to go to Craignethan? All I wanted was to hide myself away, to lie in bed in a darkened room. I wasn't fit to speak to people — not even to the grans! I must get out at the first stop and go straight back to London.

But that was nonsense, of course! The grans were expecting me and would be disappointed if I didn't arrive.

"You're just being silly," I told myself firmly. "You, who have always prided yourself on your sanity and common sense, are behaving like a hysterical girl. I'm ashamed of you, Sarah Morris."

The journey seemed very long. My head ached, as it always did in the train, I couldn't read and it tired my eyes to look out of the window. I sat huddled in my corner and bore it as best I could. The hours passed slowly . . . it was not until I had changed into the local train and I saw the bare hills, tawny in their winter coats, and smelt the cold clean air of the uplands that the cloud on my spirits lifted. I began to come alive and to look forward to Craignethan and the dear grans.

I had asked Father not to tell them what had happened to me, but just to say I was tired and was having my holiday sooner than I had expected; I couldn't have borne their sympathy and it would be easier for me to recover my balance if I had to pretend to be cheerful.

As usual Grandpapa met me at Ryddelton Station and welcomed me warmly. He was getting old now, his face was thinner and more lined, but his shoulders were as straight as ever and there was still a merry twinkle in his blue eyes.

"Have you been ill, Sarah?" he asked, looking at me in sudden anxiety.

"Just . . . not very well," I replied.

"Did you have lunch in the train?"

"I wasn't hungry."

"Well, the sooner we get some food inside you the better," he declared, taking my arm and leading me to the car which was waiting in the yard . . . and suddenly I remembered my first visit to Craignethan; the first time I had seen Grandpapa; the first time I had felt that kind old hand gripping my arm! I was a child again and my eyes were blurred with foolish tears.

As we drove along I asked for Grandmama.

"She's older, Sarah," he replied sadly. "We're both getting old, you know . . . and we miss Dorrie. We used to look forward to her September visits. But we felt a lot better when we heard you were coming. I hope this is not one of your flying visits, it would be delightful if you could stay over Christmas."

I said I could. Duncan had told Father that I must have "a proper holiday" and not return to work until I was perfectly fit . . . and as a matter of fact I felt that I was needed at Craignethan. I had come when I could but it had been impossible for me to leave home except for an occasional week-end. Now, however, with Cécile and her friend to help me at Barrington's and Mrs. Raggett coming daily to the flat, I must make a point of visiting Craignethan in September, as Mother had done.

"You mustn't let it be a burden," said Grandpapa hastily. "We don't want that, you know. We just want you to come when you need a rest and a little peace and quiet."

It was always quiet at Craignethan, but this year, after the hurly burly of Barrington's Christmas rush, it seemed more quiet than ever. When I went outside the house — and stood and listened — I felt as if I could hear the silence. Although it was now the middle of December there had been no frost and the roses in the garden were still in bloom; in the late evenings the moon rose from behind the hills like a huge luminous ball.

At first I only wanted to rest and sleep and walk round the garden with Grandpapa, but soon the fresh air and good food helped me to recover and I was eager to climb the hills. My favourite walk was up the steep path by the side of the burn to the top of Grey Ghyll and home by the old Drove Road.

Grandpapa was horrified at this idea. "You can't go alone," he said firmly. "If I were ten years younger — or maybe twenty — I'd come with you like a shot, but my legs are not as spry as they used to be."

I said no more. He had always been anxious about people walking alone on the hills and I didn't want to worry him.

"I'm sorry, Sarah," he added. "But you know my views, don't you? A twisted ankle could lead to serious trouble. If you could find somebody to go with you . . ."

"It doesn't matter," I told him, taking his arm. "We'll just walk round the garden together. I want to see the stand of conifers you've planted."

In these peaceful surroundings, familiar since childhood, it was difficult to believe that a war was raging, guns were thundering and men were being killed every moment. Only the morning papers and the nine o'clock news kept us in touch with realities. For months past we had been hearing of victories and advances — and the end had seemed in sight — but now the aspect had become less favourable: Hitler had called up boys of sixteen and was said to be preparing for a last desperate throw.

"It's now or never," said Grandpapa, who had a large map pinned up on the wall of his study and followed the course of events from day to day. "If Hitler waits until spring for his offensive the Americans will have built up their reserves. Yes, it's now or never — and Hitler knows it."

This could only mean there would be hard fighting and I thought of Lewis, of course. I wondered how many women were thinking of one particular man who would be in mortal danger.

"You often have letters from Lewis, don't you?" asked Grandmama; her thoughts had been moving in the same direction.

I nodded. "Yes, but I haven't heard from him for nearly a fortnight. He was in Brussels for a couple of days' leave and engaged a room with a private bathroom. He said he had had four baths already and intended to have another before he went to bed."

Grandpapa laughed, and said he hoped Lewis had bought himself a huge cake of scented soap, so as to do the thing properly, but Grandmama sighed and said, "Poor Lewis!"

The next morning when I came down to breakfast there was a letter from Lewis on the table; it had been forwarded to me by Mrs. Raggett. I seized it eagerly and tore it open . . . and saw that it was from a military hospital near Salisbury! For a moment or two I gazed at it in dismay but my fears were allayed when I realised that, although it was written in pencil, it had been written by Lewis himself in his own characteristic hand:

"Dear Sarah,
    Don't get in a flap. Father may or may not have got the telegram to say I've been wounded but anyhow there's no need to worry unduly. It

387

happened in a village which we thought had been cleared of Jerries, but not so! A few had remained in hiding and gave some trouble before we managed to round them up. Poor little Wilson was killed, Barnes was badly wounded and I was shot in the arm — the left, of course, or you wouldn't be getting this untidy scrawl. The bone was fractured and it was exceedingly painful. When I came to, and saw what it looked like, I thought it was good-bye to my arm. The chap in the Field Dressing Station was of the same opinion. However it seems we were both wrong. The surgeon here, John Smith by name, operated and patched it up and has made it wonderfully comfortable. He assures me that in time it will be almost as good as new ... and I'm being dosed with a marvellous new drug called penicillin which prevents wounds from going septic. It's annoying that I've been sent to Salisbury (if I were nearer London you and Father could pop in and see me), but I'm in a pleasant ward with two other fellows and the hospital is very well run: the sisters are capable and there are several V.A.D.'s who are easy on the eye — so I can't complain. Of course it's a bit sickening to be put out of action at this stage of the proceedings — I'm sorry I shan't be there to see the end of the show and the downfall of Herr Adolf Hitler — but it can't be helped. At any rate I shall be able to strip my sleeve and show my scars and say, 'These wounds I had on Crispin's

Day' like the old bore who feasted his neighbours yearly on the vigil of Agincourt.

Will write soon again — meanwhile don't worry — and lots of letters, *please*!

Love from Lewis"

As I was reading the letter for the second time Grandpapa came in. "A letter from Lewis?" he asked.

"Yes, he's been wounded." I gave Grandpapa the letter and ran to answer the telephone. The bell was ringing and I was sure it was Father.

I was right. Father had just received the telegram saying that Lewis had been seriously wounded; he would scarcely believe me when I told him that I had got a very cheerful letter written by Lewis himself.

"It says 'seriously wounded,'" repeated Father.

"Yes, but it isn't as bad as they thought. Fortunately there's a very good surgeon in that hospital; he has patched up the arm and assures Lewis that it will be 'almost as good as new.' It will take time, of course, but that's all to the good."

"All to the good?"

"Lewis is out of it, Father! He won't be in the horrible fighting when Hitler makes his 'last desperate throw.' We ought to be thankful he's safe."

"Yes, of course . . . if he isn't seriously ill."

"I'm sure he isn't," I said earnestly. "His letter is just like Lewis. It's a jokey letter. Why don't you go to Salisbury and see him? That would ease your mind."

"I'll go to-day," said Father more cheerfully.

389

Meanwhile the grans had read Lewis's letter: Grandpapa said that Lewis seemed so cheerful that his condition couldn't be serious; Grandmama said she hoped his wound was serious enough to keep him in hospital until the war was over.

I nodded and agreed.

"Just like women!" exclaimed Grandpapa. "Lewis is very disappointed; he wants to see the end of the show."

"Of course Sarah and I are 'like women,'" retorted Grandmama with asperity. "We *are* women, aren't we? Women don't want their sons and brothers and grandsons to be killed. If women had the ordering of affairs there would be no wars. Women know that wars are not only wicked, they're foolish. Nobody wins."

"Nobody wins? What on earth do you mean, Jane?" asked Grandpapa, looking at her in amazement.

"There's only one thing worse than losing a war — and that's winning it. I don't remember who said that, or words to that effect, but he knew what he was talking about."

"I suppose you think it better to sit on the fence?"

"There would be no fence to sit on if women had a say in the matter. I don't suppose German women like wars any more than we do."

"So we're to have petticoat government?"

"You might do worse . . . but it would have to be petticoat government for every nation under the sun." She smiled and added, "There might be other troubles, of course, but there wouldn't be any wars."

"What about the Amazons?" asked Grandpapa.

Grandmama hesitated, so I flew to the rescue.

"Did the Amazons wear petticoats, Grandpapa?"

The grans both laughed and the discussion ended with Grandpapa going off to his study to find a book about the Amazons, in which he hoped to discover details of their attire.

"I don't know why it's so annoying to be told you're like a woman," said Grandmama thoughtfully.

The argument hadn't been serious, but there was always something interesting in arguments between the grans. I thought of this as I sat down to write to Lewis; it would amuse him to hear about the discussion.

Immediately after lunch I set off to walk to Ryddelton; it was a pleasant walk through country lanes (perfectly safe in Grandpapa's estimation) and I wanted to post my letter and buy some things for Lewis. Grandmama suggested he might like handkerchiefs, which seemed a good idea, and I could send him sweets and a bottle of Eau-de-Cologne.

When I had done my shopping it was still quite early so I decided to call on Minnie Dell. I always went to see her when I was staying at Craignethan.

Minnie and her youngest sister were sharing a little house in the town; both were good needlewomen and, beginning in a small way by altering clothes for their friends, they had gradually built up quite a lucrative little business. As usual I was warmly welcomed and invited into the comfortable parlour.

"Our work is war work, Miss Sarah," said Minnie earnestly. "Really, it is. You see people haven't enough coupons to buy new clothes and it's good for their morale to look nice. Maggie and I have got more work than we can cope with; you'd be surprised what we can do with old rags."

Maggie was very like Minnie, but twice the size! She hadn't had "the fever" when she was eight years old.

I was regaled with tea and a slice of Minnie's gingerbread cake — which was as delicious as ever. Minnie wanted to know all about the family and was very distressed to hear that Lewis had been wounded. The news that Lottie had a baby was received with delight.

"I'd like fine to see her," declared Minnie. "Would there be any chance of Miss Lottie bringing the wee girl to Craignethan?"

I thought it unlikely but I promised to tell "Miss Lottie" that Minnie had been asking for her and was anxious to see her baby.

"And tell Mr. Willy that I've still got his totem," added Minnie, pointing to the hideous little figure which stood in the place of honour in the middle of the chimney-piece.

"And she uses his stool every day," put in Maggie, smiling. "The wee stool is terribly important. It got mislaid in the spring cleaning and Minnie was that miserable — you wouldn't believe it! She could neether sew nor take her meals without the wee stool beneath her feet."

"I'd put it away in the back of the press for safe keeping," explained Minnie, chuckling.

"Yes, she'd done it hersel' but it was me that got the blame," declared Maggie.

They both laughed. It was delightful to see them so happy together and so prosperous in their own small way; I knew Father would be glad to hear I had been to see Minnie and that all was well with her.

The grans were always a little apprehensive when I was out by myself so I had made a habit of calling to them the moment I got inside the front door. To-day I called out as usual: "Hallo, here I am! I went to see Minnie, that's why I'm a little late!"

Immediately the drawing-room door opened and Grandpapa came out. He took my arm and led me into his study.

"What's the matter?" I exclaimed in alarm.

"I've something to tell you."

"Something has happened?"

"Something pleasant," said Grandpapa cheerfully. "A friend of yours has arrived. He got here soon after you had gone. I don't mind telling you Grandmama has fallen in love with him."

"Who is it?"

"A friend of yours, Sarah."

It occurred to me that it might be Duncan. "What a nuisance!" I exclaimed. "I'm enjoying a peaceful holiday; I don't want to see anyone."

"He has come a long way to see you."

"Grandpapa, is it one of your jokes?"

"No, it's not 'one of my jokes,'" he replied. "I don't want to keep you guessing, Sarah; I'm just trying to prepare you for a big surprise."

I gazed at him in astonishment; I was still uncertain whether or not it was "one of his jokes."

"It's Charles Reeder."

"Charles?"

"Yes."

"It can't be Charles! It can't . . . possibly . . ."

"You had better sit down," said Grandpapa, seizing my arm and guiding me to a chair.

My knees gave way and I sank into it in a heap.

"Sarah, my dear!" exclaimed Grandpapa, looking at me anxiously.

"It's all right," I murmured. "I just — just can't believe it. Do you really — mean he's here — at Craignethan? How did he — get here?"

"He came in his car. He has been looking for you."

"Looking for me? That's nonsense! He could have got my address at Fairfield. Besides . . ."

Grandpapa sat down and took my hand. "I don't know the ins and outs of it, Sarah. The poor fellow was exhausted when he arrived. He wanted to know whether you were alive or dead. He was absolutely all out — and in no condition to give an account of himself. However the news that you were actually here at Craignethan, alive and well, worked wonders, and a tot of whisky and a solid meal completed the cure. Just sit there quietly and I'll go and get him."

"Wait a minute, Grandpapa!" I exclaimed, clinging to his hand.

"No hurry, my dear! Take your time. Charles says he can stay here for a few days if you want him. He's not sure if you'll want him to stay."

"What did he mean?"

"I don't know — exactly. He said there had been a misunderstanding. We didn't like to question him about it."

"Grandpapa, I don't understand! Why did he come here . . . if he didn't know I was here?"

"He thought we would know what had happened to you."

The whole thing was a complete mystery to me and was becoming more mysterious every minute. I was in a fog of bewilderment.

For a few minutes we sat in silence; then I took out my powder-compact and examined myself in the little mirror. My face had a greenish tinge and looked very queer . . . but it improved when I gave my cheeks a good hard rub and powdered my nose.

Grandpapa chuckled. "I can see you're feeling better; I'll go and fetch him."

CHAPTER
THIRTY-NINE

Charles paused in the doorway and looked at me doubtfully. I couldn't speak but I held out my arms so he came and knelt beside me and took my hand.

"Oh, Sarah!" he said softly. "There's such a lot to explain. I've been the most awful fool that ever was! I don't suppose you'll ever forgive me."

"Of course I'll forgive you," I whispered. It didn't matter what he had done . . . I had got him back safely.

He put his arms round me and for a little while we were silent. I was remembering the last time he had held me like this — it was so long ago that it seemed as if it had happened in another life.

"Listen, darling," said Charles at last. "I've been a fool — but I've paid dearly for my foolishness. When I saw the whole place in ruins I nearly went mad."

"What do you mean?" I exclaimed. "What place was in ruins? Where have you been? Why didn't you get my address at Fairfield and come and see me?"

He sighed. "Yes, I'll tell you everything — but it's all such a muddle that I don't know how to begin."

"Tell me this, Charles: did you see me that day at Barrington's?"

"Yes."

"You ran away from me!"

"Yes, I ran away. I was angry with you."

"Angry with me?" I asked in amazement.

"It's a long story, Sarah. I had better tell it to you from the beginning."

"Wait!" I cried. "Tell me first why you were angry."

Charles had got up and was sitting on the edge of the big solid table which Grandpapa used for writing his letters.

"Very well," said Charles, nodding. "There's a lot to tell you (about all that has happened to me since that cold misty morning when I said good-bye to you at Fairfield) but I'll begin at the end of the story, when Colonel Robert Loudon and I managed to escape from an internment camp near Hamburg and, after various adventures, arrived in London. The first thing —"

"Internment camp!" I exclaimed. "Is that where you've been all this time?"

"Most of the time."

"Oh, poor Charles! How dreadful!"

"That wasn't the worst of it," he said. "The worst of it was solitary confinement in a Berlin prison . . . but you can hear about that later. You want to know the end of the story, don't you?"

I nodded. I was too upset to speak.

"Well, the first thing I did when I got to London was to go to Fairfield, of course. I had been thinking about you for years — dreaming of you — picturing you at the old house, so it was a shock to find strangers there. However, Mrs. Yorke was very kind; she asked me to come in and she gave me a cup of tea. It was sad to see

397

the drawing-room — so different from what I remembered! But perhaps it would have been worse if it had looked the same with strangers living in it. Yes, I believe that would have been worse," said Charles thoughtfully.

After a moment's pause he continued, "Mr. and Mrs. Yorke were old. He was a retired clergyman and had come to St. Mary's temporarily to fill a gap. The Yorkes hadn't been there very long and were finding it rather too much for them; they were looking forward to going back to their own quiet home. Mrs. Yorke told me all this — and more — she was very chatty. She told me that Mr. Morris had gone to London at the beginning of the war; I asked if his daughter were with him. 'Oh no!' replied Mrs. Yorke. 'Mr. Morris's daughter married Sir Clive Hudson. They have a big place called Brailsford Manor about five miles from here . . . and there's a baby girl.'

" 'Are you sure?' I exclaimed. 'Yes, of course,' replied Mrs. Yorke in surprise. 'I know Lady Hudson quite well; I often see her in the village and she's always very friendly and pleasant. Some people say she behaved rather badly: she was engaged to be married to another man and broke it off when he went abroad . . . but I don't believe everything I hear.'

"She went on talking but I was too stunned by the news to listen. My one idea was to get away as quickly as I could. As we were saying good-bye she asked if I would like Mr. Morris's address — she could find it for me if I would wait — but I replied that it didn't matter and came away."

I had been listening to all this in silence, too astonished to speak, but now I exclaimed, "Charles! How could you have made such a mistake? You might have known it was Lottie!"

"I never saw Lottie."

"But you knew about her, didn't you?"

"I thought she was a child, much younger than you and your brothers (Mrs. Morris had shown me a little picture of her and had said she was 'the baby'), but to tell you the truth I never thought of her at all; to me 'Mr. Morris's daughter' meant you — and nobody else. Oh, I was a fool! It was crazy not to verify Mrs. Yorke's story, but for years and years I had been thinking of you as my very own. I had gone to Fairfield expecting to find you waiting for me. It was unreasonable — I can see that now — but imprisonment behind barbed wire does something queer to an active man. That's my only excuse."

It seemed to me an adequate excuse. "Oh, poor Charles!" I whispered.

"I was absolutely shattered," continued Charles. "I went back to Brown's Hotel where I had taken a room. I was wretched and bitter, full of resentment, but I was too proud to give in. I made up my mind to forget you — as you had forgotten me — but it wasn't easy. I had no friends in London; Bob Loudon had gone home on leave to see his family. I was sleeping badly so I went out at night and walked about the streets. One night I was nearly done for by a flying bomb; the blast bowled me over and when I came to my senses I saw that several houses had been completely wrecked. I helped the firemen to dig people out of the ruins; they were glad of another pair of hands. Some of the inhabitants had been killed but we found two women in the cellar and got them out; we found a man pinned down by a beam of wood and released him.

"Sarah, I was astonished! I had never imagined such magnificent courage and fortitude as was shown by those people, who had lost their homes and all their possessions and had barely escaped with their lives. Their behaviour made me ashamed of myself. I decided to face my trouble with the same courage and to make plans for the future; I would go to Canada when the war was over and buy a farm; I would start a new life in a new country . . ."

Charles hesitated for a few moments and then continued in a low voice. "It's very difficult to tell you what happened to me when I saw you at Barrington's. I had gone into the store to buy something — I can't remember what it was — and as I was walking through the Kodak Department I heard someone speaking German. I looked round — *and saw you!* At first I couldn't believe my eyes; I stood and gazed at you and listened to your voice. I was still gazing at you when you turned and looked up into my face . . .

"Then I went completely mad," declared Charles. "My first impulse was to seize you in my arms — but then, in a flash, I remembered that you were married! I wheeled and strode away as fast as I could, pushing through the crowd of people roughly — rudely — I didn't care what they thought of me! As I was going down in the lift I saw you again, but my anger had flared up and my one idea was to escape from you. I found a taxi at the exit . . . the man was just about to drive away but I wrenched the door open and jumped in. I went to the hotel and shut myself up in my room and walked up and down for hours — like a maniac! Seeing you like that — so unexpectedly — had stirred up my deepest feelings. I realised all I had lost! I realised that in spite of my pride, in spite of my resolutions to forget you and remake my life, I still loved you with every fibre of my being . . . and you were married to another man and had a child."

"Oh, Charles, you might have known —"

"No, wait!" he exclaimed. "Now that I've started I want to go on and tell you everything. It isn't easy, Sarah."

I nodded . . . and made up my mind not to interrupt him again.

"A week passed," he continued. "Or perhaps it was more — I don't know how long. Then one evening Bob Loudon rang me up from his club in London and I took the call in my room. He was in tremendously good form, bubbling over with happiness. He had been home and had seen his wife and children: they were all well — his two small sons had grown into sturdy little ruffians — everything was fine! He explained that he was in London for a few days on business and his brother was having some friends to dinner that night and wanted me to come. I refused. 'Oh, come on!' said Bob. 'We're having a binge and we want you to join us. I've told them about our escape and our adventures and they're all keen to see you — '

"I interrupted him and said ungraciously that I had no wish to see him or his friends. It was horrible of me," said Charles sadly. "It was thoroughly nasty of me . . . but it just seemed the last straw that Bob should be so full of joy when I was utterly miserable. I lay down on my bed in the dark and wrestled with a devil.

"Presently I heard a knock on my door. It was Bob. He came in and switched on the light. He said, 'You sounded a bit queer so I thought I'd better come and have a look at you. What on earth's the matter with you, Charles?'

"I told him. It was easy to tell him because he knew all about you (I had talked about you when we were in the internment camp together — and had listened to him talking about his wife). I told him that I had been to Fairfield and had discovered that you were married and had a child; I told him about seeing you at Barrington's.

"Bob listened in silence until I had finished and then said, 'But, look here, old boy! If she's married to Sir Clive Hudson she can't possibly be working in a shop. You said she was selling a film projector, didn't you?' 'Yes, she was telling the customer how it worked.' 'Well, then, *have some sense!*' Bob exclaimed. 'Would Lady Hudson be likely to take a job in a shop? Her husband is practically a millionaire! It can't have been Sarah.' 'It was Sarah,' I told him.

" 'Then Sarah can't be Lady Hudson,' said Bob with conviction.

" 'Listen, Bob,' I said. 'Mrs. Yorke told me that Sarah is married to Sir Clive Hudson and has a child. That's perfectly clear, isn't it? There can't be any mistake about *that*.'

"Bob shook his head. 'There's some mistake; it doesn't fit. Why on earth haven't you made inquiries instead of swallowing the story hook, line and sinker? It's that Austrian pride of yours, Charles. Put your pride in your pocket and clear up the matter.'

"'It's perfectly clear,' I told him. 'Mrs. Yorke said — '

"'It's not clear,' declared Bob. 'We're groping about in a dense fog — that's what's happening. You had better come downstairs and have dinner with me; perhaps a good solid meal and a bottle of claret will bring you to your senses.'

"At first I refused. I pointed out that Bob was having dinner with his friends. Bob smiled and replied, 'If you think I'm going to walk off and leave you moping in the dark you can think again. You didn't walk off and leave me lying in the mud when I took a toss over that piece of barbed wire, did you?'

"Bob is grand," declared Charles. "He's the best pal a man ever had. He insisted on ringing up his friends; he told them he was 'unavoidably delayed' and they were to go on without him. Then he and I had dinner together at Brown's and shared a bottle of claret. We talked a lot more. Eventually he persuaded me to let him ring up Brailsford Manor and make some tactful inquiries. He promised not to mention my name.

"I waited for him in the lounge. He was away a long time — at least it seemed a long time to me — then at last he returned, smiling cheerfully. 'You're all sorts of an idiot, Charles,' he said. 'I got on to Brailsford and spoke to Sir Clive Hudson; he was a bit sticky at first — wanted to know my business — but I told him my name and made up a little story for him. Sir Clive informed me that his wife is Mr. Morris's younger daughter and her name is Lottie.'

"'What!' I cried. 'It can't be true! Lottie is a child.'

"'Children grow up, don't they?' said Bob. He added, 'Anyway, Sir Clive told me himself that his wife's name is Lottie so the information is straight from the horse's mouth. Mr. Morris and Sarah are living in a flat in London. I asked permission to speak to Lady Hudson but he said she had gone to a party. Then I asked if he would be good enough to give me Mr. Morris's address. He said, rather irritably, that he didn't know the address, but I was very persistent so at last he agreed to go and look in his wife's desk for her address book. I waited and presently he came back with the book and read out the address. Here it is,' said Bob. 'I've written it down for you, and if you take my advice you'll go round to the place first thing in the morning.'

"'I'll go to-night!' I cried, leaping to my feet.

"'You can't go to-night,' said Bob, smiling. 'It's after eleven o'clock; Sarah is having her beauty sleep. Off you go to bed like a sensible fellow and have a good rest. You can see her to-morrow morning.'

"I went to bed but I couldn't rest. First I raged at myself for my foolishness (Bob had been right in calling me 'all sorts of an idiot'), then I thought of you! I got up and walked about the room, thinking of you, wondering what you could be thinking of me. Now that

I was sane I saw how crazy I had been. I saw myself as a miserable wretch, not fit to tie your shoe! Would you ever forgive me for the way I had behaved?

"I thought the morning would never come. At six o'clock I had a bath, by half past six I was in the street. It was too early to call on you but at least I could see where you lived. There were no taxis about at that hour, so I walked all the way to Picton Mansions. When I got there I saw that the whole block of buildings was in ruins."

"Oh, Charles, it was the wrong address! That was where we lived before we moved to Bolingbroke Square! Sir Clive must have found an old address book."

"Yes, I suppose so," agreed Charles. "I suppose that's what must have happened . . . but, of course, that never occurred to me. I thought you were buried in the ruins. I was sure you were dead. I was all the more frantic because I had seen those other buildings utterly destroyed in a moment and had helped to dig the inhabitants out of the debris . . . what had happened to them had happened to you! I spoke to several people, I spoke to a policeman, but none of them knew when the bomb had fallen, none of them knew whether anyone had been saved. I became desperate; I didn't know what to do; I didn't know how to find out what had happened. Then, suddenly, I remembered that your grandparents lived in Scotland. You had talked about 'the grans'; you had shown me their letters; we had promised to go to Craignethan and visit them on our way back from Skye . . . the grans would know whether you were dead or alive!

"I suppose I could have phoned to them . . . I never thought of it! I was too stunned by the disaster to think reasonably. I went straight to the garage and got my car. There was no petrol in the tank, and I had no coupons, but I gave the man a handful of money and told him to fill it up; I told him I was going to Scotland. He gazed at me in surprise (I suppose I looked a bit queer) but he filled the tank and gave me a couple of extra gallons without saying a word.

"When I set off up the Great North Road I scarcely knew what I was doing — except that I was going to 'Craignethan House, near Ryddelton.' I drove like a madman until I smashed into a lorry and stove in a mudguard. That sobered me. After that I was more careful . . . but all the time I kept on thinking, thinking about you and blaming myself for my madness. It was my horrible pride that had caused all the trouble! If I had had any sense I'd have taken steps to find you. I could have rung up Brailsford myself at the very beginning and discovered the mistake.

"Well, there you are," said Charles with a deep sigh. "Now you know the whole thing; you know what a first-class fool I am. You said you would forgive me but perhaps you've changed your mind."

"Oh, darling! Of course I haven't changed your mind! Oh, poor Charles, what a dreadful time you've had!"

He came to me and hid his face against me. "It isn't true," he said softly. "It can't be true! Oh, darling Sarah, am I dreaming again? I used to dream like this in the internment camp . . . and then I woke up and you weren't there."

I took his hand and held it tightly.

"Sarah, am I still the only man in the world — in spite of my foolishness?"

"Yes."

"Will you marry me?"

"Yes."

"I don't deserve it."

"Look, Charles!" I said, showing him his ring. "Do you remember when you gave it to me?"

He raised his head and smiled. "Do I remember? I offered you diamonds, but you scorned diamonds. You seized my hand and tried to drag my signet ring off my finger!"

"I wanted it because it was part of you. I had seen it on your finger the first time we met! Oh, how glad I am that I made you give it to me! It has been such a comfort to me, Charles."

He slid the ring up and down my finger. "It's rather loose; the plain gold band will have to be a size smaller."

Then he picked me up and carried me to the sofa near the fire and we sat there with his arm round my waist and my head against his shoulder. We sat there without speaking; it was a joy to be together and at peace.

The winter twilight had faded and the room was dark except for the glow of the fire and the flicker of the little flames which were licking round the apple-logs in

407

the old-fashioned fireplace. Presently the logs began to crumble into grey ashes.

"We mustn't let it go out," I said at last.

Charles went down on his knees and mended the fire carefully with small dry sticks and larger pieces of wood.

"That's lovely," I said. "I'm glad my future husband is good with fires."

"It's a useful accomplishment," he agreed, sitting back and resting his head against my knee.

He was tired. I knew he must be exhausted, for he hadn't slept last night and he had driven all the way from London "like a madman," so I let him rest like that and didn't speak. The head leaning against my knee was still dark red and the hair was thick and soft but there were quite a lot of white hairs to be seen amongst the dark ones.

I think Charles was almost asleep when there was a gentle knock on the door and Grandpapa looked in. "Am I disturbing your meditations?" he asked in a hushed voice. "I've been sent to tell you that the fatted calf has been killed — and roasted — but I don't suppose you're interested in food."

CHAPTER
FORTY

It was a happy meal. The fatted calf proved to be three plump ducklings and Grandpapa produced a bottle of champagne.

"It's to celebrate a happy occasion," he explained. "Grandmama and I have been married for exactly forty-eight years, seven months, and three days, so I thought a little celebration would be the thing."

Grandmama was smiling. She held up her glass and said, "Happy years and many, many of them, darling children."

"Hear, hear!" exclaimed Grandpapa.

Charles rose and bowed gravely. "Thank you, Colonel and Mrs. Maitland. Sarah has promised to marry me. She has always been the most important person in the world to me. This is the happiest moment of my life."

"It's a very fine thing to be engaged to be married," declared Grandpapa. "I remember when I was engaged I thought it was the happiest moment of my life . . . but there's a better kind of happiness which comes later and grows with every passing year. You'll realise what I mean when you've been married for forty-eight years, seven months and three days."

"You're very kind," said Charles.

The ducks were followed by a trifle pudding, topped with thick cream — then we had apples and pears and walnuts from Craignethan garden.

Charles cracked the walnuts in his hand, explaining that it was a trick he had learned when he was a boy and used to ride about his father's estates in Austria. "There were lots of walnut trees," said Charles. "But I never remembered to take nut-crackers in my pocket. An old man came along one day when I was breaking the shells with a stone; he showed me the way to do it. Look, it's quite easy!"

"Show me!" exclaimed Grandpapa.

Charles showed him . . . and he was so delighted with the trick that he went on cracking walnuts until there were none left.

We all laughed and teased him about his new accomplishment.

Then we went into the drawing-room for coffee and, by this time, the slightly hysterical mood had given place to comfortable friendly feelings.

The grans asked when we were going to be married.

"Soon, I hope," replied Charles. "I've applied to become a naturalised British subject and at the same time I intend to change my name by deed poll. My idea is to drop the last letter of my name; this would be easy to do and would save a lot of trouble. What do you think, Sarah?"

I nodded. "You would be Charles Reede. It's a very good plan."

"It's a good old English name," agreed Grandpapa.

410

"I must get that done before we're married. Then everything will be plain sailing."

"Charles, what happened before?" I asked.

"You mean what happened to my application for naturalisation? I had the interview, as you know, but when I disappeared and couldn't be found the file containing my papers was shelved. Now, however, Robert Loudon has the matter in hand and, as he's a live wire, it shouldn't take long to —"

"Bob Loudon!" exclaimed Grandpapa. "But he's a prisoner of war in Germany!"

"He was with me in an internment camp near Hamburg. We escaped together."

"You escaped together? Do you mean Bob is home?"

"Yes, safely home and in very good form."

"That's splendid news!"

"It's splendid," agreed Grandmama, smiling in delight. "How lovely for Elspeth and the children! I must ring her up and tell her how pleased we are. Poor Elspeth has been so worried about him."

"Are those the Loudons that Mother used to know?" I asked.

Grandmama nodded. "Yes, your mother knew them well; they live about three miles from here. Bob's parents were old; they died some time ago, so now Blacklock House belongs to Bob."

"Only three miles from here!" exclaimed Charles in surprise. "I knew Bob lived in this part of the country, he told me a lot about Blacklock House, but I didn't realise it was so near Craignethan."

411

"You said that Bob escaped with you, Charles?" asked Grandpapa, who had been waiting impatiently for a chance to slip into the conversation. "It would be very interesting to hear about your adventures."

Charles hesitated. I could see he was unwilling to talk about his escape (he had promised to tell me the whole story later) so I said rather quickly, "I think Charles is tired — he has driven all the way from London — we'll hear about his adventures to-morrow."

"Yes, indeed!" cried Grandmama. "There has been enough talk for to-night. Charles must go to bed. His room is ready, but he didn't bring any luggage so you'll have to lend him some things, William."

"That's easily done," agreed Grandpapa, rising from his chair. "My pyjamas ought to fit him none too badly. I'll come and see what else he wants."

Charles and the grans went upstairs together and left me sitting alone.

> "My heart is like a singing bird
> Whose nest is in a water'd shoot;
> My heart is like an apple-tree
> Whose boughs are bent with thick-set fruit;
> My heart is like a rainbow shell
> That paddles in a halcyon sea;
> My heart is gladder than all these,
> Because my love is come to me."

The old song by Christina Rossetti came into my mind as I sat on the hearthrug by the drawing-room fire. I hummed it softly. Long ago, Mother used to sing

412

it — and I had always loved it — but it was only now that I understood and appreciated the deep truth underlying the simple words: my heart was singing; my heart was full of gladness; the world was bright with sunshine and rich with the promise of fruit.

The fire was warm, the coals were glowing, so I sat there for a long time thinking of all that Charles had told me. He would tell me more to-morrow but he had said enough to show how much he had endured in mind and body; it was no wonder that he had lost his balance and behaved a little foolishly! I found it very easy to forgive him because, in spite of everything, he had never ceased to love me "with every fibre of his being."

I remembered what Charles had said on that sunny morning when we were sitting together beneath the apple-tree, with the pink petals drifting in the gentle breeze — how long ago it seemed! "If the girl I loved began to 'have fun with other men' I should retire from the contest and give them a clear field." The words had been said half in fun, but I had known at the time that the sentiment was profoundly true of his nature: Charles must have everything . . . or nothing.

Perhaps it would not be easy to be married to a perfectionist — but I need not worry for Charles had everything that I could give him. He had always been the only man in the world.

I had just risen to go to bed, and had put the guard on the fire, when the door opened and Charles came in; he was wearing Grandpapa's pyjamas and dressing-gown.

"Hush!" he said, smiling in a conspiratorial manner. "The two old dears have gone to bed and are probably asleep. I couldn't go to sleep without making sure that you were here — and it wasn't a dream."

"It's twelve o'clock!"

"I know. I'll just say good night." He kissed me very tenderly . . . and then turned to the window in alarm. "What's that?" he exclaimed.

It was the sound of a carriage and horses coming down the drive; they came at a good pace, approaching nearer and nearer. I heard the horses' hoofs on the gravel and the scrape of iron-shod wheels. The equipage stopped outside the front door.

"Who the dickens is that?" asked Charles in bewilderment.

"I don't think it's anyone."

"What do you mean? It's a carriage and horses; didn't you hear it?"

"Yes, I heard it once before."

Charles went into the hall and I followed him. The big wooden door was locked and bolted; he opened it wide.

There was nothing to be seen: no carriage, no horses.

A slight sprinkling of snow had fallen and the ground was white; the moon shone brightly, like a silver disc above the sleeping hills, and the trees were powdered with sparkling crystals. We stood in the doorway in silence, looking at the peaceful scene.

"There are no wheel-marks in the snow," said Charles in a low voice.

"I didn't expect to see any."

414

"You heard it before."

"Yes, once, when I was a child."

"Did anyone else hear it?"

"I'm — I'm not sure," I said slowly. "They all said I was dreaming but — but they looked at me in a queer sort of way. Perhaps they didn't want me to be frightened. Grandpapa took me out and showed me that there wasn't anything — and said again that I'd been dreaming. Then he began to talk about something else."

"What does it mean?"

"I don't know. As a matter of fact I'd forgotten all about it . . . until now."

"Could we ask Colonel Maitland what it means?"

"Well, you can if you like," I said doubtfully. I remembered how Grandpapa had changed the subject, telling me about the owls in the old tower and promising that he and I would go and see the place. Had he done it for my sake or because he didn't want to talk about the ghostly carriage and pair?

Charles nodded. "Perhaps we shouldn't," he said. "People are sometimes a little touchy about their unearthly visitors. As long as it doesn't foretell some frightful disaster —"

"Oh, I'm sure it doesn't!"

"Why are you sure, Sarah?"

"Well, it didn't last time — and I'm not a bit frightened. I feel it's — sort of — friendly. Perhaps you think that's silly?"

"It isn't silly," replied Charles. "Feelings are important and I agree that there was something friendly and pleasant about the unseen arrivals. All the same I'd like to know who they were."

Charles shut the door and bolted it securely; he said good night to me again and ran upstairs two steps at a time.

I went up more slowly to my room above the front door. When I was ready for bed and drew back the curtains I could see the moon shining peacefully above the hills.

I was a perfectly normal woman, not in the least psychic, so the ghostly carriage and pair seemed very queer to me. It was queer, but it wasn't sinister; I was sure of that. I wondered why I had forgotten about it; I wondered if it arrived every night on the stroke of twelve or only sometimes; I wondered what had happened the first time it had arrived; I wondered why Charles had accepted it so naturally.

Perhaps there were "unearthly visitors" at Schloss Roethke.

I was still wondering about it when I went to sleep.

CHAPTER
FORTY-ONE

When I awoke next morning everything that had happened seemed like a dream. I could scarcely believe that Charles was actually here at Craignethan, safe and sound . . . but when I went down to the dining-room there he was, sitting at the table, eating porridge and chatting to the grans as if he had known them all his life.

Grandpapa was still eager to hear about the escape from the internment camp.

"I'm afraid you'll be disappointed," said Charles, smiling. "There was nothing dramatic about our escape; we didn't overpower our guards and bag their uniforms; we didn't dig a tunnel under the barbed wire; we simply walked out of the place during the confusion caused by an air-raid. Then it was just a matter of foot-slogging until we fell in with a contingent of British troops."

"I don't think that can be *quite* right," declared Grandmama. "Elspeth gave me rather a different account of —"

"Elspeth Loudon?" interrupted Grandpapa in surprise.

"Yes, I rang her up early this morning to tell her how pleased we were to hear that Bob had got home safely.

She said it was all your doing, Charles. She's going to tell me about it when I go to tea with her to-morrow."

"I have told you, Mrs. Maitland," said Charles with a touch of his "Austrian pride."

"I know," agreed Grandmama. "But you haven't told us about your adventures: how you knocked out two German soldiers who had captured Bob, thinking he was a spy, and how you carried Bob on your back for miles when he had injured his leg. Elspeth said, 'Bob wouldn't be *here* if it hadn't been for Charles Reeder.'"

"Bob makes a good story out of nothing," declared Charles firmly.

There was a short but somewhat uncomfortable silence.

"It's a fine day," said Grandpapa.

"Yes, lovely," agreed Grandmama. "I'm so glad Charles will see Craignethan looking its best. The sprinkle of snow which fell last night has melted and the sun is quite warm."

"The glass has gone up," I added. I had looked at Grandpapa's barometer in the hall.

"I have an apology to make, Charles," said Grandpapa gravely. "I should have liked to entertain you this morning; my plan was to take you for a pleasant stroll round the garden. There's not much to see at this time of year but I could have shown you what I intend to do in the spring — I'm sure you would have been interested to hear my views about the rotation of vegetable crops and the best way to eliminate club-root — but the fact is I've got to see a man about a dog so I'm afraid you'll just need to make do with Sarah. The girl is poor company but no doubt she'll do her best to amuse you. I'd better warn you that her idea of a pleasant stroll is to take the path up the side of the burn and climb Grey Ghyll and return by the old Drove Road; it's five miles, more or less, and pretty steep going . . ."

Charles had looked somewhat anxious at the beginning of this apologia but now he was chuckling helplessly.

"And don't worry about the time," said Grandmama, smiling kindly. "If you happen to be late for lunch we'll just go on and you can have soup and cold chicken when you get home."

Half an hour later Charles and I met in the hall by appointment and I was amused to see that he was wearing a very ancient brown tweed coat belonging to Grandpapa.

"My host insisted that I should wear this," explained Charles. "He said it was more suitable for the hills than my 'fine London coat.' Your grans are wonderful, Sarah; they fit together like the two halves of an apple."

"Yes, they're wonderful; I love them dearly."

"I'm not surprised."

"Charles, do you feel fit for a five-mile walk or would you rather have an easy morning?"

"I'm fit for anything . . . so off we go; up Grey Ghyll and back by the Drove Road!"

We set off together up the path by the side of the burn. It was too steep going for us to talk much, but when we came to more level ground Charles began to tell me some of his adventures.

When he left me at Fairfield he had had an uneventful journey to Vienna and had found his family in the town house, as he had expected. Rudi was overjoyed to see him and thanked him again and again for coming. The two brothers had a long talk about their father's case, which seemed less serious than Charles had feared. In fact Rudi was very hopeful and repeated several times that if only their father would behave reasonably his friends would be able to get him released.

Charles pointed out that if they had stayed quietly at the Schloss this would never have happened.

"I know . . . but the others wanted to come," explained Rudi.

"That was just like Rudi," said Charles with a sigh. "He knows what's right and sensible but he's as pliable as clay in Anya's hands. I tried to put some stiffening into him but I doubt if it will last."

"Was Anya pleasant and agreeable?" I asked.

"I didn't see Anya; she was reported to be in bed with a headache," replied Charles, with a queer little twist of his lip. "I didn't see my sister either; Rudi had sent her to stay with one of our aunts."

The following day Charles went to the State Prison to visit his father, and was greeted affectionately. "He was so pleased to see me that I was glad I had come," said Charles. "At first he was very intractable, cursing and swearing at the way he had been treated, but I reasoned with him and pointed out that not only was he prejudicing his own case by his behaviour but also endangering Rudi and Anya. Rudi had told him this already but I was able to put it more forcefully. We talked for about an hour and at last I managed to persuade him to be patient and wait quietly until his friends were able to help him (Rudi was very angry with him, but I understood how hard it was for a proud man like my father to bear the indignity of imprisonment). As I was coming away he said, 'You'll come again to-morrow, won't you, Ludo? It's so damned dull in this place.' I promised to come and bring him some books."

Charles came away feeling cheerful; he had pacified his father; his words had taken effect. He decided that he needn't stay long in Vienna — perhaps no more than a week — just long enough to get things settled and make sure that his family would go home to Schloss Roethke and stay there. He must see Anya and speak to her seriously about it; that was the best thing to do.

He was thinking of all this as he came out of the prison gates. When he turned into the street a squad of Secret Police closed round him and arrested him. There were five of them, so it was useless to try to escape. He demanded what was the meaning of his arrest; what was the charge against him? They made no reply. There was no trial, nor was he allowed to communicate with his family. He was sent by train to a prison in Berlin where he was kept in solitary confinement and interrogated for hours about a plot to kill Hitler and overthrow the régime. Charles knew nothing of any such plot but they didn't believe him.

Charles told me very little about the "interrogations"; he didn't want to talk of it. He just said that his agony of mind when he thought of me was a great deal worse than anything else he had to suffer.

"Was there a plot?" I asked.

"There must have been some sort of plot but I knew nothing about it until they told me . . . and, as far as I know, it never came to anything. They wanted me to tell them the names of the men who were involved in the plot, but of course I had no idea who was involved so I couldn't tell them — even if I had wanted to."

"Why did they think you were involved?"

"At first I thought they had mistaken me for someone else. I kept on telling them I had never been interested in politics and that during my stay in Austria I had spent my time improving my father's estate and renovating the Schloss. Then one day, during a particularly long and disagreeable series of interrogations, they lost patience and said that it was useless for me to pretend to be innocent; my sister-in-law had given them the information which had led to my arrest."

"Anya!"

"Yes, Anya."

"Charles! I can't believe it!"

"I can understand your disbelief. It must be quite incredible to anyone who has never had the misfortune to live in a Police State."

"But why? Why did she do it? There's no sense in it!"

"Oh, there was sense in it," said Charles grimly. "The reason is obvious. She did it to ingratiate herself with

422

the authorities, to make life safer for herself and Rudi. Our father's behaviour had endangered Rudi — or so she thought. Anya informed against me because she was frightened of what might happen . . . and I was a convenient scape-goat."

I gazed at Charles in horrified silence.

For nearly a year Charles had been kept in solitary confinement and then he was moved to an internment camp near Hamburg. He was given no reason for the move and at first he was annoyed for it was a hutted camp, encircled with barbed wire, but he soon found that it was a great deal better than the Berlin prison. Although it was cold and dreary he had the companionship of other men. The camp was an Oflag and was full of British officers who had been captured during the retreat to Dunkirk. It took Charles some time to make friends with them (they wanted to know why he was there, if he wasn't a prisoner of war) but after a few weeks they accepted him and were very companionable. It was then that Charles became acquainted with Robert Loudon and spent a lot of time talking to him.

The British prisoners of war were allowed to write home and received letters and parcels from their friends, but Charles was in a different category and no letters from him were allowed to pass the censor. Colonel Loudon had tried to convey a message to me in a letter to his wife but the letter had been confiscated.

When Charles had been in the Oflag for a couple of months he was sent for by the Commandant and questioned about the behaviour of the British officers: were they friendly with him or were they proud and disagreeable? Did he know whether plans for escape were being made? He was told it would be to his advantage if he would answer all the questions frankly. Charles gave misleading answers — or no answers at all. It was an unpleasant interview but he was glad it had taken place for the mystery of his presence in the Oflag had now been solved: he had been sent there in the hope that he would fall foul of his companions and consent to act as a spy.

"There were several attempts to escape," continued Charles. "Three chaps managed to get away but they couldn't speak German so they were caught before they had gone far. Bob Loudon and I discussed the matter but it seemed hopeless. Then one night the R.A.F. raided Hamburg and dropped a few of their surplus bombs on the camp. My companions were somewhat annoyed at being bombed by their own people! However the R.A.F. did us a good turn; some of the guards were killed or wounded, and in the darkness and confusion Bob and I found a gap where the wire had been destroyed and walked out. Quite a lot of people escaped that night — I don't know what happened to them. Bob and I stuck together and made for Hamburg. The place was in a frightful mess after the raid but that was all to the good from our point of view. We were able to find a couple of outfits of civilian clothes. After that I didn't worry; I knew we'd be all right because I can pass as a German anywhere. As I told your 'grans' it was just a matter of foot-slogging

424

until we managed to link up with some British troops. Then Bob became the spokesman and explained who we were."

"You said he fell over some barbed wire."

"Oh yes, he gave his ankle a wrench; it wasn't serious. As a matter of fact the most interesting thing about our walk from Hamburg was some notes I made about German airfields and munition dumps. I thought a few notes might be useful later — and they were. We had very few adventures and no hair-raising escapes," added Charles with a smile.

I didn't really believe this but I let it pass.

"The only difficulties arose when we reached our objective," continued Charles. "I wasn't surprised — I'd been wondering how I'd be received by the British authorities — but Bob was furious when I wasn't welcomed with open arms."

"What do you mean?"

"It was natural that they should be doubtful about me; I could easily have been a spy! If Bob hadn't made a fuss about it I might have been interned in Britain until the end of the war. Fortunately for me Colonel Robert Loudon is a distinguished officer, so he was able to vouch for me, and he gave them rather a highly coloured account of our escape which helped considerably. They didn't take any chances of course — why should they? — I was carefully screened and all my statements verified before they decided that I was all that I claimed to be.

"Then Bob and I were flown to London and interviewed at the War Office. We were able to give them some information about conditions in Germany, which they said would be useful, and they were interested in my notes. I raised the matter of my application for naturalisation — I told you about that, didn't I? — and they promised they would put it through as soon as possible. I was told — unofficially — that they would be glad of my services at a base camp; they're short of interpreters to interview the thousands of German prisoners who have been captured. Well, that's about all," said Charles. "After that Bob got leave and went home and I went to Fairfield. You know the rest of the story."

Yes, I knew the rest of the story. "What a frightful time you've had, Charles!"

"It was pretty grim, but it's over now and I don't want to think about it any more."

"You'll have to tell Grandpapa something about it."

"Oh, I shall," he agreed. "I just wanted to tell you first. There are several things I can't tell him; about Anya, for instance."

"Of course! Have you heard anything about your family?"

"No, and I'm not likely to hear anything until after the war."

"But you won't ever go back, will you?" I asked anxiously; it was a nightmare to me that some day he might want to go back.

"No, never," replied Charles firmly.

For a few moments we walked on in silence. Then he said, "As I told you, I've promised to take on the job of interviewing German prisoners, which probably means that I shall be sent to a base camp somewhere in France. I shan't be free until the war is over, but after that —"

"I shan't be free either," I told him.

"What do you mean?" he asked anxiously.

"Well, for one thing, I shall have to stay with Father and Willy; they couldn't manage without me. After the war Father will be able to get another living, and I don't suppose it will be difficult to find a good housekeeper for him. For another thing, I can't leave my job at Barrington's all of a sudden. In fact I practically promised Duncan Barrington that I would stay until after the war."

"Who is Duncan Barrington?"

I smiled and replied, "The manager of Barrington's — and a very good friend."

"Oh," said Charles, looking at me doubtfully. He was silent for a few moments and then added, "I've told you all my adventures and of course I want to hear what you've been doing, Sarah."

"Keeping house for Father and Willy, helping in an air-raid shelter and working at Barrington's from eleven to six every day. I'll tell you all the details some time — but not now. Let's enjoy ourselves this morning and talk about what we're going to do when the war is over and we're both free."

"All I want is to settle down here, in Britain, for the rest of my life."

This was good news. "Where?" I asked. "I mean where would you like to live? Would you like a flat in London, or a little house in Oxford or —"

"Goodness, no! I'm a countryman."

"Well, where?"

"I wouldn't mind living here," replied Charles.

We had reached the top of Grey Ghyll and had paused there for a few moments. We could see for miles over the rounded rolling hills of the Border Country; they were tawny hills, covered with orange-coloured grass and withered heather, but the tops were still capped with a sprinkling of snow which sparkled in the sunshine.

"Here?" I echoed in astonishment . . . for to me Craignethan was a "holiday place"; it had never crossed my mind that we could settle down and live at Craignethan.

"It's wild and free!" exclaimed Charles, standing upon the hill-top and stretching out his arms in the gesture I knew so well. He added earnestly, "Sarah, you can't understand — nobody who hasn't been imprisoned for years can understand the blessedness of freedom or appreciate the joy of walking for miles over moors and hills!"

"Yes, but Charles —"

"Of course I don't mean we should park ourselves on Colonel and Mrs. Maitland, that would be out of the question, but perhaps the Colonel might like to sell us a piece of ground and we could build ourselves a cottage. Your 'grans' would like to have you near them, wouldn't they?"

"Oh yes! But, Charles —"

"And we should be near the Loudons. Bob is one of the best fellows in the world; I know you'd like him."

428

"Yes, I'm sure I'd like him, but —"

"But what?" asked Charles. "You keep on saying 'but.'"

"It's the weather, that's all. The weather isn't always like this."

"Who cares!" he cried. "I'd like to see a storm here — all these tawny hills covered in snow! I'd like to see them swathed in mist! I'd like to hear the wild west wind howling in the chimneys."

"You will if you live here," I told him.

"Don't you want to live here, Sarah?"

"There's nothing I'd like better ... if you'd be happy."

"I shall be happy," said Charles. "I shall have you — and books — and music — and the freedom of the hills. I shall be content with a quiet peaceful life; I've had more than my fill of adventures."

"Perhaps you could finish your book?" I suggested.

"My book?" asked Charles in surprise. "Oh, my book about Oxford! I'd forgotten all about it!" He laughed and added, "It will be many a long day before people in Austria or Germany will want to read a book about Oxford. No, Sarah, my book is a back number; it belongs to the past. Let's think about the future and all the things we're going to do together when the war is over."

I took his arm and we walked on slowly, making plans for buying a piece of land and building ourselves a cottage: I wanted a labour-saving kitchen and lots of roomy cupboards; Charles wanted a piano, shelves for books and a lavender hedge under the sitting-room window.

Presently we came to the old Drove Road and turned homewards to Craignethan ... and now, by one accord, we hastened our steps: we were eager to see the grans and talk to them about our plans for the future.

Moffat,
Dumfriesshire,
  August 1966.

Also available in ISIS Large Print:

Katherine's Marriage

D. E. Stevenson

Katherine Wentworth has married her hero, Alec Maclaren. They are on their honeymoon in the Scottish Highlands, and lost to the world. She can scarcely believe that the four previous lonely years can have been replaced by so much joy. But her unclouded happiness does not last long.

Their return to Edinburgh brings her into conflict with her old school friend, Alec's sister Zilla. A beautiful woman who had expected Alec to remain a lifelong companion, devoted only to her. Then the jealousies and greed of her first husband's family threaten to bring unhappiness upon them all when her stepson Simon is summoned as the heir to the great estate of Limbourne in the South of England. Limbourne, the home for centuries of his father's family, with its stately mansion and fine old trees and gardens — and its tense atmosphere . . .

ISBN 978-0-7531-9270-2 (hb)
ISBN 978-0-7531-9271-9 (pb)

Emily Dennistoun

D. E. Stevenson

Emily Dennistoun lives alone with her elderly tyrannical father at Borriston Hall on the Scottish coast. Her mother died many years before, and her younger brother is at Oxford, presented with opportunities that Emily can only dream of. She has few friends and lives through her writing. Then she meets Francis, and despite vicissitudes of fortune, despite uncertainties, loneliness and unhappiness, Emily holds steadfast to a love she knows is true.

Originally entitled *Truth is the Strong Thing*, this has never before been published.

ISBN 978-0-7531-8950-4 (hb)
ISBN 978-0-7531-8951-1 (pb)

The Fair Miss Fortune

D. E. Stevenson

Jane Fortune causes a stir when she arrives in the small community of Dingleford. She has bought an old cottage and plans to open a tearoom. Old friends Charles Weatherby and Harold Prestcott both fall for the newcomer, but her behaviour seems to vary wildly — she encourages first one then the other and at other times barely recognises them. Is there more to the fair Miss Fortune than meets the eye?

Never before published, this charming story was originally written in the 1930s, when it was thought to be too old-fashioned to appeal to the modern market.

ISBN 978-0-7531-8948-1 (hb)
ISBN 978-0-7531-8949-8 (pb)

Mrs Tim of the Regiment

D. E. Stevenson

Vivacious, young Hester Christie tries to run her home like clockwork, as would befit the wife of British Army officer, Tim Christie. However hard Mrs Tim strives for seamless living, she is always moving flat out to remember groceries, rule lively children, side-step village gossip and placate her husband with bacon, eggs, toast and marmalade. Left alone for months at a time whilst her husband is with his regiment, Mrs Tim resolves to keep a diary of family life.

When a move to a new regiment in Scotland uproots the Christie family, Mrs Tim is hurled into a whole new drama of dilemmas. Against the wild landscape of surging rivers, sheer rocks and rolling mists, who should stride into Mrs Tim's life one day but the dashing Major Morley. Hester will soon find that life holds unexpected crossroads . . .

ISBN 978-0-7531-8608-4 (hb)
ISBN 978-0-7531-8609-1 (pb)